PRAISE FOR
BY DAWN'S EARLY LIGHT

"Suspicion, suspense, thrills and mystifications. . . . A lively, enthralling fable forcefully told."

—*Los Angeles Times Book Review*

"Sizzling thrillers have been Philip Shelby's métier, and *BY DAWN'S EARLY LIGHT* proves no exception. . . . A keen sense of international finance and the political atmosphere charged by money and power."

—*Baltimore Sun*

"There's all kinds of intrigue and action. . . . The complexity of the novel takes on a life of its own as you hurtle towards its breathless conclusion in this perfect mix of interesting characters and cunning maneuvering."

—*Time Out* (Denver, CO)

"Shelby shines . . . in building suspense around a complex conspiracy. . . . If you like espionage thrillers, then you should enjoy this book."

—*I Love a Mystery*

"Shelby is wonderful at plotting a devious story that can totally fool the reader. This book is definitely worth a read."

—*The Pilot* (Southern Pines, NC)

GATEKEEPER

LAST RIGHTS

"At last, a strong, competent, intelligent female action-adventure hero who is believable and great fun to read about! Rachel Collins, we've waited for you for a long, long time. Jack Ryan and Dirk Pitt, give Rachel the gun and let her drive."

—Stephen Coonts

"Sizzling. . . . [A] page-turner. . . . *Last Rights* is a taut, action-packed tale."

—*Orlando Sentinel*

"A political thriller with a punch. . . . Shelby weaves a fascinating tale of corruption, greed, and jealousy. The plot twist at the end is a total surprise."

—*San Francisco Examiner*

DAYS OF DRUMS

"Electrifying. . . . A white-hot Washington thriller. . . . Lightning-fast. . . . *Days of Drums* is rich stuff, indeed."

—*BookPage*

"[A] fleet political thriller. . . . An even slicker version of *The Pelican Brief*, with the Senate sitting in for the Supreme Court."

—*Kirkus Reviews*

"Captivating. . . . [A] fascinating political thriller. . . . A plot so heinous it might be true."

—*San Francisco Examiner*

"Fast-paced, intense . . . razor-sharp characterizations . . . [and] a thrilling climax."

—*The Star* (Chicago)

"Explosive."

—*The Plain Dealer* (Cleveland)

BY
DAWN'S
EARLY
LIGHT

PHILIP SHELBY

POCKET BOOKS

New York London Toronto Sydney Singapore

This book is a work of fiction. Names, characters, places and incidents are products of the author's imagination or are used fictitiously. Any resemblance to actual events or locales or persons, living or dead, is entirely coincidental.

 POCKET BOOKS, a division of Simon & Schuster, Inc.
1230 Avenue of the Americas, New York, NY 10020

Copyright © 2002 by Philip Shelby

Originally published in hardcover in 2002 by Simon & Schuster, Inc.

All rights reserved, including the right to reproduce
this book or portions thereof in any form whatsoever.
For information address Simon & Schuster, Inc.,
1230 Avenue of the Americas, New York, NY 10020

ISBN: 0-671-01394-7

First Pocket Books printing February 2003

10 9 8 7 6 5 4 3 2 1

POCKET and colophon are registered trademarks of
Simon & Schuster, Inc.

For information regarding special discounts for bulk purchases,
please contact Simon and Schuster Special Sales at 1-800-456-6798
or business@simonandschuster.com

Cover design by Hsu and Associates
Photo credit: Christopher J. Boyle/Photonica

Printed in the U.S.A.

For my mother and father

BY
DAWN'S
EARLY
LIGHT

PROLOGUE

THERE WERE forty children in Barracks 6, the orphanage section of the refugee camp in western North Korea. The youngest was five, the oldest eleven, which was the cutoff age. Twelve-year-olds were moved into the general population.

The children lived in a universe of cold, hunger, and fear that not even sleep could relieve. Each was trapped inside a brittle cocoon of pain. The room was never silent, the days and nights filled with hacking coughs and cries as sharp as piranhas' teeth.

The older ones preyed on the young when they could, for as long as they were strong enough to do so. They stole rations and water, and, when these were not to be had, they explored the parameters of their own crippled psyches by twisting limbs and breaking joints with the indifferent curiosity of seasoned torturers.

The colonel in charge of the camp stepped across the frozen mud of the compound. A year before he had inadvertently slighted a superior and was relieved of his command, banished to run this dung heap the United Nations and the International Red Cross called a displaced persons camp. But he sensed his luck was changing, all because of the man walking beside him.

The stranger was a Caucasian, tall and loose-limbed, with close-cropped iron-gray hair and the dark, weathered features of a farmer. He was in his forties or early fifties—hard to tell because he was very fit, moving through the bitter spring air like a ghost.

The colonel had not been informed of the man's visit until the helicopter carrying him was airborne. His orders had been to cooperate fully. The camp held back many secrets from international inspectors but this visitor was to be shown anything he wanted.

Which told the colonel that the man was important. Very important. And if he served him well, it would be reported to the chain of command. Maybe a word or two from the stranger would be enough to retrieve the colonel from this purgatory.

The visitor, who was known in his trade as the Handyman, was aware of the colonel's plight. He did not care, except that it would make the man easier to handle.

The colonel threw open the door to Barracks 6 with more force than necessary. The smell of diseased flesh billowed out.

The barracks was sixty feet by thirty, divided by three rows of bunk beds. The dim lighting filtered down from weak overhead bulbs and died on the grime that covered the windows and raw plank floor. Shapes stirred on the beds and the Handyman saw feral eyes tracking his movements.

The overhead lights flickered and brightened and the Handyman gazed down upon a sight he'd witnessed in other black pits of the world—the refugee camps of Cambodia and Laos, the Bekáa Valley and the black townships beyond Johannesburg.

Most of the children lay curled up in their bunks. It was impossible to determine their sex. All had skin yellowed by malnutrition, the same sallow faces that made their eyes inordinately large, the knobby knees and elbows with skin stretched tight over bones as brittle as chalk.

Walking between the rows of bunks, the Handyman searched among the faces, dismissing those who were too far gone, weighing those who could still be saved on scales only he had calibrated.

The role of savior unsettled him. At any given time, he was regarded as one of the top four assassins in the world, doling out death on grains of metal and with an unerring eye. His employers were governments or individuals who could afford his fee. But this job was unlike any other he had undertaken. He was to select and to protect, and might never be called upon to pull the trigger.

The Handyman caught a glimpse of the child through the support beams of the other bunks, lying on the mattress, his back pressed against a wall. He was eight, maybe nine years old, thin but not yet emaciated, staring out into space, his expression vacant. But his eyes were still clear, like those of a freshly caught fish laid out on ice.

Moving closer, the Handyman drew in a sharp breath. The child was a doppelgänger, almost an exact double of the child he had been searching for up and down the frozen wastes of this godforsaken land for the last few weeks.

The Handyman slipped onto the edge of the bunk. He reached for the boy, felt him flinch when he touched his shoulder. The boy resisted for a second, then let the strong hand roll him over. There was dried blood on the seat of his pants, indicating that the child had recently been assaulted. The Handyman peeled back the filthy shirt, checked the arms, chest, and back. There were sores and blisters, but nothing was broken—except the life behind those vacant eyes, a wasteland.

The Handyman rose. He had been the instrument for some of the most audacious killings men could devise and he had carried out his assignments flawlessly. But this assignment was beyond anything he had ever imagined. Looking at the boy, he saw a perfect killing machine, a child so innocent that he would overcome every hurdle, every obstacle, every watcher between him and his intended target. The President of the United States, Claudia Ballantine, would actually feel this child's embrace before she died.

The Handyman turned to the colonel. "Who is this boy?"

"He has no name. He comes from the southeast."

The Handyman knew all about the mass graves that fertilized the fields of that region. Safe to assume that the boy's parents and other relatives would never come looking for him.

"The boy is designated number 1818," the colonel volunteered.

The Handyman gave the colonel his full attention, which caused the officer's mouth to go dry.

"Get him out of here. Have a doctor examine him for an infection and give him the necessary antibiotics. I want him clean and ready to travel in three hours."

The Handyman paused. "My report will comment on your cooperation, provided that everything is in order."

The officer's Adam's apple jutted against the knot of his tie.

"Of course."

"Then we are finished here."

The Handyman took one last look at the boy, then made his way outside. After the stench of the barracks, the cold air was welcome. Pulling out cigarettes, he offered the colonel one and lit one for himself. He hadn't been quite honest when he'd said he was finished here. The colonel was the only witness to 1818's existence. He might be inclined to talk about the man who had come looking for a special child, brag about his role in finding him. In view of the project's importance, this possibility was unacceptable. Therefore, the colonel would have to cooperate further, by dying when the Handyman returned for 1818.

1

SLOANE RYDER stirred beneath the sheets. Dawn had not yet penetrated the bedroom windows of her "sliver" condo on 47th Street, between Second and Third Avenues.

She waited until she was fully awake, then tried to shift her leg out from under Peter Mack's. He was a light sleeper, something he attributed to his FBI training. Sloane knew that the slightest sound or movement could wake him.

She rolled slowly to the edge of her bed, her leg inching out from under his. In the blue wash of the room, she could make out the stack of clothes, set out the night before, on the credenza. Reach them and she'd be home free.

Her foot came loose and she was about to lift back the sheet when a hand clamped on her hip.

"Where do you think you're going?"

His voice was husky with sleep, his intention unmistakable as his hand slid over her hip.

Sloane shifted. "The office. I told you, remember?"

His fingers continued to travel along her leg. "It's Saturday," Mack muttered, trying to spoon up against her.

He groped for her breast and she felt his stubble prick the nape of her neck.

"Peter, aren't you supposed to be on duty at Dodge French's place today?"

"Not until later. Much later."

He shifted again, trying to pull her back into bed.

Sloane, twenty-eight, was a runner and a swimmer, deceptively strong beneath her slender frame. She pulled away from his grasp, the momentum taking most of the bedding with her. Standing naked, goose bumps creeping along her skin, she finger-brushed her wedge-style chestnut hair.

Peter Mack propped himself up against the pillows. At forty-one, he was in top physical condition, his arms and torso muscled from regular visits to the Bureau's gym. In the street, his coal-black hair and green eyes made women look twice—and he knew it.

"Jesus, do you know how cold you've gone on me?" he said.

Sloane closed her eyes. There it was: Their tepid sex life was her fault, his inevitable frustration. It had been going on like this for the last few months: schedules and moods and desires clashing, bodies and needs out of sync, angry recriminations and stony silences. A relationship, once beautiful and passionate, being picked apart by crows.

And it is my fault, Sloane thought.

But as much as she wanted to, there was nothing she could change. After today, maybe. But not right now. She had managed to keep her secret this long, she could hold it for another few hours. Because if she didn't, Peter Mack would try to stop her, because he cared for her, and because it would be his duty as a law-enforcement officer. He would try to save her from herself and she couldn't afford that.

Sloane hurried into the bathroom, showered, then slipped on slacks, a denim blouse, and an old but treasured Escada jacket. She checked her sling bag to make sure it had the essentials, and looked at Peter.

"I gotta run," she said. "I'll call you."

Her heart fell when her kiss fell on unresponsive lips, and then she was gone.

It was the start of the Memorial Day weekend, and the bagel shop on the ground floor was closed, depriving Sloane of a much needed coffee. Her fix would have to wait until Grand Central station. Shouldering her sling and setting a long-stride pace, she was thinking about the man she'd left in her bed.

She'd met Peter Mack eleven months ago, shortly after she'd started at the investment banking firm of Young, Pullen. The occasion was a party her firm had hosted at the Plaza for its A-list clients. Sloane had spent the first hour being hit on by investors who professed to take more of an interest in her personal well-being than in their portfolios and was about to leave when a tall, quiet-spoken man approached and said, "You know, you can always press harassment charges."

The idea of Young, Pullen's cash cows being hauled off to the hoosegow made her laugh. Peter Mack had said a lot of things that made her laugh—then and later. He'd told her he'd been on his way to the Oak Room for an after-shift drink when he'd caught a glimpse of her through the open doors of the salon.

"So I crashed your party."

Flattered, she had listened with interest as he briefly told her about his work as a special agent in the New York field office. She had said yes when he asked if he could see her again and yes again when, on their third date, she invited him up to her condo for what she knew would be an all-night nightcap.

Sloane's worst nightmare was a needy, demanding man. Someone equally busy, who understood the demands of her fledgling career, and still appreciated the time she had to give him—that was the kind of man she could stay with. Sloane was not desperate but was keenly aware of the drought in her personal life before she'd met Peter Mack. Now it was comforting to see his shaving gear on the vanity, his change of clothes in the closet.

For a time, she and Peter had shared something good and simple and sweet: Sundays in Central Park or out on the waters off Long Island, late dinners in the West Village listening to the cool throb of jazz, Saturdays for themselves and their bodies. It had been enough for her, more than enough. Sloane came from a past that buried dreams and crushed hope. She understood the danger of wanting too much, how slippery the world could be.

Sloane turned down Park toward Grand Central station. She did not want to carry thoughts of what was happening between her and Peter to her appointment. She wanted nothing to intrude on what would happen when she reached the station—and on what she was committed to do later, to end the hell that had been keeping her at the office night after night for the past two months. Things she couldn't talk about.

It'll be okay, she told herself. *When I finally tell him, he'll understand.*

Grand Central was a near empty catacomb of lost white-collar souls rushing to catch trains to join spouses and children who had already left for the holiday weekend. But the coffee shop was busy, being the only place in the vicinity open for business. Sloane's eyes roamed over the hollow-eyed husbands and fathers, the tourists trying to make sense of maps and train schedules, then found the one man she was looking for sitting at a corner table sipping coffee.

Frank Ryder was fifty-eight and looked fifteen years older than that. Cigarettes and a past problem with alcohol were responsible for some of the damage—but not all.

Sloane approached him and said, "Hello, Dad."

When he looked up at her, his clear eyes and calm smile told Sloane that he'd been staying on his medication.

"Hello, Starbuck," Frank Ryder said. The childhood nickname that had always made Sloane feel special now saddened her, coming as it did from this husk of a man.

She sat across from him. "You look great, Dad."

He smiled lopsidedly. "I feel fine. The weather's good. I walk every day."

"That's good. How's Paulina?"

"Last week she brought me stew."

"That's great, Dad."

Paulina Sanchez was the middle-aged registered nurse whom Sloane had hired to look in on her father three times a week. Frank Ryder could clothe, feed, and generally look after himself. But he had bouts of confusion and memory loss, and it was imperative that he take his medication consistently.

Sipping her coffee, Sloane told her father about what had happened at work during the past week. The conversation was really a monologue, because Frank Ryder did little more than smile pleasantly and stare into space. Try as she might, Sloane could never get used to her father's silence. Once, he had been a gregarious, outgoing man, full of stories and blarney. Now he dwelled in self-imposed exile, his universe bounded by the walls of a small condo in a family neighborhood in Queens.

Her father had been a successful maritime engineer. In middle age, he had retired and poured his life's savings into opening his own firm. Two years later, he had developed a new process by which the metal hulls of oil supertankers could be strengthened without any adding of weight, which would help prevent spillage during a collision.

But when Frank Ryder applied for his patent, his former employer got a court injunction to stop him, claiming ownership of his process on the grounds that Frank Ryder had begun development of his process while its employee. Negotiations were initiated, stalled, lawyers entered the fray, and the financial bloodletting began.

Years later, when it was all over, Frank Ryder was a hollow man, broken, bankrupt, and ruined. He had also become a widower. In the fifth year of litigation, his wife had succumbed to a ten-year chronic depression and had jumped off the subway platform at the 34th Street/Herald Square subway stop, into the path of an incoming train.

Six months after the funeral, two Cambridge police officers came to Sloane's Harvard dorm to tell her that her father had been picked up on the streets by the New York police. When she arrived at Bellevue after a harrowing overnight drive, she did not recognize the man in the straitjacket, flanked by watchful attendants.

Sloane blinked hard and pushed away the image.

"Dad, there's something we need to talk about."

"Sure, Starbuck. Anything."

Sloane pulled a sheaf of papers from her sling bag and arranged them on the table. They included the paid-up mortgage on the small Queens condo, a receipt for the homeowners' dues for the next five years, and letters from a trust company that would deposit a guaranteed income into Frank Ryder's checking account every month.

Sloane walked her father through the details, keeping her tone light, her explanations simple. She was pleased that he seemed to grasp the mechanics of what she'd done. He did not ask where Sloane had gotten the money for all this. Nor did she volunteer that it had come from the signing bonus Young, Pullen's recruiter had promised her. In his childlike state, he simply accepted that his daughter was providing for him.

"Are you going away, Starbuck?"

The question caught Sloane by surprise. Reaching for his hand, she replied, "No, Dad. I'm not leaving."

His fingers tightened around hers and she found herself looking into his eyes. "Starbuck?"

Sloane collected herself. "It's just stuff at work. There may be some changes . . ."

"Are you in trouble?"

"No, Dad." *Not yet.*

Frank Ryder shuffled the paperwork. "Then why all this?"

Sloane took a breath. "There may be something wrong at work. If there *is* a problem, I might have to do something—"

"Do you, Starbuck? Do you *have* to?"

His question cut to the dread Sloane had been living with these past months. It would have been so easy to ignore what she had come across, which some would say was none of her business. Except that ultimately it was her business, and her responsibility to the people who had invested both their faith and their money with her.

But doing the right thing could cost her so much . . .

Sloane covered her father's hand with hers. She knew that she could not walk away from this problem. She had never walked away from anything in her life. The man sitting across from her had taught her what it meant to take a stand—and to keep standing even as the odds ground you into dust.

The offices of Young, Pullen took up the top ten floors of a building on Washington Street, a few blocks east of Battery Place. The partners' offices and the boardroom, where investment officers were invited the second Tuesday of each January to receive their bonus checks, had a spectacular view of the Hudson River.

Sloane got out of the cab at the New York Stock Exchange and walked the remaining two blocks. Not to the front doors, which were sealed and armed, but to a side entrance. It took three rings to wake up the guard. Through the thick glass, she watched him amble like a disgruntled bear, hitching up his pants by his gun belt.

There were no names on the sign-in sheet. Good. Sloane was fairly sure it would stay that way. During the past week, she'd eavesdropped on colleagues' conversations about their holiday plans, mentally crossing off names.

The elevators operated on key-coded cards. The ride to the thirty-second floor took less than a minute. Sloane walked briskly through the reception area, a designer's paean to Dickensian barristers' rooms, and into the warren where the investment officers had their suites. Befitting her one-year tenure, hers was in the center, toward the back, windowless.

Snapping on the halogen desk lamp, Sloane fired up her computer, calling up the profile of a client she had absolutely no interest in—just something to make it look like she was busy, in case someone unexpectedly came by.

She had the guards' routine down pat. On weekends and holidays, they monitored the offices from an octagonal room in the basement of the building. During her visit to security to pick up her building pass, she had noted the three banks of monitors, twelve to each row. The video cameras hooked up to the monitors worked on a relay system, scanning designated parts of the ten floors at precise intervals. There was an override if the guards wanted to survey one particular area.

The week before, on the pretext of having lost her coded parking key, Sloane had visited security again. She had mentioned that she might be working over the long weekend and asked if there were any special details she should know about. None. The procedure was the same: Log in, go up, do your thing, go home.

It was time to do her thing.

Sloane could not know when or if the cameras would catch her movements. Bathroom key card in hand, she walked briskly back into the reception area, out the double doors, and made a sharp left into a hall. She slipped inside the bathroom, listened to the door sigh behind her, and leaned back against it. She counted off thirty seconds.

If a camera had picked her up, and if the guard had been watching, he would have seen her enter the bathroom. She would be accounted for and he would go back to his coffee.

She whispered "thirty" and stepped back into the hall. Twelve quick steps brought her to the stairwell door, for which no employee had a key. As long as there was someone in the suites, the fire exits had to be accessible. That was the law.

Sloane twisted the knob and stepped into the stairwell. It took her less than a minute to run up three stories to the partners' floor. She paused at the stairwell door to steady herself, then pushed it open.

The layout was plush: wood paneling, oriental rugs over thick carpeting, recessed lighting, spacious workstations for the secretaries. The partners' suites, especially the one belonging to H. Paul MacGregor, were opulent.

Sloane had met MacGregor only a few times. At forty-nine he was a senior partner, cold, driven, aloof, with an affected mid-Atlantic accent and a British tailor. On the credenza were pictures of a wife seldom seen and children he never spoke about. The rest were vanity shots of MacGregor with the rich and famous.

Sloane made her way around the slabs of mahogany and cherry wood, the leather chairs that smelled like a Jaguar dealership. MacGregor's taste ran to antiques and dark, grim portraits of men with whom he might or might not have a blood connection. His computer, however, was state of the art.

Sloane settled herself in his rich, black leather chair. Her hands performed as though with a will of their own and the computer was running, awaiting her command. But first it required the password.

Sloane had gotten her M.B.A. from Harvard, then spent two years at Ravenhurst, an elite business college in Pennsylvania where the courses included industrial and corporate espionage, examples of shady business practices, and other things that most business graduates never even dream of. Ravenhurst's instructors, former law-enforcement agents and corporate security officials, had lectured Sloane that most business executives chose a simple code. They also taught her where and how to find it.

Sloane had minimal contact with MacGregor, no reason to visit his suite, no common projects or clients that might have provided an excuse to be present when he logged on. So she waited for him to make a mistake and leave himself vulnerable.

Six weeks before, MacGregor had done just that—by firing his secretary of ten years over a minor clerical error.

If MacGregor had done this by the book, he might have been safe. Instead, he had reduced the usual severance package and stripped the woman of her health insurance—even though he knew her son was on kidney dialysis.

Sloane had visited the woman at her home, gently worked past her resentment and suspicion, and shown her a letter from Young, Pullen's legal department. Sloane had convinced the head counsel that it would be cheaper to fix MacGregor's actions before his actions resulted in a lawsuit. Legal had seen her point and quietly ordered that the insurance be reinstated.

The secretary was a sharp woman, grateful, but waiting for the other shoe to drop. When Sloane asked her for the password to MacGregor's computer, she gave it up with a laugh. "Use it to put a stake through his heart," had been her advice.

As Sloane typed in the letters OLYMPUS, she thought that was exactly what she was doing.

The Ravenhurst instructors had taught Sloane that virtually all executives failed to have traps set up beyond the password. Such precautions were considered irritants, impediments to getting on with the job. Sloane had no reason to suspect that H. Paul MacGregor was any different.

Had she known about the quality of information she was about to access, Sloane might have reconsidered. But she did not. She tripped the first electronic wire fifteen seconds after keying in the password.

Two phones began ringing at the same time, one in a guest bedroom of a Long Island estate, the second in the offices of a two-man scramble team belonging to Guardian Security, a private intelligence and corporate protection company. Founded by a retired CIA official, it was staffed by former government agents and ex-military personnel.

Three minutes after the call, a nondescript sedan was rolling out of what had once been a limousine company depot in Lower Manhattan.

What little Sloane knew about H. Paul MacGregor had been gleaned from business and society clippings and New York's *Families Register*.

He was to the manor born, the only son among five children. His family had provided legal services to the Street since the late nineteenth century, but MacGregor had turned out to be something of a rebel, eschewing the family business in favor of working in the investment banking community.

As a first-year associate, Sloane should not have had anything to do with MacGregor. It was a mistake in the firm's mailroom that had caused the package to be delivered to her. She remembered the moment vividly: being on the phone with a client, searching her desktop for notes she'd prepared, the mail boy coming by, handing her the package, she ripping it open without looking at the label.

All Sloane had seen was the cover letter, speed-reading it before she could stop herself. Later, when she was called up to the thirty-fifth to face a seething MacGregor and two other senior partners, she swore that she had not looked at the actual dossier the letter was attached to.

MacGregor had wanted her head, but the other two partners, noting that the seals on the dossier were intact and fearing a wrongful-dismissal suit, had talked him out of it. They had made Sloane promise that as far as she was concerned, she'd never seen any of this.

Sloane had agreed, but she couldn't get the details of the cover letter out of her mind. They were sufficiently alarming for her to ultimately break her word.

The details in the letter had to do with oil. In the early and mid-nineties, the Chinese government had embarked on a fast-track program to privatize and streamline bureaucracy-bound state industries. Among them was the East China Oil Company, overseen by an official named Mi Yang, the author of the cover letter. Its contents convinced Sloane that Yang and MacGregor had been in close touch for months. With careful digging, she realized why this was so: East China Oil was planning to go public, with MacGregor spearheading the effort on behalf of Young, Pullen, the lead underwriter.

It all seemed like standard deal making until, through one of her Houston clients, Sloane got hold of a geological report stating that the proven oil reserves where East China Oil had been drilling were minuscule—one of the reasons the company was hemorrhaging money.

She couldn't stop wondering why Mi Yang, in his cover letter, had written of "new developments" and "the need for absolute secrecy," and "the special event on Thanksgiving Day."

Getting inside information on an oil company halfway around the world was a daunting task. Using her Houston client as a reference, Sloane slowly built up a network of oil-patch informants that stretched across the Pacific. Most of what came back was hearsay and gossip. It took a great deal of time to sift through it all. But slowly a stunning mosaic emerged.

East China Oil had in fact uncovered a vast pool of petroleum. It had been sitting quietly on the discovery as it slowly bought up adjacent fields that Mobil, Texaco, and Exxon were only too happy to unload to buyers they considered greenhorns. As of now, East China Oil had a patch the size of Oklahoma. No one had picked up on this or even suspected it because no one had bothered to do the spadework Sloane had done. Other oil companies and industry-related concerns only looked after their own interests. Sloane had strung together the facts and the rumors to make connections that everyone else had missed.

But the question remained: Why the overwhelming need for secrecy? And what was MacGregor's role in East China Oil's ambitions? The answer was as staggering as it was simple: MacGregor and Mi Yang were sitting on the mother lode because there was phenomenal money to be made after the news of the true reserves was released.

Given what was publicly known about East China Oil and its dim prospects, Sloane had calculated that when it was taken public, its shares would fetch between eleven and twelve dollars. MacGregor, Mi Yang, and whoever else they chose to favor could buy blocks of millions of shares, sit on them for a while, then watch as their value skyrocketed when the announcement about the vast reserves was made.

It was the purest form of insider trading—simple, greedy, and totally illegal.

At the initial public offering, Sloane had tracked the big buyers of East China Oil. It had been easy enough to do because the stock was too speculative for conservative institutional buyers. Some of the more aggressive mutual-fund managers had scooped up hundred-thousand-share baskets and the gambling public had picked up the rest.

Except for a block of three million shares that had been purchased by a Netherlands Antilles offshore company.

Sloane knew that she'd never get beyond the front wall of the bankers and lawyers who nominally ran the company. The Antilles' banking-secrecy laws were among the toughest in the world. So she waited, listened to the announcement of East China Oil's huge "discovery" of new reserves, watched as the stock orbited to eighty dollars a share in less than three weeks.

That's when she began plotting a way to get around the Antilles company's walls. There was one way in: through MacGregor's computer. Somewhere in his private files would be a connection between him and the shell company. If she could find evidence that it was MacGregor who had bought those shares at the IPO, that, along with the rest of her carefully documented research, would be enough to prevent him from ruining tens of thousands of small investors, the kind she worked for.

Sloane felt a throbbing at her temples. The fifteen minutes she'd been there felt like hours. She prayed that the cameras hadn't caught her going into the bathroom. Or, if they had, that the guard wasn't watching, waiting for her to come out. She was counting on the male inclination not to inquire too closely about things that went on behind the doors of women's rest rooms.

Sloane leaned closer to the keyboard, as though that would somehow make her fingers fly faster. The number of files was dwindling rapidly. MacGregor was an anal retentive but he was also an arrogant son of a bitch. Sloane had been counting on those qualities—that he would, first, keep files at all, and second, that he believed his inner sanctum to be inviolate. The Antilles connection had to be there.

The sedan hurtled down the ramp to the underground garage. The driver, a hatchet-faced former SEAL, braked hard in front of the electronic gate, thrust a key card into the slot, and drummed his fingers on the steering wheel as the security gate rumbled up.

Beside him, his partner, a black man with a clean-shaven head, checked the load in his Magnum.

The driver left six feet of rubber on the concrete floor and wheeled the sedan around to the elevators.

On his key chain was a small, round key for the elevator.

"What about the guard inside?" the driver asked.

His partner shook his head. "We don't need no rent-a-cop on this one."

He brought out a cellular phone and dialed the security desk, informing the guard that Young, Pullen investigators were on their way up. And by the way, who had come into the offices earlier this morning?

It was the third-to-last file, innocuously labeled "Vacation Planner."

"Vacation, right," Sloane muttered.

According to the office rumor mill, MacGregor hadn't taken a day off in three years.

It was all there, just as she had known it would be. Dates, meeting memos, signatures and countersignatures, buy orders, execution confirmations, and the amounts. Money. So much money . . .

"Why did you need to do it?" Sloane whispered, ramming in a disk and hitting the copy key.

MacGregor was a rich man in his own right. His family wealth was substantial. Yet, for some reason, he needed more. Was it greed, or the lure of getting away with it? His actions pointed to a character flaw that Sloane couldn't fathom.

Sloane popped out the copy disk and dropped it into her sling bag. Only then did she realize that she had been holding her breath. For a moment, she sat there staring at the screen. She had what she'd come for. Time to go.

She was half out of the chair when she heard the

faint sounds of footsteps hurrying on the other side of the door. Her scalp prickled as heat flooded her face.

Nowhere to run. Nowhere to hide.

Glancing at the computer, Sloane realized that she must have triggered a silent alarm. Just as the door burst open, she keyed in a set of numbers.

Behind her, she heard a hard voice. "Take your hands off the machine and stand back."

⁑ ⋆ ⋆ ⋆ ⋆ ⋆

2

THE MAIN HOUSE, stables, gatehouse, and adjacent quarters hearkened back to the late 1800s. Richard Morris Hunt, a favorite of the Vanderbilts, had been chosen as architect. Frederick Law Olmstead had laid out the gardens.

The French family, who owned 150,000 acres of the shoreline and interior of what was to become Suffolk County, New York, held a groundbreaking ceremony in August 1885. Ten years later, the Brandywine estate was formally opened.

Over the years, 90 percent of the original holding had been sold off, but the family seat was still surrounded by a grand acreage. And there was today, as there had always been, a French in residence at the grandest home of them all on Long Island.

Dodge French sipped his coffee, then pushed away the Meissen cup and saucer. He was in his early seventies, tall and lean, with scarecrow limbs and a shock of white hair. His hands were large and liver-spotted, his complexion ruddy from decades of outdoor activity. He was often mistaken for a simple New England gentleman farmer, someone who perhaps devoted his leisure time to raising prize cow flesh. Until one looked into his eyes. Brilliant blue, reflecting an intelligence as sharp as diamonds.

Dodge French had been reared in privilege and taught to respect his good fortune. Like his predecessors, he'd entered a life of public service, learning the art of statesmanship from such mentors as Henry Kissinger and the Dulles brothers.

A special presidential envoy during the Reagan and Bush Sr. years, he had fallen out of favor when the Clinton mob invaded the White House. But when George "Dubya" Bush took office, the phone call had come. The new president had wanted to know if French could help bring about in China the kinds of changes that had taken place in the former Soviet Union.

"Get it done, whatever it takes," had been the presidential directive.

French was unusual for an American in that he had a keen sense of and profound respect for history. He had foreseen America's emergence as the dominant world power and had directed his considerable intellect and will toward making that inevitable. During the Reagan and Bush eras, then under the younger Bush's successor, Claudia Ballantine, French had helped restructure the world order to fit his vision. And he saw that it was good.

Good, but not finished. The centerpiece of that vision was still missing, although it was almost within his grasp. As long as no one interfered or made any mistakes.

Dodge French fixed his gaze on H. Paul MacGregor, standing in front of the dining room windows. Beyond,

French saw his majordomo dealing with the caterers. In a few hours, the Small Lawn would sprout tents and tables laden with food and drink. By midday the ambassadors and their entourages would arrive. The Secret Service had already vetted the property in advance of the President's appearance.

French noticed that MacGregor was chewing on a cuticle, an unseemly act for a forty-nine-year-old man of his station. French sighed. He reminded himself that for all his wealth, MacGregor was, in his soul, a parvenu, not terribly bright, and a bully. But these same qualities that offended had made MacGregor ideal for the assignment French had given him. He spoke the same language as the buccaneers who ran the big multinationals and who'd signed the secret business protocols with the old men in Beijing. Having lost Iran and Iraq to the Europeans, American enterprise wasn't going to let anyone beat them to China. MacGregor had been an excellent point man—until his greed had gotten the better of him. Unfortunately, he had also just demonstrated a quality French hadn't been aware of: stupidity.

"Why did you keep records?" French asked, as though chiding a child.

MacGregor ground his molars. "Because I needed them. They were in my office, perfectly safe—"

"Apparently not," French said. "Tell me why you did it. Something to do with your wife, Elizabeth?"

MacGregor's shoulders sagged. He wasn't surprised that French was privy to what even his lawyer wasn't aware of yet.

"She won't go quietly," MacGregor said. "I offered her five million in alimony to walk away and she laughed in my face. Bitch told me she'd fight the prenuptial and go for the full fifty-fifty split unless I came up with thirty percent of my assets, in cash, in sixty days."

"So you went to Mi Yang and he gave you a million shares of East China Oil," French said reasonably.

"He understood my position," MacGregor hedged. "He's a decent man."

Yang understood your position all too well, and no, he's not a decent man. He saw a way to put you in his pocket and took advantage.

"Whatever your arrangement with Yang, that's your business. My next question is, who?"

MacGregor watched the caterers go about their business. He was not a well-liked man, knew it, and didn't care. His partners didn't either, because MacGregor was an extremely valuable rainmaker. His contacts on the Street and in the international markets were second to none. If his bringing in business meant turning a deaf ear to associates who complained of verbal abuse, arrogance, and a vile temper, then so be it.

Never in his life had H. Paul MacGregor been crossed. The idea that anyone would even dare was ludicrous. But someone had tried, and almost succeeded. *Who?*

MacGregor's cell phone warbled in the inside pocket of his suit coat.

"The security team," he muttered.

Dodge French listened as MacGregor barked questions into the tiny phone, watched his expression morph from astonishment to outright rage.

"You found Ryder in *my office?* At my computer?"

MacGregor roared. "Haul her ass out of there and down to the precinct station!"

"Paul . . . *Paul.*"

Startled, MacGregor saw French shake a finger at him. "Tell them to wait and call back. We need to talk. Now."

MacGregor hesitated, then said into the phone, "I'll get back to you in a minute. Keep her there. Don't let her touch *anything.*"

"Tell me," French asked.

MacGregor shook his head, a man baffled. "A first-year paper pusher, Sloane Ryder, somehow managed to get into my computer. Fortunately she hit the electronic trip wire and that alerted security."

"Why would she risk doing something like that?" French asked. "And what was she looking for?"

MacGregor threw up his hands. "I don't know. I've never had anything to do with her. Except that one time . . ."

He told Dodge about the incident with the package Mi Yang had sent him several months ago, how it had gone to Ryder's desk and she'd inadvertently opened it.

"But she never saw the contents. The seals were intact."

"She must have seen something, though. Something that made her suspicious."

"She couldn't have," MacGregor insisted. "If she had, she'd have blown the whistle a long time ago."

And my Chinese friends would not have made the fortune they so badly needed, French thought. "Tell me something about her."

MacGregor was on Young, Pullen's hiring committee and had excellent recall.

"Born somewhere in Westchester County," he recounted. "Not the best part. Private schools, full ride to Harvard; finished her undergrad in three years, then picked up her M.B.A. there. Could've—should've—gone straight to work from there but instead did four years in a place called Ravenhurst. Erie, Pennsylvania, I think."

French's attention ratcheted up several notches. "I'm familiar with it," he said. "Did anyone on the hiring committee think to ask why she was there?"

"I don't think so," MacGregor replied. "It was more like a footnote in her resumé."

Dodge nodded. Ryder's name didn't resonate through the sweeping corridors of his memory. Certainly it wasn't on the threat list concerning the project. But now he would have her checked out—fast.

"What was she after?" he asked.

MacGregor's expression reminded French of a trapped badger he'd once killed.

"Security said that she was into the Antilles file. She made a copy, but they have it. That makes her a thief, and thieves go to jail—some for a longer time than others."

So MacGregor was going for vengeance over this. Typical reaction—and wrong.

"There's another way to handle this," French said. He held up his hand to stave off the inevitable protest. "I don't want you drawing attention to yourself right now, Paul. You're too valuable to the project to risk any kind of exposure. This girl isn't going anywhere. As you pointed out, she is a thief. That gives us leverage. She might want to trade her freedom for silence, don't you think?"

French allowed MacGregor to turn the idea over in his mind, then continued. "Give me an hour or so. In the meantime, tell your people to keep her there. It's a holiday. No one else will be going into the office."

Dodge French's reach was infinitely greater than even MacGregor imagined. Within minutes of placing his calls, the replies he desired were pouring in.

French sifted through Sloane Ryder's life with the patience and eye of a coroner. He weighed each detail precisely before cataloging it and moving on to the next one. By the time he was finished, he knew Ryder well enough to appreciate that a possible solution to the mess was standing right outside his windows.

Sloane sat in MacGregor's big leather chair, a mere two feet from the computer console. Across the desk sat the thin, hatchet-faced security man, holding a big-bore gun on her. Slowly, her breathing returned to normal.

It had been a heart-stopping moment when she'd heard the footsteps outside MacGregor's door, then the door flying open and the two men bursting inside, guns drawn. They had flashed their IDs, which identified them as employees of Guardian Security, the private contractor for Young, Pullen. Sloane recalled the name from a company briefing.

After making the one phone call to MacGregor, neither of the men had said more. Sloane, too, had kept quiet. She had been so shocked and felt so guilty that she hadn't protested even when one of the men grabbed her sling bag, rummaged through it, and found the disk. He didn't need to ask her what it was; all company disks bore a tiny imprint of the Young, Pullen logo.

Thoughts of what might happen to her crashed through her mind. Young, Pullen could ruin her professionally. Civil and possibly criminal charges waited in the wings. She clung to the thought that maybe it wasn't in Young, Pullen's best interests to crucify her in public. Did they really want her talking to lawyers and the media? People would listen, even if she didn't have the disk as proof.

The disk . . .

It was in the hand of the black security guard, who outweighed Sloane by a hundred pounds or more. No way she'd ever touch that disk again. It would be turned over to MacGregor, who would destroy it along with the incriminating files stored in his computer.

The computer . . .

It was still on, the screen glowing, silent. The electronic door Sloane had opened was still accessible. All she had to do was reach out . . .

Across two feet of empty space, with a gun pointed at me.

The guard's cell phone trilled. Sloane assumed that it was MacGregor.

The guard listened briefly. Sloane noted his puzzled expression as he flipped the phone closed. "She stays here. No cops."

His partner looked annoyed. "How long?"

"Two hours, maybe less."

Sloane felt a tug of hope. She didn't know what it was, but something was stopping MacGregor from handing her over to the police. She still had a chance.

The drive from Manhattan out to Brandywine took two hours. Peter Mack needed most of that time to work through his anger at Sloane.

He had been with her for eight months—longer than he'd ever stayed with any other woman. Even now it was easy to recall the first time he'd set eyes on her, at the Plaza, and the tremor that had raced through him. He could no more have walked on than put his hand on hot coals.

Peter Mack had not been looking to fall in love. The Bureau was a jealous mistress and her demands always came first. But there was something different about Sloane, in the ring of her laughter, the way she held his hand in the street, the curve of her hip when she lay next to him. It took him a while to realize that she was a woman who showed him her love in the smallest acts.

Which was exactly what had made the last two months so strange. Mack had a keen sense for people hiding things from him. And Sloane was definitely holding out.

By the time he reached the tip of Long Island, he'd made up his mind: He would sit Sloane down and have it out with her. Whatever it took, he would finally find the secret that had turned her from him.

Mack rolled down his window and lit a cigarette, one of his ration of three per day. There was something else he'd have to tell Sloane—that the strain of whatever was going on with her was impacting his work. He had spent sixteen years in the FBI, years that combined into a brilliant career. At age forty-one, he was the third-highest-ranking agent in the intelligence division. Now he stood poised to make even greater leaps, and focus on his job was imperative.

Back in his early twenties, Mack had hit the recruitment jackpot. The FBI was looking for bright, aggressive, physically fit young men. The recruiting agent had been impressed with Mack's law degree from Boston University, even more with the fact that he had played varsity hockey. Mack was also as polite and attentive as an altar boy and possessed a quick, clever mind honed by Jesuits.

Mack had aced the Quantico training and, by the luck of the draw, been placed in the New York field office. It had been an eye-opening experience.

The largest of the Bureau's fifty-six field offices, the New York chapter had over twelve hundred agents working in the Jacob J. Javits Federal Building, across the street from the U.S. District Court. Because of the city's ferocious cost of living, most agents lived in New Jersey or Pennsylvania, and put up with a daily three-hour commute. Peter Mack got around that by scoring a three-room apartment in the West Village. The landlord liked the idea of having an armed federal officer on the premises and gave him a break on the rent.

For someone with ambition, drive, and little need for sleep, the New York office was the place to get on the fast track. Because of its size and volume of cases, it was headed up by a full assistant director instead of a special agent. Peter Mack made sure he caught his eye. Eighteen months after receiving his credentials, he was pulled off the bank-robbery desk and disappeared into the intelligence division.

Set up in 1919 to keep track of anarchist activities, the intelligence division is responsible for tracking subversive agents and thwarting their activities. In New York, because of the United Nations and the large number of consulates and diplomatic missions, this can be a lifer's job, the equivalent of taking priestly vows. The division is also compartmentalized from the rest of the field office and its members are notoriously tight-lipped about their activities.

Soon after his induction, Peter Mack had discovered that his talent for wiretaps was as great as his skill with sidearms. When it came to surveillance, he had the patience of Job, and the ability always to stay alert during long stakeouts. Undercover assignments, where he had to mingle at diplomatic soirées in order to keep tabs on a target, became his specialty.

In the fraternal, secretive world of the intelligence division, Peter Mack found his calling. He made GS-12, step 6, in less than five years. His fitness reports were uniformly excellent, mirroring what the assistant director had always believed: Mack was one to watch. Not only because he learned Russian and Arabic at nights, or because he had studied, cultivated, and polished the manners of the world he was sent to surveil, but because he was, to his marrow, a company man. The Bureau was both his calling and his sanctuary.

Anything, anyone, on the outside would always be regarded with a degree of suspicion.

Mack turned off the two-lane blacktop onto a paved private road and drove the hundred yards to the gates of Brandywine. He looked straight up into the video camera set into the stone pillar and waited for the two ten-foot sections of wrought-iron filigree to part.

Mack's team of six was waiting for him in one of the stables, which had been remodeled into the caretakers' quarters. Mack checked their undercover dress—red valet jacket, the striped vests of the caterer's waiters, two in somber, well-tailored business suits who could pass for ambassadors' assistants. They were the pick of the division litter. Mack had trained four of them personally; as a unit they had been in the field on a dozen operations. Confidence was not an issue. He watched as they checked their sidearms and tested their ear and throat mikes. When they were ready to disperse, he said what he always did at that moment: "Not on our watch." In the division, this was known as "Mack's Motto."

Peter Mack walked along the seawall that bordered the lawn, looked down at the thin strip of rocky beach, then slowly back across the grass toward the house. Since he'd become the number-two man in intelligence, his assignments had often taken him to places like these. He felt very much at home in consular ballrooms and in the great halls of the United Nations. But Brandywine was a world unto itself, resplendent, removed, a fantasy disguised as a home, not unlike Randolph Hearst's legendary San Simeon.

Mack checked his watch and picked up his pace as he crossed the lawn. The first of over two hundred guests were arriving. Of that number, thirty would be accredited members from the People's Republic of China embassy and consulate.

China. It had replaced the former Soviet Union as the new bogeyman, and Peter Mack had seen that coming. The Bureau had twenty-two hundred agents working foreign counterintelligence, buttressed by a lavish budget of over a half-billion dollars. Yet, in the entire FBI apparatus, there was only a handful of Chinese agents, most of them on the West Coast. Not one was in the New York field office, nor was there anyone who spoke any dialect of the language.

Mack had tried first to learn Cantonese, then Mandarin, and had found both overwhelming. But he had immersed himself in Chinese history and philosophy and found them fascinating. Fascinating, too, was the way in which modern China behaved toward the United States: bullying, arrogant, and barefaced when it came to bribing politicians or coercing American multinational corporations.

Two years ago, Mack had written a memo urging that the Bureau develop a crash course to train agents to deal with what was rapidly becoming an epidemic: Chinese economic espionage. How the contents of that memo had come to Dodge French's attention, Mack never knew. One day, he was summoned into the assistant deputy director's office and introduced to a man whose face he recognized from the evening news and whose name was synonymous with U.S. policy toward China.

The conversation with Dodge French had lasted three hours. Mack reviewed the highlights of his memo, citing historical examples and current events to support his claims. When he finished, Dodge had thanked him and complimented him on his arguments. Two weeks later, the New York assistant director informed a startled Mack that in addition to his usual duties, he would serve as the Bureau's liaison with Dodge French.

Standing near the majestic, flower-bordered fountain, in front of the house, Mack watched the way French worked his guests, with just the right amounts of deference and familiarity. Over the past two years, he had learned a great deal from the fabled diplomat. With a few quiet words in certain influential ears, French had caused Mack's career to skyrocket. Magically, extra money was found in Washington to allow Peter Mack to work up databases on all Chinese connections, diplomatic, political, and industrial, in New York. The consular stuff was scrutinized, as were the local subcontractors the Chinese preferred. Accommodating judges signed wiretap orders and authorized close-in surveillance.

Technically, all the information Peter Mack gleaned remained in the law-enforcement/intelligence community. He traveled regularly to the capitol to brief his counterparts in the CIA, the National Security Agency, and the president's National Security Council. Occasionally, he traveled to Brandywine to answer questions and offer analyses and commentaries to America's elder statesman, the man credited with coaxing China onto the world stage.

As French escorted his guests into the house, Mack

turned his attention to the valet who was showing the
Chinese driver where to park. And surreptitiously taking his picture. And coaxing a few words of conversation to create a voiceprint. Who knew who the driver
really was—or who he might become? The most effective spies appeared as underlings, invisible in the glitz
and glitter. They were the fish Peter Mack trolled for.

"How are you, Peter?"

The smell of her perfume reached Mack before the
fall of her footsteps.

Holland Tylo, senior Secret Service agent in the
White House detail, was in her early thirties. Her
ash-blonde hair, cut short, framed a heart-shaped
face, the skin burnished gold from the sun. She was
over five feet eight, and very fit. From any distance
she would be called beautiful. But close examination
revealed tiny flaws that betrayed exactly the kind of
person she was: the eyes, wary, stalking; the tight
creases at the corners of her mouth that chiseled
away what could have been warmth in her smile.
Features molded by the harsh demands of her job,
demands that Peter Mack shared. He had met Tylo
on a number of occasions and felt something more
than a professional kinship. More like a temptation
to explore certain possibilities . . .

"Agent Tylo. Good to see you again."

The last time had been in D.C., two months before,
when Dodge French had invited Mack to accompany
him to a White House function.

"Are you working the advance team?"

Holland Tylo nodded. "The President's on her
way."

From the way he was looking at her, Tylo could tell that his interest was more than just professional. She returned his smile with one of appropriately dim wattage. Mack was a handsome man, but too narcissistic about his looks. Besides that, she knew that he sat on the right hand of Dodge French when it came to counterintelligence issues, that most of his fellow agents respected him but seldom asked him to join them for a beer. And that he had a steady girlfriend in New York.

"How's business?" she asked.

Mack gestured with his chin toward the driveway where another limousine was disgorging its consignment of Chinese diplomats.

"It's picked up since they increased their consular staff by thirty percent."

Mack paused. "Listen, I'm going to be down in D.C. in a few days or so. It'd be nice to get together."

"I'd like that," Tylo replied, then after the slightest hesitation added, "Will your girlfriend be coming too?"

Tylo suppressed a grin at the way Mack's face colored. Then a voice behind them got Mack's attention.

"Peter!"

The two agents turned to see Dodge French walking toward them.

When Mack introduced Tylo, French was polite but brief.

"Peter, you and I must have a word," he said. "Agent Tylo, will you excuse us?"

"Of course, sir."

She watched them go off, heads close together,

French speaking quickly, gesturing with his hands. Then Mack's intent expression changed to disbelief

Nodding, the agent turned away and walked quickly across the lawn. French moved in the direction of the house.

Tylo went after Mack. She lost sight of him in the woods but caught him again as he emerged in a large clearing. The helicopter's blades were already spinning. Mack ducked, then jumped through the open passenger door.

Tylo turned away as the chopper rose, hovered, then tore off over the estate toward the Sound.

What the hell was that all about?

3

TWICE IN THE last ninety minutes, Sloane had asked to use the bathroom; twice the security men had refused. Their focus on her was unwavering.

Ignoring her discomfort, Sloane concentrated on time. Time was her friend. The more she had of it, the better. Her captors were waiting for MacGregor to show up. Since he hadn't shown up already, he was probably driving in from Long Island. That meant she had fifteen, maybe twenty minutes left in which to find a way to reach the computer keyboard.

Sloane deliberately kept her back to the keyboard. She didn't want to attract her guards' attention to it. Nor did she try to talk to these men, who were obviously professionals. Questions would only annoy them. She wanted them to think that she was defeated, let them get a little complacent, maybe even careless. Then, if the moment came . . .

The black security man answered the phone on the first ring, listened, and hung up.

"He's on his way up," he told his partner.

Sloane caught his wolfish grin, as if he were measuring her for the noose. She dropped her left hand to her side. Her fear dissolved and her mind was clear.

Two seconds. That's what you'll have when the door opens. They'll turn to look and—

Sloane saw the door handle move, started to twist around, then froze when Peter Mack walked into the room.

Dodge French was seated in one of the two wingback chairs in the Quiet Room, which was what he called the space that had caused Agent Tylo several anxious minutes.

Four hundred feet square, the Quiet Room was recessed in the northwest wing of the library, behind fruitwood paneling, directly opposite the Adams fireplace. French had had the old laundry area abutting the kitchen remodeled by a special unit from the Army Corps of Engineers—the same men who had designed and supervised the construction of the Pentagon's hardened bunkers.

The room had its own electrical supply and filtered air units. Its concrete walls, eight inches thick, were covered in heirloom tapestries. The carpeting was Wilton, the furniture simple Shaker antiques. The elegant trappings lent a feeling of warmth to the equipment that the room was specifically designed to accommodate: G-6 fax machines, land lines, satellite communications, and modems, all secured with the latest encryption devices. IBM's government-issue-only computer, the next generation of the 3000 Series, and its complementary software, gave French access to virtually any machine in the government's inventory. Peeking into the files of corporations or, on the odd occasion, an individual required only minimal effort. Dodge French may have reached a biblical age, but when it came to computers he'd been coached by the best byte boys on Bell Labs' payroll.

"You really shouldn't have let Mi Yang make that arrangement with MacGregor," French said.

The man in the chair opposite him caught the reproach in the words and shrugged it off. He was Chong-Pin Dan, personal secretary to the Chinese premier, and at that moment savoring cold quail eggs, a delicacy French had provided just for him.

"I was not aware that Yang and MacGregor had—how do you call it?—a side bet."

His voice was reedy, like the man, a thin, dusty mannequin in an ill-fitting blue suit on a bony frame.

French didn't buy the image for a minute, any more than he did Dan's hesitancy before employing a colloquialism. The Chinese had studied at Princeton and the Sorbonne. Fluent in six languages, a grand-master-level chess player, his intellect was almost a match for French's.

"The point is, this is not some mere bagatelle," French said. "MacGregor has exposed himself—and been caught."

This got Dan's attention, as French knew it would. "How great is the exposure?" Dan asked softly.

"Negligible—or it will be made so very shortly. I'm expecting a call. I'm suggesting, however, that Mi Yang erase all evidence of the stock transaction." He paused, then added delicately. "Concerning Yang, you might consider other measures as well. We can't allow anything to jeopardize the project at this late date."

The Chinese allowed a polite beat to go by. It would

be unseemly to decide a man's fate in less than that.

"Be assured that the matter will be resolved appropriately." Dan's eyes blinked like a sleepy lizard's. "And MacGregor?"

French's hand came to rest on the handset of a telephone. "Perhaps a job for your man in Hong Kong?"

Dan smiled.

"Peter!"

His eyes were like polished Teflon. Sloane noticed the slight tic at the corner of his mouth, saw his effort to control his anger.

"I'll take it from here," Mack said to the two security men. "Wait outside."

She watched Peter Mack walk over to the windows, stuff his hands into his pants pockets. She heard the click of the door closing, then his voice, tight, as though he were barely able to control his anger.

"You want to tell me what's going on, Sloane?"

She tried to regain her composure. This wasn't even close to what she had expected. Where was MacGregor? Peter had never even hinted that he had any connection to him, or to Young, Pullen. He'd never shown any real interest in her career at all.

"Peter, what are you doing here?" she asked finally.

When he faced her, his expression was bitter, as though she had somehow wronged or betrayed him.

"Hauling you out of the mess you've gotten yourself into. I was out at Dodge French's place. MacGregor was there when you were busted. He told security to hold you until I got here."

Sloane caught the whiff of a fix. "Are you on official

FBI business, Peter? Or did they send you because they knew about us, thought that you could—"

"Help you, Sloane," Mack interrupted. "Listen to me. You broke into your employer's computer. You copied private material. They can make that a federal case if they want to." He paused. "I'm not speaking for MacGregor, okay? It's Dodge French who wants to know what's going on."

Sloane knew Dodge French by reputation and that Peter had become close to him. But she hadn't been aware that French had any connection to Young, Pullen, much less to MacGregor. If the firm handled some or all of French's assets, it would be at the highest levels. Could MacGregor be the portfolio manager? Was French intervening to help out a friend?

Sloane glanced quickly at the computer keyboard. She could finish what she had begun and there was no way Peter could possibly stop her. Knowing that, she decided to tell him everything, gauge his reaction, then decide what to do.

"You want to know why I'm here?" Sloane said. "Okay, here it is."

She began with the package she had inadvertently opened, then walked Mack through her investigation, how she'd connected the dots on the East China Oil deal, describing the picture of corruption and lawlessness they'd eventually formed. Now and again her eyes strayed to the computer, still running.

From Peter's incredulous expression she realized that he knew none of this.

"Why didn't you tell me any of this?" he asked when she finished.

"I didn't want you involved. This had nothing to do with you." She paused. "If something went wrong, I wanted to be able to say that you knew nothing."

Sloane thought that her attempt to protect him would count for something, but found no understanding, much less gratitude, in his expression.

She stirred. "Can I get out of this damn chair? They've had me in it for two hours."

Mack watched her as she moved to the wet bar, poured a glass of water, watched the long, soft curve of her throat as she drank. What he had to do was very delicate. He recalled the details French had given out on the Small Lawn, the two of them standing in the breeze from the Sound, foreheads almost touching, French speaking crisply, his words concise, those of a field commander to his troop leader. He had barely had time to deal with the shock of what Sloane had done before French was giving him concise instructions: Talk to Sloane Ryder and find out why she had invaded MacGregor's computer.

Mack knew that Sloane had told him the truth.

"Sloane, I know you think you're on the side of the angels, but you're in a world of trouble," he said quietly. "What did you intend to do with the disk copy you made?"

"Take it to Latham, the CEO," she replied. "That was my proof."

"What did you expect him to do?"

"Cut MacGregor off at the knees so that he couldn't do any more damage, then go after the proceeds in the Antilles account."

"And?"

"Take everything to the Securities and Exchange Commission and come clean. Young, Pullen would be fined by the Securities and Exchange Commission. There would be fallout from the bad publicity. The SEC would suspend trading in East China Oil until the dust settled, then organize an orderly trading pattern to make sure it didn't bottom out in a panic sell."

"All this would happen because you want to protect investors?"

Sloane nodded. "A lot of small investors bought East China Oil near or at its peak. If it plunged, the results would be devastating."

Mack leaned against MacGregor's desk and crossed his arms. "You never considered any other way to handle the matter?"

Sloane carried her water back to the chair.

"There was no other way," she said "People go to jail for less than what MacGregor did."

"There are certain considerations."

Considerations . . . Sloane felt the air in the room become very still. "Such as?"

"There are things concerning East China Oil and MacGregor's involvement that you don't know about. That directly affect national security."

The Dodge connection. The fix. Sloane tried to keep her voice level.

"Peter, there is nothing in MacGregor's files to indicate that—"

"Don't make assumptions, Sloane. Just take my word for it."

"Your word—or Dodge French's?"

"Don't ask for details—I don't have any. All I'm saying is that there's a way out of this for you. If you forget everything you've seen, walk out of this room and never look back, then this never happened. MacGregor won't say a word, and Latham will never know a thing. Your position in the company won't change. In return, Dodge French will have handed you a marker. I don't have to tell you what that's worth."

Sloane couldn't believe what she was hearing. "Are you trying to bribe me, Peter? Are you really going along with this?"

He looked at her steadily. "Take what's on the table, Sloane. This is one crusade you can't win."

"And what happens to the investors? What's on the table for them? Some of them won't even *have* a table when this thing explodes. And it will, sooner rather than later. No one can hide something this big—even if it has something to do with national security."

Mack shook his head. "Think of yourself, Sloane— how hard you've worked. Just to throw it all away? You have responsibilities to your father—"

Her eyes blazed. "Don't you *dare* drag him into this!"

Mack didn't flinch and his next words cut her even more.

"Then at least think of what you owe me."

"Owe you?"

"I'm serious, Sloane. French held off calling the cops and sent me because you and I are involved."

Involved. Is that the best way you could say it, Peter? She felt her lower lip tremble. *Don't cry, dammit! Not one drop.*

"What's our being 'involved' got to do with any-thing?" she whispered.

"Don't be naive. What happens to you affects me. You may be ready to throw your career away, but can you live with destroying mine too?"

Bottom line, Sloane thought dully. *Rock-bottom line.*

"Are you willing to do that, Peter?" she asked. "Break the law because French tells you to?"

"I'm not an SEC enforcer," he replied. "I personally have no knowledge that any law has been broken. I've seen no evidence to that effect."

"But I have," Sloane replied.

Her hand reached out to the computer keyboard. Out of the corner of her eye she registered Peter Mack's startled expression, the realization of what she was going to do.

"Sloane, no!"

He was very quick, but he had six feet to cover before he could knock her arm away. He wasn't even close as Sloane reached out and tapped the key that completed the sequence she had typed in before the security men had broken into the office. She saw his shock and disbelief as he stared, mesmerized, at the words blinking on the screen.

NYSE—STOCKWATCH—SENT

Sloane did not spare him. "The SEC regulators never sleep, even on a holiday." She hesitated. "What happens now? Do you turn me over to the police?"

In a gesture she never expected, he reached out and covered her hand, his touch very gentle.

"No, Sloane. You're free to go."

★ ★ ★ ★ ★
★　　　　　★
★　　　　　★
★　　　★
★

4

Dodge French had spent the past hour circulating among his guests. Every ambassador, plenipotentiary, and consular official wanted something from him. Behind carefully crafted smiles, the whispered conversations were quick and succinct, sketching proposals, offers, and counteroffers.

French worked his way across the Grand Ballroom, its walls, floors, and ceiling littered with Italian treasures his ancestors had cheerfully looted over a century before. Sometimes, when the great house was empty, he came into this room to gaze at the booty. The artwork and tapestries served to remind him that he was only their caretaker, responsible for their safety and preservation. It also amused him to contemplate how quickly a man's family could go from being seen as pirates to being seen as revered custodians. Except the buccaneer streak was still very much in evidence in the French bloodline.

He murmured a few words of reassurance to the ambassador of Brunei, a tiny country that, because of its staggering oil reserves, merited attention well out of proportion to its size. He slipped into French when the Gallic ambassador buttonholed him, and into Milanese Italian to chat with the papal nuncio. When he finally came before Claudia Ballantine, the President of the United States greeted him with a soft grin.

"You sure know how to work a room, Dodge," she said. "You really should take my offer to run the State Department for a while, toughen up those candyasses we send abroad."

She was one of the few people French knew who could make a mild obscenity sound like an endearment.

French regarded her as he would a favorite niece. Claudia Ballantine, a natural redhead with milky skin and a spray of freckles across her cheeks, was exquisitely turned out, as usual. The navy Chanel suit enhanced her femininity, but also breathed power. Because of good genes and regular exercise, she did not have to do battle with her age. At fifty-three, she wore the power of her office with authority, while remaining an exquisitely desirable woman.

Her entourage, consisting of the secretaries of treasury, health and human services, and education, parted to let French through. He shook the President's hand with deference.

"Madam President, I fear the task would be beyond my humble abilities."

That earned him a laugh. "You're so sly, Dodge. So sly."

Claudia Ballantine scanned the room, picking out the knots of conversation, checking to see who was huddling with whom, always alert for the anomaly, alliances between opposites, contacts between adversaries. For statesmen, policy makers, and foreign diplomats, Brandywine was one of the most exclusive back rooms in the world, off-limits to the prying eyes of the media and the political masters back home.

Claudia Ballantine took French's arm and steered him away from the crowd. A covey of Rembrandt's burghers gazed upon them from down the centuries.

"I never had a chance to properly thank you for putting this together," she said softly. "It means a great deal to me."

"Madam President, it has been my privilege. Whatever I can do, you need only to ask."

She nodded, and for a moment her eyes became vacant. French had been a friend of her family ever since she could remember. When she was thirteen, she'd developed a schoolgirl's crush on the handsome, sophisticated man, twenty years her senior. Over time, that feeling had passed into an affection that slowly bridged the years between them. Dodge French was the first person she'd called when a bullet fired from the Statue of Liberty tore apart her husband's skull. French was with her when she accompanied the presidential candidate's body back to his home state of California and sat with her through the long vigil that had marked the beginning of her widowhood.

Two weeks after Robert Ballantine had been laid to rest, she went to French and told him that she wanted to pick up the standard. With their contender dead, the party was in disarray. Furious arguments had broken out about who should replace him. French did not challenge her wish; he waded into the internecine battle, sat the party bosses down, and outlined how they would capture the White House that November. He made sure they listened to Claudia Ballantine when she came in with her pitch. She did the rest herself. The American people swept her into the Oval Office with the largest majority since the Nixon-McGovern rout.

Claudia Ballantine looked out over the sea of faces in the room. She recognized most of them, point men for world leaders who had greeted her ascension with skepticism and trepidation. A woman at the helm of the world's richest, most powerful nation? In certain corridors, this was sacrilege.

In due course, she had changed opinions and provided reassurances. Fences had been mended and alliances strengthened. Those with a cultural bias against women, who insisted on seeing the President as weak and timid, were still smarting from her decisive military moves in the Middle East and in the Taiwan Strait. Claudia Ballantine had no compunction about using the power of her office. But only a handful of advisers, Dodge French among them, had any idea of the long vigils she kept after dispatching America's sons and daughters into harm's way.

"Madam President, it's time."

She smiled at French's fin de siècle formality. In public, he always addressed her by her title, just as he did privately, even though she had urged him, even scolded him, to do otherwise. She smiled secretly, imagining his reaction to the gift she was going to bestow upon him in November for his years of service and friendship.

Assistants hurried up to the podium that had been erected at the far end of the ballroom. Conversation stilled as the President mounted the three steps and stood before the microphone. Before saying a word, she reached behind and tugged a thick, corded velvet rope. A curtain fell away to reveal a large poster depicting children holding hands, forming a globe. The logo read: HANDS OF HOPE—HELP FOR CHILDREN WITH AIDS.

"I want to thank you all for being here today," the President began. "As some of you know, I have had two family members die of AIDS, a beloved sister and a niece who was only seven years old. It is in their memory that I have established Hands of Hope, a program that brings together the resources of our government with those of private enterprise and the medical community.

"In 1960, John F. Kennedy challenged our nation to put a man on the moon by the end of the decade. We rose to that challenge. Today I challenge the best minds in America and around the globe—regardless of race, religion, or creed—to bring an end to this scourge before the year 2010.

"I ask all nations to mobilize the resources at their disposal and to stand together with me. AIDS has no politics. It recognizes no national or political borders. It strikes rich and poor, developed and developing, without prejudice. And the victims, who are least responsible, who cannot defend themselves, are our children.

"Yes, they are *all* our children. This Thanksgiving Day, one hundred and thirty children, representing every nation on earth, will be my guests at the White House. For some, it will be the last holiday they will celebrate. For others, I pray that it will be their first day of true hope."

Standing off to the side, Dodge French observed skeptical, suspicious expressions soften as the President's words hit home. The woman had the gift to reach beyond the selfish and immediate and into one's heart and conscience.

French was no stranger to seeing good men go to their deaths. He had sent many himself. But, at this moment, he wished that Claudia Ballantine had been granted a different fate, one that would have kept her far away from the corridors of darkness where he walked.

5

THE HANDYMAN stepped out of the taxi and into the squall that had swung down from the Sea of Japan to batter Hong Kong. The police precinct station was less than a dozen steps from the sidewalk, but his suit jacket and shoes were soaked by the time he pushed open the front door.

The smell of fish heads, rice, and stale, spiced cabbage; peeling jaundice-yellow paint; resignation and defeat in the eyes of the detainees sitting on the long benches in front of the watch commander's desk. The Handyman walked past nodding heroin addicts, sloe-eyed prostitutes, and sullen street urchins who'd been picked up for vagrancy or shoplifting. The new regime in Hong Kong was not as tolerant of human foibles as the British had been.

The officer behind the desk barely glanced at the Handyman as he entered a narrow corridor behind the desk. He walked past the holding cells, alive with groans and snoring, went down a few steps to the interrogation rooms with their heavy metal doors that couldn't quite muffle the screams.

At the end of the hall was a door that opened onto a ten-foot-square room, the ceiling and walls completely sealed with state-of-the-art soundproofing material. The Handyman closed the door, sat down at the sophisticated communications console, and activated the computer. His fingers danced over the keys, opening the electronic door to a Fujian-class satellite deployed from the mainland missile station at Lop Nor four years before. As he waited for the uplink, he thought how clever it was of the Chinese to squirrel away this commo center in a grubby cop shop in the middle of Hong Kong's poorest district. Even the ethnic Chinese agents left behind by the British in a Trojan horse gesture, who had been born and bred in the colony, were unlikely ever to stumble across it.

The satellite acknowledged that it was ready to download. The Handyman keyed in the code and waited. He had devised this method of contact himself, insisting on absolutely no direct link between himself and his principal. The principal dialed his encrypted message up to the satellite, which then stored it in its memory bank. Then a second call went out, to a cheap beeper clipped to the Handyman's belt. No voice or numeric message was ever left. That the beeper vibrated was the only signal the Handyman needed.

The message was coming now, the decryption filling the screen. The Handyman committed the words to memory, terminated the reception, and shut down the console. The message was, in terms of its general content, what he'd expected. No one called him about anything else. He recalled how the people who'd hired him had assured him that his God-given talents would not be required, that they were simply taking him off the market in case he was needed. "In case" had arrived. The

Handyman imagined he could hear the dice rolling in God's hand somewhere on the rain-lashed thunder.

He left the police station the way he'd come in. No one gave him a second glance. Outside, the pelting rain and dark skies reduced him to a fast-moving shadow. He cut in between a merchant and the taxi he'd flagged, jumped in, and gave the driver an address. Fifteen minutes later, he was in a seventh-floor apartment in an old but well-maintained high-rise.

Unlike most Hong Kong apartments, this one was large, built in the mid-sixties when real estate values had been relatively sane. It was furnished Western style, blond-wood Scandinavian furniture, cheerful rugs and curtains. The only hint of the Orient drifted in on the odors from the kitchen.

A middle-aged North Korean man glanced up at the Handyman when he entered the living room. On the table in front of him were various pieces of documentation: South Korean birth certificate, school reports, vaccination certificates, medical records. The Handyman looked over the Korean's shoulder, checking their quality. They appeared authentic, down to the faded ink, cracked seals, and worn creases. All were forgeries, of course, produced by the best paper men in the service of the People's Liberation Army of China.

"You are satisfied?" the Korean asked, using the Mandarin dialect he knew the Handyman understood and spoke.

"Speak English," the Handyman reprimanded him. "Yes, they're very good. American immigration won't be a problem. What about the passports and visas for you and your wife?"

The Korean smiled. The woman coming out of the kitchen carrying a steaming bowl of noodles and spiced pork was not his wife. He wished that she were. She was ten years younger than he, with straight, shiny black hair and a supple figure that stirred his loins. They both wore wedding bands and were known in the building as man and wife, but there were two single beds in their bedroom. The man had tried to touch her once and found himself looking down the barrel of a gun held one inch from his right eye.

The woman, also North Korean, set down the bowl and politely asked the man to clear the table. When he left the room, she said, "The passports will be here next week. The visas too."

"Then you will go shopping," the Handyman said.

"I have already done so," the woman told him. "It is the easiest thing to get clothes made in South Korea. I also bought some that were made here."

"Something pretty, I hope."

The woman favored him with a tiny smile.

"How is the boy?"

Silently she led him to a room in the back. Number 1818 was sitting on the carpet, crayons clenched in his fists, intently scribbling on butcher paper. He seemed oblivious to the rain beating against the window behind him and to the eyes observing him through the partially open door.

The Handyman thought that 1818 appeared quite the normal child. He had put on weight since he'd been spirited away from the camp. The woman, among other things a highly trained nurse, had ministered to his injuries and infections and carefully supervised his diet. The child's skin was losing its jaundice-yellow color; his hair and skin shone.

Appearances were so deceiving, though. The Handyman knew that beneath the semblance of good health and the effects of a wholesome diet, 1818's body was being pillaged by a virus that was an equal-opportunity killer. Barracks 6, where he had found the boy, was the camp's AIDS ward.

"He looks . . . presentable." The Handyman had trouble saying "fine" or "good." Certainly not "well." "Can you keep him like that?"

The woman shrugged and led him into the bathroom. The shelves of the medicine cabinet were filled with vials of pills.

"The best American and European research has produced," she said. "If anything can keep him alive, these will."

"Have you had him tested recently?"

"Every two weeks, at the local clinic. The documentation will be impressive."

Another man might have flinched at her matter-of-fact tone. She could have been telling him the price of fresh ducks in the marketplace.

"Six months, a little less," said the Handyman. "Keep him alive for that long."

"I can do that."

The Handyman had no doubts. The woman was one of the finest agents he'd ever come across. At thirty-six, she had been in the field for almost a quarter century. The North Koreans did a few things well. Creating deep-infiltration agents was one of them.

The man and woman had established their cover in

Hong Kong years before. They posed as husband and wife: he, the owner of a small jewelry shop that sold trinkets of electric-plated gold, and made very little money; she, a nurse who had worked in a British military hospital. The intelligence she'd gathered had been priceless in its day.

The man and woman had been waiting for the Handyman when he'd come across what used to be the border between the colony and the mainland. They had been briefed by the second directorate of the North Korean Security Cadre that this man would be their control. He answered to Beijing; they to him. They had also been briefed about the boy, but in greater detail, about his condition and his needs. That he was their son and had to survive until Thursday, November 27, had been made clear to them. Responsibility for this lay exclusively in their hands.

The man who was bringing the boy would explain their full mission in stages, when he deemed it necessary for them to know the next step. He would not stay with them, but would be in close contact. The implication was that he was a traveling man.

It was, of course, a lie. The Handyman remained in Hong Kong, residing in an exclusive building whose apartments were leased to Western businessmen. He'd been watching how the couple handled the boy and knew that the woman had told him the truth: The child was difficult in public, but she continued to play perfectly the role of patient, determined, protective mother. The Handyman had overheard other mothers' whispers about how patient she was with the boy who seemed so difficult.

He was also aware that she knew he was never far away. Sometimes when she was with the boy, shopping or in the park, she would scan the area around her like a soldier, front to horizon, then divide it into squares and examine each one carefully. She never saw him but thought that she could smell him.

The Handyman followed her now to the front of the apartment.

"How is the man?"

The woman's lips curled in distaste. "Better now that he has learned not to try to put his hands on me. He is good with the boy. You would think he had children of his own."

"You think he hasn't?"

The woman raised her hand, her thumb and forefinger an inch apart. The Handyman did not miss the malice behind her smile.

The man was slurping at the noodle dish. He wiped his mouth and started to get up, but the Handyman gestured to him.

"You are doing well with the boy," he said, addressing both of them. "I will mention this in my report."

"Won't you stay and eat?" the woman asked.

"Regretfully, no."

"You are traveling. Busy."

The Handyman withdrew an envelope thick with banknotes and placed it next to the noodle dish. "I will see you soon."

6

THE WALK FROM the elevators to the receptionist's desk outside Charles Latham's office seemed endless. Sloane fixed her eyes on the rosewood paneled door at the far end of the partners' floor and tried not to think.

On Saturday, after her encounter with Peter Mack, she'd left the building numb. She had no recollection of how she'd gotten back to her apartment, only that the rest of the day had been spent curled up on the sofa, the comforter drawn up to her chin.

Over the holiday weekend she'd been waiting for the phone to ring. Because there was always a stock market open somewhere in the world, SEC regulators kept vigil twenty-four hours a day. The damning information she had E-mailed would have been reviewed by Sunday morning at the latest. But her phone and fax lines remained silent. Nothing from the SEC.

Nothing from Peter either. Unable to bear the silence, Sloane had twice dialed his number, only to get his answering machine or voice mail. She badly wanted to talk to him, to find out the reason for his trying to compromise her. Staring at her bed, with Peter's scent all around her, Sloane admitted that she also needed to know how badly her relationship with him had been damaged, if there was anything at all they could salvage.

But throughout the weekend, the phone never rang, leaving her with the feeling that there were things happening that she sensed but couldn't grasp, like distant thunder just over the horizon.

By Monday, Memorial Day, she was tired of the silence. She called her father and took him to brunch at the Four Seasons Hotel. He loved the fish table, returning with plates heaped with oysters, gravlax, herring in sour cream and onions, and smoked whitefish.

Now it was Tuesday. On the way to work, she had marshaled and reviewed her arguments one last time. A hard tribunal would be waiting for her, she was certain of that. When she got off the elevator, everything and everyone on her floor appeared normal. But passing the secretaries' stations and the open doors to her colleagues' offices, she glimpsed the curious looks sent her way, saw how people averted their eyes when greeting her. The long walk down the corridor made her feel like a condemned prisoner on her way to the executioner.

When she finally made it into her office and fired up her computer, she found an E-mail on her screen. Latham's office. Now.

Latham's secretary looked up as Sloane approached the rosewood double doors.

"He's expecting you, Ms. Ryder," she said, her voice chilly, then busied herself with the correspondence on her desk.

Charles Latham was from the Midwest. He had snow-white hair, shiny crab-apple cheeks, and a kettledrum belly nudging the edge of his desk. His Santa Claus appearance masked a razor-sharp mind and an appalling ruthlessness when it came to business. The majority of Young, Pullen had been family owned and operated for ninety years before inbred heirs had brought the company to the brink of ruin. The outside shareholders had finally mustered enough votes, kicked out the existing board, and brought in Latham to clean house. He had sent the heirs packing, cut away the dead wood, and, after the bloodletting was done, returned the investment bank to profitability. Now he ran it as his personal fiefdom, driving the hardest deals on the Street, protecting his turf from the takeover sharks. The company's stock kept going up and the shareholders cheered him on.

"Miss Ryder. Good morning."

"Good morning, sir." Sloane watched him relax in his big chair, gesture for her to sit.

"A beverage, perhaps?"

"No, thank you."

"Then it's to business. You've been very busy, haven't you, Miss Ryder?" Bushy eyebrows rose to punctuate his words.

"Yes, sir."

"Working weekends, holidays . . . Care to tell me about Saturday?"

Sloane had no doubt that Latham had reviewed all the reports having to do with that day, from the security guard's sign-in sheet to the one Peter Mack must have written. She wondered if Latham was giving her a chance to explain or looking to catch her in a lie.

Sloane stuck with the argument she'd rehearsed,

building her case, emphasizing the crucial points. To Latham's credit, he heard her out without interruption.

"Let me ask the obvious question," he said. "Why didn't you come to me with what you found?"

"That was my intention all along, sir," she replied. "Except, circumstances—"

"You were caught."

"Yes, sir."

"And you were in MacGregor's computer because you believed that that was the only way to get the evidence you needed. Very well, I can buy that. Unorthodox method, but it does show imagination and guts."

Sloane blinked.

"Oh, come now, Miss Ryder," Latham continued. "It's not as if you didn't know what you were doing— crossing the line because you believed the end justified you doing so. True, we have rules to follow, but you know as well as I how these rules are bent, twisted, subverted.

"You see, I don't have much of a problem with ninety-nine percent of what you did. I had no idea MacGregor was running a little scam on East China Oil, or else I would have taken him out to the woodshed, so to speak. But what I need to know is why, and at the very last second, you sent the information to the SEC."

"I had no choice," Sloane answered. "I believed that the evidence would be destroyed—or at the very least that I would never see it again."

"So you made sure someone *would* see it."

She nodded.

"It never occurred to you to send it to, let's say, your computer, or the one you have at home? Somewhere you'd be sure you could retrieve it?"

Sloane felt heat creep up her neck. "No, sir, those possibilities didn't occur to me. But since the SEC was going to see the details anyway—"

Latham's words exploded like a gunshot. "No, Miss Ryder, that's an *assumption!* If you'd had more experience in our business, if you'd really thought through your actions, you would have realized that we could have taken care of our dirty laundry without sending it out.

"MacGregor is a greedy fool. But he is our fool, Miss Ryder. If you had presented me with the evidence, I could have squared the matter away with three phone calls. The East China Oil investors, upon whose behalf you became a white knight, would not have suffered in the least. There are ways to control a stock so that it doesn't plunge, but that requires the cooperation of the Street. Getting people to cooperate is my specialty."

It's also called collusion. Sloane knew better than to voice the thought.

"MacGregor isn't the most personable fellow," Latham continued. "But he is a partner in this firm. When you went after him, you put the firm in jeopardy. Then you went even further: By exposing him, you placed the firm in a very harsh, lonely spotlight. To mix metaphors, Miss Ryder, you have tarred us with a very large, very dirty brush."

Sloane felt the room shrink, the air become thick with threats and consequences as yet undefined.

"I did what was right," she insisted.

"You did what you *thought* was right. The two are not mutually inclusive." Latham paused. "Now I must clean up the results of your good intentions. East China Oil will not open on the board this morning. Within the hour, I expect to hear from the regulators. After that, the firm will be deluged with calls from the media. Instructions on how to deal with them have already gone out to the partners and staff."

But there was nothing about that on my E-mail.

"I expect that you will be even busier than I, Miss Ryder. The SEC investigators will be spending a great deal of time with you. You will be the object of media scrutiny. Tell me, do you fancy yourself as some modern-day Joan of Arc?"

The question made Sloane shiver. "No, sir."

"But it is the result, Miss Ryder. And results are all that really matter."

"What do you want me to do?" she asked, trying to keep the desperation out of her voice, but failing.

"*Do?* You will do whatever you must. Surely you must have thought through the consequences of your actions. Or you thought you had."

Sloane raised her chin and met Latham's icy gaze. "Am I fired?"

Latham's smile revealed a row of perfect, white teeth.

"You have a long day ahead of you, Miss Ryder," he said. "Best you get to it."

Leaving Latham's office, Sloane kept her stride quick, her gaze fixed on the long corridor to the elevators.

Latham's secretary's expression would have tipped her off had she seen it. As it was, Sloane walked as far down as MacGregor's office before she sensed the stillness in the air, saw partners standing by their open doors, secretaries peering over the cloth-covered partitions.

The door to MacGregor's office was closed, but Sloane saw the dark shadows of men through the frosted glass. From behind the glass came the sounds of hasty packing, the thump of an armful of books into a case, the crackle of wrapping paper around glass and china.

A heavyset man in movers' overalls came out, pushing a dolly stacked with boxes. His buddy followed, holding an oriental flowerpot in each hand. Then came MacGregor. He stopped in mid-stride when he saw Sloane. She noted the creases in his jacket and pants, the faint ring of dried sweat on the edge of his shirt collar. H. Paul MacGregor had slept in his clothes—if he'd slept at all. His eyes raked her and she flinched at the violence lunging behind them.

MacGregor took two steps toward her then froze as Latham's voice carried across the silence.

"Miss Ryder, the SEC regulators are in your office. I wouldn't keep them waiting."

7

THE HANDYMAN CHOSE United Airlines for the Hong Kong–New York run. It is among the fifty-one airlines participating in the Advanced Passenger Information System and has the busiest schedule on trans-Pacific routes.

The Handyman traveled on a passport made out to a nonexistent French-Canadian businessman. Over time, U.S. Customs had accumulated a solid travel profile on this globe-trotting man. When the Handyman entered any major airport in the world and presented his papers at the check-in counter, he knew that the passport number would be scanned by one of thirty-five hundred machines loaned by Customs to selected airlines. The machine would read the passport and, while the flight was in the air, relay the data to a Customs office in Newington, Virginia. There it would be compared with a federal law-enforcement database, the Interagency Border Inspection System. If no red flags popped up, the traveler—in this case the French-Canadian businessman—would almost certainly be waived through the "blue lanes" at Immigration.

In spite of the usual dispensation, Customs could

still pose a low-percentage threat, because of luggage. There are three general categories of baggage inspection. One targets those passengers whose names appear in the offenders' database. The second group is the people with duty to pay or forms that have attracted the attention of a Customs officer. The Handyman was unconcerned with them. The threat to him lay in what Customs calls its control group: people selected at random to allow Customs to determine whether it is meeting its offenders quota. The Handyman had had only one such experience, a year ago at Dulles. The Customs officer had pawed through his elephant-hide Dunhill suitcase and come up with nothing more than a perfectly legal tin of foie gras.

The United flight arrived at Kennedy at 11:05 in the morning. Forty minutes later, the Handyman was in a cab bound for the Four Seasons Hotel in Manhattan. Kennedy airport held unpleasant memories for him and he hadn't tarried.

The hotel was holding a suite—one with a large, city-view terrace—in the French Canadian's name. The Handyman presented a platinum American Express card embossed with the same name. After checking in, he was given a key and a large, tightly sealed envelope, on it the name of an internationally recognized publishing house—the reason he had traveled thirteen thousand miles.

The Handyman showered, changed into casual spring-weather clothes, made himself a drink at the bar, and cut open the package. If the package had been tampered with, the thief and/or law enforcement would have been disappointed. Biographies and eight-by-ten glossy photos of America's business and financial leaders spilled out onto the Handyman's lap. The enclosed cover letter prattled on about a possible book to appeal to investors. The suggested title: *The Millionaire Within You.*

The Handyman ignored all but one biography and its corresponding photograph—that of H. Paul MacGregor.

The Handyman smiled. This would save him a great deal of legwork, which in turn minimized his exposure. Rather than stalk MacGregor, he would simply let the disgraced executive come to him.

While the Handyman enjoyed lengthy lunches at "21" and Le Cirque—venues favored by MacGregor's divorce lawyer, who billed his client $300 an hour then stuck him with the lunch tab—Sloane Ryder wolfed down sandwiches in front of the U.S. Federal Court between her depositions before the SEC regulators. Latham had been right: She'd had no idea just what was in store for her.

The SEC was represented by tag-team auditors Burnett and Reece. Their gray suits matched their dour personalities and Sloane could barely distinguish between their monotone voices. She called them Bob and Rob.

In a cramped, windowless room with laptops linked to the SEC's mainframe, and a large reel-to-reel tape recorder that squeaked, the auditors gravely commended Sloane on her actions, then threw what would be the first of many curves.

"Do you want a lawyer present, Miss Ryder?"

She blinked. "Why would I need one?"

Rob expelled a puff of Juicy Fruit breath as he smiled. "Given the circumstances, we thought—"

"We just want to make sure you're aware of your rights," Bob chimed in.

Sloane recalled every detail of her second meeting with Latham, during which he'd told her to cooperate fully with the SEC. She had gone over that conversation very carefully, sifting for snares and traps, finding none. Latham seemed to have only one desire: to get the investigation over with as quickly as possible.

"I don't need a lawyer," she told the regulators. "Let's do it."

Rob and Bob had gone through the file, but they wanted to hear the story, from the very beginning, in Sloane's own words. As she talked, the tape recorder spun and made its cricketlike noises, and the air in the room grew fetid.

Sloane had thought that the evidence she'd downloaded to the SEC and her testimony were clear enough. But each evening she was told to return, and the next day Rob and Bob were waiting for her with fat transcripts, the pages flagged with yellow stick-'ems, sentences and passages underlined in red pencil. They went to work on her words like Fulton Street fishmongers with filleting knives.

The process continued for two weeks. There were delays as details were sent to Washington to be double-checked and replies were coaxed from overseas financial institutions. Sometimes Sloane was told that she didn't have to come on a particular morning, only to have her modem line ring when she was on the phone with a client. Could she come down right away? There were "developments." More often than not these related to things she had no knowledge of, facts and figures that only MacGregor, as the central figure, could talk about. Tired and edgy, she once asked the regulators why they weren't dealing directly with him.

"Oh, MacGregor went and got himself a lawyer," Rob told her. "Willy Preston out of D.C. You've heard of him."

Sloane had. Preston had been lead counsel for a former president, defending him against a sexual harassment charge.

"Preston is keeping MacGregor out of sight," Bob added. "He says he wants to see what we have before he'll let MacGregor talk to us."

"I thought MacGregor could be compelled to cooperate," Sloane said.

"Well, technically that's true," Rob conceded. "But we don't want to burn our bridges, do we? If we get MacGregor to cooperate, who knows who else he'll serve up."

"But make no mistake," Bob said hastily. "MacGregor is going down."

Not as long as Willy Preston is holding his hand, he isn't, Sloane thought.

Sloane's brave words about not needing an attorney now tasted like ashes in her mouth.

The SEC's erratic schedule made it virtually impossible for her to do her job. Most phone calls to clients were never returned; appointments were canceled, rescheduled, canceled again. By the middle of June, the volume of calls had dropped by 50 percent.

It was the publicity blitz that ultimately did her in. Within two weeks, the *Wall Street Journal, Business Week,* and *Fortune* had run lengthy articles on the East China Oil scandal. Sloane was portrayed either as a traitor to her own kind, someone who had deliberately set out to ruin a good man's name, or a consumer avenger, risking her career for the small investor. None of it was any good for business.

The few institutional investors Sloane handled were the first to pull their portfolios. In spite of her attempts to reassure them, the reply was the same: We loved working with you, yes, you've made us money, but the people *we* represent are nervous about all the publicity. It's been swell.

Individual clients were no different, frustrated, demanding to know why she hadn't put them into this deal or gotten out of that stock. Sloane had nothing to tell them. Her research, always top-notch, had lain fallow. Opportunities she would have been the first to spot had been scooped up by her competitors. Clients mumbled their apologies and withdrew their money.

Young, Pullen's quarterly figures revealed the extent of the damage. Sloane had managed to achieve what the firm euphemistically called a "negative intake." More money had gone out of her account than had come in. In a handwritten note, Latham pointed out that the worth of her holdings—and by extension, her worth to the firm—had dropped by 70 percent. This would be reflected in her performance evaluation. The issue of bonuses wasn't even mentioned.

By the third week in June, the regulators had given her a firm date for MacGregor's hearing before the SEC. She would be the only witness, with three weeks to review her testimony. Neither party knew then that other events had already overridden that schedule.

Nights, Sloane would return to the condo, which had grown silent and grim. One evening, she discovered Peter Mack had come and gone. The key she had given him was on the hall table, his clothes, once hanging in her closet, were gone. Angered by his intrusion, she called the FBI's New York office and was told that Peter Mack was traveling and unavailable. Sloane didn't bother to ask where he was or when he'd be back. In her mind's eye, Peter Mack was becoming a ghost.

The plan had taken two weeks to flower in the Handyman's mind. Now he regarded it as he might a rare blossom, walking around it, admiring it from all sides, always intent on finding a flaw or a pest. He found none.

In that time, he had gotten to know H. Paul MacGregor intimately. He knew not only his schedule but that of his estranged wife and their two teenage daughters, twins, whom MacGregor doted on. When the Handyman was ready, he called MacGregor at his home on Long Island and identified himself as the emissary of a man to whom MacGregor could deny nothing.

The Waldorf has a deserved reputation for elegance and security. It is home to numerous celebrities, and countless presidents have stayed there during visits to the city. Peacock Alley has been given back its old name after a brief lapse into anonymity during the Iranian hostage crisis. Refurbished, part of it is a splendid indoor avenue for cocktails and people watching.

It was ten o'clock on a Friday night. The hotel was humming with activities, its ballrooms and salons full. Traffic in the Alley was heavy, which was exactly what the Handyman wanted. Conversation, music, and the clatter of service were the background noise he required.

He'd had the concierge at his hotel reserve him this table, a necessary precaution against the Friday-night crush. From his place on the red leather banquette, he saw MacGregor brush aside the maître d' and shoulder his way toward him. There was no sign of recognition when he stopped in front of him. MacGregor had been given no description of the man he was to meet, only the number of the table.

"Mr. Smith?"

MacGregor glanced down at the man in the navy blue pinstriped suit accented by a sunflower-colored tie. He seemed relaxed, with an air of quiet competence, just the kind of man Dodge French would keep on hand for errands requiring both discretion and muscle.

"Mr. MacGregor," the Handyman said. "Please, sit down."

MacGregor wedged himself into the banquette, almost knocking the arm of the waiter who was bringing his drink.

"I didn't order this."

"Single malt," the Handyman said. "From the hotel's private reserve."

MacGregor smiled and relaxed a little. He was still trying to place Smith's accent—European, but which region?

"So you're French's man," he said.

"And I understand that you've been having certain difficulties."

MacGregor snorted. "You might say that."

Forced to take a leave of absence, he had discovered that he had become a pariah among the members of his set and in the Wall Street financial community generally. Barred from any kind of financial activity, he had no idea how to fill his days. His wife, mortified by the gossip at the country club, had fled to Europe on an extended holiday; his daughters were away at boarding school and wouldn't be home for weeks.

"Dodge French tells me you might be able to help," MacGregor said.

The Handyman placed what looked like a cigarette case on the table. Inside was an electronic device that created a field of white noise around the table. Only a lip-reader would know what they were talking about.

The Handyman then brought out a manila envelope and passed it to MacGregor. "Open it."

The contents were photographs that made MacGregor blanch. He would have exploded in anger had something not warned him to keep still, something soft and very vile in Mr. Smith's voice.

"Your twins are a joy, aren't they, Mr. MacGregor?

Katie and Allie. Rosebuds, both of them. They attend Miss Farmer's School for Girls in Greenwich, and ride at the Lancaster stables. Twice a year they compete in the Connecticut Nationals, Katie on Black Squire, Allie on Little Nell.

"They are the apples of your eye, aren't they, Mr. MacGregor? You've given them everything, made excellent financial provisions for them, ones that will not be affected by even the worst outcome of your current situation. In fact, you've got quite a bit stashed in the Antilles—although by now I'm sure it's in The Hague. You want your daughters to have beautiful, brilliant lives. That can still be the case."

MacGregor didn't notice the waiter deposit the second drink. He reached for the full glass and took a long swallow.

"Who are you?" he whispered.

"That doesn't matter to you. The only thing you have to know is that no harm will ever come to your daughters as long as you do the right thing."

"What the hell are you talking about?"

The Handyman placed a carton on the table, the size of a shoe box only not as tall. The cover bore the logo of Holland & Holland, legendary manufacturers of shotguns and hunting accessories.

"When I leave, take this into the washroom. What's inside is self-explanatory."

MacGregor's eyes were riveted on the box. Suddenly he began to blubber, the words tripping over one another in a rush.

"Whatever French has in mind, tell him it's not necessary. I'll stonewall the SEC—my lawyer will gut that Ryder bitch. By the time he's done with her—"

"She's not the issue," the Handyman said gently. "You are. This matter needs closure."

"Let me talk to French!"

The Handyman handed him a cell phone. "Try. But he won't take your calls. Never again."

MacGregor mashed his finger on the numbers, jammed the phone against his ear. His eyes began to glaze over as seconds ticked away.

"Never," the Handyman repeated.

"Why? Why is he hanging me out after all I've done?" MacGregor hissed.

"To prevent me from calling on Katie and Allie," the Handyman replied.

MacGregor stared at the quiet, composed stranger, felt the chill of the grave come off him. A fresh drink had been put in front of him. He squeezed shut his eyes, then gulped it down.

"What am I supposed to do?"

The Handyman slipped out of the banquette, then leaned in close to MacGregor.

"Have one more drink. But just one. Then take what I gave you and go to the washroom. Open the box, remove what's inside, then go outside. You won't see me, but I'll be watching." A beat. "Mr. French asked me to tell you that it's nothing personal. Just the need for closure."

The stranger was gone, and there stood the waiter with one more round. When MacGregor reached for it, he noticed three fifty-dollar bills on the table. Mr. Smith, gentleman to the end, had picked up the tab.

He stared into the amber liquor, trying to make

sense of what had overtaken him. All he could see was the reflection of his twins. Their laughter filled his head with a terrible roar, until he couldn't stand it any longer.

MacGregor had been drinking on a nearly empty stomach. He was unsteady on his feet but reached the men's room without incident. He carried the box into a stall and sat down on the toilet seat. He opened the box, stared dully at the two items nestled in tissue paper, and put them in his pocket. On his way out, he absently dropped some bills into the attendant's basket. He never realized they were twenties, never heard the man's profuse thanks echoing off the tile.

The night was cool, the wind stirring the exhaust from the limousines and cabs pulling up to the hotel. MacGregor bumped into a couple on their way in, heard the woman curse, and steadied himself against a lamppost. The doorman noticed but was too busy with the parade of arrivals to intervene.

When the light turned green, MacGregor stepped off the curb and walked doggedly toward the median, hunched forward like a man plowing into a fierce snowstorm. Images of the twins had been replaced by one of Dodge French, the warm, grandfatherly face now cold and impassive, monitoring his progress like an unforgiving god.

The idea of calling French, appealing to him— begging—thundered in MacGregor's mind. But he knew all too well that having made a decision, Dodge French was never swayed. MacGregor had seen first-hand how French doled out his mercy—with the tea-spoon of a miser.

The traffic light at Park and Fiftieth Street was a long one. MacGregor could easily have crossed the whole of Park Avenue had he wished to. Instead, he broke away from the people crossing with him and, to get out of their way, stayed on the median, moving closer to the flower beds. The world was spinning all around him, the lights of the buildings fusing with the headlamps of cars whose beams first speared and then washed over him. The grinding of gears, the incessant honking, the shrill blasts of the Waldorf's doorman's whistle to summon cabs created a monstrous symphony in his head.

MacGregor looked up at the sky, which, because of the city lights, was never quite black. Blood rushed to the back of his head and he had a sudden attack of vertigo and almost tipped over. His arms windmilled and he steadied himself. A voice nearby was asking him, "Hey, buddy, you okay?"

If he didn't do it now, someone might reach him in time to stop him. The police would be called; he'd be searched and questioned. While he sat in an interrogation room, Mr. Smith would be gliding toward his daughters, to put coins on their eyes as the Romans had, or a few grains of rice in their mouths in the Vietnamese way, once they were dead.

MacGregor dipped his hand into the pocket of his trench coat. The paper the note had been printed on felt greasy, the diamond-patterned wood butt of the small revolver warm and slippery. MacGregor faced the old Pan Am building, focused his gaze on where the once proud symbol had glowed. The barrel of the gun chipped his tooth as he rammed it into his mouth. He did not understand how he could possibly be screaming with his mouth so full, never realized that it was the scream of a woman crossing who chanced to glance at him. Then the back of his head blew apart and he didn't need to understand anything at all.

8

THE INVESTIGATION into H. Paul MacGregor's death focused on his last few hours. The detectives could smell the liquor on the corpse. That, and the doorman's volunteered comment, took them into Peacock Alley. The evening shift was not allowed to leave until each employee had been questioned.

The waiter who had served MacGregor explained that he'd had four doubles. The bar chit confirmed this. He described MacGregor as just another businessman. He mentioned his companion, who'd nursed a single beer, but it had been a busy evening and the best the waiter could come up with was a vague description of the man. He unknowingly misled the detectives when he said that it was MacGregor who had paid the tab with three fifty-dollar bills, leaving the balance. The waiter remembered the generous tip, so he had a clearer image of the man he associated with it than of his companion.

When the detectives ran MacGregor's name through the computers, the stories of his problems with the SEC, his forced leave of absence from Young, Pullen, and his pending divorce painted a picture of a man who was about to lose everything. Desperation and despair were common handmaidens in such a situation. For MacGregor to have taken the coward's way out was not at all unusual. Suicide also made the paperwork that much easier.

The detectives divided their time between accounting for MacGregor's state of mind and trying to run down where he had gotten the gun. The latter proved fruitless. The .38 was a cheap Saturday-night special. In New York, such guns were easier to come by than parking spaces.

The case became driven by inevitable conclusions. The need to find the second man grew less and less compelling until he was no more than a hastily written, fading footnote in a detective's small spiral notebook.

Seven hours after MacGregor's suicide on Park Avenue, Sloane Ryder entered the gym on Varick Street for her morning workout.

After changing, she hit the treadmill to warm up, setting an easy pace of six miles an hour. The *slap-slap-slap* of rubber soles on rubber mat was comforting until a woman stepped onto the machine next to her and, using the remote, turned on the TV. Sloane heard the announcer's breathless voice and made the mistake of looking up.

There was the Waldorf at night, all lit up, serving as the geographic beacon. Police cruisers with lights flashing, patrolmen trying to direct traffic, television-station vans jostling for position. The paramedics appeared with a litter, then the patrolmen were shoving reporters and gawkers out of the way. The medics trotting with the litter between them, a sudden gust of wind whipping the sheet off the body, exposing what was left of H. Paul MacGregor's face.

Sloane had no idea that she had speeded up her stride, as if she were trying to race into the scene being played out on the television. She caught the flange at the top of the tread, stumbled, and almost fell.

"Do you want me to call one of the trainers?" the woman beside her asked.

Sloane shook her head, unable to tear her eyes from the screen, listening to the announcer repeat MacGregor's name over and over again. The stark, jiggly images chased her as she zigzagged between the rows of machines, fleeing into the locker room and a shower that lasted less than a minute. Fumbling with the padlock on her locker, she threw on her clothes, grabbed her gym bag, and raced for the doors.

She had to run as far as West Broadway before her frantic waving snagged a cab. The ride seemed interminable, but at last she caught a glimpse of the pillars and stone lions flanking the Young, Pullen building. As Sloane jogged to the entrance, she noticed the line of idling town cars and limousines. It wasn't even seven o'clock, but the partners had arrived.

Sloane took the elevator to her floor. Except for lights in two cubicles, it was empty. She stepped back into the car and went up to the partners' suites.

The receptionist was there, which surprised Sloane. She barged past the woman and discovered that all the secretaries were at their desks.

She turned to the woman nearest her. "Where's Latham?"

"In the boardroom, but you can't—"

Sloane was already moving, darting between workstations. When she got to the conference room door, she didn't bother to knock.

They were all there, seated at thirty feet of polished American walnut. Light filtered through the lightly smoked windows, glinting off a silver, crystal, and china service. Fifteen faces turned toward her as one. There should have been sixteen. The chair on Latham's right was empty.

Latham gazed up at her from the head of the table. "Miss Ryder. I take your presence to mean that you've heard."

Sloane opened her mouth, then held back the words. These men, coiffed and barbered, immaculately dressed as always, with no sleep in their eyes. How could that be? She was suddenly very conscious of the wet strands of hair plastered to her forehead and the way she had buttoned her blouse, missing one, so that it was crooked.

They didn't just happen to hear about MacGregor on the news. If someone tipped off Latham, then he called the others, got them down here.

"I heard about . . . I heard it on the news," she said. "What happened?"

"MacGregor committed suicide is what happened, Miss Ryder," Latham replied coldly. "On the median in front of the Waldorf. Shortly after eleven o'clock last night. The police say he used a handgun."

Taking a step back, Sloane braced herself against the heavy glass door.

"But why—"

"It is unseemly that you of all people should ask

that," Latham cut in. "But since you have, I shall read you a copy of the note the police found on the body. You will find it illuminating."

A note? How could Latham have gotten hold of that?

"Are you ready, Miss Ryder?"

Without waiting for a reply, Latham began to read.

"'I have always tried to live a decent and honorable life. I have tried to face these recent charges with dignity and courage, drawing strength from the fact that I am innocent. But the pain this has caused my family has become unbearable. There is only one way to stop the liars and tormentors who wish to destroy me, who are savaging my wife and children. I choose to take this way, to put a stop to their pain and suffering.'

"'May God have mercy on the soul of Sloane Ryder, who brought this upon us all.'"

Sloane watched Latham purse his lips, shake his head as though warding off a disagreeable smell, and look up at her.

"I think that says it all, Miss Ryder."

Sloane was still propped against the door, tears scarring her cheeks. "He didn't have to do that! He didn't have to kill himself."

"A great many things didn't *have* to happen," Latham shot back. "I warned you, Miss Ryder. You had no idea of the events you set in motion. Now they have reached their tragic conclusion."

"Are you saying you knew—or suspected—that MacGregor was suicidal?" she demanded. "Why didn't you get him help?"

"You are in no position to question my actions!" Latham thundered. "Throughout the ordeal that you brought upon us, I have tried to protect the good name of this firm. Now I see that I haven't done enough.

"You are no longer welcome at Young, Pullen, Miss Ryder. Clear out your personal belongings immediately. Human resources will messenger your termination pay within the hour."

MacGregor's suicide and the subsequent attention in the business media made Sloane vulnerable. It was very easy for the Handyman to track her over the next several weeks. His instructions, appended to those dealing with MacGregor, had been brief. The woman was not perceived as a threat; the information she had obtained was not intrinsic to the project. Nonetheless, steps were being taken to break her. The Handyman was to watch this happen and make himself instantly available if it turned out that she knew more than appeared to be the case.

Sloane appeared at the federal courthouse five days a week for two weeks. She had expected to be questioned by the police regarding MacGregor's suicide. She felt certain that since Latham had cut her loose, charges of criminal trespass and computer theft would be brought against her.

None of that happened. Instead, she was told to return to that suffocating little room where Rob and Bob were waiting. After murmuring their regrets about the "tragic circumstances" of the case, they revealed that Young, Pullen was cooperating fully with the investigation. New details had come to light. Sloane was asked to comment on matters concerning MacGregor's business travel, his association with

Chinese officials, certain files she might have seen while rummaging through his computer. Sloane protested that she had no knowledge of any of these matters, that she had never worked on any of MacGregor's projects, much less his itinerary. But the questions kept coming, the tape recorder spun on, and by the end of the first week, she realized that they were leading her around in circles.

"MacGregor is dead," she said finally. "There's no one left to prosecute—at least no one within the SEC's jurisdiction. What are we really doing here?"

Rob and Bob were patient to a fault. "Loose ends, Ms. Ryder. We want to get to the bottom of this."

Sloane looked into their expressionless eyes and for the first time felt a twinge of fear. These two had the authority to make her return to that room for as long as they wished. They could ask the most inane questions and she would be obliged to answer. They had all the time and resources in the world and worked on some mysterious schedule whose parameters only they were privy to. They were like the IRS or any other regulatory commission, with the power to grind a person down by sheer attrition.

The temptation to challenge them was almost overwhelming, but Sloane knew that it would be the worst thing she could do. They were isolating her, keeping her off balance, giving her no time or opportunity to defend herself in the court of public opinion. Sloane had had dozens of calls from reporters. Whenever she felt tempted to talk, she remembered Rob and Bob's warning that until the SEC report was ready, she couldn't speak to anyone about the proceedings. There would, they assured her, be plenty of time for her to tell her side of the story. It was a bald-faced lie and everyone in the room knew it. Yet the charade played on.

On the last day of the second week, the session had been indifferent, as though the regulators, too, were growing tired of the farce. Then all at once the tape recorder was turned off. Rob and Bob thanked Sloane for her cooperation and told her she was excused.

"What happens now?" she asked. "When will you issue your report?"

"In due course."

"What about Young, Pullen? I never heard you mention sanctions or a fine."

"We're working with them on that," Rob told her. "Have a nice weekend, Ms. Ryder. We'll be in touch if necessary."

Sloane got out of there fast. She knew she'd never see that pair again, that someone, somewhere, had said "Enough." Now, there was nothing except bitterness in her heart, and the images of MacGregor's torn corpse in her dreams.

Sloane never picked up on the interested pair of eyes that followed her that weekend as she made the rounds of the stationery store and copy shop, or that a hand dipped into a wastebasket to retrieve a sheet of her resumé that the copier had chewed up and she had discarded.

Sloane Ryder was behaving exactly as the Handyman expected her to: She was trying to put her life back together. The next week he walked a few steps behind her as she hit the Street looking for work and vindication. Most of the time, she would be in and out of a building in less than twenty minutes, emerging frustrated, presumably with one less resumé. The Handyman thought it would have been useful to tap her computer and phone lines, but it wasn't really necessary. He saw the results of her efforts in her eyes when she was in a luncheonette having coffee, in the listless way she checked her watch and went on to the next brokerage house or investment bank where a human resources manager would send her straight back out again.

Ryder was a pariah, and her banishment in the wilderness would, the Handyman thought, be very long.

Just before the Fourth of July weekend, a package containing a flowery, unsigned thank-you note was delivered to the Handyman's hotel. It was a signal that he could end his surveillance of Sloane Ryder.

The Handyman had been expecting the message and was surprised to discover himself a little sad to receive it. Ryder had impressed him; there was steel in her spine. It would have been nice to make her acquaintance, briefly. One came across so few interesting people.

That night, settled in his sleeper seat in the forward cabin, the Handyman looked out at the lights of New York wheeling beneath the aircraft and wondered what would become of Sloane Ryder.

Because in summer Wall Streeters flee Manhattan's canyons for country rentals on Long Island or the

Vineyard, Sloane had expected slow responses to her resumés. She was astonished—and dismayed—by how quickly the rejections poured in. From the biggest players to the boutique firms, the results were uniform: great qualifications, love to have you, but sorry, no openings at the present time.

Sloane had hand-delivered over a hundred resumés. By the middle of July, almost all the replies were in and she found herself wondering where she could turn next. Chicago, Philadelphia, Boston? She might be able to jump-start her career in one of those cities, but she had to admit that it would be going down a notch or two—or more. The Street was the pinnacle of her profession. She had proved herself there, belonged there. Except now, no one would have her. Latham had seen to that.

He had also made the MacGregor scandal go away, burying it along with MacGregor. Stories about the SEC investigation disappeared from the financial media. Trading resumed in East China Oil stock and the shares continued to move in a narrow range, giving no indication that anything was amiss. At the end of July, the *Wall Street Journal* carried a two-inch article buried in the market quotes section about a settlement between Young, Pullen and the SEC. The terms were not disclosed.

When her settlement check from Young, Pullen came in, Sloane realized that she held in her hand the last vestige of the life she'd thought she could believe in.

In early August, Sloane booked the flights, hotels, and rental cars over the Internet, then a week later picked up her father on the way to Kennedy. For the next month, they motored up the California coast, starting in San Diego, stopping in Los Angeles, then following the mission trail all the way up to San Francisco.

The sheer beauty of the coastline, the quaint comfort of the small inns they stayed at, the time Sloane had to give to her father all helped to peel away the cocoon of uncertainty and gloom that had been spun around her. When they boarded the airplane in San Francisco for the return flight, she felt rested and rejuvenated. After Labor Day, she would start hunting again—or maybe even hang out her own shingle. It would be tough at first, and expensive, but all she needed were a couple of solid clients and a few solid deals to show that she was back.

When Sloane walked through her door, she noticed the blinking light on her answering machine. She pressed the rewind button and listened as she opened the windows to air out the apartment. Then she stopped, ran back to the machine. Playing the message again, she tried to figure out why on earth the federal government was calling her with a job offer.

9

LEE PORTER always took the train when he had business in New York. Getting out to Ronald Reagan National Airport, taking the shuttle, then hauling into Manhattan from La Guardia took as much time and was far less pleasant.

Porter had a government pass that entitled him to a reduced fare. He was sixty-five and therefore eligible for a senior citizen's discount. He took advantage of both but always paid the upgrade to the club car out of his own pocket. He was a very precise man when it came to business expenses and numbers in general. He had to be. Lee Porter was a section head at the General Accounting Office, the audit watchdog of Congress.

The club car filled up quickly with lawyers and lobbyists heading to New York to grub for campaign contributions. Porter checked the breakfast menu, ordered strawberries and coffee, and settled back with the file.

Sloane Ryder had blipped on his radar as soon as word of the SEC investigation into East China Oil trades had hit D.C. Judging by what Porter had read and heard, the lady had had one hell of a summer. He'd been tempted to reach out to her earlier; he could have pulled the regulators off her back with one phone call. But he'd wanted to see how she would handle the inquisition, see whether the pressure would break her. In the end, Porter had been impressed by her survival skills.

At Penn Station, Porter slipped through the crowds at the taxi line and proceeded down Seventh Avenue. He walked briskly, enjoying the cool September weather, a welcome relief from Washington's deadening humidity. At West Eighth Street, he turned left, crossed over to Fifth Avenue, to a small, European-style hotel whose dining room offered inventive American fare at astonishingly reasonable prices.

As the headwaiter showed him to a window table overlooking the hotel's lush garden, Porter felt eyes watching him well before he saw Sloane Ryder.

Sloane followed Porter's progress across the room. She had been expecting a drab bureaucrat. But here came a tall black gentleman, with a wool cap of curly gray hair and dark amber eyes. Dressed in a conservatively cut lightweight wool suit, he carried himself with quiet dignity. She thought that he bore more than a passing resemblance to the actor Morgan Freeman.

"Ms. Ryder, I'm Lee Porter."

His handshake was firm, the skin faintly rough, like that of a weekend handyman. Sloane wondered if he had a hobby—woodworking, perhaps.

They exchanged fifteen seconds of pleasantries and ended up staring at each other.

Porter smiled. "Not one for chitchat either, are you?"

"I'm sorry," Sloane said. "I haven't used my social skills for a while."

"May I order for you?"

"Please."

Porter went along with the waiter's recommendation of venison with juniper-berry sauce, complemented by a bottle of Freemark Abbey. Then, he took a moment to study Sloane Ryder. Her skin had color, but there were dark smudges under her eyes and lines around her mouth that she probably hadn't noticed yet. Her cheeks were slightly gaunt. She sat with her back straight, her blue suit immaculate. There was a hint of stubbornness in her chin.

"I understand the SEC regulators are through with you," he said.

"They have all the paperwork they'll ever need," Sloane replied. "Plus my testimony. Except, of course, there's no one left to prosecute."

"I'm sorry about MacGregor," Porter said. "But as far as I'm concerned, you had nothing to do with his death."

"A lot of people would disagree with you."

"Do *you* feel responsible?"

"I believe that MacGregor would not have killed himself if I hadn't exposed him. That's about as much responsibility as I'll take on."

"Do you think you were wrong in exposing him?"

"No. But sometimes knowing that isn't enough."

"It can be, Ms. Ryder" Porter replied. "Do you remember Hubert Downs."

Sloane nodded. Hubert Downs had been the head of the President's commission on education, until he was caught embezzling the very funds he was supposed to be allocating to needy schools. Two days after that story broke, Hubert Downs, an avid skydiver, didn't bother to open his parachute at two thousand feet above a Florida beach.

"Downs was given a tremendous responsibility and he betrayed it," Porter said. "His actions robbed children of books, teachers, even heat for the classrooms in winter. I was the one who brought him down and no, Ms. Ryder, I don't feel responsible in the least for his cowardice."

Sloane looked into Porter's hard, wise eyes. "Your message said that you're from the GAO. But who *are* you?"

"Do you know much about the General Accounting Office, Ms. Ryder?"

"Not really."

"Briefly put, we're auditors for Congress. We monitor the financial activities of every branch of government, military and civilian."

"You're the people who ask about those six-hundred-dollar wrenches the Pentagon insists on buying."

"Wrenches and a whole lot of other things. Most of our work is open to public scrutiny, but some of it is never talked about, not even among our bosses. That's the kind of work I do, Ms. Ryder. I head up a small division called MJ-11."

"Never heard of it."

"I'd be surprised if you had. MJ-11 works under very tight security. We have almost no contact with the rest of the office. What we do have are our own mainframes and the latest encryption/decryption software from the National Security Agency."

Their lunch was served and Sloane did not speak until the waiter had departed.

"If you're telling me this much," she said, "you must have checked up on me."

"Believe me, Ms. Ryder, I know all about the events at Young, Pullen. And more."

"And you're here to offer me a job."

Porter smiled. "Let's eat before the food gets cold."

Sloane watched him cut a bite-size piece of meat, spear a wedge of roast potato, and cover both with a little creamed spinach. The movements reflected the man: precise, economical, deliberate. She managed a few bites herself before her patience ran out.

"A job," she repeated. "Working for you, in Washington."

Porter glanced up from his plate. "Exactly."

"Doing what—exactly?"

Porter set down his cutlery. "Six-hundred-dollar Pentagon wrenches really don't interest me, Ms. Ryder, except insofar as I hate waste of any kind. There are other people who handle that kind of work. MJ-11 has a much broader mandate. Anyone who is being considered for any job in the federal government, anyone who currently holds one, has been retired or fired from one falls within our jurisdiction."

"Your jurisdiction to do what?"

"Watch. Every day we scan hundreds of names of people in various positions. We search for the anomaly. Is a GS-11 making fifty thousand dollars a year driving around in a top-of-the-line Mercedes? Is he or she living in a neighborhood that's too swank, in a house or condo whose mortgage is beyond their monthly take-home? Do their kids go to impossibly expensive schools? Do they vacation in St. Kitts-Nevis and Telluride instead of Atlantic City? And if they go to Atlantic City, we want to know how often, if the hotels comp them, if their credit card receipts start to read Cartier and Neiman Marcus."

Porter returned to his food, giving Sloane a chance to think about what he'd said. She was intrigued, but still didn't know where Porter was headed. She waited until their plates had been cleared away before asking.

"You get this information," she said slowly. "You find an anomaly. Then what?"

"We establish a field file on the individual. We begin surveillance. We introduce wiretaps and other devices to help us monitor the individual's activities."

"Wiretaps," Sloane murmured.

"Are you familiar with the 1978 Foreign Intelligence Surveillance Act?"

"I know that it exists."

"Your friend, Special Agent Peter Mack?"

Sloane's eyes narrowed. "From him, yes."

"There's a room on the sixth floor of the Justice Department," Porter said. "Impervious to electronic bugging or any other kind of surveillance. Once every two weeks, a judge from one of the federal district courts comes in and signs wiretap and other eavesdropping petitions presented to him by a Justice Department lawyer. The CIA, FBI, others—all use this facility. We do too."

When the waiter came by with their coffees, Porter handed him his American Express card.

"You wiretap, you conduct surveillance," Sloane said. "To catch civil servants who play the ponies or slots and don't declare their winnings?"

Porter smiled. "Those we leave alone, Ms. Ryder. We don't even pass on our findings to the IRS because that would draw attention to our methods and resources. No, what we're looking for are Americans who have chosen to betray their country. For ideology, blackmail, money." He paused. "I am a fisher of men, Ms. Ryder. I set my lines for the spies among us."

If Porter was aware of Sloane's surprised expression, he gave no sign.

"Care to take a walk?" he asked, signing the bill.

Sloane fell in beside Porter as they moved up Fifth Avenue, trying to comprehend how she might fit into anything this soft-spoken man had told her.

"You hunt spies. What happens when you find one?"

"We are never a hundred percent sure that an anomaly means espionage," Porter replied. "Although that is the case in nine out of ten situations. Occasionally, it's a matter of a windfall inheritance or something equally innocent." He paused. "But when we are dead sure that lifestyle and paycheck don't mesh, that our surveillance indicates unconventional behavior, we call in the FBI."

"The intelligence division," Sloane said.

Porter nodded. "The unit Special Agent Mack works for, yes."

This second reference to Peter bothered her.

"Does what you're telling me have anything to do with my past relationship with him?"

"Not in the least. Although I wasn't aware it was a 'past' relationship."

The comment begged a reply but Sloane passed.

"Why have you told me all this? What do you want from me?"

"Your consideration, Ms. Ryder. For the job I have in mind for you. We recruit very carefully. Given our mandate, we have to. You came to my attention several months ago, when your troubles began."

"I came to a lot of people's attention."

"I watched your conduct throughout," Porter carried on, as though she hadn't said a word. "I heard how you defended yourself before the SEC regulators, watched how you chose not to bring the matter before the court of public opinion." His voice softened. "I felt I knew you quite well by then. I wished I could have helped you after MacGregor's suicide, but you seem to have recovered quite well."

Is that how I seem?

They had reached Fourteenth Street. Porter drew her off to the side, near a raucous monty game. Sloane watched the huckster's nimble fingers as he dealt and moved the cards around a makeshift table of orange crates, chattering incessantly at potential marks.

"Let me guess what you've done over the last while," Porter said. "Resumés have been sent out by the bushel. Replies have come back, quickly, all negative. You struggle to cope with the ugly fact that Wall Street doesn't much like you anymore. You went after one of their own, and worse, nailed his hide to the barn door. Do you really expect anyone on the Street to ever trust you again?"

"It'll take time, but I can come back," Sloane replied.

"Maybe. I'm sure you've considered all possible options. The one that looks most attractive is to strike out on your own. A hard row to hoe, Ms. Ryder."

"And what are you offering?"

"A chance to do the kind of work you excel in. Work that has purpose and meaning. I want you in MJ-11."

Sloane didn't know what to say. The offer was intriguing, but it presented obvious difficulties. She would have to leave New York and her father. She thought Porter knew about that, had factored it in before he'd made the offer.

"You know a lot about me," she said. "You must know what I made this past year."

Porter shook his head. "If you do this at all, it won't be for the money. I can't pay you what you were making in New York. You went to Ravenhurst, Ms. Ryder. You brought MacGregor down because of the skills they taught you there, and because you have the talent to make the most of them. I'm like the marines. I'm looking for a few good individuals. I think I'm looking at one now."

They walked the next three blocks in silence, Sloane lost in thought, circling the offer. The Ravenhurst reference had her snagged.

In the spring semester of her final year at Harvard, a professor who had become something of a mentor to her asked if she had ever heard of a place called Ravenhurst. When Sloane replied that she hadn't, he told her about the advanced business program the college offered.

A retired FBI agent who, during the 1980s, had been a deputy chief of counterterrorism, had designed the course. The goal of the Research/Intelligence Analyst Program was to train analysts for the FBI,

CIA, Secret Service, and other security organizations. In the '90s, the course had been expanded to include competitive business intelligence.

By and large, American companies had woefully inadequate information about their competitors, foreign and domestic. Business decisions were being made with no thought as to how to get a leg up on the competition, how to collect, collate, analyze, and present readily available information on a competitor's products—present and future—and how to ensure that one's research and development remained secure. In the global economy, America was just beginning to learn that there were no real allies, just competition.

"Most of your graduating class can't wait to get to Wall Street and start making money," her mentor had said. "But that's a short-sighted approach. Ravenhurst will teach you how to survive in the world—not just in business. The skills you'll acquire will always be in demand. You'll learn how to stay one step ahead of the herd. It's your choice, but you always struck me as a leader, not a foot soldier."

It was the mention of survival that resonated with Sloane. Her father's experience had shown her how a man's life's work could be stolen from him. If Ravenhurst could give her the tools to prevent her from ever becoming a victim, then both the time and the money spent would be well worth it.

Sloane spent as much time outside the classroom as in it. She and other students cruised the streets of Chicago in unmarked vans, homing in on cell phone conversations. There was nothing unethical or illegal about this. They were only measuring the strength and range of two competitive carriers, determining which signal was strongest, which company had a decided advantage in a very lucrative market—and what the other company could do to make up for lost ground.

In Milwaukee, she analyzed the wastewater from three different breweries, a key factor in the analysis of exactly which ingredients each company was using in its product. If a lagging brewery wanted to emulate the competition's product or improve on its own, the elements in the wastewater would be very helpful.

On a trip to the giant rail yards of Pittsburgh, Sloane took along a metallurgist who measured the thickness of the rust on the tracks leading to a steel mill. If a competing company was thinking of going into business in the area, the amount of rust would be proportional to the volume of rail traffic into and out of the yard. The less rust, the more traffic, the more business, all of which meant that there was enough business for a second facility.

In Seattle, Sloane tagged along with a joint FBI–Boeing security team as they watched Chinese trade officials tour the plant. Nothing seemed unusual. The tour was open to the public, and the Chinese never strayed from their group. Then a Boeing security officer beckoned to Sloane and pointed out the shoes worn by every member of the Chinese tour group. The soles were soft rubber, gummy. On a concrete floor, they sounded like tape being peeled back.

"The soles pick up shavings of the latest alloys we've used," he said. "As soon as the group's back on the bus, the shoes are collected, sealed in plastic bags, and air-freighted to their aerospace engineers, who break down the metal and try to copy it."

"And you let them walk out, just like that?" Sloane asked.

The Boeing man grinned. "Sure. Whenever we know they're coming, we vacuum the assembly floor, then seed it with chrome or nickel shavings. Must drive them nuts in Beijing."

After she graduated from Ravenhurst and was hired at Young, Pullen, Sloane applied the techniques of competitive intelligence to the marketplace. Her clients—and Young, Pullen—prospered.

Had prospered, she corrected herself.

"You never really had a chance to practice what you learned at Ravenhurst, did you?" Porter said.

"No," she replied. "No chance."

"Well, you have one now."

Madison Square Garden loomed over them as they approached the small plaza that fronted the Seventh Avenue entrance to Penn Station. Lee Porter turned to her, his voice urgent.

"Come work with me in Washington, Ms. Ryder." He gestured at the crowds bustling around them. "There's nothing left for you here. Make a fresh start. Make a difference."

He didn't give her a chance to reply but gripped her hand and was gone.

Sloane stared after him, his figure distinct among the stream of travelers heading to and from the station. She'd had enough experience with people to realize that he was a remarkable man—principled, honest, dedicated. She tried to remember the last time she'd met someone like that.

Walking crosstown to her apartment, Sloane thought that the city was different for her now—but how different she hadn't realized until that moment. Just a year ago, she had participated in everything it had to offer. Now, it seemed distant, anonymous, and indifferent.

And Lee Porter of the General Accounting Offices was looking for a few good people . . .

10

IT WAS THE second day of October, the last time the Handyman would be face-to-face with 1818. The boy had gained seven pounds and grown three quarters of an inch. The length of bone made for knobby knees and elbows. The boy's sallow cheeks and unnaturally large eyes made him appear sickly but not sick, a child one would still reach out for and embrace without worrying about infection.

The Handyman gave 1818 a coloring book he had brought with him from New York. Its oversize pages were filled with line drawings of things American: the Statue of Liberty, the Capitol, the White House, Mount Rushmore. He watched the boy flip the pages, his face expressionless. Then he reached for the crayons, most of them reduced to stubs, clutched one in each fist, and proceeded to mash the colors against the pages. His violent seesawing motion shredded the paper. What was left of the stubs skidded across the linoleum floor. Drool began to run from the corner of 1818's mouth.

The Handyman observed the boy, then looked around the room. A few months ago, this had looked like any ordinary bedroom belonging to an eight-year-old. Now the walls and floor were covered in a frightening crayon chiaroscuro. The colorful bedding had been torn apart, its stuffing ripped away. The ordinary glass in the window had been replaced by a thick industrial-grade pane, the kind used in prisons and insane asylums. Decapitated toys were scattered across the floor.

The Handyman understood why this was happening. No one knew how long 1818 had been on his own before the military patrol had picked him up, what horrors he'd seen, what terrors might have been perpetrated on him before he'd reached the camp. With intense psychiatric supervision and the ministrations of those who genuinely loved him, there might have been hope. But not here, with these people.

The North Korean woman did not see any change in the Handyman's expression, but she immediately sensed his anger.

"You want to know about the boy's room," she said. When he said nothing, she continued. "The episodes started a month ago. First, nightmares, then the bedwetting. I gave him small doses of diazepam and for a time that helped. Then the episodes became more frequent and intense. They lasted longer. I began adding twenty milligrams of chlorpromazine to his milk, morning and night." She shrugged. "You can see the results."

"Explain."

The woman shrugged. "The monsters finally climbed out. He damaged the furniture before we bolted down the bed and removed everything else. Then he tore apart the bedding. The window was broken twice before the new glass was installed."

"Why didn't you take away the crayons?"

"Have you ever lived with a wolf howling at your door? The neighbors were already complaining. There were threats of calling the police. Leaving him the crayons was the only way to keep him quiet—most of the time."

"Why not a heavier dose?" asked the Handyman. "Or different medication?"

"That's what I said," the North Korean man snarled.

He sat in the corner of the sofa, his short-sleeved shirt exposing a large bandage on the upper part of his right arm.

"And I warned you that he bites," the woman retorted. She turned back to the Handyman. "I increased the chlorpromazine to thirty milligrams. In less than an hour, he went into convulsions. I managed to contain them, but until there is full blood work we won't know what he is or is not susceptible to." She glanced around the apartment. "I don't have the facilities to do that here. Asking the local clinic would arouse suspicion. The wrong medical report could bring inquiries, possibly even cause problems with the travel papers."

"I know," the Handyman said. "But it is a long trip. You need an effective sedative."

The woman's eyes narrowed. She accepted that she was responsible for all things medical relating to the boy. Still, she did not care for this man's cold, accusing tone.

"Diazepam," she said. "As much as it takes to keep him quiet. There is no time to try anything else."

The Handyman turned to the man. "What about your business?"

The man shifted, scratched the skin close to the bandage. It took him less than five minutes to explain his plan.

A lot of bodies, the Handyman thought. What Americans euphemistically called "collateral damage." There would be a lot of that coming their way soon. He wondered what the American media would call it then.

The Handyman sat down at the dining table.

"Your plan is good," he said. "Now bring me all the documents."

The following evening, when the streets were clogged with people returning from work, the man and woman slipped out of the apartment building, holding on to the child between them. They carried no luggage because the Handyman had already taken their bags to Hong Kong International Airport and stored them in a locker.

The Handyman followed the three as they walked two blocks and then darted into a taxi. As soon as they were out of sight, he walked to the man's jewelry shop, shuttered for the night. He went farther up the street, to a vendor, and bought a bowl of rice mixed with fish. He did not touch the food, did not take his eyes off the shop, not even when the street quaked and shuddered.

The shop's iron accordion gate buckled. The crisscrossed metal bars helped to splinter the glass that blew out into the street. The air was red, filled with the terrible screams of victims mown down by the shrapnel. Flames erupted from somewhere deep within the store. Oblivious to the chaos around him, the Handyman dropped the rice and fish into the gutter. He had exactly six minutes to reach his second destination.

There were lights in the windows up and down the apartment building where the North Koreans had lived. Some of the windows were open and the odors of cooking wafted down into the street. Tenants hurried through the front doors, carrying mesh baskets bulging with food. The Handyman carefully chose a vantage point catercorner to the building, behind a large delivery truck. Looking over the hood of the truck, he could see a sliver of the apartment window.

The *crump!* was like a distant artillery shell. A split second later the blast tore through the exterior walls, blowing out jagged pieces of concrete, rebars, and plastic. The force of the blast demolished the windows of the equivalent apartment in the adjacent building. Splintered furniture rained down on the alley between the two towers. A large piece of a stove, buckled by the heat and the explosion, hurtled down onto the truck and caromed off the hood.

Now came the flames, flickering out of the gaping hole like snakes' tongues. The Handyman listened to the screams, watched as the brave and the foolhardy rushed to help victims laid low by the falling debris. In the alley, a woman was crawling blindly on all fours, her face a bloody mask.

The Handyman turned and walked away. All traces of the North Koreans, and, more important, of 1818, were gone. The police and emergency services would have a lot of casualties to deal with. Some of the fatalities would be burned or torn apart beyond recognition. Identification would be a long and frustrating process, especially in a neighborhood where many had no papers of any kind.

Eventually the authorities would run down the name of the jewelry-shop owner. They would link his name to the apartment tenants. Neighbors would volunteer information about a boy. The police would go back to the dead to try to find a match. Impossible. Even relatives of some of the dead would be unable to make a positive ID. The police would never know who belonged to which arm or what torso. No one would come to ask about the Koreans or the boy.

Emphasis would then shift to the jewelry shop. Evidence of triad involvement would be found, so the focus of the investigation would shift again. Criminal gangs were something the police understood. It was easier to deal with the familiar than to waste time reading inconclusive coroners' reports.

There was an outside chance that some enterprising detective might run a computer search on the North Koreans. Maybe they hadn't been in the shop or their apartment, and they hadn't been heard from because they had left the colony before the explosion, on business or for a holiday. But any scan of departing passengers at Hong Kong International would yield nothing, since the North Koreans were traveling under new identities. As for the ferries that plowed between the island and the mainland, their passenger volume made any checks a nearly impossible task.

The Handyman took a taxi out to Hong Kong International and went to a row of oversize lockers. Inside one, he found the attaché case and garment bag that he'd placed there earlier. These were props, what an expense-account publishing executive would be expected to carry. He cleared the security station and, on his way to United's private lounge, walked by the gate. Beyond the floor-to-ceiling windows stood the airline's flagship, the new, long-range Boeing 777. And there were the North Koreans, seated at the end of a row of seats, the boy between them, sleeping in the woman's embrace as she stroked his hair. The perfect family portrait. Heartrending.

The Handyman did not break his stride. The digital-time readout at the bottom of a departures monitor indicated that he had forty minutes. His eyes shifted to the arrivals monitor. The incoming flight was on time, but even so, it would be close.

The Handyman hurried up the steps of the escalator. He entered United's lounge, presented his first-class ticket and passport to the attendant, and stowed his carry-on items in an open closet next to the reception desk. Then he asked for directions to the nearest newsstand.

The Handyman did not get off the escalator at the departures level but continued down to the arrivals area. Copying the American model, Chinese Customs and Immigration had established entry points at the principal airports throughout Asia. One of these happened to be at Seoul's Kimpo International, which meant that passengers on Korean Air flight 104 had been cleared prior to takeoff. This would save precious minutes and he needed every one of them.

The flight was in. The Handyman scanned the faces of friends and relatives, waiting to catch a glimpse of the familiar. He saw the one he was searching for, a young Asian woman dressed in a crisp, blue business suit and carrying a softshell attaché case. He moved through the crowd, got close enough to exchange eye contact with her, then moved away.

A minute later, the woman broke into a smile and waved her hand. The Cho family had arrived.

Making the Cho family disappear had been the most delicate part of the operation up to this point. When the news broke that their son had become Korea's AIDS poster boy and had been invited to the White House, there was a flurry of media interest in the child. But South Korea is a fast-moving, volatile country. Labor unrest, a banking crisis, and tensions along the demilitarized zone quickly pushed the Chos off the front pages. The fact that they lived in an ugly industrial suburb of Seoul did nothing to romanticize their image. Also fortunate was the fact that the Chos had no friends other than those who worked with them at the Hyundai Heavy Industries ship-building plant. Their only relatives were a pair of senile grandparents. Everyone knew the family was going to America. They expected postcards and maybe souvenir trinkets. International phone calls would be too expensive.

The ploy that had gotten the Chos to Hong Kong had been worked and reworked by the best analysts in the service of the Chinese military. The Handyman had reviewed each scenario and fine-tuned the one that had ultimately been selected.

Like many Asians, Koreans are ferocious gamblers. When Lee Cho received a confirmation in the mail that he had won a small lottery, he could not count enough blessings. That neither he nor his wife recalled entering the lottery, or even hearing about it, was not an issue. One always seized good fortune with both hands, never questioned it.

The prize the Chos "won" was an all-expense-paid trip to Hong Kong a week before they were to leave for the United States. A charming young lady in the employ of the Chinese Secret Service visited their modest apartment, showed them bogus credentials that made her out to be a representative of the Lucky Seven lottery. She brought flowers and excellent cognac and the Chos never got around to asking who or what Lucky Seven was. The representative also showed them the airline tickets and hotel vouchers, walked them through their itinerary, and presented them with the equivalent of one thousand U.S. dollars in Hong Kong currency. Before she left, she said that she would meet the Chos at Hong Kong International for "orientation."

Naturally, the Chos shared news of their windfall with their friends and neighbors. There was a party to drink the cognac and show off the tickets. By the next day, the whole neighborhood knew where and when the Chos were going. Hyundai Heavy Industries had already given Lee Cho the medical leave for their son, with pay.

Following in their wake, the Handyman saw how excited the Chos were. As promised, the representative had been there to greet them and they flitted around her like sparrows, firing anxious questions, the boy mesmerized by the Mylar balloon she had brought him.

A porter appeared with a cart to handle the luggage. Seconds later, a uniformed chauffeur walked up. Both were big, competent-looking men, Chinese agents who were under orders to smile pleasantly, put the Chos at ease. Given their training, this was not an easy task. But the Chos suspected nothing. They followed the representative like lambs to the slaughter, she talking over her shoulder, laughing, all looking around in wonder.

A warning bell should have sounded when they saw that the vehicle waiting for them wasn't a sedan but a van, with tinted windows and no livery logo on its side. It never did. The Handyman watched as the chauffeur offered his arm to Mrs. Cho, made sure she was comfortable, then helped the boy with his balloon. Mr. Cho asked a question, something to do with the van, because the chauffeur brought him around to the front and pointed to the Mercedes-Benz logo on the hood. Mr. Cho was impressed.

The Handyman watched the father climb inside to sit beside his wife. Their son was bouncing the Mylar balloon off the ceiling of the van. The porter pulled the door shut and got into the front seat.

But the vehicle did not pull away from the curb. The Handyman was standing less than thirty feet from the van, and he heard nothing. The van rocked slightly. The din of traffic at the arrivals area obscured the slaughter taking place in the van. In his mind's eye, the Handyman saw the horror and disbelief on the Chos' faces as the sound-suppressed pistols began to spit. There would have been no time even to scream. The boy would have been killed last. The Handyman blinked away the image.

Now the woman representative was moving to the van, pulling back the sliding door. For an instant the Handyman saw an arm, blood-slicked from the wrist up, hand an envelope to the woman. The door was pulled shut again from the inside and the vehicle moved slowly off into the traffic streaming out of Hong Kong International.

The woman walked toward the Handyman, never missed a step as she handed him the envelope. The Handyman took it and headed in the opposite direction. Five minutes later, he was back in the departures area for the United flight. By now, most of the seats were taken and travelers were lining up at the counter to check in or upgrade. The attendants were busy, the families preoccupied with bags and children, the business travelers impatiently flipping through magazines. No one noticed the Handyman wend his way over to where the North Koreans, the newly resurrected Cho family, were sitting. No one saw the envelope drop from his fingers onto the floor next to the woman, who promptly retrieved it and slipped it into her purse. Just in time.

The letter the Handyman had turned over to the North Koreans bore the presidential seal and the logo of President Claudia Ballantine's Hands of Hope project. One of the pages was an invitation for the Cho family and their son, Sun, to come to the special Thanksgiving Day dinner at the White House. Eight-year-old Sun Il Cho, HIV-positive since birth, had been chosen as the South Korean representative to the event. The letter and the attached documents were essential if the North Koreans were to successfully pass themselves off as the Chos.

The Handyman watched as a gate attendant came toward the family, manifest in hand, her features full of concern and sympathy. She spoke to the couple, who handed over their passports and the envelope. The attendant cursorily checked the passports; she slowly and carefully read the letter contained in the envelope.

Handing back the documents, the attendant beckoned the "Chos" to follow her. The man lifted the boy, draping his arms over his shoulders, and fell in step behind the woman, who followed the flight attendant to the jet way.

The Handyman waited until the new Chos disappeared into the jet way before making his way back up to the United lounge. He retrieved his bags, assured the hostess that he was going directly to the gate, and was the last person to board the aircraft. As he stepped in, he glanced to his right. The curtain between business class and economy class was drawn back and he saw the replacement Chos sitting together in bulkhead seats where there was more legroom, a consideration on the part of the flight attendant. The North Korean woman must have been scanning the passengers because she looked directly at him, a hint of a smile on her thin lips.

The Handyman stowed his garment bag and brief-case and asked the flight attendant for some mineral water. He thought that the plastic surgery had made the new Chos look very much like the deceased ones. The forged documents they carried were perfect in every respect. As for the boy, he was a ringer for the original Chos' son. He was the key to it all.

11

THE NEW YORK TIMES

CHINESE CANCEL
MILITARY EXERCISES, U.S. PROTESTS
SEEN AS KEY TO REVERSAL
BY JOAN TAMBORELLI

LATE YESTERDAY, PENTAGON SOURCES REVEALED THAT A PLANNED EXERCISE BY THE CHINESE NAVY AND AIR FORCE IN THE TAIWAN STRAIT WAS CANCELED.

WHEN ASKED ABOUT THESE DEVELOPMENTS, A PENTAGON SPOKESMAN CONFIRMED THE PULLBACK. WHITE HOUSE SPOKESMAN LARRY GINZBURG SAID THE WHITE HOUSE HAD RECEIVED ASSURANCES FROM PREMIER ZHEN XI YANG THAT "NO PROVOCATIVE ACTION WOULD BE TAKEN IN THE INTERNATIONAL WATERS OFF THE CHINESE MAINLAND." HOWEVER, THE SPOKESMAN ADDED THAT THE CHINESE "RESERVED THE RIGHT TO HOLD AMPHIBIOUS EXERCISES SHOULD THE ARMY OF

THE PEOPLE'S REPUBLIC DEEM THIS NEC-
ESSARY."

PRESIDENT BALLANTINE, AWAY AT CAMP
DAVID, WAS UNAVAILABLE FOR COMMENT.

MILITARY SPECIALISTS LAUDED THE
CHINESE MOVE.

"'Military specialists lauded'?" The speaker was
James Trimble, the President's national security adviser.
He was whippet thin but his ruddy complexion was evidence of dangerously high blood pressure. He blamed
this equally on the two men he was addressing, Dodge
French and General Samuel Murchison, the chairman
of the Joint Chiefs of Staff.

"What specialists would those be, Sam?"

Murchison was a big man and he shifted gingerly on
the fragile-looking chair. The Oval Office had under-
gone a distinctly feminine turn, warm pastels, Donghia
upholstered chairs, love seats. Murchison longed for
the good old days of the leather wingbacks and solid
sofas favored by President Ballantine's predecessors.

"My boys and girls are some of the best analysts we
have, Jim," Murchison said, dreaming of a cigar, tast-
ing it. "They read satellite and fixed-wing intel like a
preacher reads the Bible. The Chinese have bugged
out. And they took their rusty tin cans and creaky subs
with them. I've had overflights going 'round the clock.
That's what the specialist—who happens to be my
chief aide—was talking about."

"They bugged out and they're not coming back,"
Trimble sneered. "Why do I find that hard to swallow?"

Murchison's temper rose a notch. "I didn't say they weren't coming back, Jim. Or that they'd never try this stunt again. The one thing I *can* tell you is that they're not going to invade Taiwan today, tomorrow, or the next day."

Trimble ran his hand through what was left of his hair. He had lost most of it, along with all his teeth and his left arm, during his six years as a prisoner of war in North Vietnam. The face of his enemy was never farther away than the reflection in a mirror. The images of his torturers had leached into his soul.

"Let me quote something, Sam," he said. "This is from one of your counterparts, Lieutenant General Mi Zhenyu."

"Yeah, I know him," Murchison growled. "Vice commandant of the Military Sciences Academy in Beijing."

"Right. Listen to this. 'Regarding the United States, for a relatively long time it will be necessary that we quietly nurse our sense of vengeance. We must conceal our abilities and bide our time.'"

Trimble gave the chairman a pointed look. "Sound familiar, Sam?"

"I've read Zhenyu—"

"And you've read all the reports on the 1994 incident. The carrier *Kitty Hawk* was in the area to show the North Koreans that we meant business about having the international nuclear arms inspectors check their plants. Hell, that had nothing to do with China. But what did Beijing do? It sent a five-thousand-ton Han-class submarine to within twenty-one nautical miles of the *Kitty Hawk*. We scrambled everything on the deck—and had a Sea Wolf sub redo her target package—before the Chinese sub got the hell out of there."

Trimble's eyes burned with the fervor of an exorcist railing on about the devil.

"But the sub *did* go, Jim," Dodge French said, his voice level, reasonable. "And the Chinese have gone away this time too. We told them that exercises in the strait, especially with live munitions that could—if an accident occurred—hit Taiwan, were unacceptable. They blustered and postured and their editorial writers called us some nasty names, but they did go." French paused. "Just like they did this time—and they didn't even send their ships to sea. I'd say they learned something back in '94."

Trimble fixed his gaze on the President's special adviser. He never underestimated the influence French had in the White House. But he also believed that French was much more dangerous than Murchison. The soldier would challenge Trimble, debate and argue with him. But if Trimble made his case, Murchison would open up his arsenal and use whatever means were necessary. Not so, French. More the diplomat, the negotiator. The deal maker and the fixer. The old China hand. *China lover.* Trimble saw through all this to what he believed was French's true face, one belonging to that of an appeaser.

"You think Zhenyu is posturing, Dodge?" Trimble asked, his tone level.

French shrugged. "Zhenyu doesn't sit on policy councils. His business is to train his military. You might consider some of the literature the Citadel and West Point are serving up to motivate *our* boys."

"Not the same," Trimble replied. "We have no expansionary designs, no interest in taking over another nation." French was about to speak but Trimble held up his hand. "Something that strikes me as curious, Dodge. Been meaning to ask you about it. The *Times* writes that the Chinese backed off because of our protests. But our ambassador delivered the letter *after* the exercises had been canceled. How could the Chinese have known we were going to get in their face in the first place?"

French chuckled. "Even the *Times* isn't infallible, Jim. The point is, we're back to the status quo in the area and that's what we wanted, yes?"

"Yes, it's what we wanted. But no, I don't believe that's what we have. Something doesn't mesh here. Traditionally, the Chinese conduct their saber rattling in late November; this year, they're seven weeks early. Why? And have they really backed off? The ships scheduled to take part in the exercise haven't gone back to their home ports, have they?"

"Satellite surveillance indicates their fleet is strung out along the coast," Murchison concurred. "They could have an armada ready to steam in less than ten hours. And Taiwan is just a hop away."

"*Do* the Chinese have designs, militarily speaking, on Taiwan?"

Seated behind her desk, Claudia Ballantine had been monitoring the debate among her advisers, weighing their arguments. She thought that Trimble wasn't faring that well.

A former department head at Princeton's Office of Strategic and International Studies, Trimble possessed a first-rate analytical mind and espoused a global view. More, he was a keen student of the human personality. Trimble always dug into the psyches of those who had, could, or were in the process of initiating events.

But for all his brilliance, Trimble had his blind spot—a deep suspicion of all things Asian. He was not a racist. He simply understood the workings of Chinese, Japanese, and Koreans better than most, accepted how different the thought processes and the cultural divides really were.

Trimble had predicted both the Japanese economic miracle and its inevitable collapse. He had lobbied against the British surrender of Hong Kong, arguing that giving back the colony to mainland China would only fuel China's designs on Taiwan. He had foretold North Korea's drive to acquire chemical and biological weapons, with their attendant delivery systems, and how this policy would result in a bankrupt economy, mass starvation, and international tensions.

He's been right so far, Ballantine thought. *But the China thing . . .*

"Jim?"

Trimble was up and pacing, his prosthetic arm swinging at his side, the sunlight glinting off the double hooks.

"Madam President, I believe we have to take the Chinese at their word," he said at last. "Historically, they have always looked upon Taiwan as part of greater China. They want it back, they have the military force to *take* it back, they're waiting for the right opportunity."

"And that would be . . . ?"

"One of several possibilities. When we're preoccupied in another part of the world, say the Middle East. Or if they succeed in destabilizing the Taiwanese government to the extent that some mouthpiece politician 'requests' their intervention, or if there's some kind of domestic situation in this country they feel they can take advantage of."

"Militarily, we're prepared to fight a two-front war," Murchison said. "We have forward bases on Okinawa and in Japan, two carrier battle groups in Singapore, not to mention the new Sea Wolf submarines."

"What's your recommendation, Jim?" asked the President.

"We contain China. Just like we've done up to now. We make it clear that any attempt to move beyond already agreed upon territorial changes—Hong Kong and Macao—are unacceptable."

Trimble paused. He had more to say, but he hadn't thought through his arguments as thoroughly as he needed to. He didn't want to give French an easy shot at discrediting them.

'Is that it, Jim?"

"For now, Madam President."

"General, you've given me the military angle," the President said. "Dodge?"

French crossed one long leg over the other.

"Madam President," he said quietly. "Kentucky Fried Chicken's busiest franchise is located two hundred yards from Mao's mausoleum. *Sesame Street* characters entertain Chinese schoolchildren. Procter and Gamble sells more soap on mainland China than it does in the United States. Motorola was—until recently—the leading cellular phone company, with over two billion dollars in business last year; Boeing did double that. Inexorably, our economy is becoming linked to that of the Chinese. In two, maybe three years, they'll be our biggest trading partner."

"With a trade deficit on us that just keeps on growing," Trimble snapped.

"Which is one reason we must not allow the Chinese to think that our intentions are to hem them in," French said, carrying on. "Did you know that in Chinese the word 'America' translates as 'beautiful country'?"

"I also know that 'China' means 'middle kingdom,' with all its surrounding neighbors paying tribute," Trimble shot back.

French ignored him. "My point, Madam President, is that we alienate China at our peril. We virtually give away our trade advantages to everyone else." He looked pointedly at Trimble. "And that would create a disastrous deficit."

"You've been saying the same thing for years, Dodge," the President remarked. "You've been right about events most of the time. But what about human rights and the forced labor that makes all those cheap goods they send us?"

"We have always differed on the issue of human rights," French said respectfully. "I believe it is a component of foreign policy, like global warming or the destruction of the rain forest. But it is not *the* issue. China has made great strides in government reform. I think we can all agree on that. Sometimes we in this country expect too much, too quickly."

"Bottom line, Dodge. Will the Chinese make a play for Taiwan? Are Jim's concerns valid?"

"With all due respect, Madam President, no. China will do everything in her power to gain political influence in Taipei. She'll use money and propaganda. But force, no."

The President turned to the chairman of the Joint Chiefs. "Sam?"

"Madam President, all I can tell you is that if push comes to shove in the strait, the Yellow Sea, or anywhere in the area, we're ready to shove back—hard."

"Colorfully put, General," Claudia Ballantine said dryly. "Gentlemen, thank you for your thoughts. Jim, would you stay for a moment?"

When the others had gone, the President went over to the bar.

"Can I get you something, Jim?"

"Whatever you're having, Madam President."

"Something with a little kick."

She poured them stiff shots of bourbon and branch water. Both took long sips, savored the whiskey.

"Okay," she said. "You were holding out on me back there. Give."

"Madam President, the analysis isn't complete yet—"

"Then let me go first," Claudia Ballantine interrupted. "I've known Dodge French for years. He's been a China hand forever. And he's been right about a lot of things that have happened over there. But this time I think he's wrong. The Chinese want Taiwan badly. They're not going to screw around with this Asian 'patience' and 'face' nonsense. It won't be like Hong Kong where they waited out the British. This time they'll take what they want." She looked at Trimble. "So what's your counterpunch?"

Trimble sipped his drink, then said, "I call it the Necklace Option," he said softly.

"Necklace," Claudia Ballantine murmured. "At least it sounds better than noose. Tell me about it."

The Oval Office is the apex of power in the White House. Degree of power equals proximity to power. The vice president's suite is three offices removed from the Oval Office, separated by the president's study and spaces occupied by the deputy chief of staff and the chief of staff. This had never sat well with Vice President Anthony Foster, who coveted the deputy chief of staff's office.

Foster had not been the President's first choice of running mate. In fact, his name wouldn't even have made her short list. Foster had been a compromise candidate the party had foisted on her late husband. Foster knew this and couldn't have cared less. Ten years younger than Robert Ballantine, Foster had shown the candidate token respect. He'd believed that Ballantine had no more than one term in him. After that, with the right support, Foster figured to become the party's standard bearer. He came from a long line of political animals. His late father, a long-standing senator from Virginia, had shown him where bodies were buried and which politicos on the Hill needed to keep them that way.

After Robert Ballantine's assassination, Foster was certain the party would turn to him. He had never given a thought to Ballantine's wife, never suspected that Claudia would step into the breach and, using her grassroots organization America Forward, build what had eventually amounted to a fucking tsunami. No one was left standing—not Foster, not Ballantine's opponent, not sixty defeated congressmen who suddenly discovered they had to work for a living. This woman, whom Foster had never liked because he believed she could see right through him, had become a one-person wrecking machine. The only thing Foster had been able to salvage was his name on the ticket. Even Claudia Ballantine hadn't had enough juice to change that.

"You're letting her get to you again," Dodge French said, watching the throbbing vein at Foster's temple.

Foster leaned forward and stubbed out his cigarette, jabbing it hard in the crystal ashtray. Claudia Ballantine's White House had a strict no-smoking policy. Like he gave a shit. He'd had special air scrubbers installed and paid for them out of his own pocket.

He rose, a slim, compact man with a long, equine face and lusterless cocoa-brown eyes. Eyes that, except on photo ops and public occasions, were hooded, as though they peered out at the world from a cave.

"She's keeping me out of the loop, Dodge," he said curtly. "I don't know about a damn thing that's going on here. Makes me look stupid whenever some wonk asks me a question."

"There are exceptions," French replied. "To the things you don't know, I mean."

"Sure. You feed me goodies, but I can't use most of them. That prick Trimble cuts me off at the knees whenever I try to say something."

"Trimble is a problem," French agreed. "But like a kidney stone, he, too, will pass. The question is, how are the Chinese deals coming along?"

Foster smiled, showing off ten thousand dollars' worth of cosmetic dentistry.

"Boeing, Sheraton, Freeport Pharmaceuticals, Chase—everyone we talked about is on board. The Europeans and the Japs will be shitting bricks."

"What's the final dollar amount?"

"A trillion, maybe more."

"And the man who brings home that kind of bounty gets to walk into the White House," French said softly.

"But only if Ballantine gives up on Taiwan," Foster reminded him.

"She'll give it up," French said.

"Care to share a few details?" Foster ventured.

French shook his head. "There's nothing you need to know." He paused. "Or want to know. You've set up the ducks, Tony. The rest is up to me."

Foster shrugged. He was a pro: He understood the priceless value of something called plausible deniability.

In the next office down, the special assistant to the national security adviser thought that his boss had never looked or sounded better. Marty Garrett had been one of Trimble's prize students at Princeton, class of '81. Since then, he'd worked as an analyst for Brookings, the Hoover Institution on War, Revolution, and Peace, and Rand. When his former mentor headed to the White House, the call came and Garrett packed his bags.

Sandy-haired, with a trim beard and mustache, and wearing round-frame glasses, Garrett was often mistaken for a pollster or media rep. His corn-fed Iowa smile hid a first-rate mind that defied conventional IQ measurements. His politics mirrored those of his boss. At least, that was what James Trimble believed, because he trusted Garrett implicitly. The younger man had never given Trimble any reason even to suspect otherwise.

"Boss, you want to tell me what's going on, or is this going to be like pulling teeth?" Garrett asked.

"I'm savoring the moment, young Martin," Trimble said. "When you get older, you'll understand how sweet that can be."

"In that case, do you mind if I go to lunch? There's a young lady in town named Patty whom I haven't seen for a while." He grinned. "My wife."

"Sure," Trimble said casually. "And on your way, stop off at the vault and get the Necklace file."

Garrett's jaw fell open. "Necklace . . . You mean she—I mean, the President . . . she bought it?"

"She wants to see it, Marty. She isn't going along with French on this one. Necklace is in play. You and I are up."

"I'll be right back with it," Garrett said, heading for the door.

"What about your lunch?"

"I'll call Patty, make it up to her."

Trimble's laugh was cut off when Garrett closed the soundproof door behind him. The national security adviser had no idea that the last words Garrett had flung over his shoulder while hurrying out were only a half-truth. It wasn't his wife he'd be getting on the line.

In her office, Claudia Ballantine reached for her phone. Porter answered on the first ring.

"Lee?"

"Madam President."

"Jim Trimble wants me to examine the Necklace Option. I think I might green-light it. What's the situation with your ferret?"

"I'm pretty sure she's going to come on board."

"'Pretty sure' isn't enough, Lee. Things are starting to move fast. Isn't there anyone else you can use?"

"My team has been on this for months, Madam President. I need a fresh face, an outsider." After a pause. "Believe me, ma'am, I'll bring her on board."

"Soon, Lee. The Chinese are screwing with us and I need to know why."

THE FIRST TIME Sloane Ryder saw Whip Alley, he was wearing a flouncy red housedress in an African print, topped off by a matching headdress. She thought the dress was quite original—daring, even. But Alley's lipstick and makeup needed work.

It was a great day for the run, even in a fresh, crisp dress, with a snappy breeze that cooled the sweat. Whip Alley, his partner, Paco Santana, and four hundred other men were all decked out in red, from demure long-sleeved shifts with white collars and cuffs to bustiers and see-through negligees with skimpy lace bodysuits. They had begun their run at the small reflecting pool in front of the Capitol, taken Madison Drive to Fifteenth Street, circled the monument, then trotted alongside the large Reflecting Pool in front of the Lincoln Memorial, and up past the Federal Reserve to Seventeenth Street, toward the White House. The idea was to turn left on Pennsylvania Avenue and head to Georgetown, where the bars would just be opening.

Alley took the turn at the Renwick Gallery and waved to the tourists gaping at the sight of hundreds of men, decked out in fashion nightmares, racing past the most powerful office in the world. The locals lined the sidewalks and cheered. Their town was viewed by most of the nation as a formal, fussy place. The Hash House Harriers, as the runners called themselves, livened things up.

Alley was on Pennsylvania, imagining the taste of that first sip of beer, when he spotted a slouching, ferretlike figure in the crowds. Without breaking his pace, he veered toward the sidewalk to try to get a better look.

The face belonged to a follow-home car jacker and thief who called himself Tip. Alley had arrested him twice and had been furious to learn that two weeks ago, the felon had qualified for an early-release program.

Tip liked to hang out at the malls at Tyson's Corner and Potomac Mills, watching for single women coming out of the stores. He favored the over-sixty crowd, burdened with packages and boxes, paying attention to whoever might be lurking in the parking lot but forgetting to check their rearview mirrors once they were on the road. Tip followed them home in a nice, new-model sedan he'd boosted the night before, the kind of car that was a staple in the suburbs. He'd watch the target's vehicle pull into the driveway, wait until the woman had her hands full again, then screech up, pistol-whip her, grab the cash and jewelry, and run.

Until last night, all Tip had been wanted for was another car jacking and assault, this time in Bethesda. Sashaying down the street enjoying the weather and a lollipop, he probably had no idea that his latest victim had died from a massive coronary as a result of the attack or that he had made it to the top of D.C. Homicide's hit parade. Alley thought he could mosey up to the felon and drop him hard before Tip knew what had hit him. Bringing out his gun would create instant chaos.

"Ooh, I *love* your hat!"

Alley glanced at the woman who'd shouted the compliment and realized that her shrill voice had attracted Tip's attention.

Tip was feeling good, watching the parade, all those dudes in skirts pounding along, sweating like hogs. He made it for some gay event.

He heard the woman's shout, saw a really ugly dish break out of the pack and head toward him. For a second, Tip thought the guy was going to hit on him. Then he saw the eyes. Tip had a rap sheet twenty years long. He could pick out a cop in the crowd at a Redskins game. The one charging at him looked hard and mean despite his red dress.

Reaching inside his jacket, Tip pulled out a cheap Saturday-night special. Screams erupted from the crowd. He saw the cop fumble in his dress, trying to get at his piece, yelling for Tip to stop.

Tip clawed his way through the crowd, straight-arming the idiots who didn't move fast enough. He saw an alley up ahead. Get in there and let the cop try to chase him over fences wearing *that* outfit.

Whip Alley plunged into the panic and confusion Tip had left in his wake. Catching a glimpse of metal, he knew that a gun was in play. Alley slammed his shoulder into the people milling around him, watching as tourists backpedaled or dropped to their knees. In the melee, Tip was almost clear when it happened.

The felon was charging toward a lane between two buildings when Alley saw a young woman jogger wearing shorts and a tank top run across his path. Tip brandished the gun and she fell away, crouching. Then she balanced herself on her right leg and on the fingertips of both hands. She pivoted slightly, then her left leg shot out and caught Tip on the ankle, sending him sprawling. As the gun flew out of Tip's hand, Alley pounded up behind him and grabbed a fistful of greasy hair, jamming one knee into the small of the felon's spine.

"Do you have any idea how long the alterations took for this dress?" he demanded. "Now it looks like my dog slept on it."

"Alley?" Tip groaned. "That you, dawg? You're breaking my back."

"Really? Okay." Alley released his grip and pushed. Tip's forehead connected with the pavement with just enough force to leave him glassy-eyed.

After handcuffing him, Alley pulled out his cell phone. While he dialed the precinct, his eyes strayed over the young woman with her long, taut legs below blue running shorts, her chestnut hair, shot through with blonde by the sun, held in place by a sweatband. Her green eyes were still wide, the residue of shock, but other than that she seemed fine.

Finishing his call, he searched inside his dress and came up with his ID. "Whip Alley, detective, D.C.

Homicide. Nifty move you put on him back there."

Her hand felt cool in his. "Sloane Ryder. Why was he running?"

Before Alley could reply, a shadow fell over them. Sloane looked over her shoulder and saw a giant Hispanic with a fierce Zapata mustache and a gold earring in his left lobe.

"Paco Santana, my partner," Alley explained.

Sloane nodded. The giant wore a red cocktail number with pearls and long gloves. Sloane figured he had to be at least a size twenty-four and wondered where he'd gotten the outfit. The unspoken question must have shown on her face, because Santana gazed down at her like a friendly Kodiak bear examining a promising picnic hamper.

"My mother sews," he said gravely. "By the way, I saw you take him down. Nice work." He turned to Alley. "Tip?"

"Tip. You want to read him his rights?"

Two patrol cars, lights flashing, pulled up. The officers pushed back the small crowd, then their mouths fell open when they saw Alley and Santana.

"What?" Santana growled. "You a fashion critic?"

He pulled off his blonde wig and scratched a perfectly bald, shiny pate. Igniting a large cigar, he gave Tip his Miranda warning.

"You're a runner, right?" Alley asked Sloane.

Sloane's attention swung back to Whip Alley. "Yes, I am," she said, wondering what was coming next.

"I really have to finish this last leg. Club rules. It's only up to Georgetown. Care to join me?"

Sloane glanced at Santana, who was pushing the thief into the back of a cruiser. "Don't you want to ask me some questions?"

"Sure I do—over a cold longneck at J. Paul's."

"I'll join you after I finish booking this dirtbag," Santana called out.

"So?" Alley asked

"So let's run."

It took them less than thirty minutes to hit M Street, where they had to slow down for the Saturday shoppers and the tourists. Sloane appreciated it that the detective didn't try to make conversation along the way but concentrated on his rhythm and pace. Running beside him, she stole the occasional glance. His legs, peeking out from under the dress, were lean and muscular. He had sharp features, witchy eyes, and thick, black hair that curled out from under the headdress. She thought he might be in his late thirties, but it was hard to tell whether the lines and creases were there because of age or his job.

Alley got a round of applause as he made his entrance into J. Paul's. The saloon was filled with red-dressed runners thirstily working on mugs of beer. In spite of the crush, there were two empty stools at the end of the bar. Alley pulled off the headdress, mopped his forehead, and held up two fingers to the bartender. The two bottles of Beck's appeared instantly.

"Here's to close encounters," he said, handing a bottle to Sloane. "That was a very smooth move you put on Tip back there."

Sloane took a long swallow, held the icy-cold bottle to her cheek.

"When I was living in Erie, I took a self-defense course taught by a retired Israeli soldier. Nothing transcendental or spiritual, just straight in-your-face moves that give you the edge."

"Love it," Alley said. "Is that where you're from, Erie?"

With the Rolling Stones belting out tunes in the background, Sloane gave him snapshots of her life: how she'd packed up and left New York, the job at the GAO she was going to start on Monday, her attempt this past week to try to get a feel for Washington.

"Mind if I ask which department you're with?"

Sloane hesitated. Porter had never said she couldn't divulge where she worked or for which branch. The idea was to make it sound as boring as possible so people wouldn't press for details.

"It's a small unit," Sloane replied. "MJ-11."

"MJ-11." Recognition flickered in his eyes, then was gone.

"Tell me about the race," Sloane said quickly. "What's that all about?"

"It's called, appropriately enough, the Red Dress Run," Alley explained. "A bunch of Englishmen started it back in the 1930s, deciding that Washington was a little too uptight. So they formed the Hash House Harriers—don't ask me where they got the name—put on red dresses, and ran through the streets. Go figure. Somehow the thing stuck. Now we have about four hundred guys, all working stiffs, who, once a year, dress up like hookers and run. By Monday, everything's back to normal."

"So it's a running club."

He gestured around the saloon, where bartenders and waiters could barely keep up with the orders.

"Actually it's more like a drinking club with a running problem. And here comes our clotheshorse."

Alley leaned close to Sloane as Paco Santana bellied his way through the crowds. "Personally, I think some of us take this a little too seriously. I mean, having your mother actually sew something when there's plenty to choose from off the rack."

"I heard that," Santana rumbled. He squeezed in beside Sloane, causing a tectonic shift along the bar. "He's talking about my outfit, isn't he? Do *you* see anything wrong in wanting custom work?"

"No," Sloane said hastily. "Absolutely not."

"But you went and changed, didn't you," Alley needled him. "Didn't want to show off in here."

"I changed because I was beginning to chafe," Santana replied primly. "Not that it's any of your business." He paused to order a two-liter mug of Coors before continuing. "Speaking of business, would it offend you, miss, if we took care of a few details?"

"Please do."

Santana pulled out a tiny notebook and a slim gold pen.

"Before you get into that," Alley interrupted "where did you stash Tip?"

Santana offered him a crocodile smile. "At the precinct. Right about now he's telling the Borget brothers everything about his follow-home jobs, and whatever else he thinks we might find interesting."

"He's facing murder in the commission of a felony," Alley explained to Sloane, then turned back to

Santana. "Tell me they're not going to offer him a deal."

Santana looked hurt. "Of course not." He wet his finger and turned to a fresh page in his little book. "Name, please," he said pleasantly to Sloane.

"While you're doing that, I'm going to change," Alley said. He reached for the sports bag Santana had brought with him and made his way through the crush, to the bathrooms.

Sloane gave Santana the address of the furnished corporate apartment she was leasing by the month, her phone number there and at work, and Lee Porter's name as a reference. Santana stopped writing.

"MJ-11," he said softly.

Sloane thought he was looking at her differently, wariness mixed with respect.

"You're familiar with it?" she asked.

Santana's voice dropped an octave. "Washington's a small town, especially when it comes to law enforcement and security. Cops, feds, and spooks tripping over one another. Whip and I were in the army's Criminal Investigation Division, counterespionage. Once in a while we hooked up with someone from your outfit."

Alley returned, wearing jeans, sneakers, and a soft tan leather jacket over a chambray shirt.

"Hold on a sec," Sloane said. She dipped the corner of a napkin in a glass of water and wiped off some lipstick he'd missed. Because of the light, she couldn't quite tell if Alley was blushing.

"You have the details?" Alley asked Santana, who patted his little notebook.

He turned to Sloane. "Ms. Ryder, it's been a pleasure. I'd love to stay but I'm already late for my shift. In case I have any more questions—"

"Paco has my number in his little book."

Alley crimsoned. "Your number. Right."

Sloane gave him a pointed look. "Which means you don't have any excuse not to call me."

13

THE UNITED FLIGHT from Hong Kong landed at Kennedy at 9:03 on Monday morning. The Handyman was one of the first people off, but he tarried to allow the Cho family to catch up with him. Even though he had only carry-on, he followed them to the baggage-claim area and fell in step behind them to Customs and Immigration.

Several overseas flights had come in and the lines to the Immigration booths were long. When the Chos finally stepped forward, the Handyman turned his attention to the young black Immigration officer. He scanned the Chos' passports and was asking them questions when he unfolded and read the White House letter. His expression softened and he leaned forward across the counter to look at 1818, sleepily clutching his "father's" leg. The officer scrawled something on the Chos' I-90 form and sent them on their way.

The Handyman caught up with them at Customs, watched as they and their cart full of luggage were waived through, then trailed in their wake.

Outside, in the private limousine lane, was a van, idling; the driver, a North Korean agent whom the

Chos had been told to expect, waited by the passenger door. He helped them stow their bags, then closed the doors.

With his garment bag swung over his shoulder, the Handyman watched the van head for the airport exit. The Chos' entry into the United States had been the last dangerous hurdle. Had something gone wrong, if someone had been watching for them, that's where they would have been taken. Now, 1818 was only a few hundred miles from his intended target. More would be done to him between now and the time he and his keepers arrived at the White House. The Handyman knew what these things were, how painful they would be, and he did not dwell on them. He had his own business to attend to, the second half of the contract.

While the Chos were on their way to Long Island, Marty Garrett, assistant to National Security Adviser James Trimble, walked past the paddleboat rental dock at the Tidal Basin. He stayed closer to the road than to the water's edge, even though it was noisier with the morning commute.

Garrett came to the Tidal Basin for its serenity and beauty. On weekends, he would lay out a blanket and sit for hours gazing at the Jefferson Memorial, across the water. Occasionally, he went inside and read excerpts of Jefferson's writings inscribed on the walls. Although he wasn't aware of it, Garrett tended to seek out the passages having to do with patriotism. He did not ask himself why he had such an affinity for those particular words. He did not realize that, like most traitors, he was seeking justification for his actions in terms that helped make treason something other than the stark reality that it was.

Garrett heard a car horn behind him. A black Lincoln town car was pulling up alongside him. The driver got out first, followed by a bodyguard who opened the back door for Dodge French.

French, elegant as always in his black suit with the faintest hint of a pinstripe, coiffed and barbered as though he'd been up for hours, which, Garrett reckoned, was likely the case. He was suddenly very conscious of his Dockers and old blazer, how greasy his hair felt because there hadn't been time to wash it.

Garrett had gotten very little sleep since Trimble's last meeting with the President. Most of the time had been spent at work, but when he'd returned to his apartment, sleep had proved elusive. Last night, Garrett had lain awake staring at the ceiling in the dark, his pillowcase and linens sour from his sweat. Doubts gnawed at him like worms through a corpse. Sleep had come only with exhaustion. Then the alarm had gone off and there'd been almost no time to get ready for this meeting.

"You're looking a bit peaked, Marty. Trimble got you burning the midnight oil, eh?"

"Good morning, sir," Garrett replied. "Yes, it's been busy, given what's happened."

French took the young man's elbow and steered him away from the road, onto a footpath that meandered among the trees.

Garrett glanced over his shoulder. The Lincoln trailed them on the road; the bodyguard was thirty paces behind and off to the right, upwind. He would hear nothing. Nor would anyone else. Laser listening devices required glass as reflectors; more conventional equipment needed transport—a van or at the very least a sports utility vehicle. In this setting, neither of those could remain stationary long enough for the surveillance to be effective. Garrett was sure that the driver of the town car kept one eye out for any vehicle that didn't belong in the morning traffic.

"I'm sorry I couldn't get to you sooner," French was saying. "The weekend was impossible." He looked at Garrett. "You wouldn't have been able to get out either, right?"

"It would have been difficult," Garrett replied.

Not impossible, though. He could have cut a few corners in order to establish contact. But that wasn't how French operated. He never made contact until he controlled the time and place. Garrett felt very safe when dealing with French.

"Tell me about the Necklace," French said quietly.

Garrett organized his thoughts.

"The Necklace Option . . . Pretty much as the name implies: a blockade of China. Primarily by sea, from just outside the territorial waters of Vietnam all the way up Qingdao, across to the Korean peninsula at Inchon, down to Pusan and across again to Japan, at Fukuoka.

"NSA estimates call for four battle groups, each one centered around an aircraft carrier. Three fighter wings out of Okinawa, four from Kagoshima, for support."

Dodge French folded his hands behind his back, inclined his head. "Bombers?" he murmured.

"Secret protocols have already been concluded with the Filipinos. We get Clark Air Force Base back on a lease arrangement for as long as we need it. That gives us a forward position for the B-1 Liberators and B-52s. The B-2s will come out of a black base in Queensland, Australia."

So the Filipinos and Aussies are on board. Curious that Claudia didn't mention that.

"Subs?" French asked.

"Five boomers on station, pulled out of the Indian Ocean. Three Los Angeles class, two Wolfs. Target packages have already been programmed. We're talking thirty missiles per boat, ten warheads per delivery system."

"Non-nukes?"

"On board the Aegis cruisers and Torrance-class destroyers. Same payloads like we used in the Gulf, only we've added Stealth technology to the Tomahawks. There was a rumor that the Chinese had developed an ultra-low-scan radar. Maybe, maybe not. In this case, it won't matter."

"I'm sure it won't. Satellites?"

"Once the President gives the order, escalation will begin at zero one. Our laser platforms take out the Chinese satellites, military and commercial. We leave them blind."

"And that's as far as Necklace would take it?"

"Lasers don't come into play again until we've reached escalation zero seven, two steps before the nuclear option."

"The nuclear option. Over a silly little piece of dirt most Americans couldn't find on a map."

Garrett was surprised by the disgust in French's voice.

"What's Trimble's pitch?" French asked.

"He'll argue for Necklace to be put in play if the Chinese flotilla doesn't pull back to its home ports. He's very nervous about their ability to race across the Taiwan Strait."

"He's too young to know anything firsthand about Korea," French said tartly. "The days of the yellow hordes coming at us in human waves, regardless of casualties, are over." He paused. "What does Trimble see as the Chinese response, if their forces are threatened or attacked in the strait?"

Garrett stopped and faced French. "Chemical-biological. He figures they would have lost so much face by that point, they'd resort to C-B payloads against our ships."

"Damn right they would!" French muttered. "Trimble wants a war and they'll give him one."

"Sir, these are only options, at least for now," Garrett said nervously. "We've got hundreds of them on the shelf. He's just dusting off a few to give to the President."

The young man's anxious tone told French that he should have guarded his tongue where Trimble was concerned. Garrett was nervous enough as it was.

French laid a hand on his shoulder. "I know they're only options," he said quietly. "But I've seen them take on a life, a momentum, of their own. I pray that you never do."

Garrett nodded and seemed to settle down. French was silent as they continued walking. This boy was very good, he thought, one of the best he'd ever recruited.

It was French's great strength that he was able to see beyond the immediate threat or opposition presented by his competitors for the President's ear. He took it as a given that men such as Trimble and General Murchison could go overnight from being allies to being vehement opponents. In the corridors of power, nothing remained static.

So French learned about these men. To whom were they close? Whom had they mentored and where were the mentees now? French, who had happened to hear about Garrett's personal situation from a member of his staff, set out the bait.

In the past, Trimble had been out of touch with Garrett at precisely the time the analyst had needed him. Garrett had married his childhood sweetheart, and their first child had been born with a hole in his heart. Over the years, the emotional costs were staggering, the medical expenses crippling.

Trimble effectively lost touch with his assistant long enough for Garrett to seek out new opportunities and allegiances. French had come to Garrett when the young man was looking for a surrogate Trimble, someone who would not only appreciate his talent, but would guide and enhance his career. He'd had an associate introduce him to Garrett and began cultivating the young man, taking him to certain clubs where he met with ranking members of America's think tanks. Flattered by the attention and grateful for French's patronage, Garrett began to spend more and more time with his mentor.

Through this same associate, French arranged for Garrett to receive a very large loan to quietly pay off his child's medical bills. The bank that floated it mysteriously accepted an absurdly low interest rate, with a payout schedule that wouldn't be met even if Garrett lived to be a hundred.

French stoked Garrett's ambition and made him feel a part of an inner circle. By the time he was done with the young man, Garrett was thoroughly corrupted and completely unaware of what had been done to him. He had two distinct lives—one that he led before the world, the other dark and removed, which revolved around the people French had put in his way, through whom all things were possible. It was a credit to the effectiveness of French's brainwashing that even when Garrett was reunited with Trimble, he never allowed his superior so much as a glimpse of what he'd become.

They had walked as far as the Jefferson Memorial and now stood facing it. The day's first tour buses were arriving, the visitors stumbling off, their cameras bumping against their chests as they gathered around their guide. Standing in front of the memorial, Garrett felt better about what he had done. Jefferson had written that the path of liberty is never straight and wide, that it takes many twists, can be arduous and trying. The warmth and respect Garrett felt for Trimble had nothing to do with his association with French. The two relationships were compartmentalized in his mind, like watertight holds in a ship. What went on in one had nothing to do with the other. Trimble was a man who thought about—and might have to act on—the unthinkable. Dodge French was the pillar of reason and sober thought, the legend who had guided the country through terrible mistakes and disasters to its shining place in the world. To continue to do this, Dodge French needed Marty Garrett's insight, gleaned from the information that crossed his desk every morning.

For all his vaunted intelligence, Garrett never grasped the notion that patriotism and treason are two sides of the same coin. He couldn't imagine that what he was doing was in any way wrong.

"What happens now?" he asked.

"Something must be done to neutralize the Necklace Option," French replied, his tone heavy.

He wanted to give the impression of shouldering a great burden, which required the young man's help. It was a convincing performance.

"Is there anything more I can do?" Garrett asked anxiously.

French pretended to consider, then nodded. "Keep your ear to the ground. There may be developments that Jim Trimble will not like. He might decide to do an end run around the President. I need to know his intentions."

"You can count on me."

"Yes," French said softly as they turned in the direction of the road. "I'm sure I can."

The Chinese embassy, at 2300 Connecticut Avenue, consists of two '60s-vintage high-rise apartment build-

ings set at right angles to each other. Gutted and
remodeled, their roofs bristling with satellite dishes, the
buildings front a tiny plaza. The front doors are guarded
by a pair of highly stylized marble lions that are neither
particularly valuable nor aesthetically pleasing.

As Dodge French walked to the front doors, he felt
the hair on the back of his neck push against his collar. He was being photographed and despised it. His
tame FBI agent, the eager-to-please Peter Mack, had
told him all about the twenty-four-hour surveillance
the Bureau conducted on the buildings. The cameras
were in a room in a building across the street, next to
the Ethiopian embassy. They were electric, with battery backup in case of a power failure. The tapes were
changed each day, reviewed, and copies made if there
was anything of interest on them.

French was not concerned that the Bureau would
take a special interest in his arrival. His visits to the
embassy were frequent, his calendar full of entries of
such meetings. But this was a delicate time. In the
aftermath of what was to come, the movements of
those who'd had any dealings with the Chinese would
go under the microscope. The outrage and the investigations it would fuel would focus even on those who
were usually beyond suspicion, untouchable. Evidence
of this visit would be available to investigators because,
as Peter Mack had so helpfully volunteered, the Bureau
hung on to the original tapes for sixty days before recy-
cling them.

The woman waiting for French in the plain, third-
floor office was Mai Ling. She was of indeterminate
age, anywhere from sixty to seventy-five. Her hair was

drawn back in a tight bun and her complexion resembled the hue and topography of a baked apple. Dodge French thought she looked like a wizened bat, but he had nothing save the greatest respect for her.

Mai Ling had outwitted—and therefore outlived—the politicians of China's old guard. She had been instrumental in helping reformers such as Deng Xiaoping and his successors, and had subverted the last attempts of diehard Maoists to reinstate the old ways. Now she had only one dream left to fulfill before she died: to see Taiwan reunited with its homeland.

"It is good to see you, French," Mai Ling said, the words slipping out between teeth that were clamped to an ivory cigarette holder yellow with age.

She always called him by his surname, her way of showing affection. But her black eyes searched his face. To arrange this meeting, French had contacted her personal secretary. Mai Ling knew that it was always risky for him to be seen coming to the embassy. She wondered what could be so important that it couldn't wait until she and French were at some social event that would give them both cover.

"There is a matter that requires your assistance," French said. "Time is a consideration."

"You are as old as the Xuan warriors, French," she cackled. "Time should hold no fear for you."

"I have yet to approach the level of your wisdom," he parried, and drew a barking laugh in response.

Mai Ling waved a bony hand. "Say it then."

He told her about Trimble, the President's call to put the Necklace Option on the table, to use it if the need arose. As he spoke, he listened to the woman's short, labored breaths, an accurate gauge of her growing anger.

"So the President is prepared to use force," she muttered. "Maybe I should let her—this one time. You know the men in Beijing cannot bring themselves to take her seriously. After all, she is only a woman."

"As you are. And they take you *very* seriously."

"Flatterer! They take me seriously because there is enough in this old skull to bury them and their next ten generations. They have no such fear of Claudia Ballantine."

"Yet."

"Yet," Mai Ling agreed. "What is it you propose?"

"Demote and exile Mi Zhenyu. Pull back some of your warships."

"You do not ask for much, French," Mai Ling said dryly.

"Only for what is absolutely necessary."

"This will be a difficult thing to achieve. The men in Beijing will feel insulted. Male pride and its attendant foolishness."

"I believe you can persuade them. Because the only really important factor is Zhenyu. The naval pullback will take time, as my military commanders appreciate."

"How shall I persuade them, French?"

"By informing them several days later that the Necklace Option has been put back on the shelf."

"And that would come about as a result of . . . ?"

"Of your using Code Purple to communicate with Beijing and they with you."

"But your National Security Agency has broken our Code Purple—"

"Exactly."

Mai Ling's eyes sparkled as she grasped what French was getting at. "I use Purple to message Beijing. Your government, which doesn't know that *we* know they have broken Purple, is made aware of the correspondence. They presume it is genuine. James Trimble, who considers Zhenyu his nemesis, is suddenly left without an adversary. General Murchison is placated because our fleet is moving to home ports. Yet none of this actually happens."

"Zhenyu is taken off the board," French corrected. "This must happen. It would be too easy for our CIA assets to determine his whereabouts. If they found him stewing in his country retreat, they would report as much."

Mai Ling puffed furiously on her cigarette holder. "You wrap the big lie in the small truth. If Claudia Ballantine has proof that Zhenyu has been neutered, she will accept the rest as fact too."

"I believe she would."

"Sometimes the greatest display of vanity lies in self-effacement," she scolded. "However, from you I will tolerate it."

"Code Purple?" French pressed her.

"Code Purple. You will gain a degree of satisfaction from Trimble's reaction, will you not? They say he suffers from heart ailments."

"High blood pressure. And yes, I will be satisfied, because his intentions are an obstacle to ours."

Mai Ling screwed in another cigarette. "There is something else, yes?"

French nodded. Something had suggested itself to him on the ride from the Tidal Basin.

"Your new best friends, the Iraqis. It could prove useful if they were to suddenly announce a series of naval exercises or something equally provocative."

Mai Ling's smile was wreathed in smoke. "Useful how?"

Twenty-two miles from Washington's Zero Milestone, on the Baltimore–Washington Parkway, stands the National Security Agency, a tan, nine-story structure surrounded by a green, three-story A-shaped building. In the spring and summer, the surrounding foliage does a fair job of obscuring not only the complex but the rows of ten-foot Cyclone fences topped with multiple rows of razor wire.

Two hours after Dodge French left the Chinese embassy, one of the two giant radomes mounted on the roof of the smaller building intercepted a communications burst originating at 2300 Connecticut Avenue. Computers assigned to that address automatically logged and taped the coded transmission, and began decryption.

Ten minutes later, the results appeared on the monitor of a cryptanalyst, interrupting his perusal of *Esquire* magazine. The analyst read the decoded message and dialed his supervisor.

"Twenty-three hundred's on-line."

One floor above, the supervisor brought the material up on his screen.

"They're still using Code Purple," he said into the speakerphone.

"Suckers," the analyst replied.

"Yeah, well. We take our breaks where we can get 'em. One of these days, they'll wake up and realize we've been peeking at their mail. Then you'll have to work for a living."

The analyst snorted. "The machines are working overtime on their new experimental code, Orange. What I think, it's so screwed up even the Chinese don't know how to use it."

The superior broke the connection. He called up the "readers list" for 2300 intercepts on his computer: James Trimble at National Security, Murchison over at Joint Chiefs.

The supervisor activated a secure modem, dialed in the numbers, and flashed the traffic across the scenic Maryland countryside.

A DOZEN BLOCKS from where the NSA message was being received by National Security Adviser James Trimble, Sloane Ryder was finishing up her first morning as a GAO staffer.

Established in 1921, the General Accounting Office had been Congress's counterbalance to the President's then newly created Office of Management and Budget. Its mandate was to help Congress monitor the spending of federal dollars.

Over the next seventy-five years, the GAO's mandate did not change much. The most compelling change came in the mid-1960s, when its oversight activities were honed on two particular issues—program evaluation and policy analysis.

At that time, the makeup of the staff also underwent a change. Although accountants and auditors were still in the majority, they were joined by scientists, health care professionals, computer and other specialists.

Operating out of a 1950s period piece on G Street, 3,200-odd employees continually monitor the state of the nation's fiscal health. They are headed by the comptroller general of the United States, appointed by the president to a fifteen-year term, giving the office a continuity unparalleled in most government agencies. The GAO's independence is also safeguarded by the fact that its workforce is made up almost exclusively of career employees, hired on the basis of skill and experience. The GAO looks after its own, which is vital in attracting and keeping highly trained and motivated personnel.

Officially, GAO investigators have the power to examine any and all government records and documents, with two exceptions: those relating to the intelligence community and to certain functions of the Federal Reserve. In the early 1950s, in the wake of the arrests of the atomic bomb spies, a presidential fiat created a new, secret division within the office. MJ-11 was designed as an oversight body to monitor the financial activities of any and all government employees involved in sensitive military work or research. In the mid-1970s, this mandate was extended to include workers for civilian contractors such as Boeing, Lockheed, and General Electric, which was involved in the construction of nuclear submarines, and Hughes, which designed and built the country's spy satellites.

"We scan half a million people a year," Lee Porter told Sloane as he walked her through a door with electronic locks. The yellow-lettered imprint on the door read ARCHIVES. "Out of that number, less than two thousand are red-flagged. Further investigation clears ninety percent of them. The rest go under the microscope."

"What happens to them?" Sloane asked.

"If we're fortunate, we find out where their money comes from—lucky streak at the gaming tables, an inheritance from a relative who died outside the country, things like that." He paused. "A good year for us means we *haven't* fingered anyone."

Beyond the electronically locked doors was a self-contained working area that Sloane reckoned took up half the second-floor wing. The decor was a cheerful blend of ocean blues and greens; the sealed windows were thick, one-way glass. There was a large conference room along the left wall, three rows of individual workstations, and Porter's office at the far end. He led Sloane into the conference room where the staff had gathered to meet her, all twelve of them.

Porter noted her surprised expression. "That's right, only twelve," he confirmed. "A baker's dozen, counting you. We're lean and mean and do more work in a day than most folks put in in two."

Sloane shook hands with them all, from a seventeen-year-old black girl who already had a doctorate in computer science from MIT to a sixty-something, ponytailed former FBI undercover agent with the nose of a bloodhound. Porter's crew, as they called themselves, came from all over the country and had a breadth and depth of experience that astonished her. Most welcome, there seemed to be no egos involved. Contributions were considered equal, the goal a common one: protect and defend the country from those who wanted to harm it.

After the introductions, Porter showed Sloane to her workstation. She glanced at the high-tech computer hardware and whistled softly.

"Everything we have here is on a par with what they use over at NSA or the National Reconnaissance

Office. The mainframes are in the basement, under armed guard. All landlines, fax lines, and cellular communications are outfitted with the latest scrambler technology. With that"—he tapped her keyboard—"you can get into any government machine anywhere in the world."

"Why don't we start with the President's PC?" Sloane joked.

Lee Porter didn't blink. "You can. The code is 1600 backward." He paused. "Just make sure you have a damn good reason and run it by me first." He handed her a thick stack of printouts. "You're familiar with the Microsoft Dragon, right?"

"Of course."

Dragon was the latest software from the Redmond, Washington, giant. A variation of it had been adapted for stock trading, and Microsoft engineers brought in by Young, Pullen had trained Sloane in its use. Although this one had a totally different, much more sophisticated application, Sloane felt confident she could master it.

"Okay, then," Porter said, pulling out his pipe and tobacco pouch. "Dazzle me."

Porter walked into his office, closed the door, and picked up the phone. James Trimble was on the other end instantly.

"She's in place and ready to move," Porter said. "Where do we point her?"

Trimble's voice was tight with rage. "You're not going to believe what I just got." He went on to describe the latest intercept from NSA-Fort Meade.

"What makes you think it's bogus?" Porter asked.

"It's too damn convenient, is what it is," Trimble shot back. "I'm ready to present the President with Necklace but the reason for it might just have evaporated. Someone had to have tipped off the Chinese."

"Where do you want me to start?"

"NSA. Where the intercept originated. I'm thinking someone must have been waiting for it, ready to pass it along."

"Very fragile territory," Porter said quietly.

"I know it. But it's our best bet."

"I'll put Ryder on it immediately. You have a short list?"

"Check your fax."

Porter heard a soft hum in the corner of the room. The fax machine was spitting out paper.

"I'll be in touch," he said.

Porter sifted through the pages. The National Security Agency employed over four thousand people, but Trimble had sent only the names of those involved in the Chinese intercepts, anyone who might have been primed to wait for it and then pass it up the food chain. Still, the count was 341.

Porter understood that Trimble was in a hurry, but he checked every name against the roster in his head. At any given time, Porter knew the names of every individual currently subject to scrutiny by MJ-11. He was searching for a match, a connection, anything. Nothing rang cherries. The name Martin Garrett was as meaningless as the others on the list.

Marty Garrett's work for Trimble would not have put him on any NSA list. The national security adviser

chooses his staff from various walks of life, usually
academia or the military. But seven years before, when
Garrett was still a graduate student at Princeton, one
of his papers had come to the NSA's attention. He had
been invited to Fort Meade to extrapolate on his thesis
of the feasibility of a secret Sino-Japanese protocol by
which Japan, in return for guarantees of territorial
integrity, would turn a blind eye to China's invasion of
Taiwan.

The computers that had logged him in had also designated him as a China hand. Because a large part of
Garrett's lecture had concerned covert communications, the machines cross-referenced his name with
categories that included Chinese intercepts.

The incident, buried under seven years' worth of
much more important events, had completely slipped
Garrett's mind.

The printout swinging in his hand, Lee Porter
walked to Sloane Ryder's workstation. He slipped
around the cloth-covered partition, pulled up a chair,
and began to explain what he needed her to do.

The modified Dragon system was the most sophisticated piece of software Sloane had ever used. It was
also the most frightening.

Frank Anderson, thirty-seven, married, a wife and
three children, house in Bethesda, State Department
evaluator, South America for five years. Cross-reference
Equifax and TRW, clean. Cross-reference IRS, payments current. Cross-reference state and county tax
rolls, payments current. Telephone records, local
except for two or three calls a month to Hawaii.

Cross-reference Hawaii, mother, living there, widowed, retired. Cross-reference HMO, no health problems in the family. But here was something: registration for a thirty-eight-foot sportfisherman made by Harrier. Cross-reference Harrier, that particular model, with all the bells and whistles—which is the only way the company turned them out—would have set Anderson back over $140,000. Way too much on his salary. Plus, he held the pink slip.

Back to the IRS, returns for the last seven years. Scanning for the anomaly . . . There it was, on the '97 filing. Anderson's mother had deeded him a parcel of land on the Big Island, which, as Sloane knew from her travels, had become very hot, propertywise, in the mid-1990s. Anderson must not have liked the island very much. He'd sold the parcel less than three months later, paid the requisite taxes, and within the next couple of weeks had gotten himself his toy. The red light around Frank Anderson dimmed, faded away.

The scrutiny of Anderson's life had taken Sloane all of twenty minutes. Dragon was that quick, that accurate. *That intrusive.* Sloane shivered. Her fingers crept up to the laminated ID hung around her neck. No clips, because the card could become snagged or come loose and fall off. Porter had made a point of telling her that getting a new one was only slightly more difficult than obtaining a presidential pardon. The white IDs were reserved strictly for MJ-11 personnel. They closely resembled the day passes for visitors coming to the GAO on official business, but the other employees knew the difference. Earlier, Sloane had had to venture into another part of the building and had been very much aware of the eyes that smiled when they met her face, then instantly hardened in wariness when they noticed the card.

Sloane stared at the printouts Porter had dropped on her desk. He'd said he needed them handled ASAP. But he hadn't said she had to pass up her lunch hour. Nor did she intend to, since it was a beautiful day and Whip Alley was coming to join her.

Alley had called her the night before. Sloane had hoped she'd hear from him, but hadn't expected it to be so soon. Her heart gave a little lift when Alley said that he would be at the First District Station at Fourth and E Streets tomorrow and maybe he'd come over if she wasn't doing anything for lunch. That morning, Sloane had declined Lee Porter's invitation to eat with him.

She was outside, waiting to cross G Street to get to the National Building Museum, when she heard her name called out over the bustle of people and traffic around her. She looked around, trying to spot Alley, and found herself looking right at Peter Mack.

"Hello, Sloane," he said quietly. "It's good to see you. Got a minute?"

Her throat was dry. She stared at Mack in shock.

"Peter, what are you doing here?" she managed at last.

"I just want to talk, Sloane. You can give me two minutes, can't you?"

She followed him to the overhang by the front doors of the GAO as the lunchtime crowd poured out of the building.

"What are you doing here?" she repeated, her voice steady now.

"I left half a dozen messages on your machine," Mack replied. "You never called back. I had to come to Washington, so . . ."

"I wrote you a letter," she replied, then decided not to spare him. "Not long after you took your things from my apartment—without so much as a word."

"It was a bad time, Sloane," Mack said. "For both of us. I had a hell of a lot on my plate. I didn't understand what was going on with you."

"It's over between us, Peter," she said. "I healed and moved on."

Mack moved closer to her. "We had something good, Sloane. If you had told me what was going on with MacGregor, maybe I could have helped. At least I would have understood."

Sloane wasn't going to trip over that. "You would have understood until Dodge French asked you to compromise me. That would have happened no matter what."

"Given what happened to MacGregor, do you really think French was wrong in asking you to back off?" he asked softly.

Sloane stepped back from him. "You made your choice then, Peter. I made mine. Let it go. Let *me* go."

"Is there someone else, Sloane? Is that it?"

Sloane turned and didn't look back. She fell in step with the crowd at the crosswalk and walked quickly toward the National Building Museum. She had her head down and ran right into Whip Alley.

"Whoa! What's the hurry?"

Sloane saw him glance across the street, where Peter Mack stood watching them. There was knowledge in Alley's eyes and she knew that the detective had seen it all.

"Let's go over there."

Pointing to a small park next to the museum, he guided her to an empty bench, then went over to a hot dog cart, returning with two giant pretzels, packets of mustard, and sodas.

"Interesting thing happened yesterday," Alley said conversationally, smearing mustard on his pretzel. "The switchboard routes this call to Paco because some guy is calling him. It's not a homicide, but the guy won't speak to anyone else. So Paco gets on the line and hears whispering. He tries to get the guy to speak up but he won't. Finally, he gets a name out of him. It's a longtime perp Paco used to bust, with an outstanding burglary warrant. Paco says, 'Look, why are you calling me? There's a warrant out for you.' And the guy says, 'Yeah, I know. I want to turn myself in.' All this time he's whispering, begging Paco to come get him right away. Finally, he tells Paco that he's at this girl's house. Her father and brother just walked in on them and now the guy's locked himself in one of the bedrooms. He was calling Paco for help, figuring that turning himself in on the burglary rap would be a lot less painful than what was waiting for him outside the door."

Alley munched thoughtfully on his pretzel and took a swig of soda. "Takes all kinds, don't it?"

Sloane stared at him sitting there shaking his head, grinning, and started to laugh, harder and longer than the anecdote was worth. Then the story about what had really happened in New York and her relationship with Peter Mack, how it had begun and ended, spilled from her lips.

Sloane was aware of talking for a long time. Occasionally she would glance at Alley, trying to catch something in his face. She was looking for distaste or condemnation, or the kind of white-knight-on-a-charger attitude that men take on when a woman tells them about a love affair gone bad. She saw nothing at all. It was rare to find someone, man or woman, who was nonjudgmental.

Whip Alley drained his can of soda. "Is it over between the two of you? I mean, really over?"

"Yes, it is."

He covered her hand with his. "I'm glad."

They stayed like that for a moment, sitting close together, silent, the sun shooting through the last of the autumn leaves, dappling their faces.

Sloane said, "I have to get back to the office."

Alley got to his feet. "And I have to catch me some bad guys. What do you think—dinner? Considering you didn't even eat your pretzel. But it would have to be late. I'll be tied up till nine or so."

"I'll be starving by then."

"Clyde's on M Street?"

"Don't be late."

She watched him walk away, stop once to look back and smile at her, and it was as though those ugly moments with Peter Mack had never happened.

When Sloane returned to her cubicle, she set to work on the printout. The names were in alphabetical order and she didn't get to Marty Garrett until close to five o'clock. Her date with Whip Alley was at least four hours away and Sloane didn't much like the prospect of spending that time in her unfamiliar apartment. When Porter came by on his way out, she told him she'd be staying on a while.

Sloane made tea at the beverage station and returned to her desk. The office was silent except for the burbling of the tropical-fish tank that belonged to one of the analysts, and the soft clicks as she worked the keyboard.

Martin Garrett . . . All the cross-references indicated a solid, upstanding citizen. A brilliant analyst. James Trimble's golden boy. But Sloane noted that Garrett had had his share of grief. The HMO records relating to his son spoke for themselves. There had been many—and very costly—procedures performed to mend the boy's defective heart. The bills were staggering. And all of them had been paid off . . .

Sloane cocked her head, then became very still. A tendril of a thought circled around her, just beyond her grasp.

The medical bills had been paid off. How? Quickly she scanned Garret's tax returns. Not on that income, as respectable as it was.

She scrutinized the tax records more closely. There it was: Ten months after Garrett's child was born and the hospital charges were threatening to bankrupt him, he'd gotten a bank loan.

Using what as collateral? The Garretts didn't own a home at the time. They had nothing in the stock market and their savings account was tapped out. Who had co-signed the loan?

Sloane got into Garrett's account at First Fidelity Bank in Alexandria and called up the loan records. She sifted through the paperwork until she found the documents she needed: the payoff note to the HMO, the attendant loan documents that Garrett had signed at . . .

At 2.5 percent interest?

Not damn likely, Sloane thought, plowing through the paperwork until she spotted it: the cosigner's name, a Dr. Susan Ostroff, a Georgetown resident.

Sloane scanned the surnames on the printout beginning with O. Ostroff wasn't there, which meant that she was not on Porter's radar—for the moment.

Was Ostroff a relative? That didn't seem likely on Garrett's side. His wife's maiden name was Franklin, born in the Midwest. No likely connection there either.

A former colleague at Princeton or one of the think tanks Garrett had been associated with?

Sloane accessed Bell Atlantic's phone records and discovered that Ostroff had an unlisted number. Next she called up Garrett's phone bills and searched for a match. Garrett lived in McLean, Virginia. The calls to Georgetown were toll calls. In the last three months, Garrett had averaged two calls a month to Ostroff's number.

Sloane sat back in her chair and let out a deep breath. Something was out of kilter here, but she cautioned herself not to jump to conclusions. There could be perfectly reasonable explanations for this situation. But Ostroff had co-signed for over $200,000. At 2.5 percent interest, the monthly payments were so low that Garrett's child would reach middle age before the last payment was made. Why had the bank agreed to such patently absurd terms? Had Ostroff had any leverage in the bank's agreeing to those terms in the first place? If so, what kind of pull did she have? And why use it to benefit Garrett?

Sloane resisted the temptation to call Porter at home. First, she had to finish scanning the rest of the names on the list. Maybe she would find a third-party connection that would provide her with a clue.

Sloane checked her watch. She could get through most of the names before she had dinner with Whip Alley. Then she'd come back and finish off the rest.

15

THE CHO FAMILY and 1818 settled in the small Long Island community of Corona, in Nassau County. Their host, Kyung Sik, was ostensibly the woman's cousin. In reality, he was a deep-penetration North Korean agent who'd slipped into the country on false papers during the large South Korean influx in the early 1990s.

Like most of his fellow immigrants, Sik had worked hard and had prospered. Having started with a single gas-powered lawn mower and a battered pickup, he now ran a large gardening service and nursery. He paid his predominately Hispanic workers well, was active in the Catholic Church, and gave generously to local charities. He was so well liked in that family neighborhood that on the day he took the citizenship oath, his neighbors threw him a block party.

The only lingering question about Sik—and it was seldom raised—was why such a hardworking, God-fearing man had never married. It seemed a shame.

Sik had been thoroughly briefed on the arrival of his relations. The neighbors were gossipy, so he short-circuited their inevitable nosiness by having a Saturday-afternoon open house. Over barbecue and beer, he introduced the Chos and discreetly told the folks from next door the real reason for their staying with him. Within the hour, word of 1818's condition had made the rounds. When the Chos brought the boy out briefly, introducing him as Sun, the women surrounded him, clucking like hens.

The Chos' cover was thus secured.

The American hospitality shown the Chos did not end there. Their son was the South Korean poster boy for children with AIDS. Arrangements had been made for him to receive first-rate medical attention while they were guests of the President. After the party, the cousin showed the Chos the letter he'd received from a famous hospital about a half hour's drive from Corona. The director of the AIDS research section welcomed them and hoped they would find it convenient to stop by the day after tomorrow so that their son could be given a comprehensive physical.

The woman had no problem with this. The disease 1818 carried in his blood was still in its earliest stages. There was nothing any doctors could do or prescribe that she wasn't already doing. The examination would be thorough, the results satisfactory. She would have to endure some glad-handing by the staff, but a lapse into broken English would terminate that quickly enough. She would be told to bring the boy back in two weeks, sooner if there were complications. That was the usual procedure and the woman did not expect any changes to it.

Except one: 1818 would miss his last appointment, toward the end of November. She would have to come up with an acceptable reason. The truth was that on November 24, 1818 had an appointment at a different medical facility. After that, no one except for the three in the house would be allowed to see the boy unclothed, never without his shirt and pants on. Any doctor who did would think that he'd glimpsed hell.

JOHN KEMENY and Sara Powell were always the first ones in the office, carpooling in from Silver Springs. Kemeny, the oldest member of the group, liked all the people who worked at MJ-11, but he had a soft spot for the mathematics prodigy who, at age twenty-two, was a Wellesley graduate. She was the daughter Kemeny, a bachelor, had never had.

The first thing they noticed was the smell of coffee. Kemeny and Powell looked at each other. The door to Porter's office was closed, but the blinds across the glass wall were up, revealing an empty space. From across the room, behind one of the workstation partitions, came a soft mumbling. When Kemeny and Powell wandered over, they could make out the words: "It's wrong, all wrong. *You're* all wrong!"

For such a big man, Kemeny was very quiet on his feet. Long ago, he'd made it a habit to clear his throat or make some other noise to announce his arrival. He did so now. Sloane Ryder looked up from her monitor, blinked, and said good morning.

Kemeny, Powell, and the others had known all about Sloane Ryder even before Lee Porter had approached her. Porter's policy was to let the team review an applicant's resumé for potential conflicts of interest or irregularities. In Sloane's case, her credentials intrigued the team. Several were Ravenhurst alumni themselves and vouched for her training. And after initial introductions, the consensus was that Sloane Ryder might be a perfect fit.

"Good morning, Sloane Ryder," Kemeny said. His words carried a slight accent; behind his cheery greeting his eyes were alert. "Didn't Lee tell you that there's no overtime bonus?"

"Have you been here all night?" Sara Powell asked. She was a slender, small-boned woman whose movements were as quick and light as a robin's.

"Not quite," Sloane replied. "I had dinner, went home, but couldn't sleep. I logged in around five o'clock." Sloane pushed a pile of printouts across her desk. "You guys want to take a look while I freshen up?"

The washrooms on the floor were clean, spacious, and well lit. They included shower stalls, complete with an array of soaps and shampoos for those not-infrequent all-night sessions.

Sloane splashed cool water on her face, feeling it take the sting out of her eyes. She searched for a pleasant memory to transport her out of this place and found it in the image of Whip Alley sitting on the stool beside her at Clyde's, where they had gone for dinner. The restaurant bar had been crowded with the young hustling set—congressional aides, greenhorn lobbyists, lawyers of every stripe—all of them talking a little too loudly, trying to get their points across.

Their conversation drifted around safe, congenial

subjects. Sloane learned that Alley was a Broadway musical aficionado who traveled to New York rather than wait for the road productions to come to Kennedy Center. He had grown up playing hockey, so, in addition to running, he skated at the outdoor rink flanked by the west wing of the National Gallery of Art and the National Museum of Natural History. She also noticed that he had a particular rapport with the city's service staff. The first time, at J. Paul's, the bartender had treated him with a brotherly familiarity. At Clyde's, the bartender had twice passed him folded napkins, obviously messages. Alley had pocketed them without comment.

She could tell he was disappointed when she mentioned that she had to return to G Street. Because of the hour, she accepted his offer of a lift in an aging sedan that still had the faint outlines of taxi-service decals on its doors.

"So it doesn't look too much like an undercover car," Alley had explained.

There was an awkward moment when they'd arrived at the GAO building, neither of them knowing quite what to say while waiting for the security guard to unlock the door. Then they both started talking at once and broke out laughing.

The memory of Whip Alley reaching for her hand and squeezing it gently pleased Sloane. For the first time in months, her doubts about men and her choice of them were stilled.

Lee Porter had arrived and was at Sloane's workstation along with Kemeny and Powell. He looked up from his reading.

"Good morning," he said. "Looks like you might have snagged something."

"Martin Garrett," Sloane said. "Everyone else on the printout comes up clean. Garrett's the only one with an anomaly. A big one."

"I think Sloane's got a hit," Powell chirped. "This business about the bank loan? Something's not right."

"And the connection to Ostroff," Kemeny added. "There doesn't appear to be any, except for the cosignature on a two-hundred-thousand-dollar loan and some toll calls to her home. Too many blank spaces."

Porter brought out his pipe, turned it over and over in his fingers like worry beads. There was a hum in the room now as the rest of the staff filtered in.

"Forget Ostroff," he said. "For now. Concentrate on Garrett."

"Active file?" Kemeny asked.

Porter nodded. "Full-blown audit. I'll call Henrietta over at Justice and arrange for the warrants. The FBI'll have the wiretaps in place at Garrett's house by tomorrow morning."

"What about his office?" Sloane asked.

"We'll tap that line too," Porter said. "And all the public phones within a ten-minute walk of his office."

Sloane was shocked by how quickly events were moving. Everything Porter was ordering carried far-reaching implications.

As if reading her mind, Porter told her, "It's got to be this fast. We need to find out Garrett's agenda, how far along it's come, what its goal is."

"What if the relationship with Dr. Ostroff and the low-interest loan can be explained away?" Sloane asked.

"That's exactly what I want," Porter said. "To have it explained away. As soon as it is—*if* it is—then we pull off everything. Garrett will never know that we were interested in him. No harm will come to him, his family, or his career. But we do need to know." He turned to Sara Powell. "You better head over to Justice. John, contact Charlie Weathers at the Bureau's surveillance unit, let 'em know what we need. I want everything up and running by the time the warrants are signed."

Sloane watched them hurry away. "What about me?"

"I want you to handle Garrett," Porter said. "Call and tell him that the GAO has been reviewing the national security adviser's request for increased satellite production. We're inclined to give a favorable opinion but there are questions. This is Trimble's pet project. Garrett will give you all the time you want."

"*What* satellite production?"

"The paperwork's in my office. Really, it's more like two ledgers. I hope you're a fast study."

Porter was right about everything. Garrett took Sloane's call at once. After she had explained the reason for her call, he cleared his lunch hour.

Both in the classroom and in the field, the instructors at Ravenhurst had taught their students the importance of using a legitimate cover to mask covert intentions. In this case, Sloane was relying on the GAO file she carried into Garrett's office to give her the authority to deal with him in his official capacity. It contained blueprints and specs related to the KH-15, the new generation of spy satellites Hughes had developed and was proposing to build for the National Reconnaissance Office. James Trimble was a vocal proponent of the new platforms, their fifteen-billion-dollar price tag notwithstanding. Garrett was his point man in the Senate Intelligence Oversight and Finance Committees.

The Ravenhurst instructors had drummed something else into their pupils: A man who wants something from you will inevitably talk more than he should. Garrett was no exception. He offered Sloane a refreshment and, after she declined, launched into a paean about the KH-15. The more he talked, the longer Sloane had to take her measure of the man.

Marty Garrett appeared to be everything that his personnel file indicated: bright, enthusiastic, his arguments coherent and concise. Sloane never got the impression that this was a man under any pressure other than that generated by his job. His approach to the subject matter was frank and straightforward; his answers to her questions were thoughtful and on point.

Sloane smiled, made notes, and gently steered the conversation. Referring to Porter's notes, she gave Garrett a rundown of the GAO's concern about the project estimates and Hughes's reluctance to provide a guarantee against cost overruns. Garrett was visibly relieved that these were her only concerns and promised answers as quickly as possible.

And would Ms. Ryder care to meet the national security adviser himself? A few minutes could be arranged.

Ms. Ryder thought not. James Trimble was a much older and wiser fox than Garrett.

Garrett buzzed his secretary to see Sloane out. The reply came back: "Ladybug is on the floor."

"You'll have to wait for an escort," he told Sloane.

As soon as he'd spoken the words, there was a knock on the door and a Secret Service agent entered.

"Ms. Ryder? I'm Agent Tylo. I'll see you out." Holland Tylo noted Sloane's startled expression and added, "It's standard procedure. Please, come with me."

Sloane said good-bye to Marty Garrett and fell in step behind the blond Secret Service woman in the chic beige pants suit.

When they were in the corridor, Holland Tylo turned to Sloane, her gaze falling on the pass draped around Sloane's neck.

"You're with the GAO, right?"

"MJ-11."

Sloane knew that the Secret Service would have asked and been told exactly which GAO department she worked for.

"Is this your first visit to the White House?" Tylo asked.

"Does it show?"

Tylo laughed. "Not that much. I was going to take you out the back way, but let's take the long way around."

Sloane's arrival at the White House had been so hurried that she had never really stopped to appreciate exactly where she was. Her first impression of the President's residence was of bomb-sniffing dogs doing a walk around a sedan.

She mentioned that to Holland Tylo, who replied, "That's only the beginning. We have guards on the rooftops and the grounds, as well as motion sensors and cameras. Plus a few other refinements we'd rather not publicize. Your clearance came in an hour before you did; otherwise you never would have been issued that pass."

Tylo walked her past the vice president's office and the President's study, then paused in front of the Oval Office.

"Gary, what's the status on Ladybug?" she asked the agent stationed there.

The agent gestured with his chin. "In the nest."

"Sorry," Tylo said to Sloane. "I thought you might get a peek."

"A peek at what? Me?"

Sloane recognized the voice instantly. She turned to see Claudia Ballantine standing in the doorway to the Oval Office, coffee cup in one hand, a red-lined letter in the other. She wore a flattering emerald-green skirt with a white blouse that set off her red hair, and had about her the air of a harried executive trying to get some annoying matter off her desk.

"Madam President," Tylo began to say, but Claudia Ballantine waved away the words.

"And you are?"

"Sloane Ryder, Madam President. From the GAO."

Claudia Ballantine looked at her keenly. "You're one of Lee Porter's, aren't you?"

"Yes, ma'am."

"Please tell Lee I said hello," the President said. "You'll have to excuse me, but I'm trying to stave off a crisis on the Hill."

"Yes, ma'am," Sloane said weakly. "I will. Thank you."

Tylo laughed as she and Sloane went out on the portico. "I think she took a shine to you."

She stepped back to allow the driver to open the back door of the sedan.

"It was nice to meet you, Sloane. MJ-11 does business with the Service from time to time. If you ever need anything, give me a call."

Lee Porter was watching Sloane make her way to his office when his private line rang.

"Good morning, Lee," said the President. "You sent me a visitor—without informing me beforehand."

Lee Porter was accustomed to surprise calls from Claudia Ballantine.

"You're referring to Sloane Ryder, Madam President."

"One and the same."

"I sent her over to have a chat with Martin Garrett, Jim Trimble's assistant."

The President toyed with a gold Mark Cross that had belonged to her late husband. "I see. Is there anything I should know about Jim? Or Garrett?"

"I'm not concerned about Trimble."

Claudia Ballantine allowed a sigh of relief. "Garrett, then?"

"It's still too early to tell, Madam President. Have you spoken with Jim today?"

"Not yet."

"He'll probably want to see you, if he's not on the agenda." Porter gave her a précis of the NSA intercept from the Chinese embassy, the national security adviser's volatile reaction, and the course of action that had been decided upon. "Personally, I didn't think the NSA scan would turn up anything, but Sloane Ryder tripped across something having to do with Garrett. We're running down more details right now. I sent her to get a firsthand look at Garrett."

"Woman's intuition?"

"Ryder was sharp enough to spot the anomaly. I thought maybe she'd see something in Garrett too."

"Lee, are you telling me that he might be the source of the leaks?"

"I will not jump to that conclusion, Madam President," Porter said firmly.

"But within seventy-two hours of Jim Trimble bringing out the Necklace Option, the Chinese are pulling up stakes and going home. I don't like this, Lee. Not one bit."

Claudia Ballantine remembered the scandals endured by one of her predecessors when evidence of Chinese money in the American electoral process had resulted in a slew of charges, countercharges, special investigators, Justice Department probes. Much of that had come to naught, yet it was clear that the Chinese had tried to corrupt the election—and in some ways had succeeded. Now, maybe because of the ineffectual investigations, they had set their sights higher. Funneling money into candidates' coffers was one thing. But being on the receiving end of policy-making decisions was a matter of national security.

And therein lay Claudia Ballantine's problem: The very agencies designed to root out treason were the ones that might have been corrupted. The vaunted resources of the intelligence community were useless to her.

Which was why she had called on the one person she knew she could trust, the government's ultimate watchdog, who, because of his low profile, was overlooked by everyone. To the power brokers, the GAO was a backwater and the name Lee Porter meant nothing.

"Lee, how far has the rot spread?"

"I don't know, Madam President. But it won't stop with Garrett. *I* won't stop either. I don't think you'd want me to."

"Of course not. On the contrary, I want you to move as fast as you can. Trimble's nervous about the Chinese. He's making *me* nervous, while Dodge French keeps saying we have to stay the steady course. Contradictions make for mistakes, which can lead to disaster. You've got to tell me what I'm up against, Lee."

A moment later, Sloane Ryder was in Porter's office, describing her meeting with Martin Garrett.

"He was glad to see someone from the GAO," Sloane said. "The satellite project is clearly important to him, and not only because Trimble has thrown his weight behind it. Garrett believes that it's essential to national security.

"I found him calm and personable. If he was hiding something, or was worried about my visit, he didn't show it. That makes him either a damn good actor or someone who believes that whatever he's doing is for a greater good."

"You're saying that Garrett comes across as a regular guy because he believes that's exactly what he is, that whatever crime he's committing is not a crime in his eyes?"

"If he's a criminal at all, that would be the pattern to his thinking."

Porter pulled out an ancient tobacco pouch, the leather worn shiny from his skin oils, and began to fill his pipe.

"You say 'if.' You're not about to cut him loose?"

"I might if it weren't for the bank loan. He might be able to explain that away—"

"—but we can't go up and ask him because that'll spook him. Your call would be to proceed with the wiretaps?"

Sloane nodded. "Yes. In the meantime, I'm going to keep digging into the financial records—and his trips abroad. Garrett's been doing a lot of traveling lately on Trimble's behalf. I want to know exactly where he went, what places he stayed at, how long, if there were any detours from the official itinerary."

"You think he might be using the trips as a cover to pass on information and collect a paycheck?"

"That's what Ames used to do."

Porter considered this. "Okay. I'll get Kemeny and Powell to help you. But be careful. Garrett would have been using both the White House travel office and the military. I don't want anything being traced back here."

17

TWENTY-ONE HOURS after Lee Porter had given the go-ahead, Sara Powell was standing in a small, nondescript office on the sixth floor of the Justice Department. The room was furnished in General Services Administration leftovers—a trestle-table desk, nicked and scratched, a few leather chairs, the hides cracked for lack of conditioner. The floorboards were bowed with age and creaked even under Sara's modest weight.

Henrietta Beaumont, the federal circuit judge on duty, looked out of place in the dusty, windowless room. She wore a tailored Armani suit set off by a colorful Versace scarf. Seated at the trestle table, she read through the GAO petition for wiretaps on Marty Garrett's office and home phones and a half dozen pay phones near the White House.

Although Lee Porter had called the judge, it was Sara Powell who had been up all night putting together the necessary brief. She wasn't sure whether she looked worse than she felt or vice versa, especially in front of this well-turned-out woman.

"Lee isn't asking for much, is he?" Beaumont commented.

"Just what we believe is absolutely necessary, Your Honor," Sara replied. Her voice sounded as if she had sand in her throat.

The judge initialed the wiretap orders. "Good for sixty days. Will that do it?"

"Yes, Your Honor."

"You should get some sleep," Henrietta Beaumont advised. "Tell Lee I said so."

Sara smiled. "I will, Your Honor. Thank you."

Like many a psychiatrist's office, the judge's chambers had an entrance separate from its exit. Sara Powell had no idea that the person coming in after her was FBI Special Agent Peter Mack. She could not have been aware that, like Lee Porter, Mack had come up in front of Henrietta Beaumont on numerous occasions to obtain warrants. Nor could she have known that the judge, secure in this specially protected room, never bothered to cover the petitions. They lay haphazardly along the side of the table, in clear view.

Peter Mack passed the judge his request and settled back as she flipped through the particulars. What happened next was more a result of training than deliberate intent.

Mack's eyes strayed to the papers at the edge of the trestle table. Reading upside down was a skill he had honed a long time before. He had no problem making out the petitioner's name or that of the target, Martin Garrett, who was described as the assistant to the national security adviser. Beside the name, in parentheses, was what really caught Mack's eye: (CHINA).

This was not the first time in his career that Peter Mack had seen something not intended for his consumption. On almost all the other occasions, he had simply turned a blind eye or suffered a convenient memory lapse. Almost. There had been three instances when he'd been able to use such information, suitably disguised so that its origins could not be traced. In this case, had it not been for the GAO designation on the cover sheet, he might have let the matter slide. But Mack was still smarting and angry over Sloane Ryder's shutting him down like that in the street.

Plus, Sloane had embarrassed him with Dodge French. Although French had assured him that his failure to convince Sloane to play along at Young, Pullen was ancient history, the agent still felt that he owed French. Now, he had just the thing to clear his marker.

Peter Mack had three numbers for Dodge French: one in the capital; one at Brandywine, the Long Island estate; and one hooked into French's personal satellite phone. Before heading out to national airport, he tried the D.C. number and was surprised not only that French was at his Kalorama home but that he was put through instantly. Careful whenever using public phones, Mack simply said that he'd come across information that French should be aware of immediately and that it could only be delivered face-to-face. French gave him an address.

Mack was reasonably familiar with the Kalorama district, north of Sheridan Circle. The upscale neighborhood was also known as Embassy Row. Dodge French's residence was a turn-of-the-century brick and gables mansion on Wyoming Avenue.

A manservant who, judging by his size, also doubled

as a bodyguard escorted Mack into a double parlor that seemed frozen in the nineteenth century. Dodge French stood by a marble-framed fireplace, warming his hands.

"Peter. It's good to see you again."

"And you, sir."

"May I offer you something? Coffee?"

"No, thank you. I have to be getting back to New York. This was just an overnight trip to appear before the FISA court."

"I trust you obtained what you needed?"

"Yes, sir."

Mack hesitated. He wasn't sure how to segue into the next part. He needed to say what was relevant without giving away the details.

French sensed the younger man's discomfort. "FISA deals with a great many issues. As you probably know, I'm on good terms with most of the federal district court judges who oversee it. It would have been Henrietta Beaumont today?"

"Yes, sir. She was looking after some petition brought by the GAO."

"The General Accounting Office? That's unusual."

"That's what I thought, sir. Especially since their request involved someone called Martin Garrett, from the national security adviser's office."

The mention of Garrett's name set off alarm bells in French's mind.

"I see," he said slowly. "I appreciate you bringing the matter to my attention, Peter. If there's a problem at the national security adviser's office, I need to know about it."

French gestured toward the dining room. "Are you

sure you wouldn't care for something before your plane leaves?"

"No, thank you, sir. As it is, I'll just make it."

"Then I won't keep you. We'll talk soon, Peter. Promise."

French let his manservant see the agent out, then retreated to a tapestry-weave wingchair. He focused on the gift Peter Mack had brought him, a gift that was not unlike Pandora's box: Once opened, its contents would be difficult to put back in. One of the things it contained could certainly never be returned. As for the rest, if he moved quickly enough, he might be able to contain the impending damage.

French had never met or broken bread with Lee Porter, but he knew him by reputation and had seen the results of some of his handiwork. Once Porter began his hunt, he never gave it up until he brought his quarry to ground. Which meant it was time to make a phone call he'd never believed he'd have to make.

As he reached for the phone, French thought of the woman who'd been Mack's lover, the one whom he had been unable to intimidate or bully, who'd forced all that unpleasantness with MacGregor. Sloane Ryder . . . Wasn't she now working for Lee Porter?

18

THE HANDYMAN had received the message on a Friday via the mail drop at the Four Seasons Hotel in New York. The contents had caused him to terminate his stay sooner than anticipated and take the first Amtrak of the day to the capital.

There he checked into a modest Howard Johnson's off Massachusetts Avenue that advertised special monthly rates for transferred executives needing a place to stay while waiting for a house or an apartment to clear. It was not a place where any one face would be remembered.

On Sunday morning, the Handyman joined the throngs of locals and tourists who trooped under the ornate arch marking the entrance to Chinatown. In the crowds, he was just another middle-aged man armed with an environmentally correct canvas food bag, poking through the food stalls that held all manner of delicacies.

The Handyman slipped inside a butcher shop called the Lucky Moon. Pushing his way past the Chinese housewives milling in front of the counter, he slipped into a tiny dining area in the kitchen—a feature most whites did not know existed. In a corner near steaming vats and a vertical roaster, its racks heavy with duck, he found Mai Ling.

The sheet of butcher paper covered the table's lime-green paint. There were two place settings, consisting of chopsticks, napkins, and chipped cups. Aromatic steam, tinged with jasmine, escaped through the teapot spout.

"A blessing on your generations," Mai Ling said in Mandarin.

She sat with her back to the wall, oblivious to the shouts of cooks, the pounding of cleavers, the rattle of heavy roasting pans.

The Handyman slipped into a chair and replied in the same dialect: "May all your sons be fertile, Mother."

Mai Ling cackled. She knew that the Handyman had never married, had no offspring. He was the last of his line, and when he died, his great talents and secrets would be interred forever.

For his part, the Handyman had learned that Mai Ling was barren. The only things she could conceive were political intrigue and death. They understood each other perfectly.

"You appear well and fit," Mai Ling observed as one of the cooks slammed down dishes of octopus, pork, and entrails.

Mai Ling heaped rice into his bowl and pushed the dishes toward him. For a few minutes they scooped food into their mouths, the sticks moving in a blur.

"How is your friend Fat Lee?" Mai Ling inquired.

"Well," the Handyman replied.

"You sought him out before agreeing to work with me."

"Of course."

The Handyman wasn't particularly surprised that she was aware of his connection to Fat Lee, possibly the most eminent astrologer in the West. The Handyman was a student of the art. He believed in the portents and influences that swirled around men, guiding their actions as a slight breeze pulls a fallen leaf across a still pond. He never agreed to undertake an assignment without first knowing the principals involved and, second, putting as much information as he could about them at Lee's fingertips. Then the horoscopes would be drawn and Lee would guide him through their meaning. If the portents were not favorable, the Handyman refused the work.

In this case, the portents had been good. But he had known early on, when he began his search for 1818, that in one crucial way Mai Ling had misrepresented his mission. She had all but assured him that his assassin's skills would, beyond the North Korean camp colonel, not be required.

"The one you are looking out for believes he is in jeopardy," Mai Ling said. She pushed a photograph across the butcher paper. "He believes this man, a link in the chain, has come under suspicion."

The Handyman did not touch the photo. The three-quarter profile showed a young man in his late thirties, his lips slightly open as though he were about to laugh. The Handyman could not have recognized the brown and green background blur as Martin Garrett's yard behind his ranch house in McLean.

"What kind of suspicion exactly?"

"Inquiries have been made about him by people whose business it is to do such things. I am told they are very good at their business."

"Inquiries that have made him"—the Handyman tapped the photo with his knuckle—"expendable."

"Exactly so. But to protect the principal, to remedy the matter, will require extraordinary methods."

The Handyman's instinct for self-preservation was like a finely cast tuning fork. Mai Ling's words had been as gentle as a butterfly alighting on a flower. But the tuning fork still vibrated.

"'Extraordinary methods,'" the Handyman murmured.

Mai Ling jammed a cigarette into her ivory holder. "I understand your preference for the long gun. But this man's death cannot be taken for an execution. It must seem an accident that the authorities will never question. He must die, be mourned, and be buried— along with any questions."

"Because he may not be the only link."

Mai Ling nodded. "True. And if there is an investigation, these others may be found out too. Each one is closer to the principal. Each one represents a greater danger."

"The principal can never be found, otherwise everything that you have structured will be wasted," the Handyman reasoned. "The Chos, 1818—everything will become ashes."

Mai Ling's eyes were wide and unblinking, like two full moons. "There is another consideration."

"The reason this one is suspect. The man who made him so."

"The *woman* who made him so."

The Handyman's only reaction was a slight intake of breath, but it spoke volumes. A woman had been involved in his last assignment. She was an amateur, an innocent who had no idea that she was being used. She was supposed to have died after helping bring the Handyman to the United States from his exile in Marseilles. But she had not died in that deserted airline lounge at Kennedy. Even at this moment, somewhere in the world, she was searching for him, waiting for a glimpse of the shadow that she hoped would betray his coming.

"A woman," the Handyman said. "Who works for the hunters. What is her name?"

"You already know her. Sloane Ryder. You cannot touch her. Even if you stage the accident perfectly, should any harm come to her, the hunters will know she was right. To kill her would be self-defeating."

"Do you have any idea how much she knows about the target?" the Handyman asked.

"Not enough. If she did and had passed this information on to her superiors, the target would be under physical surveillance. We know for a fact that their investigation is in its earliest stages."

"You said 'physical surveillance.' How are they watching him?"

"Wiretaps. I suspect at the office and at home. Possibly other communications he has access to."

They were doing more than that, the Handyman reasoned. But they were moving cautiously. They weren't sure. Had they been, there would be full-blown FBI surveillance.

So it's not the FBI.

"I need to know who is conducting the surveillance," the Handyman said.

"I will get you as much information as possible. But remember: Every day the investigation progresses, the hunters come closer to finding something that will allow them to take the target. You must deal with the target while he is still out in the open, not in some safe house, his tongue nicely loosened by the thought of what his life would be like after he has been convicted of treason."

"I'll need a few days to position myself," the Handyman told her. "After that, he is no longer your concern."

"May the gods rot your tongue," Mai Ling said somberly.

It sounded like a curse, but like so many things in Chinese culture, it was exactly the opposite, a blessing.

The Handyman watched her reach under the table and grasp a pair of white plastic bags filled with leafy vegetables. The bags were as much a prop as her dowdy dress, threadbare coat, and sturdy shoes.

Affecting a slight limp, Mai Ling left the kitchen looking like any one of a thousand Chinese grandmothers out shopping on Sunday, the reason the FBI surveillance team never gave her a second glance whenever she left the embassy on Connecticut Avenue. In an hour, the woman who was registered as one of the cooks and who had been seen leaving would be videotaped as she returned. All parties would be present and accounted for.

* * *

Dodge French might never have contacted Mai Ling, never have had her set in motion events that could not be stopped now had he known exactly how little information the MJ-11 team actually had.

Throughout that weekend and into the following week, Sloane, John Kemeny, and Sara Powell picked apart Martin Garrett's life. Because of his connections in the military and the intelligence communities, Kemeny took the lead in investigating Garrett's international travel.

Since the national security adviser had access to various means of transportation, his assistant was accorded the same courtesy and flew on military and government jets as well as commercial liners. Doggedly Kemeny checked all the flights Garrett had boarded, both at Andrews Air Force Base and at Dulles. He ferreted out the reasons for these trips and pieced together Garrett's itinerary as he moved between a NATO conference in Belgium to a secret visit to Tel Aviv where he and Trimble had met with their Israeli counterparts to discuss the transfer of antimissile technology. They continued on to St. Petersburg, where Garrett had presented a position paper on the Muslim threat in eastern Russia to the Russian armed forces high command.

It would have been easy for Garrett to find time to slip away from an official function, or to get together with a contact at any one of the dozens of meetings he attended. Kemeny had no way of ascertaining whether that had happened, so he went after the phone records Garrett had left behind. The only calls Garrett had made from his hotels were to his wife. Business calls had been made from the security of an embassy or a consulate.

Kemeny was still working on these when he reported to Lee Porter and the group. The places Garrett had traveled to were not sophisticated financial centers. If he was taking money, it was unlikely he'd bank it in institutions that had no secrecy laws. That would have been too risky, especially since during the Belgian visit, he could easily have slipped across next door, to the Netherlands, whose banking records were as compartmentalized as a wasp's nest.

Sara Powell wasn't faring any better on the domestic front. She put Garrett's wife, Patty, under the microscope. Patty Garrett had received a master's degree in social work from Columbia and had worked for two years for the city of New York before marrying Garrett. She had moved her career to D.C. but left social services after less than a year to give birth to her son. Records indicated that Patty Garrett had had every intention of returning to her job, but that was before her baby had been diagnosed with the heart ailment. Patty Garrett had stayed home with the boy, but she and her husband still had to hire a private nurse for him.

It seemed to Sara that Patty Garrett lived a life of quiet desperation. She was an only child and her parents had passed away when she was in college. There had been some insurance money, enough for living expenses to see her through to her degree, but she still needed student loans.

There was no other money that Sara could trace. Like millions of Americans living close to the edge,

Patty Garrett used credit cards even for grocery shopping. It wasn't difficult to track her progress through the supermarkets, as well as Wal-Mart, Kmart, and other discount emporiums. Patty shopped carefully and frugally. She bought a lot of sale items.

Sloane and Lee Porter handled the wiretaps. The tapes of Garrett's phone conversations were delivered three times within a twenty-four hour period, at eight A.M., four P.M., and midnight. If there was anything of interest on them, the team's reaction time would be that much quicker. It also meant that neither Sloane nor Porter left the office before three in the morning.

But the tapes of Garrett's office calls yielded nothing. Many of the business conversations were with the same people, people whom Garrett had legitimate reasons for calling. The personal ones went to his wife, to the doctor who monitored his son's condition, a car-service shop, a mail-order hardware company— reflections of the suburban life.

After almost a week of sifting through tapes, Sloane pressed Porter to let her return to the money trail. She argued that their best chance to discover the reason behind Garrett's loan was to go after the mysterious Dr. Susan Ostroff. Porter vetoed that.

"I've already started looking at her," he said. "She's a much bigger fish. We have to be very careful how we handle her. I want more on Garrett before we turn to her."

"At some point, we'll either have to confront him or cut him loose," Sloane replied. "The wiretap order doesn't run forever."

"You can ask your friend Detective Alley for a little help if you want," Porter suggested.

Sloane blushed, but she wasn't surprised. She had not made a secret of seeing Whip. And if Porter hadn't already vetted both Whip and Paco Santana, he never would have made the suggestion.

There weren't many places open at three in the morning. Popeye's on Fifth Street, next to Judiciary Square, was the most popular—and the safest because its regulars were cops going on and off shift.

Whip Alley had pulled the graveyard shift at the same time as Sloane had started her work on the tapes. They began meeting at Popeye's, a vintage fifties diner with polished-chrome-and-red-leatherette seats, for either very late dinners or early breakfasts. Most of the customers were cops, truckers, or assorted government types leafing through the bulldog edition of the *Post*.

Tonight Sloane picked at a light salad while Alley worked on a Denver omelet.

"You're quiet tonight," Alley said.

Sloane looked up from her food. "I don't want you to take this the wrong way," she said. "It's something I had to do. Part of my job."

Alley grinned. "You told your boss about me and he ran me through his machines."

"You knew?"

"When you told me you worked for MJ-11, I knew it might happen. In this town, running background checks is like catching a cold."

Alley flagged the waitress for coffee refills, then asked, "So what's up?"

Sloane gave him a sanitized version of the investigation she was working on.

"You definitely think there's something bad to this guy?" Alley asked.

"At least something not right. But I can't crack it."

Alley did not ask her to elaborate. From his days at the army's Criminal Investigation Division he knew the vast resources that were available to MJ-11. But the investigation was still young and proceeding quickly. Avenues might have been overlooked or not gotten to yet. He suggested one now.

"Have you run the name through NCIC?"

He was referring to the FBI's computerized database, the National Crime Information Center. Police across the country can access it, from a patrol car if necessary, to check whether the vehicle they have stopped is stolen or if the occupants are fugitives.

Sloane frowned. "No, we haven't. This individual has a high security clearance. It's unlikely that NCIC would have anything on him."

Alley let that slide. It was his experience that sometimes the most obvious tool at hand got the best results. But he could see another reason for Sloane's not having gone that route. She was already using the FBI for wiretaps. She wouldn't want to cozy up to the Bureau any more than was absolutely necessary.

"I'll do it for you," he said. "I could bury it in a bunch of names and no flags would go up."

Sloane looked at him carefully. Porter had given her leave to bring Alley in on the investigation. If she went ahead, she'd have to give him the name. It was her call. All right then.

"Martin Garrett," she said quietly, then spelled the surname. "He's the assistant to the national security adviser."

Alley seemed unimpressed. "No problem." He checked his watch. "By ten o'clock. That work for you?"

Alley was as good as his word. Sloane took his call at nine forty-five.

"Your boy's clean—at least as far as NCIC is concerned," he said.

"It was worth a shot," she replied. "I owe you."

"Maybe we're not done yet. Have you had any physical surveillance on the guy?"

"Only wiretaps and one contact."

"The weekend's coming up. What say you and I tag along if he heads out, see where he likes to hang, who he talks to?"

Sloane hesitated. This was not, strictly speaking, part of her mandate, nor did she have experience in shadowing individuals. But Whip did.

"You're on," she said.

"Let me know where and when."

Martin Garrett was completely unaware of MJ-11's interest in him, nor did he have even an inkling that for most of that week another shadow, roving much closer, was with him and his family. None, that is, until his wife spoke up.

The Handyman had rented a Buick Regal because it would fit in with the Garretts's neighborhood. Every morning he drove out to McLean and, after buying coffee at the local Coffee Bean 'n Tea Leaf, slowly

cruised past the Garrett residence. Just another working stiff in a suit on his way to the Beltway.

Except that after following Garrett into D.C., the
Handyman doubled back. He had no intention of trying the impossible—following Garrett into the White
House. As long as Garrett was there, he was accounted
for. There were other ways the Handyman could learn
about him.

Patty Garrett kept to a fairly strict routine. On alternate days, the Handyman heard rock music coming
through a partially open window as Patty jogged her
five miles on a rented treadmill. Thursday was laundry
day. The washer and dryer were located in the garage;
conveniently, Patty kept the door open in between
loads. With Garrett's car gone, the Handyman was
able to see the Peg-Board with its array of inexpensive
but well-cared-for tools, and fraying aluminum patio
furniture stored for the winter.

One morning, the Handyman saw mother and son
come out the door and followed them to a local hospital. There he made small talk with a nurse, a plain,
middle-aged woman who responded to the charms of
an older, handsome man asking about a patient whose
name she couldn't find—not surprising since the
patient existed only in the assassin's imagination.

The nurse had been with the hospital for a long
time and knew Danny Garrett well. When the
Handyman asked about him, she replied that he was a
great kid. A miracle that the surgery had been successful. The boy loved to play baseball and could swing a
bat like nobody's business. But every two weeks, like
clockwork, he was brought in for a cardiac checkup.

She confided to the Handyman that it must feel like living on a leash.

The reference to baseball alerted the Handyman. Among the items in the Garretts's garage were a box of old softballs and a clutch of aluminum bats. He mentioned to the nurse that he had a pair of nephews, Danny's age, coming out to visit. Maybe there was a game they could join?

The nurse beamed and told him about a softball game scheduled for Saturday down at the Tidal Basin, in West Potomac Park, between Ohio Drive and West Basin Drive. Danny Garrett never missed one. The Handyman thanked the nurse for her kindness and turned to leave.

The Handyman drove down to the Tidal Basin, parked, and strolled along the grounds. The open, grassy area, bordered by two arteries of traffic and the Tidal Basin itself, was perfect for his purpose.

He could envision it all quite clearly on a crisp, sun-streaked weekend afternoon: the picnic tables laden with trays of food under plastic wrap, the wives digging soft drinks and lemonade out of the coolers while the fathers walked off the distances between the bases, tattered old outdoor cushions. There would be some good-natured argument about how the teams were picked and who would be the umpire. A cheer would go up when the first pitch was thrown. The fathers would settle down with their wives to root their kids on.

What would the fathers be drinking?

Beer, soft drinks, or iced tea. Iced tea would be better for his purposes. Its dark color made it easier to work with than clear soda.

There was another important factor: spectators. People strolling by would pause and watch for a few minutes. Another amiable, suitably dressed stranger wouldn't cause concern or even be noticed, with everyone's attention on the game. It was all quite perfect.

The Handyman reviewed the plan, spreading slowly across his imagination like a bloodstain, as he drove out of the city. He took Route 50, which skirts Dulles International Airport, and headed for Middleburg, in Loudoun County, the heart of Virginia's hunt country. In less than an hour, he was driving by sprawling equestrian estates where horse breeders indulged in the sports of fox hunting, polo, and steeplechase. After an early lunch of cold seafood salad, the Handyman set out to find what he needed.

The veterinarian's office was elegantly appointed and well stocked. The Handyman had deliberately chosen the lunch hour to come by, hoping that the owner would be away. He was, his place taken by a polite, earnest young apprentice who sympathized with the plight of the nonexistent gelding that the Handyman told him about. The drug that the Handyman was interested in was on the list of controlled substances in most states. But the equestrian contingent in the Virginia legislature had quietly lobbied for it to be removed from the list, a wish the governor, himself an avid horseman, had granted with a stroke of his pen.

The Handyman was careful to buy just the amount indicated by the condition he had described. Since he paid cash, the only record of the sale was in the veterinarian's computer, buried among dozens of other orders. Even if the drug were detected in the victim's toxicology—unlikely given that only a minuscule amount was needed and the residue was quickly flushed by the body—the investigators would be hard-pressed to trace it back to the upscale office in Middleburg. And if the young apprentice was interviewed, the best he'd be able to give the investigators would be a general description of an unremarkable middle-aged man who really didn't look anything at all like the Handyman.

Whip Alley picked Sloane up at her apartment building promptly at seven o'clock Saturday morning. He brought a big thermos of coffee, and bagels still warm from the bakery. They dug into the food as he cleared the city limits and headed east on the Baltimore–Washington Parkway, getting off just before BWI Airport.

The route took them through an area of industrial parks, along a road that dead-ended at a huge warehouse surrounded by a Cyclone fence topped with razor wire. The sign on the gates read MARYLAND STATE POLICE DEPOT.

"You said this would be a surprise." Sloane looked around at the silent, desolate surroundings. "You really know how to romance a girl."

Alley grinned and held his badge in front of the video camera. The gates rolled back and they drove to the warehouse. Paco Santana appeared from out of nowhere, holding a half-eaten piece of melon in the palm of his hand. He opened the door for Sloane and greeted her with a shy smile and offered her a bite of the fruit.

Alley led the way into a cavernous hold filled with state trooper sedans, wreckers, and an assortment of other vehicles. He checked in with the officer in the glass-enclosed office, then turned to Santana.

"Paperwork?"

Through a mouthful of melon, Paco Santana mumbled that it was all done, using the fruit as a pointer. Standing under the fluorescents was a dark blue, conventional-looking Chevrolet Suburban.

"It's nice," Sloane commented. "If you're considering hauling a dead elk."

"This one's a little different," Alley explained. He led her around the vehicle. "Outside, you have run-flat tires with an inner plastic rim. You can go for fifty miles at fifty miles per hour even if they're all deflated. There's a bullet-resistant battery, exterior armor plate, and the gas tank is anti-explosive."

He opened the driver's door and elaborated on the interior. It was sheathed with ballistic steel. The windows all held bullet-resistant glass. There was a remote control that scanned for bombs and an oxygen tank in the back if tear gas became a problem. "The doors can only be opened when you release this switch here," he finished, reaching behind the door handle.

Sloane took all this in carefully. "Don't forget that." She pointed to a shotgun stand mounted by the dashboard.

"Right. There are a couple more weapons placements I'll show you."

Sloane put her hand on his arm. "Excuse me, but are we going into a war zone?"

"Not as near as I can tell," Alley replied cheerfully.

When he walked back to the trooper's office, Santana took Sloane aside. "The troopers let us borrow things now and then. They confiscated this from a drug dealer." He added confidentially, "It's really very good. The dealer survived the attempt on his life."

"Wonderful endorsement," Sloane murmured.

A few minutes later, they were headed back to the parkway. At College Park, Santana, driving an undercover sedan, honked and peeled off onto an exit.

"He forgot to bring his lunch," Alley explained. "He'll meet us at the Tidal Basin. We have plenty of time."

The latest batch of wiretap tapes that Sloane had listened to had Martin Garrett calling friends and telling them to be at West Potomac Park by ten o'clock to stake out their turf for the game. They had more than an hour.

Forty-five miles to the west, Martin Garrett finished packing up his Volvo station wagon. It had once been beige but now the paint had dulled to a muddy brown. The rust spots around the wheel wells and bumpers, courtesy of D.C. public works winter road salting, looked scabrous.

Garrett glanced at Patty fussing with Danny and his seat belt, the boy squirming, saying he could do it himself. Her face was pinched and her skin had an unhealthy pallor. She deserved better than this. Garrett wanted better for her, for all of them. But the hole in Danny's heart had done more than bring them to the brink of financial ruin; it had sucked years out of Patty, stolen her laughter and zest, tired her out for life and love.

And things seemed to be getting worse. A few days before, Patty had told him that she thought she'd seen a man watching their house. She had caught a glimpse of him through the window when she was on the treadmill and again when she'd gone out to do the laundry. Garrett had pressed her for a description and wasn't surprised that it was vague. Patty was good with numbers, bad when it came to recalling names or physical features. Still, he had listened patiently and talked to the neighbors. No one could corroborate Patty's sighting.

Garrett would have let it go had his wife not stuck so firmly to her story. Her continual references to the stranger had bothered Garrett enough that finally, as he'd been instructed so long ago, he contacted Susan Ostroff and told her that he might be under surveillance. She wasn't aware of this, she said, and hinted that Patty was imagining things. Garrett had dropped the subject and put it out of his mind.

Most of the crowd was there when Garrett pulled into the parking lot. As Garrett waved to his neighbors, Danny grabbed his outfielder's glove and dashed for the grass. Patty made a move to follow, but stopped when Garrett touched her arm.

"It's okay. Let him go. He'll be fine. Give me a hand with the food."

His wife smiled faintly and did as he asked. Garrett was aware that her eyes never left Danny as they walked to the picnic table. He noticed the green Suburban parked at the edge of the lot and felt a pang of envy.

Patty could use an SUV like that, especially in winter. It would be much safer and more dependable than the Volvo.

Garrett greeted the other fathers and swung his legs over the picnic-table seat. The sun felt good on his face as he popped open a Coke and poured it into a tall plastic glass filled with ice. Taking a swig of his soda, he plucked a crispy drumstick off the top of a heaping plate, and strolled down to where Danny was listening raptly to his coach. On the way, he passed a smartly dressed older man with a pair of small but expensive binoculars hanging from a leather strap around his neck. Garrett noticed a book on ornithology in the man's hand and wondered what kind of fowl the enthusiast might be hoping to spot. As far as he knew, the Tidal Basin was not prime bird-watching territory. The man smiled and nodded at Garrett as he passed, then Garrett heard his son shouting for him.

The Handyman continued without breaking stride, heading directly for the picnic table where Patty Garrett was sitting with two other women.

"Excuse me, madam."

The Paris-accented English rolled grandly off the Handyman's tongue. He saw Patty Garrett start and the two other women look up at him with interest and curiosity.

"How can I get to the Holocaust museum?"

Patty Garrett was flustered. She knew where the museum was, but couldn't think of the quickest way to get there. Her friends offered suggestions, then the three of them were talking to one another as the Handyman smiled and looked on. By now they had decided he was a harmless tourist, a camera around his neck and a book in one hand. No one noticed that his other hand was slightly closed, the folds of the palm hiding a tiny plastic pouch.

The Handyman moved slightly so that his hand was directly over Martin Garrett's glass of Coke, the sides wet with condensation. He brushed his thumb against his palm, opening the plastic, the gray powder sprinkling into the beverage, dissolving instantly, blending in with the color of the soda.

Having agreed on the best directions, the women turned to him and pointed to the path curving around the Jefferson Memorial to Raoul Wallenberg Place. The Handyman thanked them and, with a courtly bow, moved off.

Sloane Ryder shifted in the passenger seat and turned her attention from Garrett and the ball game to the wives. She saw a man's back, tan houndstooth jacket, and dark brown pants. He walked casually toward the pathway. She also noticed that one of the women at the picnic table was looking at the retreating figure, then turned to the others and joined the conversation. Something nudged itself in Sloane's mind, the way an errant foot touches one in the middle of the night, the thought that the woman and the man might somehow be connected. But now the man had disappeared from her line of sight.

Sloane glanced at Whip Alley, who hadn't taken his eyes off Garrett since they'd driven up.

"I'm beginning to think that I jumped the gun with Garrett," Sloane said. "It was only one anomaly that put me on to him. It seemed enough at the time . . ."

"If it was enough then, it's enough now," Alley replied, watching Garrett leap to his feet as his son made a wobbly catch in the outfield, ending the inning. "You have a piece of information that doesn't fit. You have the instincts to recognize it, to work it."

"I know. But the guy's doing what every normal father would on a weekend morning."

"But that anomaly of yours is still there, right?"

"Sure is."

"Then trust your instincts. This guy looks like he should be on the cover of *Time* as dad of the year. Maybe he should. But if he's dirty, he'll show it. They all do."

While Whip checked in with Paco Santana, positioned on the other side of the park, Sloane watched Garrett talk with his son. The boy clutched a bat, but there were four other hitters in front of him. From the boy's expression, Sloane thought he knew he didn't have much of a chance to step up to the plate this inning.

Now Garrett was walking away from the diamond, toward the picnic table. Sloane watched him hug his wife, then reach for his drink. He gulped it down thirstily.

One hundred thirty yards away, standing in a copse of trees, the Handyman saw the same thing. It wouldn't be long now.

In humans, ketamine works as a hallucinogen, creating seizures and memory loss. In the quantity that the Handyman had dropped into Martin Garrett's glass, it attacked the nervous system immediately.

The Coke tasted fine in Garrett's mouth, strong and sweet. He was reaching for the plastic bottle for a refill, replaying Danny's catch in his mind, when the sweetness in his mouth became overpowering. He coughed, then started to gag. The image of something warm and wet slammed into his brain. He saw it clearly now, a giant slug caught in his throat, slowly sliding into him.

Patty Garrett had seen her husband choke, had come up beside him and hit him on the back with an open hand, hard. She was leaning close to him when he screamed and started clawing at his mouth, forcing his fingers as deep as they would go.

The other people at the table shrank away in horror as Garrett reeled away. His screams were muffled by his fingers, but they were loud enough to draw the attention of passersby. Patty ran to him and threw her arms around him. Martin Garrett never heard her cries. He leaned forward, taking her weight on his back, then with a savage roar he broke her grip, sending her sprawling. A second later, something red and dripping wet flew onto the picnic table. In his frenzy, Garrett had bitten off a piece of his own tongue.

Garrett's mouth was a gaping, bloody maw. He had no way to convey the terror that gripped him. Short, guttural grunts escaped his mouth, and each time, more blood erupted. By now the front of his shirt and pants was sticky. He was vaguely aware that he had torn something out of his mouth but could still feel the slug inching down his throat and into his chest, eating him up. His brain seemed set on live coals. Wheeling away from his wife and friends, he staggered through the middle of the ball game, the players and spectators shrinking away as he windmilled past them. Such was the power of ketamine that Garrett never recognized his son as he swept by him. Danny's anguished cries were lost in the maelstrom roaring through his father's head.

Sloane and Alley were out of the truck and running hard, fifty yards behind Garrett and closing fast. Alley was yelling into his lapel mike. Seconds later, Sloane saw Paco Santana charge toward Garrett like a Cape buffalo, moving diagonally, trying to cut him off.

Garrett beat all three of them. He reached West Basin Drive and ran across, into traffic. The driver of an oncoming tour bus managed to swerve but the vehicle jumped the curb, tore up the flower beds, and sideswiped a tree before coming to rest.

Sloane lost sight of Garrett momentarily as he staggered into the cherry trees on the other side of West Basin Drive. Alley was holding up his badge, trying to slow traffic. Sloane saw an opening and raced through it. Behind her, she heard the pounding boots of Paco Santana.

"He's at the water!" she yelled to him. "There's nowhere to go. Cut around the other side."

Sloane thought she would come in from the right, Santana from the left, and Alley would cover the area between the trees and the waterline. Garrett would be trapped.

She was wrong. Garrett never stopped at the bank. Driven by a terrible need to kill whatever was devouring him, he plunged into the Tidal Basin and immediately opened his mouth. He would drown the thing.

Sloane tore off her jacket, kicked off her sneakers, and plunged in. The icy water made her gasp, but she swam on, to the point where Garrett had gone under. She took a deep breath and disappeared into the murky water. It wasn't very deep, but she had to feel her way through it. She touched the cold, soft bottom mud and recoiled. Then her fingers brushed something else—fabric. A pant leg, then an ankle.

Sloane clamped her hand around the ankle and kicked hard with both feet, trying to drag Garrett up. Suddenly Garrett's thrashing stopped. Sloane made the mistake of relaxing her grip a fraction and the leg was pulled away. At the same instant, something hard slammed into her temple. Sloane spun away, holding her head, and tried to kick her way to the surface. But a pair of arms locked themselves around her waist, pinning her, squeezing the breath from her laboring lungs.

Sloane clawed at the hands locked around her diaphragm. Blackness spilled over her consciousness. It seemed impossible for Garrett to be so strong, not to have run out of breath by now.

For a split second, Sloane didn't realize she was free. There was no air left in her, and the narcosis created by nearly drowning had numbed her. She felt herself floating. *You don't have to die*, she told herself, and found the idea quite odd. But the survival instinct was triggered and she thrashed for the surface.

Sunlight. Paco Santana standing waist deep in the water, lifting her effortlessly onto the bank, turning back and plowing into Whip Alley, who had just surfaced. Coughing and retching, Sloane saw Alley's face, dripping with mud and blood. There were long, angry marks where Garrett had clawed him as he'd freed Sloane, breaking Garrett's wrist in the process.

Alley had his forearm under Garrett's chin, in the classic rescue position. He held it until Santana took Garrett from him, flung him over his shoulder, and waded out of the water. Sloane watched the big detective lay Garrett down on the incline and begin CPR.

Alley dragged himself over to her and collapsed. "Are you okay?"

Sloane nodded. "He needs mouth to mouth."

Alley held her back. "We don't know what happened to him—"

"But he'll die!" Sloane cried.

"It doesn't matter. Not anymore," Paco Santana said.

He passed his hand over Martin Garrett's face, closing the jaw, bringing down the lids over wild, sightless eyes.

Then Patty Garrett, who'd fought her way through the knot of onlookers, screamed.

19

CLAUDIA BALLANTINE stepped into the Oval Office and glanced at her national security adviser. Jim Trimble's complexion was pasty, his eyes reddened by lack of sleep. With his left hand, he absently rubbed his right shoulder, trying to relieve the phantom pain where the prosthetic arm was attached.

"Jim . . ."

Trimble rose with effort. "Madam President."

"Any word on Martin Garrett?"

"The autopsy results should be available in a couple of hours. We'll know more then. His wife is still under sedation at Georgetown University Hospital. Danny's being looked after by neighbors."

"I'm so sorry, Jim. Was there any medical history to indicate that something like this could happen?"

"No."

The Secret Service, which monitors all newscasts for references to senior White House personnel, had alerted Claudia Ballantine to Martin Garrett's death.

Looking at Trimble, the President silently cursed the whole problem with China. She wanted to tell him to go home, to rest and mourn, but she couldn't. Something was happening on the other side of the world. She felt it the way a sailor senses a swell coming at him, unseen and still miles away.

"The Chinese have pulled back their fleet, Jim," she said. "They've sent General Zhenyu packing. Putting the Necklace Option in play now might be seen as a provocation."

Trimble had known this was coming. Under different circumstances, he would have delivered a host of arguments supporting Necklace—that it was the proper defensive posture, that even if Chinese or Russian satellites detected the American maneuvers, they could be explained away as an exercise. But Martin Garrett's sudden death had created a dark, cold hole within him, sapped him of his strength, destroyed his concentration.

"We still don't know *why* the Chinese pulled back," he said.

"That's not reason enough to pursue Necklace," the President said flatly.

Trimble understood that. He had relied on Lee Porter to get him some information, any lead, on how Beijing had executed such an abrupt policy turnaround at the exact time when Washington was looking for just such a gesture. It was too convenient and Trimble did not believe in coincidence. But Porter had not called, meaning that he had nothing.

Trimble decided it was time to play his trump card. He would have preferred to save it for another time, another crisis. But he could not afford to have Necklace relegated back to the dusty shelves of the war-games room.

"There's still the matter of Peter Lin," he reminded her.

Lin had been a thorn in the side of the Taiwanese government for years. A first-rate journalist, he was an ardent Chinese nationalist who lobbied tirelessly for the island's unification with the mainland. The Taiwanese premier regarded Lin as Beijing's stooge, and in fact Lin made no secret of his ties to and influence in Beijing. Nor that he controlled a large pro-unification organization on Taiwan.

The government had branded Lin a traitor and, after a kangaroo-court trial, had thrown him in jail. This attempt to silence him had backfired. Lin had become a martyr, and the ranks of his believers had swelled a hundredfold. However, Washington still believed that Lin headed a powerful fifth column that would seize the island's infrastructure in the event of an armed invasion.

"What about Lin?" the President asked.

"He's running for parliament in next week's elections," Trimble said. "If he wins, he might be in a position to form a puppet government."

This interested Claudia Ballantine. But she also knew that internal Taiwanese politics was not Trimble's area of expertise.

She buzzed her secretary. "Find Susan Ostroff and tell her I want to see her, please."

A half hour later, a Secret Service agent opened the door to the Oval Office. Susan Ostroff was in her early forties, all business in a severely cut camel-hair suit and jade-green blouse. Her shiny black hair was pinned back in a tight bun, her Donna Karan black eyeglass frames offering a startling contrast to her white skin. Behind the trifocal lenses, her dark eyes were hard and alert. Ostroff, who held two doctorates in Chinese civilization and politics, was known in some quarters as the go-to gal on things Chinese.

"Madam President," Ostroff said formally.

"Susan. It's good to see you again. You know Jim Trimble."

"Of course. Although we haven't had a chance to see each other since the Singapore conference."

Where you almost caused an international incident because you didn't clear your speech with me, Trimble thought.

Ostroff had taken Singapore's strongman to task over Indonesia's treatment of its ethnic Chinese population. Trimble had had a hell of a time papering over that one.

"Nice to see you again, Susan," Trimble managed.

Ostroff headed the State Department's China division, so there wasn't much Trimble could do about her presence and so had accepted her as a cross to bear. Besides, Ostroff was the President's college pal. That and an undeniably first-class mind had made her one of the world's leading experts on China, guaranteed to have Claudia Ballantine's ear.

"Susan, Jim and I were discussing some issues surrounding Peter Lin," the President said. She sketched the latest military developments and the debate over activating the Necklace Option.

"The question is, if Lin wins a seat in the Taiwanese parliament next week, will he become enough of a destabilizing factor to push Beijing into thinking they could take over the island and get away with it?"

Ostroff nodded slowly, absorbing the question. Her

gaze fell to her lap, her hands, a finger that had never been graced by a wedding band.

"I think that's a distinct possibility," she said at last.

Trimble looked up sharply. "Did I hear you right?"

Ostroff regarded him coolly. "You and I have had differences of opinion, Jim. But this time, you must have come to the same conclusion."

"As a matter of fact—"

"So would you recommend that Necklace be implemented, as a precaution?" the President asked.

"No, I wouldn't," Ostroff replied firmly.

"But you just said—"

Ostroff held up her hand. "If you'd let me explain . . . The election is a week away. I admit that Lin seems to have a very good chance of winning a seat in the chamber. But if Necklace is put into play and word gets out, Lin would have cause for his unification argument. And an issue to campaign on."

Ostroff directed her full attention to Claudia Ballantine. "Madam President, it is my considered opinion that Necklace should not be activated until after the election. And even then, only if it's absolutely needed. To introduce it sooner is to court political disaster."

Trimble slumped in his chair, watching as Claudia Ballantine weighed Ostroff's argument.

I'm going to lose this one, he thought. *First, French shows me up, now Ostroff.*

"Jim? Any thoughts?" the President asked.

He fought to match Ostroff's cool calm, but his words came out sounding stubborn, petulant.

"Madam President, Beijing is not acting true to

form. Getting rid of Mi Zhenyu, pulling back their flotilla—that's totally out of character."

"But that's exactly what we wanted," the President interjected.

"Yes—yes, it is," Trimble stumbled on. "Maybe it was coincidence. I don't know. The thing is, we can't let Beijing even begin to think that they can cross the strait and take Taiwan."

Claudia Ballantine looked at him sympathetically. Suddenly this was not the adviser she trusted and respected but a tired, grief-stricken man.

"No one's going to take Taiwan," she said. "Susan has a point. There's a big downside to going with Necklace. I'm going to table it for now, Jim, and see where we are after the elections. If Lin gets in and the rhetoric heats up . . ."

Susan Ostroff smiled to herself at Trimble's rout. She knew that Trimble had always thought she was soft when it came to China. She'd made sure not to give him any direct evidence to that effect. No one, especially not Claudia Ballantine, could ever say that Dr. Ostroff's position papers and recommendations were anything but level and pragmatic in their approach and execution.

These were a seamlessly stitched cover for the place where Susan Ostroff really lived, for the pain and loss and ache within the bleak walls of her life.

For eight incredible weeks a decade before, Susan Ostroff had been very much in love. He was an extraordinary man who not only matched her intellect, but coaxed out a carnality she'd never thought herself capable of. She had been on a leave of absence from

Berkeley, touring Asia; he was a fiery journalist whose articles inflamed the local population and incensed the Taiwanese government.

For those precious weeks, Susan Ostroff had a kindred spirit, the kind she had long despaired of ever finding. She and Peter Lin melded as one, talking late into the night, snatching hours in the day to punish and pleasure their bodies. He opened her eyes and mind to a single, reunified China, and everything she had been taught and thought she believed fell by the wayside. She understood only the need to be one, craved it.

Then one night, while they were making love, the doors to the apartment splintered. Taiwanese security forces burst in, seized Lin, and beat her senseless. For two days, she lived with the agony of not knowing whether he was dead or alive. Then one of his disciples rushed to her with the news that Lin had been found, his battered and bleeding body thrown from a speeding car onto the steps of the office where he worked.

Ostroff stayed by him, helped nurse him back to health. Each time she touched a cut or changed the bandages that held him together, she felt her anger grow richer and more powerful. In a white-hot epiphany stoked by the pain of the man she loved, Ostroff saw the righteousness of his cause, the purity and unswerving correctness of his vision. China had to be one. China was one. Taiwan was a political aberration created by long-dead politicians and defeated warlords. Her place in the world was beside the man who would tear that down.

But Lin would not let her stay. "It is too dangerous

here for you," he had told her through a mouthful of broken teeth. His nose and cheekbones would require reconstructive surgery and it tore Ostroff apart to look at him. "They will come for me again—and you if they find you. When they do, they will realize that they can use you to reach me. A man is most vulnerable when someone he loves is threatened."

She fought him every step of the way, using every weapon, from cold, reasoned arguments to tears. But Lin would not cede. In the end, it was he who had packed her bags because she couldn't bring herself to do so.

"You must never call or write to me," he had told her at the airport as she waited to board the plane to San Francisco. "No one must ever be able to connect us." Then he had told her why, and what she must do, and had given her the name of a man: Dodge French.

Susan Ostroff remembered that day ten years ago as if it had been yesterday. Every career move she'd made—from leaving Berkeley, entering the State Department, working day and night to become the undisputed China specialist—all of it had been to further a vision she shared with Lin. And the higher she moved in the Washington decision-making bureaucracy, the closer she felt to him.

Claudia Ballantine's presidency had been an unexpected stroke of luck. Ostroff had used the connection between them to advance herself even further. Now, because of China's growing importance in U.S. strategy, she was the State Department expert Claudia Ballantine relied on most.

In all these years, no one had ever uncovered that remote connection between her and Lin.

Very soon, Ostroff would get her reward for those years of solitude. As she hurried from the White House, she knew with absolute certainty that her watch was almost over. Soon China would be one. Soon she and Lin would be one.

Sloane Ryder had never been in a morgue. She was surprised that her first reaction was not repugnance or sickness but awe. The pitiless lights and cold stainless-steel trappings brought death into vivid clarity.

Whip Alley was standing next to one of the cutting tables, chatting quietly with the coroner. Then the swinging doors burst open and a young female technician hurried in and handed the coroner a computer printout.

Sloane watched Alley read what she presumed were the autopsy results on Martin Garrett.

"You sure about this?" he asked the coroner, indicating a line on the printout. The coroner's name was Grant Lane; he and Alley went back a long way.

"Bizarre is what it is," Lane muttered. "Let me double-check with the lab." He moved off to a phone, scratching behind one ear.

"What is it?" Sloane asked Alley.

He showed her the reference, couched in scientific jargon. "Ketamine. Know what that is?"

Sloane shook her head.

"A hormone drug. It's pretty common in these parts. Vets use it on horses."

"And it showed up in Garrett's blood? Is there a human application?"

"Only among the worst drug freaks. Or someone

looking to screw up someone in a really bad way. Ketamine brings on hallucinations. It also creates seizures and memory loss."

The image of Garrett's bloody mouth, his inexplicable attempts at self-destruction, and his delusional behavior flashed through Sloane's mind.

"Did you double-check his medical history?" she asked. "Could his actions have been brought on by something else?"

"Sure, but that isn't the case here."

Sloane knew that Alley had gone through Garrett's medical records. Aside from an occasional rash associated with seasonal allergies, Garrett, a nonsmoker and moderate drinker, was in perfect health.

"You're saying that someone fed him this . . . ketamine."

"Looks that way."

"But the people he was with were his friends. Could it have been in the food he ate?" She caught herself. "No, the food was just being put on the table. I didn't see Garrett pick at anything. But he did have a drink."

"Didn't he, though." Alley said softly.

Sloane recalled newspaper headlines, television lead stories: an outbreak of salmonella because of spoiled beef in hamburger patties; schoolchildren falling ill because of pesticides in imported strawberries; bottles of Tylenol, their contents laced with poison, being swept off drugstore shelves.

"Something in Garrett's soda," Whip explained. "Yesterday, while the medics were checking you, Paco and I went through the trash can by the picnic table. We took everything. The women were able to identify what each one had made or brought, right down to the tuna salad. We gave it all to the FBI lab. Turns out the food was clean. The cans and bottles too. But not the plastic glass that Garrett drank from."

He turned to Lane, who was still brooding over the report. "You'll want to sit on that detail for a couple of days," he said quietly.

The coroner was startled. "Whip, you know I have to give the next of kin a full report—"

"We don't have a complete report yet. You say you found ketamine in his Coke and we have a full-blown national—no, make that international—panic. Anyone who's had a Coke in the last twenty-four hours will be calling the emergency rooms. People will be dumping the stuff in the sewers. And let's not forget that this guy was the chief assistant to the national security adviser. Do you really want to go out with a statement over your signature that might piss off 1600?"

Lane had spent his entire professional career in D.C. and knew his way around the city's politics.

"I can tell his wife that the results are inconclusive. But if she starts hollering . . ."

"That's not likely to happen anytime soon," Alley said.

The one time the doctors had taken Patty Garrett off sedatives, she'd started screaming for her husband and tearing at her bedclothes. Now she was being kept under sedation until an aunt arrived from Los Angeles.

"What about the media?" Lane asked. "They've been nosing around. Someone in the park shot some video showing this guy wig out. The networks are using it on every news cycle." He made a face. "Great entertainment value, huh?"

"'Inconclusive.' That's all you have to say."

Lane thought about that for a moment

"Whatever it is you're going to do, you have until Mrs. Garrett comes around and starts asking questions," he said finally. "That's the best I can do."

Tapping Alley on the shoulder with his copy of the printout, Lane left the room.

Alley turned to Sloane. "I need to talk to Lee Porter."

"Why?"

"The glass Garrett drank from was contaminated," Alley reminded her. "But not the bottle. That means someone deliberately poisoned him."

"But we were watching him from the time he reached the park. I didn't see anyone even approach him."

She paused, then said slowly, "Oh my God. That man who came by the picnic table. Did you ask the women about him?"

"They remembered an older guy who came up asking for directions—a Frenchman, they said."

Sloane closed her eyes and envisioned the women clustered around the table. One of them is looking at . . . *Looking at what?* She couldn't get an image, only colors. A houndstooth sport jacket, dark brown pants. A man walking toward the footpath that leads to the Jefferson Memorial. But she couldn't see his face.

Whip Alley's voice intruded. "Sloane, what is it?"

"The older man who asked for directions. I remem-

ber seeing him out of the corner of my eye, thinking
that there was something about him. I can't explain it.
I can't *see* him."

"Maybe he slipped by us. Maybe he'd been watching
the whole thing unfold—the picnic, the game, Garrett
opening up the soda, pouring it into a glass, walking to
the game and leaving the glass behind. Not an easy shot
because there are women at the table. But he's very
good, very smooth, charms them with his accent, dis-
tracts them just long enough to dump the drug into
Garrett's drink."

"The assistant to the national security adviser was
murdered and we watched it happen," Sloane said in
disbelief.

"And that's why I need to speak to Porter. Before
yesterday, this was your case. Now it's my business too."

George Washington University Medical Center complex starts at the block bounded by Pennsylvania
Avenue and Twenty-second Street. Its proximity to
Washington Circle and the university itself makes for
a great deal of traffic, vehicular and pedestrian. Even if
Sloane and Alley had known what the Handyman
looked like, they never would have spotted him standing under the portico at the Pennsylvania Avenue
doors near a parked ambulance. Wearing black pants
and a blue nylon jacket with an orange caduceus pur-
loined from the university cafeteria, he looked like an
on-call paramedic.

From a hundred yards away, the Handyman had
seen the ketamine rip through Martin Garrett's system, reducing him to a demented marionette. Then the

woman from New York, Sloane Ryder, and the man obviously with her began chasing Garrett. Finally, a third, very big man joined the pursuit from the opposite side of the park.

The presence of the second man confirmed that there had been a stakeout. That all three individuals were in civilian dress indicated surveillance or a counterintelligence operation. But what was Sloane Ryder's role? Yesterday, she seemed nothing like the innocent he'd watched moving from office tower to office tower on those hard New York streets.

Two hours later, the Handyman had returned to the butcher shop where he'd met Mai Ling. The roll of film, suitably bagged, and secreted in the cavity of a freshly slaughtered duck, was delivered to the Chinese embassy.

The next morning the Handyman had breakfast at the Ana Hotel on Twenty-fourth Street, where he found a small envelope tucked into his morning paper. He studied the photographs in the privacy of a stall in the men's room, committed the faces and details to memory, tore up the pictures, and flushed them down the toilet. Now he had everything he needed on Sloane Ryder and Whip Alley and his partner.

The Handyman let Ryder and Alley mingle with other pedestrians before he fell in behind them. He wanted to see, for himself, where Sloane Ryder lived.

Porter dropped the autopsy report on his leather blotter and looked at Sloane, Alley, and Santana.

"You want in on this investigation?" he asked Alley.

"It's a homicide," the detective replied. "Technically, it's already mine."

The background Porter had on Alley indicated that the detective was straight up but tenacious. He wouldn't give up turf, but he might share. Porter decided to try that route first.

"D.C. Homicide can't be involved in this. It's too sensitive. If you come on, you're part of my team."

Alley raised an eyebrow. "Fine. Paco stays too."

Porter glanced at Santana, who smiled, displaying his perfectly white teeth.

Porter dialed the police commissioner's number, spoke briefly, then passed the receiver to Alley. The conversation lasted all of fifteen seconds.

Alley turned to Santana. "The commissioner says we're off the boards, on special assignment."

"I'm sure he won't miss us," Santana murmured.

"Sloane," Porter said. "Tell them everything, from the beginning."

Sloane spoke for a full half hour. When she was finished, Alley turned to Porter. "What's the White House position on this?"

"The President has expressed her 'grave concern,'" Porter said. "The national security adviser is taking it hard. He wants details."

"And?"

"And when we're done, I'll give them to him."

"What about Garrett's wife, his friends?"

"The autopsy will show that he was suffering from an undiagnosed brain tumor."

Porter held up his hand before Sloane could protest. "We have no choice," he continued. "If we go with the ketamine, we either implicate an innocent multi-national company in a potential consumer scare, or the media throw the murder of a high-ranking official on the front page and keep it there. Either way, it lights up our investigation, and we can't afford that. I don't like lying to anyone, much less the next of kin, but under the circumstances, there's no alternative."

"What's the circulation going to be on this?" Alley asked.

"The President, Trimble, the four of us, and John Kemeny and Sara Powell."

"What about the FBI? Any chance they'll horn in?"

"They haven't heard about it yet and they won't. Sloane, are you okay with this?"

"Martin Garrett died because I was investigating him," she said. "Someone got wind of that. Someone felt threatened and murdered him. I want to find out who that was."

The room was very still.

"You can't be sure that it comes back to you," Alley said at last. "Garrett seemed like a regular guy, but he worked in national security. There may be things in his classified file that we don't know about."

Porter shook his head. "We have it all."

"Then maybe Sloane is right," Alley said. "But I still don't think that the killer is the same individual who felt threatened by her investigation."

"Why?" asked Porter.

"Because the murder was sophisticated," Santana rumbled, leaning forward in his chair. "The killer knew Garrett's movements, his habits, that he would be in the park that morning, with a lot of people around. This requires patience, planning, and experience."

"What kind of man would have it?" Sloane demanded.

"The kind I saw operate in Latin America," Santana said quietly. "Professional assassins. Only a professional would know exactly how he could get to Garrett under any given circumstance. How he could approach him, execute him, and leave the scene without anyone being suspicious. Or even noticing him. Given the circumstances, the choice of ketamine was perfect."

In her mind's eye, Sloane saw the retreating back of the man in the houndstooth jacket.

"We have to interview Patty Garrett's friends again about the French guy they spoke to," Alley said.

"Do it," Porter instructed. "But very carefully. No need to raise their suspicions."

"Maybe we can do better than that," Sloane added. "The video shot by the tourists. When the network buys something like that, it makes copies. The seller is given back the original with the understanding that he won't peddle it anywhere else. If we can run down the people who shot it, see the whole thing, not just the network clips, we might get something on that mysterious Frenchman."

Alley nodded. "I like that."

"Which leaves us with the one person Garrett was close to," Porter said. "Susan Ostroff. She made that bank loan happen. Time to ask her why."

"Just like that?" asked Sloane.

"We can't afford to wait," Alley explained. "Whoever took out Garrett knew a lot about him. That would include his association with Ostroff. If she tells us something useful, we can get her into protective custody while we run down what she gives us."

"Go talk to her," Porter said.

As everyone stood to leave, Alley said, "There's one thing we haven't touched on. If the killer knew that Garrett was under the microscope, then he knows who put him there."

He looked at Sloane. "I've seen your apartment building. The security isn't great. I know a better place."

20

THE SURRATT CLUB is headquartered in an elegant, century-old cottage on R Street off Wisconsin Avenue. Founded in 1934, its original members believed that Mary Surratt, who allegedly left field glasses and guns for a fleeing John Wilkes Booth, was in fact a martyr, railroaded to the gallows by public outrage, not evidence.

Like most current members, Susan Ostroff didn't have an opinion about Mary Surratt. Over the years, the club had been transformed from a historical shrine to a place where Washington women ranging in age from thirty-five to eighty, whose careers included a seat on the Supreme Court and a U.N. ambassadorship, quietly helped one another to influence the policies of the nation.

Beyond the principal rooms of the cottage was a small conservatory retreat overlooking a brick-lined patio with a fountain. Club rules dictated that no one ever disturbed a member while she was in there.

Dodge French was seldom a guest at the club, preferring to have Susan Ostroff pass him her information through other, less direct channels. Now he sat opposite her by the window overlooking the patio where sparrows splashed in the fountain.

"This has to do with Peter Lin," Ostroff said after they had exchanged greetings.

It was a directness French appreciated, although it served to underline Ostroff's hard edge.

"Claudia is worried about what might happen if Lin wins a seat in the next Taiwanese parliament."

"Worried how?"

"That he would start lobbying—publicly—for reunification. And that this time he might actually get enough support to force a referendum."

"If that were to happen, then what?"

"Trimble's Necklace Option goes into effect." The curl to her words revealed her distaste. "I thought you should know right away."

"I already know."

Ostroff saw that she'd struck a nerve.

"So Necklace has come up before. Was Garrett involved?"

"To a degree."

It was the kind of answer Ostroff expected. French rarely gave anything away. His informants were compartmentalized. Only on rare occasions did he make direct contact with the people who quietly provided him with information. Ostroff had been Garrett's contact, guiding him and analyzing and evaluating the intelligence on China that he passed to her before she sent it up the food chain to French.

"What happened to him?" Ostroff asked intently.

"I'm still waiting for the coroner's report," French replied.

"Too long . . . It's taking too long." She drummed a finger on the leather sofa arm. "It doesn't make sense. He was in perfect health. Unless you know otherwise?"

"I do not."

"When was the last time you spoke to Garrett?" she asked.

"At least a year," French lied smoothly. "Why?"

"So he wasn't in touch with you in the last few days?"

"No."

"Because he called me Saturday morning, said that he thought he was under surveillance."

"An overactive imagination," French remarked sadly.

"His wife told him she saw a strange car in the neighborhood," Ostroff continued. "And a man who looked like he was watching the house."

"We both know that Patty Garrett is a fragile woman," French said. "And Trimble is under a great deal of pressure at work. I'm not surprised Martin was feeling some of that."

"So you don't think this had anything to do with Garrett's death?"

"Some *supposed* surveillance? No."

Ostroff nodded. She was sure she was getting worked up over nothing, yet a little voice deep in her skull still nagged.

"The President's going to do it, isn't she?" she said. "Activate Necklace no matter what."

"That won't happen," French replied quietly. "You and I and others will not permit that. But certain measures will have to be taken."

Ostroff sensed what was coming and dreaded it. Sometimes she wondered how French, who never cringed before a necessary sacrifice, ever slept at night.

"What?" she asked quietly.

French reached out and patted her hand, as if reassuring a child. Susan Ostroff was a brilliant but desperate woman. The furnace of a love ten years old and eight thousand miles distant still burned fiercely within her. She had come to French because Lin had told her that French was the only hope of China's reunification. That made him the only hope Susan Ostroff had of ever being reunited with her lover.

Now French told her what had to be done in the wake of the information she'd given him, explained how it was the only option. He told her the truth, not out of compassion or to comfort her, but because he needed her to understand exactly why certain things were going to happen. He could not take the risk that she might, if she heard about it after the fact, do something foolish.

He watched her shoulders sag and her eyes burn with fierce anger. He could almost see the counterarguments churning in her mind, being weighed, examined, and ultimately discarded. Susan Ostroff would try to save everything that Lin had built because that was her bridge to him. But ultimately cold reason would prevail. The bridge could be destroyed if she believed French's promise that very soon she would be with Lin.

A silence descended after French finished, broken

only by the noisy sparrows. Somewhere in the cottage, a grandfather clock struck the hour.

"You can still do it, get in touch with Lin?"

Susan Ostroff looked up from her lap, her eyes glistening. There was a way. She and Lin had arranged it before she'd left Taipei. But the security of the communication could not be guaranteed. He had made her promise that she'd use it only in the most extreme emergency. Throughout her long, lonely vigil, even at times when she would have killed for the sound of his voice, she had kept that promise.

"He will hear from Beijing," French was saying. "But he needs to hear it from you first. He needs that in order to believe how necessary it is for him to do what Beijing will ask. He needs to believe."

"I'll get it done," she told him.

There was a knock on the door. Ostroff ran the back of her hand across her eyes and frowned. The staff knew better than to disturb her here. She opened the door and accepted the note held out by the club manager.

"What is it?" asked French.

"Strange," Ostroff muttered. "Why would someone from the GAO want to see me?"

French's heart lifted slightly. "Who?"

"Sloane Ryder."

"Really."

"What is it, Dodge? What does she want?"

French gestured at the door. "Have them tell her you need a few minutes."

Ostroff frowned but did as he'd asked. When the manager had left, she said, "So?"

"This young woman is part of the team investigating Garrett's death."

"*Investigating?* Why? What do the police suspect?"

French shushed her gently. "Not to worry. Sloane Ryder won't get in our way. But she has to be handled carefully. The only possible reason she has for being here is because she's connected Garrett to you. The bank loan. The GAO does random screens on federal employees. You know that. They picked up on the loan, which, if you look closely, would seem a little suspect. Once you explain it, she'll go away."

Ostroff felt something askew but couldn't pinpoint it.

"That loan was buried so deep I didn't think anyone would find it," she said. "If they were digging that hard—"

"Don't panic," French said smoothly. "You have nothing to hide. Tell her the truth. Your bank records will back you up."

He rose and stepped out onto the patio. "Call and tell me how it went."

The meeting in the presidential study adjacent to the Oval Office had started auspiciously enough. The President had cut short her photo op with the Girl Scouts of America; Trimble was there, as Porter had requested. Porter had entered the White House using the tunnel that runs from the Treasury building. No one except the Secret Service escort and the President's secretary knew he was in the building.

The President and her national security adviser were on the last page of the autopsy report. Both had read the complete text even though Porter had attached a one-page cover précis. Now Porter could see Trimble's jaw working furiously, his eyes bright and angry.

"You're telling us that Martin Garrett was murdered," the President said.

"All the evidence points to that, Madam President," Porter said.

Now that Claudia Ballantine had had the first word, Trimble waded in. "And you've sat on this for over twenty-four hours?"

"There's a reason for that."

"You should have notified me at once," Trimble carried on. "I could have put people on it—"

"Jim." The President's voice was gentle and firm. "Let's hear Lee out, okay?"

From the many dealings Porter had had with Trimble, he'd come to respect and like the man. But Trimble was reacting now instead of listening and absorbing. Porter had prepared himself for this.

He explained how the two D.C. Homicide detectives had become involved in the matter, and that all the witnesses had been interviewed and the physical evidence studied. That was how the ketamine had been spotted so quickly. He described how watertight the investigation was and the need to keep it that way.

"All right, Lee," the President said. "I see your point. It seems to me that you've covered the bases. A couple of questions: How long will the coroner keep his mouth shut?"

"Forever—if the request is based on national security considerations and you authorize it."

"And so a widow never learns the truth about her husband's death?"

Porter felt the sting of her words. Claudia Ballantine was a widow. To this day, she did not fully understand why her husband had been made an assassin's target. Her heart reached out to Patty Garrett.

"Madam President, the murder of Martin Garrett, by a person or persons unknown, for reasons unknown, constitutes a security threat."

"Which is exactly what makes it a law-enforcement matter!" Trimble said.

"If you bring in the FBI, you might as well splash the story across the media," Porter said.

"I have a second question, Lee," the President said to him. "Why, exactly, did you have Martin Garrett under surveillance in the first place?"

Trimble blinked, stunned. "Goddammit it, Lee. What were you thinking?"

"Because of the investigation you knew I was running," Porter said. "You remember, don't you, Jim? One day you lay out the reasons for the President as to why Necklace should be implemented, a few days later the Chinese make moves that wipe those reasons off the board. You suspected a leak."

"Sure I did!" Trimble replied. "But you told me it was NSA that made the intercept, that someone was there waiting to pass the information along from the original source. That couldn't have been Marty. He never had anything to do with NSA."

"He did, Jim. You sent me a list of all the NSA people working on the Chinese. But you never checked it. Garrett's name was on it because a long time ago he delivered some Sino-Japanese position papers at Fort Meade. The computers had him logged on the China intercepts. We ran all the names. Garrett was the only one with an anomaly we couldn't account for. So we started walking back the cat."

Porter paused. "You put us on to him in the first place. We took it from there. But we couldn't take it far enough. We didn't have anything hard to confront him with. Maybe if we'd had, we could have saved his life."

Trimble was devastated by the irony.

"Lee told me about Garrett, Jim," the President said quietly, then turned to Porter. "Lee, you said that Garrett's murder constitutes a threat to national security."

"I believe that to be true."

"So once again, circumstances bring us back to China," the President said. "Since I thought that might be the case, I asked two people to stand by in case we wanted their input. Now I think they need to come in on the ground floor. Lee, do you have any objection to General Murchison and Dodge French joining us?"

It wasn't so much a question as a courtesy. But Lee Porter remembered what he'd promised his team and he always backed his word.

"I told my people that this would be a limited-circulation situation," he said. "I need that assurance to preserve the integrity of their investigation."

"I'll bear that in mind," Claudia Ballantine said, then asked her secretary to show in the two men.

Dodge French noted how brief the introductions

were and how somber the mood in the room. He shot a glance at Sam Murchison, but the chairman of the Joint Chiefs only shrugged. The two men had spent the last twenty minutes exchanging small talk, neither knowing why they had been summoned.

"Gentlemen," Claudia Ballantine began. "Lee Porter has something to tell you. Please listen carefully and save your questions until he's finished. Lee, from the top, please."

Lee Porter laid out the details that Trimble and Claudia Ballantine were already privy to, then got to the part about a possible assassin and the person directing him. That got everybody's attention. When he was finished, there was a stunned silence.

"You serious about this, Lee?" Murchison said finally. "You've got the evidence you say you have?"

"Yes, I have," Porter replied. "The part about the assassin—that we can't confirm, obviously. But the facts point in that direction."

"I can't believe this," Trimble said softly.

"But catching this killer is the problem," Dodge French said quietly. "That's not something you're equipped to do, Mr. Porter. You have no mandate to conduct law-enforcement activities, nor are your people trained in the science."

"That's true, sir."

French shook his head, as though this whole business were bewildering and repugnant to him. In truth, however, he had been fascinated by what Porter had laid out, amazed, impressed, and not a little afraid at how quickly and effectively Porter's hunters had cottoned on to Garrett. He knew exactly what he had to do here to stop Porter, and he had to do it very carefully.

"Has your investigation of Garrett led you to any conclusion as to why he might have been passing information to the Chinese?"

"No, sir."

"Have you traced him to any second or third party he might have used to help him?"

"No."

"Marty Garrett was not a traitor!" Trimble shouted.

French nodded. "If I offended you, Jim, I apologize. But clearly Mr. Garrett was involved in something. He had some connection to information that came from these premises—information upon which the President bases her decisions."

French then turned to Claudia Ballantine. "Madam President, I believe that we must first decide which law-enforcement agency will become involved in this case."

"That's premature," Porter cut in.

"Really, sir? Would you rather wait until this assassin murders again? Because for all you and I know, he might. We're operating in the dark. We have no idea of this individual's agenda, whether Garrett was all or just a part of it. And we need to know."

"There's already a law-enforcement component involved. I explained that."

"Yes, you did. A Washington Homicide detective. Does that *really* satisfy you, Mr. Porter?"

Porter was losing control of the meeting and felt it keenly. French was going somewhere with this and Porter was sure he wouldn't like where it ended up.

"All right," Claudia Ballantine said sharply, her patience worn thin. "Dodge, let's have it. Bottom line."

"Madam President, I believe professional law enforcement must be introduced into this investigation as soon as possible. I think the FBI would be the best player." French held up his hand to stave off the protests. "Please let me finish. I understand and appreciate the need for controlled circulation, as Mr. Porter phrased it. Therefore, I recommend that we bring in only one agent, someone senior, experienced, with a background on things Chinese. Someone who can call upon vast resources at a moment's notice if need be."

"Obviously you have someone in mind," the President said.

"I do. His name in Peter Mack. Let me tell you about him."

"Thank you for seeing me, Dr. Ostroff," Sloane said.

"I was curious as to what the GAO could want with me," Ostroff replied coolly.

She indicated the bay window where two chairs and a small table were set in the recess. Walking beside Sloane Ryder, she took a measure of the woman, recalled what Dodge French had said about her.

After they were seated, she said, "Now, how can I help you?"

"Do you know Martin Garrett?"

"Jim Trimble's assistant. Yes, I do. Terrible what happened to him. The news said it was some kind of seizure."

"Dr. Ostroff, did you know Martin Garrett well?"

"You mean, were we friends? No. Professional acquaintances would be more like it. Martin was a general analyst, but his particular area of interest was China. As mine is. I'm sure you know I head the State Department's China division."

"So over the years you've maintained a working association."

"We usually ran into each other at conferences and seminars. And the odd time I'd call him if something came across my desk that I thought Jim Trimble should know about."

"And vice versa?"

"Sure. Martin would send material up to State if he felt I could use it. Ms. Ryder, where exactly are you going with this?"

"You arranged for and co-signed a large loan for him, to cover his son's medical expenses."

"I did. I wanted to help him out."

"That was very generous of you."

"Ms. Ryder, you're with MJ-11. Believe me, I know what your department does. You people must know that I'm quite wealthy."

Ostroff's great-grandfather had founded a jeans company that had, over the years, become as synonymous with America as Disney or McDonald's. Susan Ostroff wasn't "quite wealthy," she was enormously rich.

"On your recommendation, your bank lent Garrett this money at a very favorable rate," Sloane said.

"Are you implying that there was some conflict of interest?"

"I'm just wondering if all those calls Garrett made

to your office and home were related to the loan—or if they were about something else."

"Ms. Ryder, my financial records are available to anyone with the proper credentials. I imagine that includes you. If you and your auditors want to check them, be my guests. You won't find a thing. I have very conservative accountants.

"As for the calls Martin made to me, at work and at home, most of those were business related. And I will *not* divulge their content or context until you either subpoena me—in which case I may fight you—or you tell me why you're nosing around in issues that, on the face of it, appear to have nothing to do with his death."

Decision time, Sloane realized. Ostroff was pushing; she could either push back or fold. Instinct urged Sloane to stay on the offensive. She had to rattle the woman, even if it meant giving Ostroff a glimpse at the cards she was holding.

"We have a record of a telephone conversation between you and Martin Garrett two days ago," Sloane said. "In it, he sounds very agitated. He suspects that he may be under surveillance—that his phone may be tapped and that he's being followed. Do you recall that conversation?"

Ostroff's eyes were as hard as ten-penny nails. "I assume that you had a warrant to listen in on that conversation?"

"We did."

"Let me tell you something about Martin Garrett that you might not know," Ostroff said. "He was something of a professional paranoid. In his business, you have to have that quality. But Martin had a little too much. If you check the transcript of that conversation, you'll find that I said something to the effect that at any given time half the phones in D.C. are tapped. Especially in security-sensitive areas."

"This call was made from a pay phone."

Ostroff shrugged. "Like I said, a paranoid," she paused then said: "Ms. Ryder, it seems to me that there's a lot more to Martin's death than you're letting on or letting people know—given that you had him under electronic surveillance. And if you want to ask me any more questions, then first you better damn well explain your interest in Martin and how that's connected to me."

Sloane met the woman's gaze. "I don't have any more questions—for the moment."

Ostroff rose. "Then you'll excuse me. I have another appointment." She paused. "A word of advice, Ms. Ryder. I get the feeling you're new in town. Don't get on the bad side of the wrong people."

Susan Ostroff's first instinct was to race back to her office. There were stacks of computer disks sitting in her safe, disks that contained information that Martin Garrett had, over the years, passed along to her. A great deal of what was stored on them was intelligence-grade analysis, well beyond her security clearance. If anyone asked about the disks, explanations would be difficult.

Instead, Ostroff went into the tiny lounge—four tables, eight chairs, a horseshoe-shaped, leather-topped bar, and asked the bartender for a single-malt scotch, no ice. She sipped the liquor, felt it steady her.

Then in her mind she replayed the first part of her conversation with French.

"I'm still waiting for the coroner's report." That's what French had said when she'd asked about Garrett. She'd pressed him because the report was taking too long, but he'd deflected her concern, said what he'd come to say, pierced her in the place where Lin's image dwelled.

Was it possible that French hadn't known that Garrett was under surveillance? Had she been the first—and the only—person Garrett had telephoned with his suspicion? That call had come the morning of Garrett's death. He had been doing just what his instructions called for: In the event of an emergency, real or imagined, contact the person above him. Her.

Ostroff took another sip of her drink. Garrett's actions were logical. The sequence was correct. French's explaining away the coroner's report had been convincing, his tone firm but patient. Yet Susan Ostroff recalled the fleeting change in French's demeanor when Sloane Ryder's name had been mentioned. He hadn't volunteered that he knew the woman from MJ-11; Ostroff had had to press to get him to say that she was on the team investigating Garrett's death. Then, before she could ask more, he'd segued into the business of what Sloane Ryder was doing there, and the business about the bank loan.

But you never mentioned that Ryder might want to go in other directions.

Sloane Ryder was using the bank loan as a kind of probe. Her real interests lay in Garrett's calls to

Ostroff, their professional relationship, connections
between the two of them . . .

*You know more about Garrett's autopsy than you told
me, French. You know more, period. Are you getting ready
to cut me loose?*

Ostroff forced down the panic threatening to choke
her. Two conflicting impressions kept colliding within
her. Dodge French, the man she'd trusted for ten years,
had never done anything to make her doubt him.
Dodge French, the master manipulator, might be turning his talents against her. Which was it? To determine
that, Ostroff knew she would have to proceed very carefully.

But now she needed to deal with the concrete: the
disks in her office vault. She knew they were still
secure, otherwise her unexpected visitor wouldn't have
been Sloane Ryder but a pair of quiet men from the
State Department's internal security who would have
asked her to accompany them back to her office and
open the safe.

Ostroff had kept the disks for two reasons. The first
was visceral: They were a living record of her actions on
behalf of Lin, a kind of lover's diary. The information
Garrett had given her, the intelligence that came across
her desk and that she passed along, was a record of her
contribution to Dodge French's grand scheme.

The second reason was more practical. Susan
Ostroff was a Jew. She'd grown up listening to relatives' stories about pogroms and holocausts, about
gold coins sewn into the linings of coats and diamonds
secreted in shoe heels. She knew that prudent Jews
always had something—money, favors, influence—to

trade for survival. Careless Jews were herded into boneyards. The disks were her insurance policy. If they ever came for her and accused her of treason, she could give them the man whom she served and who watched over her. A compelling case could be made that she was merely a single link in the chain of American patriots who stood on guard for their country.

DR. SUSAN OSTROFF came out of the Surratt House, the hem of her tan Burberry coat snapping in the wind. Alley wore Docksiders and a tweed jacket, and carried a battered briefcase. He looked exactly like the young, untenured college professor she took him to be. That Ostroff bothered to check him out at all—and others in the street—told him that she was watching for surveillance.

Falling in behind her, Alley matched her brisk pace. He had talked to Sloane after her encounter with Ostroff. According to Sloane, the good doctor was pure Teflon and that their encounter had been futile. Alley wasn't so sure.

Ostroff headed down Wisconsin without pause, but she continued scanning, mostly cars, but sometimes pedestrians. She slowed near the corner of N Street, walking into a Western Union office next to a Gap. Alley had no play. There were no other customers, so he could not follow her inside. He went into the Gap and loitered by the mannequins in the window, waiting for her to come out.

Ostroff spent less than five minutes at Western Union, which led Alley to think that she had drafted

her message before she got there. She was now on the
move again, turning down M Street, walking past the
Four Seasons, then along Pennsylvania Avenue all the
way to Washington Circle. From there, it was a clear
shot down Twenty-third Street to the State Department, but that's not where Ostroff went. She disappeared into the Metro station on the corner of I
Street.

Ostroff had her choice of two routes from that
station. She got on the Blue Line headed for Franconia-
Springfield. She got off halfway there, at the Pentagon.

Alley had not expected that. The move was both a
blessing and a curse. Ostroff was showing him a connection—the fact that she went to the Pentagon so
quickly after her confrontation with Sloane could not
be a coincidence. However, Alley couldn't follow her
inside. The most his police credentials would get him
were questions from the military police.

Alley followed Ostroff as far as the public spaces
permitted, watched her flash her State Department
ID and then disappear. Cursing softly, he retraced his
steps to the Metro. A quick glance at an overhead
clock told him that if he hurried, he could retrieve the
Suburban and still make it out to BWI airport before
getting back to G Street.

"I'm not happy about it either, but that's the way the
President wants it."

From the tenor of Lee Porter's voice, Sloane knew
that he was frustrated. She looked at John Kemeny
and Sara Powell. Kemeny ran his hand through his
hair and muttered something in Hungarian. Powell

seemed to be giving her full attention to her finger-nails.

Sloane realized that Porter was talking only to her now. "I'm sorry that it's Peter Mack," he said. "John and Sara will run some interference, but you'll be the one dealing with him. Can you handle that?"

"Yes," Sloane said quietly. She caught Sara's sympathetic look and shrugged.

The three of them had known that something was wrong the minute Porter returned from the White House. The fact that Dodge French had managed to convince the President to bring a second party in on the investigation was bad enough, but Sloane couldn't believe it when Porter mentioned Peter Mack's name. She had taken a few minutes to sketch for Kemeny and Powell what her relationship with Mack had been, the dismal note on which it had ended.

"What does French expect Mack to do, exactly?" Kemeny asked. "If he convinced the President to bring in the Bureau, why only one man?"

"First, because he could sell the President on one agent," Porter explained. "This way, it looks like we're still a tight little group."

"That, and he asked for a specific agent," Sloane added. "I'm sure he told the President he knows Peter. The truth is, he knows which buttons of Peter's to push. Peter craves advancement. French can give him that." She looked at Porter. "Peter will want everything we have so far on Garrett and Ostroff."

Porter smiled thinly. "Only Garrett. I didn't bring up

Ostroff's name. Couldn't think of a good reason to."

Sara Powell chuckled. "You're *so* sly, Lee."

"Mmm."

"So he'll get our information on Garrett," Sloane continued. "It'll take him a few days to get up to speed. After that, be prepared for suggestions."

"Meaning he may want to start steering the investigation," Kemeny said flatly.

"You bet he will. And he'll use French as the big stick."

Sara Powell sighed. "It would be so much easier if he stayed in New York."

There was a knock on the door and all heads turned in the direction of Whip Alley, who entered the room followed by Paco Santana, fresh off a plane and looking like it.

Santana walked up to Sloane and handed her a small package.

"The videotape shot by the Wisconsin couple," he rumbled.

"I ran the video in the truck on the way in from the airport," Alley said. "There are a lot of faces on it. The quality's not bad, but the images need enhancement."

"We can do that," Porter told him. "The first order of business is to make copies. John?"

Sloane handed Kemeny the tape and he was gone. Then Porter brought Alley and Santana up to speed on what had happened at the White House. If Alley was annoyed or surprised by French's interference and Peter Mack's inclusion in the investigation, he didn't show it. He smiled when Porter mentioned that he'd omitted Ostroff's name from the discussion.

"That gives us at least a few days before Mack cottons on to her," Alley said. "We need that time to find out exactly how she fits into this thing."

He went on to explain how he had followed Ostroff from the club to the Western Union office, then to the Pentagon.

"We need surveillance on her," he continued. "Paco will take the first shift, outside her town house in Georgetown. I'll relieve him. If someone's going to make a play for her, it'll be there. She's pretty safe when she's at work, given the security at the State Department."

"You won't be able to keep surveillance going indefinitely," Porter pointed out.

"That's why I'm counting on you to come up with something to tweak her. She was a lot tighter with Garrett than she wanted us to think. Sloane rattled her just enough so that she hit Western Union and the Pentagon right away. Western Union to send a message. The Pentagon, maybe to meet someone?"

"I'll get wiretaps on her phones," Porter said.

"The other thing is, she's being careful now," Alley said. "She's reached out to somebody. You can be sure that person won't be calling her back at home, or even at work. It'll be a face-to-face meet."

"The dominoes are starting to fall," Sloane said.

When Whip Alley had convinced Sloane that, in the wake of Garrett's murder, she could not stay in

Washington on her own, she'd thought he wanted to move her into a police safe house. Only reluctantly had she agreed to what he'd actually proposed.

That was then. Now, as she rode with Alley into Fairfax County, she felt herself relax for the first time in days. The last of the foliage was still turning and the countryside teemed with color. Alley had told her he lived in the country, and Sloane was surprised when he got off Route 620 while still inside the Beltway and headed into the quiet retreat he called Brook Hill Estates.

"Estates they're not," he commented as they drove into what looked like a nature retreat. There were almost no sidewalks or street lamps. The houses, ranging from 1950s rambling ranch homes to two-story Colonials, sat on very large lots. The driveway of the one Alley pulled into was bordered by a pond. In the crepuscular light of late afternoon, Sloane caught a glimpse of ducks moving about placidly on the surface.

"It's beautiful here," Sloane said.

"My dad bought this back in the late fifties," Alley explained as they pulled up in front of a low-slung timber and fieldstone house with enormous picture windows. "After he passed on, it was just me and my mother. Until she needed private care."

Alley's home reflected a weekly visit by a housekeeper. The furniture was period-piece sixties, some of it reupholstered, the wood accents carrying the sheen of lemon oil. Alley walked her through the principal rooms and into the self-contained guest quarters. The dresser, mirrors, lamps, and queen-size bed were all new. Sloane glanced at the rug and spotted the imprints of what had been there before. She knew exactly what Alley had done. After his mother had been institutionalized, he'd stripped the room, gone out and bought all new pieces, objects that held no memories for him, that he could bear to look at. Sloane had done the same thing two weeks after her mother had gone into that subway station.

"It's private," Alley said, showing her the en suite bathroom. He gestured toward the sliding glass doors that opened onto the patio. "Used to be we'd have deer come up and eat the impatiens."

For dinner, Alley barbecued the steaks. There was good red wine, and a fire going in the hearth, filling the house with the strong scent of seasoned oak. Sloane found herself talking about her father, what she had done on Wall Street and how her career had ended there, and how she'd come to be in Washington.

Afterward, they sat at opposite ends of the long couch, wedged into the corners. Sloane tucked her feet under her and watched as Tom Hanks and Meg Ryan began their comedy of errors that was *Sleepless in Seattle*. She did not see much after the opening credits.

The next time Sloane opened her eyes, it was past midnight. The fire had burned down to a pile of embers. She had shifted in her sleep, spread out along the couch; lying alongside her was Whip, asleep, one arm draped around her.

Her first thought was to get up. She would wake him and they would go off to bed—to their separate beds. She told herself that it was the fear of breaking his sound sleep that made her hesitate, not the warmth and soothing sensation of his body next to hers. Her hand crept across his chest, past the buttons that had come undone at the top of his shirt, and along the hard, flat muscles of his chest. She let it stay there for a moment, held her breath as he sighed and shifted, then spooned herself against him.

Two hundred miles away, while Sloane and Whip Alley slept in the rosy glow of the fireplace, Peter Mack raced out to Long Island on the expressway.

The last few days had been long and difficult. Without warning, the Chinese had rotated their entire mission to the UN. Mack had stayed up nights poring over the files of the new arrivals, getting their particulars into the computer, sifting through hundreds of still photos and miles of surveillance video to familiarize himself with the new quarry. His eyes were red and his temper short. All he wanted to do was go to his apartment and collapse. But he could not ignore this unexpected summons from Dodge French.

Brandywine was blazing with lights, as though a party were in progress. Mack was shown in by one of the bodyguards and excused himself to use the washroom. He splashed the grit from his eyes, combed his hair, and straightened his tie.

"Good evening, Peter. Or rather, good morning," French said when Mack was shown into the library.

Mack thought the room resembled a college professor's cluttered office, albeit much grander.

"Sir."

"I'm sorry to have dragged you out here at this hour, but we have something of a crisis. Drink?"

Mack declined the Armagnac French offered. If there was a crisis, he would need his wits about him. He opted for mineral water.

French studied the younger man over the rim of his snifter. He would have to be very careful in handling Peter Mack. That the agent was dead on his feet worked to French's advantage. He would be easier to lead and to misinform. The seeds of prejudice against common enemies would fall on fertile ground. Mack wouldn't be thinking fast enough to ask difficult questions.

"There have been disturbing developments in Washington," French said.

He opened with details about his meeting with the President and her advisers, then briefed Mack on the death of Garrett, a suspected informant who might have been passing information to Beijing, how Garrett had had connections to at least one other highly placed individual in government service. Finally, he gave him Susan Ostroff.

This was a gamble because Ostroff's name had never come up in the meeting. Lee Porter had held out on everyone. French was certain that Porter and his people had already connected Garrett to Ostroff but were keeping that card to themselves. But in order to be effective, Mack had to know she was a player.

French explained Porter's subterfuge, then said, "Under no circumstances are you to bring Ostroff's name up first. It's to your advantage that Porter and the others believe you don't know as much as they do."

Mack had been listening hard, careful not to show his incredulity at what he was hearing. The effect of Dodge French offering him a seat at the most powerful table in the world swept away his exhaustion.

"I've spoken with the director," French continued. "You're relieved of your current duties and will report to Washington headquarters. The full resources of the Bureau will be made available. Your job will be to go through everything that Porter's people have accumulated on Martin Garrett. They dropped the ball and let him get killed. Now you're coming in to find out who killed him and whether or not Susan Ostroff is a potential second target. She's your key. Lock in on her. Any suspicious movements, anything that's out of the ordinary, I want to know about it."

"What's the chain of command?"

"You report directly and only to me."

"Garrett's killer, does Porter have any idea who it is?"

"As far as I know, none." French paused. "The President is watching this, Peter. We've got some fancy footwork to do with the Chinese, and someone is showing them our dance card. We're talking hard intelligence here, which was why Porter was brought in and not, say, Bureau counterintelligence. That's all changed now. I convinced the President that we need a professional on this. She agreed. I recommended you. She agreed to that too." French let his last words hang. "I trust you're up to this."

Mack's thoughts strayed for a moment. He pictured Sloane the last time he'd seen her, his hurt and anger pushing her away. Into the arms of another man.

"Whose jurisdiction comes first, sir, mine or that of Sloane Ryder and her team?"

French smiled to himself. The boy was hooked. He had thought that Ryder might be a problem for Mack, but obviously that wasn't the case.

"Ryder is obliged to share everything with you. Conversely, I place no such restraints on you. How you deal with her and her group is up to you."

Walking Mack out to the front steps, French said, "Look after yourself, Peter. And remember, whoever is leaking this information is our enemy, no matter what position he or she is in."

As he watched the agent climb into his car, French's expression hardened. Less than three weeks remained until the plan would, literally, explode. French's greatest fear was that Sloane Ryder and her detective, Alley, would keep circling Ostroff until they found a weak spot, then move in on her. He needed Peter Mack to stay one step ahead of them, keep Ostroff isolated for as long as it took Mai Ling's assassin to get rid of her.

By this time, Peter Mack was back on the expressway. He was no longer tired. French's words pounded through him like raw adrenaline. He was driving by rote, itemizing the things he had to arrange before leaving for D.C.

Maybe that was why he never remembered the voice-activated tape recorder in his jacket pocket. It was the latest model, nearly weightless and equipped with a very sensitive microphone. The tape contained the last notes Mack had dictated before leaving Manhattan, bits of music and news he had listened to on the radio while driving out to Brandywine, and every word Dodge French had said.

Somewhere near the border of Nassau County and Queens, the tape ran out and the recorder shut down. Mack thought he heard a small click but was unable to place it. He scanned the readouts on the dashboard. Everything was functioning normally.

Sloane had thought things might be awkward between them the next morning, but when she awoke, Alley was up and in the kitchen. The coffee he handed her smelled strong, and his eyes had a twinkle to them. They drank in silence, listening to the sounds of morning filtering in from outside. There was a difference now, unspoken but understood and accepted. The question was what they would choose to do with that change, lying in their palms like a rare, fragrant bloom.

Driving into the city, they began to fill in the day's schedule.

"First, I have to relieve Paco," Alley said. "He's going to be cranky by now."

"What about when Ostroff goes to work?"

"Not much we can do there. I'll make sure she gets in okay, then go back just before lunch. There's no point in sitting outside all morning. The State Department building has thirty ways in and out. If she's going to leave on the sly, it won't be through the front door."

Sloane was worried about this but had no alternative to offer.

"I'll work on the Pentagon connection," she said. "Kemeny and Powell and I will scan Ostroff's phone records, see if we get a hit. If we're lucky, there'll be a pattern of calls to one particular number."

"All this time we've been thinking about Garrett and Ostroff," Sloane said. "What about the killer?"

"He's always on my mind," Alley replied. "I'll try to run down the ketamine, where he might have bought it and when. But don't expect too much."

"Why? It's an exotic substance."

"Not around here." He explained why. "Even if I manage to luck out and find where he bought it, it's not likely anyone will remember much. This guy's a long-range planner. He wouldn't leave much to chance. He probably disguised himself before he went shopping."

"There's the video Paco brought back. If we can separate the faces on it, enhance them . . ."

"It'll all help. But we need luck too."

Paco Santana was parked catercorner to Susan Ostroff's town house in upper Georgetown. He got out of the sedan, yawned and stretched, and ambled over to Alley's Suburban. He glanced from Sloane to Alley, then back to Sloane, and the glint in his eye made her blush.

Santana told them that Ostroff had stayed in all night. There had been one delivery, from an Indian restaurant on Wisconsin, around eight o'clock. The lights went out two hours later.

Alley sent Santana home to bed, then pulled into the space his partner had vacated.

Paco Santana was very good on surveillance, but he had made a basic assumption that was incorrect. He pictured the assassin as a white male who, given what had happened to Martin Garrett in West Potomac Park, preferred close-in work. To counter that, Santana had created a hundred-foot perimeter around the front of Susan Ostroff's house. He never thought to check the area behind him.

From his perch on the roof of the Maybe Baby vintage furniture boutique, the Handyman had watched the scene below unfold, the details enhanced by Israeli army-issue field glasses. As the big man had kept watch, so had he, chewing on dried fruit and nuts for sugar and protein, sipping bottled water.

Now came the changing of the guard, the big man leaving, the slender detective pulling into the space, the girl getting out. The Handyman attributed her rosy cheeks to something other than the brisk morning air. Sloane Ryder lingered by the open window of the SUV, speaking to the man who was obviously her lover, then left.

A pity, he thought, that they had picked up on Garrett so quickly. The Handyman could not have predicted how Garrett would act once he was in the drug's grip. He had hoped that Garrett would race into traffic and into the path of an onrushing vehicle. That would have been best. All the panic and screaming and confusion, precious moments lost to crowd and traffic control. By the time the pathologist got around to the corpse, it would have shed the real reason for its demise.

Instead, Sloane Ryder had interfered. The Handyman recalled his meal with Mai Ling in Chinatown, how she'd warned him that the woman had cut

Garrett from the pack, that she was investigating him but didn't have enough information to justify physical surveillance. *Not officially.* But Ryder had been at the park. Resourceful and independent, she was not afraid to play her hunch.

The Handyman never took his eyes off Ryder, not even as his fingertips played over the hard-shell plastic case that held his weapon. Instinct whispered to him to get rid of her now, while Mai Ling's admonitions rang in his ears. He pictured the tremendous, intricate plot he was helping to steer and moved his fingers off the case. Sloane Ryder was not the key. It was the woman in the town house.

The night's vigil had given the Handyman the exact scope and nature of the protection surrounding Susan Ostroff. It would be pitifully inadequate if he used the long gun. But, like Garrett's death, Ostroff's demise had to be surrounded by question marks. Mai Ling had promised that when the time came, Susan Ostroff would be vulnerable. The Handyman would be guaranteed a clear pass at her. Very well.

"As usual, you're fine, Sam. Fit as a horse."

Dr. Billy LeBonte was a tall, thin man with a stoop resembling a stork's and the gentlest hands in the hospital. He'd known the chairman of the Joint Chiefs for over thirty years.

Murchison slipped off the tissue paper that covered the examination table. The suite at Walter Reed Hospital in Bethesda was identical to the one next door to it, used by the President. Its large windows opened onto a grassy quadrangle; inside, there was every amenity, from a stocked wet bar to a comfortable sitting area with a plasma television set on the wall.

Climbing back into his uniform, Murchison chatted with Billy LeBonte about this year's hunting trip. Politically, the doctor was a pacifist, yet those same hands could steady a rifle barrel on an elk or a bighorn sheep five hundred yards away. The two men had been hunting together since college.

There was a knock at the door. "Come in," Murchison called out.

His adjutant, a career captain, poked her head in. Murchison was only half dressed, but neither he nor the captain was fazed. They both knew she'd seen a lot more of him than that. Billy LeBonte hid his smile.

"You have a visitor, General," the adjutant said crisply. "A Dr. Susan Ostroff from the State Department."

Murchison glanced up from buttoning his shirt. The captain wondered why he looked so perplexed, and then alarmed. The thought that Murchison might be two-timing her flashed through her mind.

"Give me a minute, then show her in, Captain."

"Yes, sir."

"You finding more ways than one to keep your heart rate up, Sam?" Billy LeBonte said slyly on his way out.

"This is business," Murchison replied dryly. "If you don't believe me, wait until you get a look at her. She's a fucking ice queen."

When he left the suite, Billy LeBonte had to admit that this woman looked pretty glacial. Not Sam's type at all.

"Hello, Susan," Murchison said after the door had closed behind her. "This a surprise. How did you know where to find me?"

"My assistant called yours, saying that there was an urgent matter at the State Department that needed your input," Ostroff replied.

Murchison noted her quick, sharp movements, how tightly wound she was. This was highly unusual for the ice queen.

Over the years, Susan Ostroff had provided Murchison with excellent, high-grade intelligence that, despite his position, he otherwise might never have seen. She had enabled him to steer the military's China policy in the direction he and Dodge French wanted.

Sam Murchison had cut his career teeth in Vietnam. He'd lost more friends in that Asian muck than he cared to remember. He'd watched as civilians—politicians—had continually hamstrung the chain of command, and consequently the ability of the fighting men and women to perform their duties. He swore that he would never again permit their decisions to cause unnecessary bloodshed.

Although he had kept that pledge during the Gulf War, Murchison understood that China was not the Middle East. Another president, a *civilian*, would soon ask Murchison to pony up young cannon fodder in the defense of Taiwan. Claudia Ballantine had made it clear that she would never give up the island to Beijing. So Claudia Ballantine had to go.

Three weeks. Less. All we have to do is keep it together that long.

But French's intricate operation was starting to fray. Pencil pushers were nosing around. The first casualty—Garrett—had been recorded. Murchison finished adjusting the knot in his tie and turned from the mirror, to Ostroff, pacing in front of the big, wide windows.

"Okay, Susan. What's on your mind?"

"We have a problem."

Ostroff told him about Sloane Ryder's unexpected visit to the Surratt House, the questions she'd asked, the feelers she'd put out.

"She doesn't have a damn thing," Ostroff concluded. "But she's still digging. And this morning, when I came out the door, there was surveillance posted, some guy in an SUV checking me out."

"Did you get a plate number?"

"Of course. I'll run it when I get to the office."

"I don't know what I can do about the surveillance," Murchison began.

"I'm not asking you to do *anything*," Ostroff snapped. "I can handle the lightweights at the GAO. You need to know what French intends for Peter Lin."

Murchison noted how Ostroff's features softened at the mention of Peter Lin. He thought he knew what was coming.

"French wants Lin to take a fall," she said, trying to hide her disgust, knowing she'd failed. "He's to withdraw from the election. I've already made initial contact. He'll be waiting for the second one."

She explained the reason behind this latest turn of events.

"It seems you have a handle on the situation," Murchison said, careful to keep a neutral tone.

"Right. I do. Like you, I'm the good soldier."

Murchison was shocked by the bitterness in her voice.

"I need you to promise me something," Ostroff continued. "Peter Lin has worked all his life to bring about reunification. You don't know half the sacrifices he's made. Now French wants to push him off to the sidelines. I need you to guarantee that nothing will happen to him. When things start unraveling over there, Lin will be one of the first people the police will go after. I won't stand for him to be hurt or taken. I won't leave him there to be tortured. I want you to promise me you'll bring him out."

Murchison had never imagined Susan Ostroff capable of tears, but he saw a hint of them now.

"I can do that," he said quietly. "I can bring him home."

Ostroff nodded and turned away. She dug in her purse for tissues and mashed them against her eyes. She did not turn around as she spoke.

"All right then. I know you'll do this. I don't think French would, but you . . ." When at last she faced him, Murchison was shocked by her brittle appearance, shocked even more by the words she spit at him. "Because if anything happens to Lin, I'll blow French and this whole thing out of the water. You understand that, don't you, General?"

The general did.

Earlier in the morning, Peter Mack had come by Susan Ostroff's town house, spotted the Suburban parked in the street, and immediately made it for what it was. Behind the tinted windows, the driver was only a vague silhouette. Mack assumed he was Whip Alley, and he appeared to be alone.

Mack decided to use the detective as cover. Hanging back, he watched Susan Ostroff get into her BMW and back out of the narrow driveway. The Suburban dutifully fell in behind the import, and Mack tailed both vehicles through the crowded Georgetown arteries.

Like Whip Alley, Mack was surprised when Ostroff headed out of the city. At the hospital perimeter, she slowed at the security post at Walter Reed Hospital and flashed her ID. Alley decided not to follow, and Mack knew why. A Homicide detective would draw the attention of security personnel.

Mack waited until Alley had turned around before he drove up to the post. His credentials elicited a bored wave from the guard and he was through. The only problem was timing. There was Ostroff's BMW in the visitor's lot, but she had already disappeared. She could have entered any one of a half dozen annexes to the sprawling compound.

Mack decided on the direct approach. With his ID in plain view, he got directions to the security office. There, he spoke to the duty officer, whose first reaction was to ask whether Dr. Ostroff posed any kind of threat. Mack assured him that that was not the case. But he needed to speak with her immediately. Whom had she come to see?

The duty officer punched up Ostroff's name on the computer and politely gave Mack directions to General Samuel Murchison's suite.

To play out the charade, Mack actually took the elevator to the designated floor. But he had no intention of talking to Ostroff. He had what he'd come for—the name of the person she was visiting.

Why was Ostroff meeting with the chairman of the Joint Chiefs at Walter Reed? What was so important that it couldn't wait until after Murchison had left the hospital?

Mack saw Ostroff coming out of Murchison's suite, heard the pistol-shot echo of her heels, and smiled at her as she passed him on her way to the elevator. When the doors opened, he followed her inside.

General Murchison never saw the FBI agent because he didn't follow Ostroff out of the suite. Instead, the minute the door closed after her, he snapped open his encrypted telephone. French's voice sounded scratchy on the secure line.

"Ostroff was just here," he said without preamble.

"What did she want, Sam?"

Murchison told French about Ostroff's concern for Lin, her demand for his safety, the threat she had thrown down.

"She's dangerous," Murchison said flatly.

"You needn't concern yourself with her," French replied. "Are *you* ready to proceed?"

"Yes. But I need Trimble and the President in a box." The double meaning of the word "box" shook him.

"It's being taken care of."

23

LEE PORTER'S HOME was a modest ranch house in one of the older sections of Chevy Chase. Sloane Ryder headed up the flagstone walkway lined with rosebushes, pressed the doorbell, and heard chimes strike somewhere in the house. She wasn't expected and now regretted not having called ahead.

"Hi. Can I help you?"

The young woman behind the screen door was nineteen or twenty, wearing a baggy Georgetown U. sweatshirt over jogging pants. Her skin was the color of dark caramel, her eyes as black as Porter's.

Sloane held up her ID and introduced herself. "I'm here to see Mr. Porter. He's not expecting me—"

"Camille, who is it?"

Dressed in jeans and a denim work shirt, Porter came into the foyer and hovered behind the young woman. Sloane noticed drops of water glistening in his hair.

"Sloane . . ." He turned to the young woman. "Camille, honey, why don't you go finish your breakfast. It's just some office business. I'll be along."

"Okay," she said, not sounding very sure.

Porter waited until she was gone, then pushed open the screen door. "My niece," he said. "She's a sophomore at Georgetown."

Sloane stepped into the foyer. "I'm sorry to intrude. I should have called."

Porter looked at the stuffed briefcase in her hand, at her puffy, red eyes. "You've been up all night. Let me get you some coffee."

He led her into the house, into a small study where the walls were paneled with knotty pine. There was an impressive workstation and an aging sofa whose contours suggested that it had often done double duty as a bed.

Porter left her alone for a few minutes. Sloane heard voices and the rattle of crockery in the kitchen. Then he was back, handing her a cup of coffee and settling into his chair.

"Thanks," Sloane said, and started to tell him about Ostroff. "According to Whip, Peter Mack tracked Ostroff to Walter Reed yesterday. While Whip was tailing her, he saw Mack behind him."

"Did Alley follow her into Walker Reed?"

"No. He figured that would send up flags."

"What about Mack?"

"He went in and stayed about forty minutes. We have no idea what happened inside."

"You haven't talked with him?"

"I've left two messages on his cell phone."

"Do you think he's holding out?" Porter asked.

"He's been in Washington for five days and still hasn't contacted us," Sloane replied. "Not even a courtesy call. But he's on Ostroff's case. How did he even learn about her? You said her name never came up in the White House briefing."

"It didn't. I don't know how he got it."

Porter sipped his coffee. "Tell me about Ostroff first."

"She came up clean. John, Sara, and I ran her home-phone records, credit cards, travel itineraries. Nothing. We won't be able to get to her office phone until Monday. She hasn't been out of Washington in six months. Before then, it was to Saint Thomas for a week's holiday at Frenchman's Reef.

"We went over her tax returns and bank statements. She was telling the truth—her accountants are conservative. The family money went into blind trusts when she joined the State Department. Ostroff gets quarterly statements—that's the extent of her involvement in the portfolios. The bank loan to Garrett is perfectly legitimate although the interest rate is obviously suspect. But we can't get to the loan manager who did the paperwork because he's out of town until the middle of next week."

Porter looked away. Sloane and the others had worked very hard for very little.

"You didn't come here just to tell me that."

Sloane dipped into her briefcase and pulled out a file. Color glossies spilled across the coffee table. Each one was numbered in the top-right-hand corner. There were twenty-two photographs.

"There was a lot of tourist stuff on the videotape shot by that Wisconsin couple," she said. "The lab cut out the usual monuments footage. Only ninety seconds was shot at West Potomac Park. Every frame was blown up into a still. I went through them all, setting aside the ones that showed no people. Then I culled the ones that were shot before Garrett and his softball party arrived. This is what's left."

Porter examined each still. Some had better definition than others; he could make out faces of men, women, and children. There were some of the kids playing ball.

"What do the red marks indicate?" he asked, rubbing the grease-penciled *X*.

"Faces we know. Whip matched them against the men at the game and the women at the picnic table."

That eliminated seventeen of the twenty-two. Porter scanned the remaining five once more. Two were undoubtedly women. The resolution was so good that there could be no mistake. Black middle-aged women, each carrying a Bible in her hand. And one had a tote bag over her shoulder with the logo of a travel agency clearly displayed.

That left three. A man lying on a blanket on the grass, his face turned to the sun, a German shepherd sprawled across his legs. The second was of a forty-year-old man, give or take, with bland features and a startled expression, as though he'd been surprised and annoyed to discover a camera pointed at him. The third photo had the grainiest resolution of the three. The distance was substantial and the lighting poor; the picture caught the man turning away from the camera. Less than three quarters of his face was visible. The enhancement had caused his houndstooth jacket to become a blur.

"What do you see here?" asked Porter.

"Whip thinks that the killer may have stuck around," Sloane said. "Garrett wasn't murdered by a gun or a knife—not in a way so that the killer could be absolutely sure he was dead. So he'd want to stay close, watch the results of his handiwork, make sure that Garrett went down. I think he watched us try to save Garrett, maybe even waited until he went into the body bag."

Porter recoiled at her cold tone. Perhaps it was just her exhaustion talking. Perhaps something else.

"Where are you going with this, Sloane?"

She set down her coffee. "Whip ran these three pictures through the D.C. Homicide computers, looking for a hit on known felons. He came up empty. He also called in favors from the Virginia and Maryland state troopers. Nothing. I want to cast the net farther, using the FBI data bank of wanted or suspected killers, and the Secret Service computers."

Porter felt a slight twinge in his stomach. "Why the Secret Service? You think that one of these three could be a foreigner?"

"I don't know. But the Secret Service's foreign intelligence branch might."

"Something's spooked you, Sloane. What is it?"

"I've been going over and over the sequence," she replied. "First I thought that Garrett had been murdered because we were investigating him. But what if there's another reason? What if he was murdered because he had done whatever it was he was supposed to do and had outlived his usefulness? What did he pass on that made him expendable?"

"Passed on to Ostroff?"

"Probably."

"But during your face-to-face with her, she didn't exactly grieve for Garrett."

"Makes you wonder why, doesn't it? Right after I saw her, she took off for Western Union. Why would Ostroff, who has the best communications systems at her disposal, do that? Privacy. This was not a message she would trust to her phones or faxes—not after she and I had spoken."

"You're saying that Garrett carried out some kind of assignment—successfully—and was killed not only because you were watching him but because he was no longer a necessary component. Now you tweak Susan Ostroff and *she* reacts in an uncharacteristic way. This Western Union message might be her last assignment and now she can be taken off the board too. Am I reading you right?"

Sloane nodded. "She's out there all alone, Lee. Whip and Paco are covering her as best they can, but they can't do that indefinitely. And Whip will tell you that the surveillance is full of holes, any one of which an assassin could slip through."

Porter picked up one of the three photos. "Houndstooth jacket. You keyed in on him before. You think he might be the one?"

"He was the closest one to the women at the picnic table. They remember speaking to him. He was close to the food and drinks on the table. He had ten, maybe fifteen seconds to spike Garrett's Coke. My money's on him."

Porter looked at the photo again, straining to see

something beyond the grain and the whorls, some secret hidden there. He knew that Sloane had spent hours doing the same thing.

The problem was, given the GAO equipment, this was as good as the photograph was likely to get. There were other labs, like the ones down at NASA's Cape Canaveral facilities where they enhanced the Mars Rover pictures, and at the Jet Propulsion Lab in Pasadena, California. Porter could overnight copies of the pictures to those two facilities.

"Or we could ask the Secret Service," he said. "They have excellent equipment."

Sloane nodded. "That's better. When I was at the White House, I met an agent there, Holland Tylo. I think I can work with her."

"She'll want to know if this guy is in any way a threat to the President."

"We have no indication of that. Despite her college connection to the President, Ostroff doesn't have much to do with the Oval Office. And Garrett, even though he worked inside the White House, wasn't close to the President. Let's see if Tylo's machines score a hit."

Porter knew of Holland Tylo, the President's eternal shadow. "What about the Bureau?"

Sloane shrugged. "Not much choice, is there?" She gathered up the photos and rose. "I called Mack's office earlier and told the switchboard to get hold of him for a ten o'clock meeting."

Sloane called the White House Secret Service number on her car phone. She was in luck. Holland Tylo was just going off duty and agreed to meet her in the lobby of the Willard Hotel, two blocks from the executive mansion.

The Willard's old world grandeur had been painstakingly restored through years of renovation. Surrounded by mahogany and gilt-edged moldings, Sloane and Tylo met in an alcove close to the concierge's desk. The steady traffic of guests seeking assistance and the constant ringing of the phones masked their conversation.

Sloane gave her an envelope containing the three photos. "I need your help," she said, and went on to explain.

Tylo didn't look at the pictures until Sloane was finished. Then she took her time examining each one.

"I don't recognize them from the threat list," she said at last, and that was true enough. What Tylo didn't mention was that the image of the houndstooth man fanned the ember of a distant memory that she could not quite grasp. "Is there anything I should know regarding the President's safety?"

"No. What I need is for you to run these pictures through the Secret Service threat list computers, in case the machines can correlate some of the facial features of the men in the pictures with someone the Service might be watching or have background information on."

"I'm on my way to Service headquarters right now," Tylo said. "I'll drop these off and flag 'em with a bullet. But we're still looking at twenty-four, maybe forty-eight hours."

"Whatever you can do, I'd appreciate it." Sloane

then mentioned that NASA and JPL would be working up enhancements. If they could sharpen the images, she'd get them to Tylo right away.

Watching Sloane, Tylo heard a little voice in her head. She felt confident Sloane was telling the truth about there being no threat to the President, but . . .

Tylo decided to do better than a bullet; she would walk the pictures through the threat list section herself. And if the section came up empty, and if the little voice continued to nag, there was another pair of eyes—and different machines—that would see the photos. Especially the one of that houndstooth man.

Sloane waited for five minutes in the FBI headquarters' reception area before a guard came to escort her upstairs. She suspected that Peter Mack was playing mind games with her.

Inside the elevator, the security escort did not press the button for the fourth floor, which was where the intelligence division was headquartered. The car stopped two floors above, and she walked down a wide corridor that ended at doors marked SPECIAL OPERATIONS.

Sloane could not have known that she was about to enter one of the Bureau's most restricted areas, devoted exclusively to Megahut. In FBI parlance, this section is known as an "off site." Here, the Bureau works hand in hand with the National Security Agency to intercept communications originating in U.S.–based foreign embassies, communications that include satellite, phone, fax, courier, and mail. Black-bag assignments are conceived there, too, approved, and forwarded for execution. A black-bag job might entail the break-in by federal agents of a foreign embassy to install bugs, or the interception of a very junior embassy staffer whose low rank is merely a cover for his being a courier entrusted with sensitive transactions.

Behind the double doors, in the reception area, a pleasant young woman wearing a sidearm scanned Sloane's temporary ID, then asked her to take a seat. Special Agent Mack was expecting her and apologized for the delay. He was still on the phone.

Sixty feet into the warren of soundproof offices behind the receptionist, Peter Mack was speaking to Dodge French, finishing his report about Susan Ostroff's encounter with the chairman of the Joint Chiefs at Walter Reed.

"What I don't understand, sir," Mack said, "is why she would go to see him. There's nothing in Ostroff's records to indicate that she's had any dealings with Murchison at all—no briefings, no consultations, no special assignments. Yet she knows that he'll be at Walter Reed and that's where she meets him."

French's voice sounded very far away, but Mack knew that was only because of the scrambler phone.

"Are you sure it wasn't just a coincidence, Peter? Could she have gone there for another purpose?"

"No, sir. That floor is reserved for the President and other top officials. Murchison was the only patient there at the time. That, and I saw her leave his room."

"So you believe there's some connection between them." French's voice had a thoughtful quality to it and Mack did not interrupt. "I find this very strange indeed, although I wonder if we're not missing the woods for the trees. Sam Murchison has a reputation, discreet, of course, for being something of a ladies' man. Is that a possibility?"

That he's screwing Ostroff and she came by for a nooner?

"That may be the case, sir," Mack said diplomatically. "I'd have to get more background on Ostroff to determine if that's a possibility." Which made him remember: "Sloane Ryder is waiting outside my office now. Maybe she can help."

"Be careful," French cautioned. "Let Ryder show you her cards on Ostroff first. But if she's already tied her to Murchison, find out what she knows."

Mack hung up and buzzed the receptionist to show in Sloane. Like all the offices in Megahut, the one he'd been assigned was small and windowless. A predecessor had mounted a mirror on one of the walls to give the illusion of more space and Mack checked his appearance in it. He knew he looked fine, but he still caught his breath when he heard the knock on the door.

"Peter . . ."

"Sloane. I was surprised to get your message. It sounded urgent." He gestured for her to sit. "You look tired."

Sloane took in the office. This was not what she'd expected. Small, sterile offices often held dark secrets; the executive suites, where she thought she would find Mack, were for show. Mack was moving up.

"I tried to call you, at your apartment," Mack said.

"I've moved. Peter, it's not going to be a problem, us working together?"

"I don't see why. I was calling you to get your files on Garrett and the investigation. I assume you've been briefed on my participation."

"Yes. But it seems you're already participating. Why did you follow Susan Ostroff out to Walter Reed? How did you know about her?"

Mack was startled. "How did *you* know?"

"Because we were watching her too."

Mack shrugged. "Fine. I was just doing my homework, Sloane. MJ-11 isn't the only agency with access to information about Garrett. I made the same connections you did."

And quickly too.

Mack's glib reply rang false, but Sloane didn't press.

"Okay. You've made the same connections. That's good, because I want to talk about Ostroff. Do you know who she went to see at the hospital?"

"No. I lost her inside."

Sloane bit her lip. Mack was lying again. Why? Because he wanted the glory, or to show her up?

"Peter," she said slowly, "Garrett's death is an official Homicide investigation. I'm not the only one who'll be asking these questions."

"You're talking about Detective Alley? If I have anything relevant to add to the investigation, Alley will be the first to hear. Promise."

His supercilious tone stung.

"Let me put it another way," Sloane said. "According to the reports you've read, what did Garrett die of?"

"Some kind of brain tumor."

"Wrong. Try ketamine."

Sloane ignored his astonishment and explained what the coroner had found in Garrett's system, how the drug worked, and how Garrett had ingested it. Mack seemed stunned when she talked about the killer and Paco Santana's take on him.

"Garrett may have been the target of a professional assassin," she said. "By association with Garrett, Susan Ostroff might now be in danger. That's why we have her under surveillance. Now, are you going to keep trying to make points with Dodge French, or do we work this thing together?"

Mack had regained his composure, but his mind was churning. French had never even alluded to autopsy results or an assassin. What else didn't French know?

"Okay," Mack said. "We got off on the wrong foot. My fault. Like I said, I've been backtracking Garrett, which led me to Ostroff. But I sure as hell don't know anything about any assassin. Help me out here."

Sloane spread the three photographs across the desk blotter, explaining where and when they had been taken. She mentioned the enhancement work being done by other agencies and outlined what she wanted from Mack.

"I can run them through our computers," he said. "If you want to wait a day or so, I'll have our lab try to enhance the definitions."

"Why not do both at the same time? Maybe we'll get a hit off the originals and won't have to wait."

"Fine."

"Now Ostroff. Who did she meet at Walter Reed?"

Mack hesitated, recalling Dodge French's advice. But new variables had entered the picture. Mack called it.

"Murchison. General Sam Murchison, chairman of the Joint Chiefs of Staff."

Sloane slumped back in her chair. First, Susan Ostroff goes to the Pentagon, then she's out at Walter Reed . . . a military connection . . . all the way up to the nation's highest-ranking military commander.

"You didn't know?" Mack asked.

Sloane shook her head. "We've been going through her phone logs. Calls to the Department of Defense, but not to the Pentagon."

"That's how she might have fooled you," Mack said. "The DOD operators will patch you into the Pentagon. Say Ostroff calls some number, talks for a bit. Before she hangs up, she presses the pound or star sign on her phone, connects with the operator, who then puts her through to the Pentagon. The Pentagon number never shows up on any record."

So simple, Sloane thought. *How could we have overlooked it?* And Murchison, what was she going to do about *him?* How could they throw a surveillance net over someone like that?

Then she realized she was headed in the wrong direction. Murchison wasn't the one she should be thinking about. She needed to concentrate on Ostroff.

"Do you know Ostroff's schedule?" Sloane asked.

Mack dug a printout from a pile. "There's a gala at the new Meridien Hotel tonight, a benefit warm-up for the President's Hands of Hope ceremony on Thanksgiving." He handed her the pages.

"A *Who's Who* of Washington," Sloane murmured, scanning the list.

Everyone from the CEOs of major corporations to social and political luminaries would be there. Individual tickets started at $25,000; tables went for over a million. The Hands of Hope foundation would make a killing. Ostroff would attend because of her family's contributions.

"Peter," Sloane said quietly, "I want you to get me and the detectives into this thing tonight."

"If you're worried about Ostroff, don't be. The President will be on hand tonight—with all the security that implies."

"For the President. Not Ostroff."

"You seriously think someone would make a play for her under those circumstances?"

"I don't know. I can't be sure. Do you want to take that chance?" She paused. "All I'm saying is that we baby-sit her until tomorrow."

If it hadn't been for the revelations about Garrett's death, Mack would have argued with her. Now, he, too, had questions for the State Department's China specialist.

"Have you been to the Meridien?" he asked.

"No," Sloane replied.

Mack pulled out a large, blueprint-style layout of the hotel. "Okay, this is the service entrance, this is where security checks in . . ."

THE NORTH KOREAN woman known as Kim Cho sat in the waiting room of the Nassau County Doctors' Hospital. There were four other people present, mothers and fathers flipping pages of magazines they were pretending to read, glancing repeatedly at the wall clock as if trying to speed up the maddeningly slow sweep of the second hand.

Cho had a newspaper in her lap, the late edition of the *New York Post*. Splashed across the center pages were photographs of the new Meridien Hotel in Washington. The text about tonight's gala was couched in breathless, gushing prose. Cho stared at the photo of the American President. She was a beautiful, well-fed, pampered woman, like some goddess far removed from the hunger and misery her actions had caused in Cho's homeland. American embargoes on North Korea's products, the blockade of her harbors and inspections on the high seas by U.S. naval vessels—all had contributed to grinding down her country's economy. Without trade, people had no work; without work, they starved.

Kim Cho knew that the operation she was part of had not been conceived of or financed by Pyongyang.

The Great and Devout People's Leader had neither the money nor the resources to strike alone against the American leech. But a confluence of interests with a far greater power had come about, had made Kim Cho the warden for her country's revenge. Soon the Americans would experience the grief and terror and helplessness that saw two thirds of the world to bed every night.

"Mrs. Cho?"

The doctor, in his mid-thirties, was prematurely bald and had peppermint-scented breath that Cho found offensive. Nonetheless, she went into her act, nodding and smiling anxiously like a coolie.

The pediatric AIDS specialist prattled on about how well 1818—whom he knew as Sun—was doing. He was especially happy that the boy was putting on weight but cautioned that he should exercise more.

"I don't want any heart problems down the road," he explained gravely.

Kim Cho bobbed her head. "Yesee yesee . . ."

A nurse brought out 1818 and handed him a hard candy. The doctor ruffled 1818's hair and said he'd see him in two weeks.

Yesee, yesee . . .

Except that 1818 would not keep that appointment. In ten days, he would be taken to another facility, in Rhode Island. There, a team of specialists, flown in allegedly to participate in a medical conference in Boston, would attend to him. When they were done, 1818 would be ready to leave for the White House.

* * *

By the middle of the afternoon, Sloane was back at Whip Alley's home in Brook Hill. She sat at the dining room table, sifting through the pages Mack had faxed to her office.

She had told Whip and Lee Porter about her meeting with Mack. The agent had been as good as his word. A courier had delivered security credentials for the three of them and for Paco Santana. An hour later, a copy of the guest list and details of the security arrangements came through the fax machine. The consensus was that the safest place Susan Ostroff could be that night was the Meridien. The Secret Service had done its usual impeccable job.

The issue of General Murchison's connection to Ostroff had been tabled.

"There's nothing anyone can do about it today," Porter had said. "Tomorrow, we have a quiet chat with her."

Sloane knew that Murchison's sudden appearance in the mosaic had caught Porter off guard and had created enormous complications. Porter had sat across from Murchison during Oval Office policy debates and discussions. He was well aware of how much intelligence the chairman of the Joint Chiefs was privy to. Was it conceivable that a man of such proven loyalty and dedication could be trading in his country's most intimate secrets?

"Still at it?"

Sloane glanced up and managed a smile as Alley let himself in the front door. "You ready for tonight?" he asked.

"As ready as I'll ever be," she replied listlessly.

He went over to the table, glanced at the faxed paper-work and her notes, then covered everything with a newspaper.

"Leave it alone," he said. "Just for tonight."

Sloane nodded. "We should eat. We might not get a chance later."

She helped him unpack the groceries he'd bought and arranged the cold cuts on a platter while he tossed the salad. They took their plates into the living room and watched the early news on CNN. Foreign visitors had been slaughtered at the foot of the Luxor tombs in Egypt; Colombian drug lords were killing Mexican government prosecutors; a German security official had been arrested for spying for Saddam Hussein. The world remained a dark and dangerous place and suddenly Sloane was tired of it all. She wanted to close her eyes and make it all go away.

Alley cleared away their plates, and when he returned there was soft music on the stereo. Sloane lay back in the cushions of the oversize sofa, her eyes lightly closed. He walked past her, not wanting to disturb her, but he felt her fingernails brush his hand.

"Sit," she murmured. "You know, one day this'll all be over."

"One day."

"And then what are you and I going to do?"

"What did you have in mind?"

"Well, we haven't done anything yet, have we?"

Sloane let her palm travel along his cheek, past his temple, around to the back of his head, and gently grabbed a fistful of his hair. Pulling him to her to taste his lips, she could smell the lingering scent of soap on his neck.

Her fingers nimbly pried open the buttons of his shirt, reached lower to unbuckle his belt. All the while, her mouth made his a prisoner.

Now he was lifting her, stripping away her sweater and slacks while she shook her hair free and reached to undo her bra. His kisses made her lie back, shudder as his lips caressed her breasts, then trailed across her belly, hesitating, teasing, making her groan before they reached the soft folds between her thighs.

Time was lost to her. She had three tiny orgasms as he savored her, then surrendered to the long, undulating waves that cascaded through her. When she could no longer stand it, she drew him up to her, her legs enveloping him, her hips rising to meet him, a sharp sigh escaping as he entered her.

For the longest time, Sloane was lost in that rocking sensation, cleaving to him as he moved within her. When she cried out in release, she felt cleansed, reborn, and when he did not stop, when he coaxed her to come still one more time, she tightened her grip and melded against him until their movements were one.

Then it was done, as softly as it had begun, as softly as a feather falling. Sloane falling, her eyes burning brightly, skin wet, all of her wet, his breathing deep and hard, the pulse of his neck savage. When he stirred, she shushed him, and kept him inside her even as he grew soft.

They stayed like that until the last shadows of the

day disappeared and the room darkened around them. The CD had spun itself out long ago, leaving only the slow pounding of their hearts and their whispered endearments. Their eyes were set on each other's, as wide and unblinking as a cheetah's, marveling at this treasure they had found.

Fifteen miles from where Sloane and Whip Alley lay in a tangle of arms and legs, Secret Service Agent Holland Tylo stood in the vast lobby of the Meridien Hotel. She glanced down at the paperwork that detailed the workings of the hotel.

A Paris-based international resorts company had built the Meridien on a choice parcel of land on Kalorama Road, not far from the French embassy. The cost overruns had been extravagant, but the results were stunning.

The centerpiece was a rose-colored marble atrium that soared high above the lobby. At the top of the atrium was a lounge, complete with an infinity pool whose water flow was controlled by an electric motor. The water ran over the edge of the pool and cascaded down to a lush, tropical-like pond surrounded by dense growth and captive jungle birds. If one looked up the waterfall at the right angle, in the right light, the outlines of a bronze chute could be detected. This directed the flow of water into the pond. Not visible were the two-foot-long bronze plates, like the steps of an escalator but with much sharper edges, that caught and broke the water, creating the froth and white-water effect.

As impressive as the waterfall was, it wasn't Tylo's

main concern. The President's movements would be restricted to the temporary podium set up in the lobby and the De Gaulle Salon, where she would host the A-list crowd. After dinner, the President would visit the other four salons to press the flesh of contributors. So far so good.

Even better, the hotel was not yet open to the public. Tonight would be its public debut. That alone saved enormous manpower that would otherwise have been given over to securing the Meridien's 640 rooms. All the elevators, save one that would service the protection detail's command post on the second floor and the glass one that went to the lounge at the infinity pool, would remain frozen. All the fire doors would be locked, their alarms armed. That left the front and service entrances, the garage, and the kitchens.

Tylo had already checked the entrances. The agents responsible were happy with the layouts. Same for the garage, a section of which would be cordoned off for the presidential motorcade. Ladybug's entry would be through the corridors that ran behind the kitchens. At that time, agents would make sure the staff was buttoned up in the food-preparation area.

As for the staff itself, the Meridien hired very qualified personnel whose references and IDs were easy to check. The cooks were French, naturally. The evening's waiters and support staff had been provided by the company that serviced state dinners at the White House.

Holland Tylo was satisfied with the arrangements and reported as much to her boss, the chief of the

White House detail. They stood together in the center
of the cavernous lobby, surrounded by dozens of workers—carpenters, electricians, florists, hotel assistant
managers—who were turning the last screw, arranging
a bud just so. A large Hands of Hope banner was
being lifted above the podium.

"What're you wearing?" asked the security chief.

"Just a little off-the-shoulder number."

"Mmm. Sounds fetching."

"Practical."

It was. The gown was cut at the thigh, allowing
Tylo to draw her weapon instantly.

"Those pictures you bulleted to the lab?"

"Uh-huh?"

"Should be ready first thing in the morning. We've
already run the faces against the threat list. No hits.
Although that last guy, in the checkered coat, he could
be anybody."

"Maybe he'll be ID'd by the morning."

"Let's hope so."

Tylo and the chief turned to admire the waterfall.
The lighting wasn't the best and neither noticed the
sawtoothed bronze plates hidden in the curve of the
chute. Nor did they know just how fast, how very fast,
the current was in the infinity pool high above.

The Handyman knew. These and other details had
been provided for him in the hotel's engineering specs,
delivered by courier to his modest room at the Howard
Johnson's.

The Handyman could not say for sure how it was
that these events had unfolded. He suspected that the
principal, whose life he'd been hired to protect, was in

ever more danger of being exposed. Hence the message from Mai Ling, which included the time and place of execution.

Among the details was a guest list for this evening's gala. There was the name Claude Besson, listed alphabetically, along with a matching passport and invitation. Besson was a senior vice president of the conglomerate that had built the Meridien. He was responsible for the company's hotel interests in Brazil and worked out of São Paulo. There were no other company officers from South America attending. Since the conglomerate would be represented by over fifty executives from its various international offices, and the entire guest list ran to over a thousand, it was safe to assume that Claude Besson, reinvented, would not be likely to bump into anyone who knew him. As for the real Besson, the Handyman had it on good authority that he was in fact in the United States at the moment, hauling his querulous wife and whiny children around Disney World.

The Handyman finished dressing, then, with a bib around his neck, he began to apply cosmetics that would alter his appearance slightly. He was not concerned about matching Besson's description. No need for that. But, as he'd seen from that cold, dark Georgetown roof, his target was under surveillance and he couldn't take any chances at being recognized. After Martin Garrett's demise, Sloane Ryder and her detectives would stay very close to their charge.

However, the Handyman knew that they would be working at a disadvantage. Invariably the focus of security would be the President, which would deflect attention from his task. And when the killing occurred, security's first reaction would be to protect Claudia Ballantine. With so many people milling about, plus the added chaos of the ensuing panic, the crime scene would render no clues. The chaos would also provide cover for his escape.

The Handyman checked his work, washed his hands, and made a last-second adjustment to his black tie. Outside the hotel, he handed a flower girl five dollars for a single white rose. He clipped the bloom from its stem and inserted it in his lapel. Now he was ready.

Susan Ostroff kept her trim figure thanks to a careful diet and punishing hours on a Lifecycle and a StairMaster. Slipping into the clinging Norma Kamali evening gown was no problem for her.

Ostroff had spent most of the day at an exclusive spa, having a complete makeover. She was quite sure no one had followed her there. Once inside, she was surrounded by women being kneaded, pounded, mud-packed, bathed, and clipped. The gossip was all about the pecking order of the seating assignments at tonight's gala.

Between the shiatsu massage and the herbal wrap, Ostroff had excused herself and gone into the lounge. In the privacy of a booth, she had made an international call. The time had been prearranged, the duration of the conversation painfully brief. Ostroff had not heard Lin's voice in ten years except on television news. Its sound cracked her heart.

She had succinctly related Dodge French's message.

When she was done, there was silence on the line. Finally, a universe away, the voice of the man she had never stopped loving floated to her, telling her it would be done French's way. His final words to her, "I love you," had bored into her soul.

Examining herself in the foyer mirror, Ostroff was satisfied. She picked up her evening bag and stepped from her home into a black Cadillac limousine. The drive to the Meridien took only a few minutes. At the hotel, the driver slipped the car into the line of vehicles inching to the Meridien's porte cochere.

Inside the lobby, Susan Ostroff handed over her evening bag to a polite young man who looked as if he would have been more at home in a linebacker's uniform than black tie. She passed through an airport-style metal detector and fell into the swirl of voices and movement in the magnificent atrium.

Such events usually brought out her family, and Ostroff knew where to find them—the A-list room. Her father, a courtly figure, greeted her with a strong embrace. Benjamin Ostroff was a strong backer of the President; paying a million for a table was both politically pleasing and shrewd. Her mother, bejeweled and overly plump, gave her delicate pecks on each cheek, inquired about a man—any man—in her life, her health, and her latest travels, in that order. Bernice Ostroff's greatest fear was that her daughter would be a spinster.

Susan Ostroff spent a few minutes with her older brother, who now ran the family business and whom she genuinely liked, and her sister, a hard-bitten, anorexic divorcée on the prowl for fresh upkeep.

Ostroff had her maximum of two drinks as she worked the lobby, touching base with foreign and domestic officials at her level or higher. When dinner was announced, she found herself seated between an earnest Dutch diplomat who rambled on about the need to revalue the Euro against the dollar, and the scion of a Mexican banking fortune whose thigh brushed hers under the table in what might or might not have been an accident.

Claudia Ballantine's speech, between the main course and dessert, was forceful to the point of passionate. Ostroff put on her attentive look, but having never had an affinity for children, she found the address turgid. Her thoughts were miles away, with Lin, his face in her mind's eye.

Ostroff stirred when everyone rose and started clapping. When the applause died down and dessert was being served, she seized the opportunity to excuse herself. All the talk was giving her a headache.

"Looks like she's headed to the ladies' room," Whip Alley said.

Standing beside him, Sloane watched Ostroff cross the lobby and disappear around the corner. She would have followed her inside, but she knew that no one had gone into that rest room in the last twenty minutes.

Sloane glanced at the mini rain forest and saw Mack walking past the caged macaws.

"Anything?" he asked.

Sloane shook her head.

"My bet is that she's going home."

Alley watched the people coming out of the salons.

Somewhere a band began to play. "She might stick around for a dance or two," he said.

Mack looked at him. "She didn't come with a date and it doesn't look like she's met anyone." He paused. "Look, you two can leave if you want. If Ostroff stays, I'll keep an eye on her."

Sloane wondered about Mack's offer. Mack was already in the hotel when she and Alley had arrived. There had been a tense moment when the two men had taken stock of each other. Sloane had wondered whether Mack could still read her as well as he once had, if he'd picked up on the bond between her and Alley. If he had, he hadn't shown it. He'd greeted Alley and Santana courteously and then launched into suggestions as to how best to cover Ostroff. They'd immediately agreed on one thing: Since Ostroff knew Sloane's face, Sloane had to keep her distance. The three men would take turns shadowing her.

"I'd just as soon stay," Sloane said.

In the few minutes they'd been talking, the lobby had become crowded. Women were headed for the rest rooms in droves. Sloane strained to catch a glimpse of Ostroff coming out.

"Something's not right," she said, and before either Alley or Mack could stop her, she was gone.

But it was too late. Susan Ostroff had emerged from the women's room just when the three watchers had been huddling. Now all eyes were on the crowds, Alley and Mack knifing swiftly through the throngs, scanning faces. No one bothered to look up at the glass-enclosed pod that was rising silently to the lounge high above the atrium.

* * *

"Out of the way!"

Chefs, cooks, and pot washers scattered before the phalanx of armed men who'd burst into their kitchens. Somewhere in the bristle of Uzi submachine guns and large-caliber handguns was General Samuel Murchison, in full uniform, striding as if he were Odin coming from Valhalla.

"Mon dieu, c'est la guerre!" he heard one of the chefs exclaim. The man cowered under Murchison's glare.

The general's bodyguards got him into the stairwell that led to the main floor. They followed him into a cinder-block corridor that ran along the side of the building and dead-ended at a fire-escape door. Two men stationed themselves at the doors, another pair by the door to the hotel manager's private suite. When Murchison entered, the Secret Service advance team was already checking it out.

In the De Gaulle Salon, Claudia Ballantine was leaning over to exchange words with Benjamin Ostroff when Holland Tylo caught her eye. The President recognized the agent's silent signal and pulled back from her guest. At the same time, she saw Jim Trimble snaking his way around the tables, his expression grim.

Claudia Ballantine immediately glanced at the air force officer within the Secret Service perimeter, at the briefcase chained to his wrist. The case was known as the Football, and the officer was never more than steps away from the President. The Football contained the communications apparatus that would allow the President to activate, in a nuclear emergency, the GO codes.

She noted the officer's impassive expression. That meant he had not received instructions, via his earpiece, to move next to her. But there was Trimble, leaning close enough so that his lips brushed the hair around her ear.

"We have a situation over Iraq. Satellite recon shows deployment of Scud missiles near suspected biochemical weapons sites. All indications are that Saddam is getting ready to load and launch."

Claudia Ballantine was intensely aware of how quiet the room had gone, how everyone was focused on her. She could not allow even a hint of her horror to reach them. She turned and smiled and waved at the crowd. She kept her pace deliberately even and didn't break it until she and her handlers were clear of the salon.

"Damn gown!" she muttered, moving as quickly as her dress would allow.

Fortunately, the manager's suite was nearby. Holland Tylo raced ahead to check the advance team's report. She wouldn't allow the President inside until they'd green-lighted the suite as secure. It was. Tylo hustled Claudia Ballantine inside, then took up her post outside the door.

"All right, Sam. What the hell's going on?"

Murchison was ready. "At 0400 Baghdad time, one of our satellites picked up thermal activity near the Basra Valley area. Photo reconnaissance produced these."

He handed over digitally enhanced satellite photos. There was no mistaking the mobile missile launchers and their deadly cargo.

"Thirty minutes later, the convoy arrived at this

complex." Murchison produced two more photographs.

"It looks like a hospital," Claudia Ballantine observed, puzzled. "The ambulances, Red Crescent trucks . . ."

"That's what they want us to believe," Murchison said. "Here's the latest U.N. weapons inspection team report on the site. It's conclusive: The place is in the business of making biological soup." He handed over one last picture. "Those aren't X-ray machines or MRIs, Madam President. They're warheads designed to carry loads of mass destruction. Saddam's loading his six-shot. The only questions are when he'll fire and at whom."

The President forced herself to remain very still in order to grasp what she'd been told. Then she turned to the national security adviser.

"Jim, your recommendation?"

"B-52s out of Diego Garcia are already airborne. Their cruise missiles are locked on this target. Everything on the carrier *George Washington* is on alert-one status. The planes are fueled and armed."

"How many?"

"Fifty all told."

"Fifty?" It seemed such a small number given the enormity of the threat.

"Of course, we're scrambling everything we have on the ground in Kuwait and Saudi Arabia—"

"Where we have to wait for permission to use them," Murchison cut in. *One hand tied behind the back—it always turns out that way.*

"Can we neutralize the immediate threat with the resources on hand?" the President asked coolly.

"Yes," Murchison replied. "If the order to attack is given soon."

"How soon?"

"You have no more than thirty minutes, Madam President. Once the warheads are loaded and affixed to the missiles, they can move those trucks around or fire at will."

The President looked at Trimble, who nodded. "What about the Israelis?" she asked.

"No one's told them yet."

"Tell them now. I'll speak to the prime minister from the car. Tell them what we know—and what we're going to do about it!"

Claudia Ballantine's eyes bore into her two advisers. "You're sure about the details? These pictures don't lie?"

"No, ma'am," Murchison replied.

"Then you're good to go."

"We'll need backup right away," Murchison added quickly. "We're stretched thin out in that sand."

"What do you need?"

"At least two more carriers. And an immediate air-lift out of the U.S."

"Do it," the President said flatly.

"Where are you going to get those carriers, Sam?" Trimble demanded.

"Out of the Taiwan Strait. At flank speed, I can have them on station in six days."

"That leaves Taiwan without any sea protection," Trimble protested. "You can't take away two entire battle groups just like that!"

"Taiwan isn't being threatened!" the President

snapped. "The old men in Beijing aren't getting ready to rain down anthrax on anyone."

"But, Madam President, it's a cardinal principle of warfare that once an action starts in one location, it will start in another, and a third, and so on. The key is to always maintain the established perimeter, not to break it up."

Claudia Ballantine held up her hand and Trimble fell silent. Tonight she had gone before her party and the country and once again asked for generosity so that a vicious disease could be driven off the face of the earth. Now a madman, who should have been put down years ago, was threatening to unleash a viral holocaust.

"Jim, if I'm about to send American men and women into harm's way, I have to give them every possible advantage and all the support at my disposal. Sam, you've got your battle groups. I'll deal with Beijing if the old men try to capitalize on this. Now let's get to the car. I want calls to Israel, Great Britain, Russia, and France lined up, in that order."

In the atrium lounge high above the lobby, a jazz combo was doing an excellent interpretation of a moody Miles Davis piece.

The lounge was circular, with a half-moon bar ringed by tables and chairs. There was a small dance floor off to one side that ran right up to the hip-high railing that separated it from the infinity pool. The ceiling was studded with pinprick lights arranged to mirror the constellations.

The lounge was crowded with a younger crowd

that had drifted up from the benefit. Susan Ostroff had to settle for a stool at the end of the bar, where she ordered a Chardonnay. She sipped the wine and took in the faces around her. This was where Dodge French had said he would meet her, where she would tell him that she had passed along his message to Lin.

Ten minutes ticked by. Then another five. Ostroff's glass was half empty and she was feeling a little buzz. The chicken Cordon Bleu had been greasy and she'd left most of it on her plate. What was keeping French? He was always so punctual. Now here she was, sitting like a bumpkin while all around her wanna-be studs put the moves on barely legal-age barons' daughters.

Feed 'em, fuck 'em, then deduct 'em, Ostroff thought cynically, watching a *GQ* type caress the back of a blond's neck.

"Would you care to dance? Seems a pity to waste such a beautiful piece."

Susan Ostroff shifted on her stool. She'd already given the man sitting beside her the once-over. He was probably the oldest one there, but damn if he wasn't the best looking of the lot. Swept-back silvery-gray hair, strong jaw, fine, long-fingered hands, the nails perfectly manicured. She wondered what it would be like to be touched by those hands, held, caressed . . .

She surprised herself by saying, "I'd love to."

She threaded her way to the crowded dance floor and turned as he took her hand. His touch was so light, his steps slow and sure, moving to the music, leading her through the notes. She edged closer to him, telling herself it was because of the other dancers. But it was his musky scent, beyond the expensive cologne he wore, that drew her. She hoped he wouldn't break the spell with words. The music was so soothing . . .

The Handyman had no intention of saying anything. He knew that Ostroff had come there to meet a man and that that man would never show. He had expected at least one of the baby-sitters to accompany her, but she'd come alone. Now he had a clear shot, but not much time in which to take it. With most of the hotel closed off, the baby-sitters would soon pay a visit to this lounge.

The Handyman glided closer to the railing. There the burble of the water being fed through the pumps blended with the music. He used his fingertips on her back and her hand in his to guide them to edge of the other dancers. For an instant, the Handyman almost didn't want to let her go. He'd studied her reflection in the bar mirror. This was a woman alone, dry and unloved for a long time. Yet there burned a fire within her eyes, and he knew she was imagining holding another man. An old lover, someone dead or otherwise beyond her reach? It didn't matter.

Time.

The Handyman slid his left hand up Susan Ostroff's back. He did not feel her stiffen until his thumb touched the bare skin of her neck. But any protest was far too late. The Handyman drove his thumb against the soft pulse of the carotid artery and Ostroff went limp. At the railing, he gave her a gentle push and let gravity do the rest—carry her over the railing and into the infinity pool.

Because of the music, the sound of rushing water, and the fixation the other dancers had on one another, no one cried out for several seconds. That was all the Handyman needed to move into the middle of the dancers and head the other way as they crowded around the railing.

Susan Ostroff regained some consciousness as soon as she hit the cold water. She flailed her arms and tried to move her legs, but they were trapped by the Norma Kamali gown. The wet fabric clung to her like a mummy's shroud. The current created by the pumps pulled her inexorably to the edge of the infinity pool.

The pool was only four feet deep, but Ostroff didn't have the presence of mind to stand up. She clawed at the water, and when the current dragged her to the edge, she tore her fingernails trying to grab hold of the smooth, curved cement wall of the infinity pool.

When the dancers screamed, the Handyman, standing by the glass elevator pod, knew she'd gone over the edge.

Sloane Ryder heard those screams too. She'd returned to the lobby after helping Alley check one of the salons. She craned her head, and the image of Susan Ostroff hanging on the edge of the pool became fixed forever in her mind. Because in the next instant, she disappeared into the cascading waters, dropping, only the black of her dress visible.

Suddenly there was a dull thud and the cascading water turned red. Ostroff's body reappeared from the water, her spine curled at a peculiar angle. She continued to fall that way, disappearing, reappearing. Only when Sloane had rushed up and jumped into the tropical pool where the waterfall ended did she look up and see the bleeding sawtoothed plates that had reduced Susan Ostroff to a mangled doll, floating among the lilies and the crazed, screeching birds.

25

DODGE FRENCH carefully timed his arrival at the gala. He was not interested in putting on his diplomatic face and socializing, nor did he want to hear more about the President's Hands of Hope crusade. He had come to witness only one thing, and it was now unfolding before him.

From his vantage point on the mezzanine balcony above the lobby, he saw Sloane Ryder plowing her way through the tropical pool, the waterfall drenching her as she tried to pull Susan Ostroff's body toward the edge. The two detectives were there, too, the bigger one blocking the straining onlookers, the other climbing into the pool to help Ryder.

French's eyes flitted across the faces below. Word that an accident had occurred brought people into knots of three or four, rapidly exchanging questions. The lobby was becoming even more congested as guests continued to emerge from the salons, having heard about the tragedy.

There was commotion by the soaring spiral staircase next to the glass elevator that serviced the lounge. French recognized Peter Mack, his hands gripping both rails, his arms braced to prevent lounge guests from stampeding into the lobby crowds. What the devil was he doing?

Witnesses. He's keeping the witnesses together.

Mack yelled over his shoulder and a big detective bulled his way to the staircase just in time to corral a slew of guests.

French clenched his teeth in anger. He had ordered Peter Mack to *use* Ryder and her detectives, not help them. Under the circumstances, it was clear that Mack had betrayed French's trust.

Unpardonable.

French quickly examined the possible consequences. He was not afraid of witnesses. Mai Ling's man, and French's protector, was reputed to be the best at his trade. His work tonight was testimony to his skills. No, witnesses weren't the issue. But there were other areas in which the killer's skills could be applied.

French used the long walk along the mezzanine balcony to the sweeping staircase to collect himself. Garrett and Ostroff had been eliminated in ways that raised more questions than answers. Ryder and her flatfoots—now with Peter Mack in tow—would try to make the next connection, to Murchison. But that, French reflected, would be substantially more difficult.

On the broader front, the Iraqis had acted exactly as Beijing wished. There would be some saber rattling and heated late-night meetings. In the end, American air power would wipe out the facility in the Basra Valley, Baghdad would sue for a cease-fire, and hostilities would be suspended. But the time French needed would have been bought. The two U.S. battle groups would have arrived on station in the Persian Gulf and would stay there, grim reminders of further punishment that could be inflicted for Saddam Hussein's mischief.

Meanwhile, the Taiwan Strait would remain defenseless.

"Grab her feet! We'll swing her over."

Alley crouched and pushed his hands under Ostroff's limp arms. He made sure Sloane had a good grip on the woman's ankles and together they lifted the body over the tiled edge of the pond. Sloane's muscles were screaming as she gently lowered Ostroff to the floor.

The doctor on call for the gala pushed his way through the crowd. Shivering, Sloane watched as he crouched beside the body, looking for signs of life. She read the conclusion in his eyes.

"I'm sorry," he said. "She's gone."

The crowds parted as the paramedics arrived. Someone threw a blanket over Sloane's shoulders and she wrapped it tightly around herself. With the paramedics came the police, and slowly the lobby was cleared except for the people who'd been in the lounge.

"How many do you think we got?" Alley demanded, watching patrol officers herd the potential witnesses toward the open area around the reception desk.

"Not all of them," Peter Mack replied. "I saw at least two elevator loads come down. Who knows how many scattered before I got to the stairs."

"We have the staff and the band," Alley said tightly. "The bartenders and waitresses can tell us if she was with anyone. Musicians usually look around at their audience. Maybe one of them saw something."

"We should go up there. Now."

Both men turned to Sloane, who shrugged off the wet blanket and headed for the elevator.

The exodus from the lounge had turned into a stampede. Tables and chairs had been overturned. The floor was slick with spilled drinks and broken glass. Cautiously, Alley approached the railing in front of the infinity pool. He did not touch it, but from what he could see it seemed solid enough—no cracks or breaks.

"How the hell did she fall in?" Mack whispered.

"She didn't fall in," Sloane said dully. "Someone pushed her. Maybe he knocked her out first—I don't know how—and then he pushed her."

Alley swore under his breath. He pointed to the water slipping over the concrete embankment into the infinity pool. The pumps were still running.

"There goes our trace evidence," he said bitterly. "There were what—fifty, sixty people up here? Even if we found and fingerprinted all of them, we'd never get a match. The water washed her clean."

"There's a chance the body will talk to us," Mack said in a low voice. "Garrett's did."

Alley shot him a hard look. "Didn't do us much good, did it?"

Below, more police had arrived and were quickly clearing the lobby. The emergency medical team had bagged Ostroff's body and were set to wheel it out to the coroner's van. The first team of detectives was on the scene. They were talking to the hotel manager, who pointed alternately at the witnesses by the reception desk and up at the three people on the lounge level.

"Time to go to work," Alley said.

"You could use an extra body," Mack offered. "To question the witnesses."

Alley nodded, then turned to Sloane. "You need to get out of those clothes. I'll radio for a patrol car to pick you up at the loading dock."

He squeezed her hand and was gone, following Mack down the staircase. Sloane shivered in her wet clothing. Whip was right, she had to change. But she had to do something else first.

She picked her way through the litter toward the railing, her eyes fixed on the floor. There were several purses lying around, forgotten in the melee, and she opened them all. Only one had any ID, and not the one she was looking for. The gruff voices carried up from the lobby. She had only seconds before the detectives would swarm up and seal off the lounge.

She was closer to the pool's edge now, wishing that she had more light to work with. What if Ostroff's bag had dropped into the water? It could be anywhere by now—in the pool below, snagged in the chute, caught in one of the drains or pumps.

But it wasn't. Sloane didn't really see the bag—the toe of her shoe nudged it. It was small enough to have become wedged in a crevice between the floor and the tiled border of the pool. Her fingers raced through the contents, ignoring the makeup kit, tearing open the zipper to a tiny compartment. There was a thin fold of hundred-dollar bills, an American Express card, and Ostroff's driver's license. And two other cards: one a State Department picture ID, the other a plain white card with a magnetic strip. Sloane took them both and left the purse behind.

"Hey, what are you doing there?"

The detective's voice boomed across the empty space. Sloane rose, palming the cards.

"I'm with Detective Alley," she said.

"Yeah, well, he's downstairs and you're disturbing a crime scene." He jerked his thumb toward the staircase.

Sloane hurried past him. A few minutes later, she was through the kitchens and on the loading dock. As Alley had promised, a patrol car was waiting.

The President's chief of staff learned about the tragic accident at the Meridien thirty minutes after it happened. Since the President was occupied, in a heated exchange with a recalcitrant French prime minister, he wasn't about to pass on the news. The incident had occurred after Claudia Ballantine had left the hotel. From initial reports, there was nothing to link the death to the White House or to the events that were unfolding tonight across the globe. The chief of staff thanked his D.C. police liaison officer for calling in the incident, asked for a follow-up report when one became available, and switched to another call.

With its siren screaming and light rack flashing, the patrol car made good time out to Brook Hill. Sloane thanked the young patrolman and ran into the house. Seconds later, she was under a shower, the water as hot as she could stand it. After driving the chill from her bones, she slipped into a turtleneck sweater and wool pants. Twenty minutes later, she was on the road again, headed back to the capital in Alley's car.

Given its transglobal responsibilities, the State Department was one of the government agencies that never closed. Sloane hoped that to get in at this time of night all she would need was the white coded card.

As she drove through the deserted Washington streets, Sloane wondered if she should have called Lee Porter and told him what she intended to do. Maybe he would have told her to go ahead. *Or maybe he would've shut me down, told me to wait till he got a warrant.*

The image of Susan Ostroff's body breaking apart in the waterfall pushed against her eyes. She'd already waited too long. Ostroff could give her nothing now. But maybe she'd left something useful behind, something her killer might also be interested in—something he couldn't be allowed to get to first.

Sloane turned off Twenty-third Street and drove toward the blinking orange lamps at the top of the garage ramp on C Street. Inching the car down the incline, she found, on the driver's side, a key-card slot and a video camera. Beyond that was a shuttered steel door. Sloane knew that if the key card wasn't accepted, not only would alarms go off, but tire-shredding spikes would pop up behind her car. She'd be trapped.

Holding her breath, she inserted Ostroff's card. The camera continued to regard her with its unblinking eye. The scanning machine didn't seem to reject the card, but Sloane had her hand on the stick shift, ready to slam it into reverse.

The steel-shuttered door groaned and started to

rumble up. Sloane exhaled slowly, retrieved the card, and gently rolled into the garage, descending two levels before she found Ostroff's reserved space.

Sloane hurried toward the elevators. Having studied Ostroff so thoroughly, she knew exactly where to go. The question was whether she could get there in time. The fact that Ostroff's card had been accepted meant that State Department security was unaware of her death. So far.

Sloane swiped the card again and the elevator doors parted. Inside was the ubiquitous camera. Sloane ignored it. She pressed a floor button and her stomach lifted as the car began its ascent.

The reception area was deserted; pools of light illuminated the gray carpet. Sloane had to swipe the card again to get into the main office area, then she hurried down the hall. Ostroff's office was at the very end, a spacious corner suite with handsome furniture and a small sitting area. Sloane flipped on the lights and went immediately to the computer. In less than ten seconds, she realized that the machine was impenetrable, the contents of its hard drive guarded by NSA–designed encryption and lockdowns.

It doesn't matter, Sloane told herself. *It's history I'm after, not her current projects.*

The desk drawers were unlocked and yielded nothing except State Department memoranda. The bookshelves held volumes ranging from the latest edition of *Jane's Fighting Ships* to back issues of *Foreign Policy*. And then there were the storage cabinets underneath the shelves. The doors of the middle one opened to reveal a squat, steel cube.

The keypad on the front of the safe was alphanumeric. Sloane stared at the simple letters and numbers. They might as well have been hieroglyphics.

Think about her. Think like her. What is she? Very smart, very cool, a professional. What would she use? What would you use?

Sloane rifled through everything she knew about Ostroff. The combination could be anything—a phone number, part of a DMV tag, a birthday . . . All these were things Sloane knew about. That *everyone* either knew about Ostroff or could uncover.

Exactly the things Ostroff would never use.

What wouldn't be in her 202 personnel file? Or in the department's security-clearance computers? Or unknown to a close friend or even her family?

She is a woman alone. By personality, by choice—by design.

Sloane thought she had it then. She looked at the safe carefully, but it refused to offer any hints. She couldn't tell whether it was hardwired into an alarm system that would go off if the wrong combination was entered. Sloane looked down at her hands, her fingertips still puckered from the icy water through which she'd hauled Susan Ostroff's body.

Go for broke.

Crouching in front of the safe, concentrating on keeping her hands steady, she pressed the keys one at a time: G-A-R-R-E-T-T.

The red light on the keypad blinked off, replaced by a green one. Sloane blinked away sweat, twisted the handle, and pulled.

Computer disks, at least fifty of them. Sloane shoveled all of them into her sling bag. She felt inside again, but found nothing else. Locking the safe, she closed the cabinet doors.

Sloane was in the corridor, walking swiftly, when the call came into the State Department security office. The duty officer checked the speaker's ID in the computer, then listened to what he had to say.

"Dr. Susan Ostroff, head of the China section, suffered a fatal accident this evening. You can check with the D.C. police for details. In the meantime, a security team from NSA is on its way to remove sensitive documents from her office. The agents are not to be interfered with."

"Yes, sir," the duty officer said. "But someone's got his wires crossed."

"Meaning?"

"Dr. Ostroff logged in twenty minutes ago. She's up in her office right now."

Sloane swiped Ostroff's card at the elevator. She lost a few seconds because she looked away and didn't notice that the light on the pad was still red. The elevator doors weren't opening. Then she knew.

She whirled around and dashed for the stairwell door. She wasn't familiar with the building's shut-down procedures. The elevators were frozen. Security would be swarming to the third floor. The garage doors . . .

She refused to think about that. The clatter of her shoes created a hellish racket in the cement-walled stairwell. Each time she passed a door, she expected it to fly open, revealing a man pointing a gun at her.

She was on the main level now, fingers sliding off the slippery gun-metal banister paint, shins and knees skimming off rails as she careened around the corners. She hit the door to the garage at full speed, heard it slam against its rubber stopper and hit the wall. Racing for her car, the vehicle looking tiny in the concrete tomb that was half a football field long.

The lights blinded her first, the high beams of an oncoming car. Before Sloane could react, the sedan was upon her, veering away at the last instant, the stink of hot brake pads and tire rubber filling the air. "Jump in!" a voice shouted.

Because she recognized it, Sloane did just that. She barely had time to slam the door before the car rocketed toward the exit ramp to the first sublevel.

"Are you okay? Are you hurt?"

Sloane glanced at Lee Porter, his hands working the wheel as he steered through tight curves, taking shortcuts to another ramp.

"I'm okay."

"Did you get what you came for?" Sloane stared at him. *"Did you get what you came for?"*

"I don't know. I think so."

"Well, I sure as hell *hope* so. Because the shit has really hit the fan." Porter paused. "Now listen to me. Whatever happens, don't say a word. Not a word. Understand?"

"How did you know—?"

"Later. First, we have to get out of here. Get ready."

Through the windshield, Sloane saw the steel-shuttered garage door and three armed men standing in front of it, their automatic rifles held at port arms.

Porter cruised up to them as if he was slowing down at a tollbooth. He held up his ID for the security guard.

"The person I came to see wasn't in," he said amiably. "Must have gotten the appointment time wrong."

The guard's eyes flashed to the video monitor. "Mr. Porter, you were cleared to enter, but we have no record of this young lady."

"She's with me. Show 'em your picture, Sloane."

Sloane pulled out her MJ-11 credentials. The guard scanned the monitor again. "We have no record of her arrival."

Porter shrugged. "It's late. We have an appointment to keep. Is there a problem?"

"The problem, sir, is that we're in lockdown mode because of an intruder."

"Well, I'm not your intruder and neither is Ms. Ryder."

Out of the corner of her eye, Sloane saw the guard hesitate. "I'll have to detain the young lady, sir."

Porter reached for his phone. "The number I'm dialing belongs to the national security adviser, who is now in the White House Situation Room. With the President. Who is expecting Ms. Ryder and me immediately. Maybe you'd like to explain why we're not on our way."

Porter stuck the phone out at the guard. Sloane could hear ringing on the other end, then a low, gravelly voice: "Trimble, NSC. Hello? *Hello?*"

The guard backed off and signaled his men to raise the door. Calmly, Porter broke the connection and replaced the phone in its cradle. Laying six feet of rubber, he raced into the night.

Sloane felt relief wash over her. Her sling bag, with the disks safely inside, was between her knees.

"How did you find me?" she asked.

Porter's eyes cut to her, then back to the road. "You'd left the hotel, no answer at Alley's house except the machine, so I took a guess."

"Lucky for me."

"What's going on, Sloane?"

"That's a question I should be asking you. The minute you learned that Ostroff's card was missing, you knew I'd be here."

"I thought that whoever Ostroff was reporting to might try to sanitize her office," Porter said.

"Someone from MJ-11?"

Porter worried his lower lip. "All right, I would have told you eventually. Listen to me. What is one common denominator between Garrett and Ostroff?"

Sloane thought for a moment. "China. They were both experts on things Chinese."

"And what was it that totaled your career in New York?"

"MacGregor."

"Not only him."

"Mi Yang. The business with East China Oil."

"Right," Porter said. "We've been monitoring Chinese financial activity very closely since the '92 and '94 elections, when there were charges that their money might have been funneled into various political campaigns. Since then, we've learned a lot about how they move money, where, through whom, and why. MacGregor and his Chinese counterpart, Mi Yang, had set up a huge oil deal. Question: Why were the

Chinese, who need every drop of energy they can get, ready to go public with East China Oil instead of keeping it a state monopoly? What was more important than a steady, reliable energy source?"

"Money. Cash. A lot of it."

"Tens of billions. The Chinese were raising capital and they needed it fast. Almost as if they had some deadline."

"Related to what?"

"We don't know yet. Then you come along and pull the rug out from under MacGregor. A little later, he ends up killing himself in the middle of Park Avenue. You take the fall and become everyone's black sheep."

"Then you come along because you think I might know something more than just MacGregor's arrangement with Mi Yang," Sloane finished.

"We were already tracking the Chinese on our end," Porter said. "We know they're reading our mail, but we can't prove it. We don't know who their postman is. I start thinking that you might be the one to stir things up for us, maybe point us in the right direction."

"'Fresh eyes, no baggage.'"

"What?"

"That's what you said about me. Instead, I've become a ferret." She turned to him. "Goddammit, why couldn't you have been up-front with me?"

"Because I didn't want to prejudice your instincts. I didn't want to tell you anything that would make you go in one direction as opposed to another. *You* had to decide that."

"I did—and two people are dead."

"Not because of you!" Porter said fiercely. "Listen to me. This thing is accelerating. People don't get killed until the endgame. And that's coming up fast. You took an incredible risk tonight and maybe you came away with something we can use. What do you say?"

Sloane stared at him. "I say we find out what's on these disks."

By first light, the last witness was allowed to leave. The lobby was almost deserted except for a skeletal investigation crew checking the drains and the chute in the now silent waterfall. Whip Alley, Paco Santana, and Peter Mack had pages of notes to show for their interrogation efforts.

Susan Ostroff's evening clutch had been found; most of the contents were intact, but her State Department ID was missing.

Paco Santana looked around at the vast, empty lobby with only police techs going about their business.

"We missed him," he said flatly. "He was here and we missed him."

"Who did we miss?" Mack snapped. He flipped through the pages of his notebook. "Here's the piano player: 'The guy was an older dude, with a ponytail.' The guy on bass: 'Yeah, she was dancing with some guy, maybe forty or something. He looked a little like Mel Gibson.' And the bartender: 'I don't know. It was pretty crazy up here. I know she had a glass of wine. There was an older guy sitting beside her. The next time I turned around, they were gone.'"

Mack held up his hand as if to say "And?"

"There was too much going on," Santana muttered.

"The crowd up there was trolling for someone to go home with. Between the booze and the drugs, they could have tripped over a potbellied pig and not known it. The question is, what was Ostroff doing up there? That wasn't her kind of scene."

"Maybe she was looking to get lucky too," Mack suggested. "She may come off as all prim and proper but—"

"She was set up."

Alley said, "Paco's right. She was out of place in that crowd. Her family was downstairs, along with the other movers and shakers. There was no reason for her to be in that bar . . . unless she was waiting for someone special, someone who knew that it'd be the one place they could have some privacy and anonymity. Sure there'd be a crowd, but not *their* crowd."

"And that someone killed her," Mack finished.

"No. That someone set her up for the killer."

Mack rose and went over to the coffee service that the hotel had provided for law enforcement.

"Ten of the witnesses we've interviewed agree that she was dancing with this guy," he said. "Problem is, his description is all over the map. Plus, no one actually saw her fall into the pool. No one said her dance partner pushed her or hit her, or did anything."

"Except that one minute he's there, the next he's disappeared," Santana rumbled.

"Which is why I'll go along with you: Ostroff was murdered. But there's nothing I can take to the Bureau." Mack paused. "And keep in mind, all the witnesses talk about one guy, not two."

"The setup man wouldn't have been close by," Alley

said. "He was someone Ostroff knew and trusted. Otherwise, why bother to follow directions? She agreed to a meet outside her element, figured she was safe enough because of the crowds. Whoever set her up is one clever son of a bitch. Ostroff never saw the hit coming—just the way it was intended."

"The bottom line is, we have no proof that it was a hit," Mack said. "Without that—"

Alley's cell phone went off. He flipped it open, listened, then turned to the others.

"Sloane. She has something for us."

The lighting in the GAO offices is better than in most government buildings, the expensive kind that mimics sunlight. Nonetheless, Sloane felt it grind behind her eyes like sugar glass.

But what was on the computer screen more than made up for the nonstop work she'd put in since she and Porter had arrived. She was checking the sequence one more time when Alley and the others came in.

"Gentlemen," Porter said, putting aside his pipe. "A long night, by the look of it."

"And zip to show for it," Alley said.

"Tell me."

A few minutes later, Porter understood why the trio was so frayed around the edges.

"Sloane, show them what you found."

She turned the monitor so that all of them could see it. She told them about her unauthorized foray into Ostroff's office. Sloane couldn't say who wore the more incredulous expression, Whip Alley or Peter Mack. Paco Santana beamed proudly.

"What you see on the screen is information Ostroff had been storing on disk for years. Some of this stuff goes back to the late eighties."

She worked the mouse and documents flashed on the screen.

"This is all classified secret or higher," Mack said softly. "Coming out of places like the Rand Corporation, the Hoover Institution on War—"

"All the places that Martin Garrett worked before Trimble brought him into the White House," Sloane said. "And there's a common denominator to everything he passed on to Ostroff."

"China," Alley said. "Everything so far has been about China."

"It gets worse," Sloane continued. "Here are position papers, war-game scenarios, economic and political digests that Garrett passed to Ostroff after he'd started working at the White House. All of this material is highly sensitive. It was meant to stay inside the office of the national security adviser. Ostroff had no business seeing any of it."

"And you're sure it couldn't have been anyone but Garrett?" Mack asked.

Mack's tone revealed how sickened he was by this deep and long-running breach of security. Sloane wished there was something she could say to help him, but there was more to come, and none of it good.

"It's Garrett," she said. "We have his signature on some of the documents. We have Ostroff's notes on the source."

"And?" Alley asked quietly.

"And we now know that Susan Ostroff once had a

brief but passionate affair with a Taiwanese Chinese by the name of Lin. He's seen as the major voice for reunification. He's unabashedly pro Beijing."

"Shit!" Mack whispered.

"There's no indication that Ostroff was feeding Lin anything she received from Garrett."

"That doesn't track. Why wouldn't she?"

"Because she was sending it elsewhere."

"To Murchison," Alley said. "His name is all over her entries."

Mack's face was ashen. "The chairman of the Joint Chiefs? She was feeding *him* information?"

"The kind Murchison might never see, or see too late for it to be useful to him. Come on, Mack. You know how compartmentalized the intelligence community is. It's all about one-upmanship, making sure you know something the other guy doesn't so that you can beat him over the head with it and at the same time make yourself look good."

"Okay," Mack said slowly. "So what we have here is classified information about China that's been taken out of channels and is being passed along a pipeline. *But that pipeline is within our own government.*"

Lee Porter spoke up. "No one creates this kind of system just to stay in the know. This pipeline was created to feed one individual, someone so trustworthy that the mere thought of his being a traitor would be outrageous. Whoever he is, he's the one who finally connects to the Chinese."

"You're talking about a conspiracy ten times more intricate and effective than Robert Hanssen's treachery," Mack said, referring to the FBI agent who had turned out to be a notorious double agent.

"Is it Murchison?" Alley asked. "Is he the last link? Christ knows, he can do pretty much what he wants, see anyone anywhere and not raise eyebrows. The perfect conduit."

"We don't know if the chain stops with him," Porter said.

"Why don't we ask him?"

Porter looked at him curiously, then realized that Alley might not have heard the latest news.

"Come over here."

He walked the group into his office, where a television flickered, the volume low. The scene could have been documentary footage from the Gulf War: the Iraqi sky all lit up by tracers and missiles, creating a phantasmagoric fireworks display, a quick cut to a U.S. Navy warship launching a Tomahawk missile, the reports from correspondents all over the Gulf.

"This started about five hours ago," Porter said. "Satellite reconnaissance and overflights indicated that the Iraqis were loading Scud missiles with biochemical warheads. The President ordered an immediate preemptive strike. This"—he gestured at the screen—"is a little extra, taking out the Republican Guard barracks."

Porter looked at Alley. "That's why we can't ask Murchison. He's off in some command bunker pounding salt up Saddam's ass."

26

LIKE MOST OF the nation and the world, Sloane and Alley were consumed by the news coming out of the Gulf during the next seventy-two hours. In the evenings, they huddled together on the couch, watching the round-the-clock air raids carried out by U.S. fighters, bombers, and missiles. Military briefings offered bird's-eye pictures of direct hits on Iraqi weapons sites; correspondents on the ground confirmed the carnage.

"A slap on the wrist it's not," Alley observed.

During the day, Sloane hunted, putting General Sam Murchison's life and military career under a microscope. She began at West Point and paid special attention to his tours in Southeast Asia, always searching for a Chinese connection she knew had to be there. There were tangents and digressions, most of them leading to dead ends. But slowly the number of individuals who were instrumental in Murchison's career dwindled to a manageable handful. One of these men, Sloane thought, had to be Murchison's master.

When the list was pared to one, Sloane asked for a meeting with Lee Porter and Peter Mack. She knew what Peter's reaction to her conclusions would be and had debated including him. She decided that in the end, he would honor his oath to his profession and carry out his duty.

In Porter's office, she watched Porter and Mack read her report, then felt Mack's bright and angry eyes bore into hers.

"You're kidding, right?" he said. "Tell me this is a joke."

"No joke," Sloane replied.

"You're sure about this?" Porter asked quietly.

"This is the man Murchison calls and meets with on a regular basis," Sloane said. "The common connection is China."

"It's inconceivable!" Mack replied.

"Most traitors are inconceivable."

"I know. But this . . ."

She could feel Mack struggling with his disbelief.

"There's something else to consider," Porter said. "Because of the current situation in Iraq, there may be a problem laying this out for the President. What we know—and suspect—will undermine her confidence in Murchison's ability to do his job."

"Which he seems to be doing damn well," Mack said.

Porter agreed. "Plus, there's been a development concerning Lin. It seems that he's *not* going to run for a seat in the Taiwanese parliament. The rumor mill in Asia is working overtime, wondering what the hell that means. But all indicators are that Lin will not be a factor."

"Which means that Trimble has lost another argument about how Taiwan might be vulnerable to a Chinese attack," Sloane said.

Porter had told her and the others about Trimble's concerns at the last White House meeting.

"It's almost as though someone is deliberately undercutting Trimble, making him look bad, or at least incompetent, in front of the President," she concluded.

"Careful where you go with that," Mack warned.

"Where *can* I go with it?" Sloane shot back. "Susan Ostroff was Lin's lover. Lin is rabidly pro unification, and suddenly he abandons his life's goal just as he's on the brink of achieving it? Not without a very good reason. Not unless someone told him that he had to."

"Ostroff?" Porter queried.

"My money's on her," Sloane said. "She had more than enough chances to contact him. Or to get Murchison to do it."

"Let's get back to Murchison," Mack said. "What's our play on him?"

"Nothing until he's back in the country," Porter replied.

"And then?"

"We sit him down with Ostroff's disks and listen to what he has to say."

"Jesus, Porter! You're talking about interrogating a soldier who's going to come home a hero," Mack said.

"I'm not questioning Murchison's battlefield command," Porter said flatly. "They can give him all the medals they want for that. I want to know about other things."

Sloane looked carefully at Mack. "Peter, do you have a problem with any of this?"

Mack used the tip of his pen to push away the paper

that had the name on it, as though he didn't want to dirty himself by touching it.

"This is what I have a problem with," he said, struggling to choose between competing loyalties—to his oath as an FBI agent, to the man he believed was above reproach.

In the end, Peter Mack realized there wasn't really any choice at all.

Mack drove to the Four Seasons Hotel in Georgetown through the evening rush hour. Tuning in National Public Radio, he heard the breaking news of a cease-fire in the Gulf.

The bar in the hotel was filled with talk of nothing else. A cheer went up when the television commentator detailed the terms of the cease-fire and just how devastating the aerial assault had been. Mack did not join in the celebration. He sat at the end of the bar with a glass of Old Weller Antique bourbon, drinking too fast. The more his thoughts turned over, the clearer his course of action became and, staring down into the amber liquid, he saw no reprieve. Pulling out his cell phone, he made the call.

Thirty minutes later, he was negotiating the driveway of the grand home. A manservant opened the door and ushered him into the library with its scent of wood smoke and pungent tobacco. Dodge French greeted him in black tie.

"There's a party at the country club," he explained, and looked at Mack carefully. "You said this was urgent, Peter."

Mack stared into that wise old face full of concern

and anticipation. He thought back to Sloane and Lee Porter. No. He had to go his own way.

"MJ-11 is moving very fast," he said. "You gave me the tip about Ostroff, but Sloane and the others were already on to her. Her death was no accident."

French used a poker on the logs in the fireplace. He turned around slowly, the iron still in his hand.

"Really? That's contrary to the reports I've heard. If not an accident, what then?"

Mack watched French's expression become incredulous as he recounted Sloane's assassination theory.

"Does Porter have any proof?" he asked when Mack finished.

"Nothing about the assassin, but Sloane connected Garrett to Ostroff and Ostroff to someone else."

"Has she now?"

French wondered about that—since it was he who'd made the call to State Department security, alerting them to the fact that Susan Ostroff had had a fatal accident and that her office should be sealed forthwith. But security had gotten there too late. Ryder had been inside that office and, worse, in the safe. The minute Sam Murchison had conveyed Ostroff's threat of exposure, French had known that Ostroff must have had something to back up her words. He had intended to have the office looted the night of the gala, but he'd waited too long. He'd wanted her dead first to ensure privacy.

French listened with dread and fascination as Mack recounted what was on the disks Ryder had hauled out of Ostroff's office. In the end, he realized that her motive for betraying him was rooted in something that he, who had never married or ever carried a torch, could not understand: being in love.

"You have no reason to doubt the authenticity of the information on those disks, Peter?"

"No, sir."

"And Ostroff named Murchison as her conduit for the information she and Garrett had been gathering?"

"That's right."

French shook his head. "I find this all so incredible. Sam Murchison involved in espionage. It's unthinkable."

"Ryder and Porter don't believe so, sir."

"Proof, Peter, proof! What is Murchison doing with this information? Whom is he passing it to?"

"Ryder and Porter don't know—yet," Mack replied. He paused. "I can't believe that a man like Murchison could be guilty of treason, sir."

"Nor should you believe it!" French moved around the room, pounding a fist into an open palm. "I know what to do. With the cease-fire in effect, I can get through to Sam. I'll explain what's going on—"

"Sir, do you think that's wise?"

"Wise? It's absolutely necessary. Sam is one of my oldest friends. Believe me, he cannot lie to my face and get away with it. And if he is guilty of even a minor infraction of some sort, Peter, I will bring him to you myself!"

After Mack departed, Dodge French went to the River Run club, which his family had helped found. There he toasted the President's victory in the Gulf and traded in speculation as to what events might follow. Punctually at midnight he was back at Kalorama. The rooms were quiet now, and he drifted through them like a ghost.

Finally, from his bedroom, he made the call—not halfway across the world, but across town.

Like French, Mai Ling worked late and slept little. She was awake and alert when she took the call. French heard her sucking on her cigarette holder.

"There have been some developments you should be aware of," he said, and went on to explain. "You realize that if they get to Murchison, he will serve me up," he concluded.

"Yes, he will," Mai Ling agreed. She also agreed with the remedy French proposed. "Only nine days, French. We only have to keep things as they are for nine more days."

"Nine days," he repeated.

Dodge French knew, better than most people, just how much blood could be spilled in nine days.

General Sam Murchison left the Gulf two hours after the declared cease-fire, aboard an SR-71 spy plane. Code named Blackbird, the aircraft was capable of flying at four times the speed of sound at an altitude of 125,000 feet. Three hours after its departure, Blackbird touched down at Andrews Air Force Base. There Murchison showered and changed and was driven to his appointment at the White House.

The President rose from her chair and stepped across the great seal, woven into the carpet of the Oval Office.

"Hello, Sam. It's good to have you home. Congratulations."

"Thank you, Madam President."

Murchison thought Claudia Ballantine had lost weight. Her eyes were puffy and her movements quick, almost brusque. He could not know that part of her condition was due to grief over the senseless death of a friend, Susan Ostroff.

"Do you think the cease-fire will hold?" Ballantine asked.

"You've set the terms, Madam President. The question is whether or not Saddam will comply. Preparations for a second strike are under way." He paused. "We're good to go at any time."

"Give me the full background, please."

Murchison kept his briefing succinct, but still it took over an hour.

"Bottom line, Sam?"

"We should go in and finish the job."

"But the civilian casualties would be high."

"Only because civilians are being used as human shields, forced to sleep outside Saddam's palaces. That they do so makes them frontline fighters, soldiers like any other."

"I'll have to consider that, Sam."

"Of course."

Beneath his impassive expression, Murchison was seething. Years ago, he had been forced to deny the commanders of Desert Storm their finishing off of Iraq once and for all. Given the way Saddam had toyed with the West in the intervening years, this time the go order should have been automatic. But again a civilian was showing that she didn't have the stomach to give such a command.

After leaving the West Wing, Murchison had his driver take him home, to the house he and his wife, twelve years gone now from cancer, had bought in the mid-seventies in Chevy Chase. The sprawling one-story bungalow was set on a wooded double lot and backed onto a ravine that was virtually impassable. The front had a rolling lawn and low shrubbery that afforded no cover. The neighboring homes were ninety feet away, separated by high hedges, and their owners had been Murchison's friends for years.

A two-man security team had been stationed at the house since the outbreak of hostilities. The residence was absolutely secure when Murchison stepped inside.

His first order of business was to go into his study and pour a large scotch. Drink in hand, he did what he always did when he returned from abroad: He went over to the credenza, its gleaming pecan top filled with framed photos, and gently ran his fingertips over the pictures of himself and his wife. It was a pictorial history of twenty-one years of marriage, cruelly cut off just when he was about to reap the rewards of a lifetime's service to his country.

Murchison carried his drink into the master suite. He took a quick shower, then bundled himself up in a fleece jogging outfit. He topped off his whiskey from the small wet bar and went to the sitting area. The telephone console there, like the one in his study, was equipped with satellite capability and a digital scrambler. Murchison speed-dialed French's number.

"Dodge?"

"Sam. Where are you?"

"Home. I flew in a few hours ago. The President wanted a one-on-one update."

"And?"

"The usual." Murchison gave him the gist of his meeting with Claudia Ballantine. "She doesn't have the stones to finish the job."

Dodge French picked up on the soldier's frustration and anger. "Nine days, Sam. How long will you be here?"

"At least forty-eight hours. That's how long the cease-fire's supposed to last."

"Good. Because there's something that needs to be done."

"I heard there was an incident at the Meridien."

"Susan Ostroff suffered a fatal accident."

Murchison closed his eyes. "Of course she did. That's it, then."

"I'm afraid it isn't. Ryder and her team know that she's connected to you. If they had any idea that you were back in the country, they'd be on your doorstep right now."

Murchison took a deep swallow of his drink, the liquor making him cough. "Christ almighty, Dodge! How could you let this get so out of hand?"

"It's not out of hand," French replied smoothly. "It just means that we have to neutralize the situation."

Murchison's laugh had a hysterical edge to it. "Neutralize the situation? And how many more people are going to die?"

"A whole lot less than if we do nothing," French replied coldly. He could hear ice rattling in a glass at the other end of the line. "One more mission, Sam. That's all we need. Just one."

It's always one more, Murchison thought. *To bury the mistakes and stupidities and to rewrite history.*

"All right," he said. "I'm listening."

West of the capital, along Route 66, at Tyson's Corner, was a megamall anchored by a Nordstrom's, a Bloomingdale's, and a Ritz-Carlton Hotel. Tens of thousands of shoppers passed through it every day, more as the countdown to Thanksgiving and the pre-holiday sales kicked in. Surveillance of an individual in such a vast place was virtually impossible. Even if the FBI shadow teams had been aware of Mai Ling's true standing in China's embassy, she would easily have eluded them in the crush of the crowds.

The Handyman found her in the cavernous food court, sitting at a long counter opposite a row of fast-food outlets. The area was jammed with shoppers bolting a quick snack, the floor littered with their bags and packages.

Mai Ling had a cup of steaming tea in front of her.

The Handyman took a seat beside her and sipped what was a barely passable café latte. Living in France for so many years had spoiled him for American coffee.

Mai Ling pushed a sealed envelope over to him. Opening it, the Handyman was intrigued by the photographs inside.

"This must be done very soon," she said. "The day after tomorrow, no later. There is flexibility about the time, but not the place." She told him where that was.

The Handyman knew the area Mai Ling referred to. It was a popular memorial in Washington, a beating heart beneath an old, deep scar. Thousands visited every day; many lingered for hours.

He turned the image over in his mind, examining it from every angle, searching for the site's vulnerability. The geography stymied him.

But not the time of day.

The Handyman pushed away the cold coffee. "It will have to be done at night. The sun sets between five-thirty and a quarter to six, so between six and half past. It'll be rush hour, and that will help too."

Mai Ling smiled and nodded. "That can be arranged."

Forty-eight hours after Peter Mack's visit to Dodge French, Lee Porter's secure phone rang.

"Mr. Porter, this is General Murchison."

Porter activated the recording system on his line.

"Yes, General. Are you calling from the Gulf?"

Murchison's voice was harsh and aggressive. "No. Listen, I understand that you've been investigating the deaths of Martin Garrett and Susan Ostroff."

"Yes, I am, General. Are you calling to suggest that you might be able to help me out?"

"Don't fuck with me, Porter! I know what Ostroff kept in her safe—and how much *you* know."

"Then you can understand why I'd like to talk to you."

"You have no idea what you've opened up. This thing is bigger than you realize. It goes beyond Garrett and Ostroff, even beyond me."

"Then talk to me about it, General. I'll meet you wherever you like."

Porter listened to the labored breathing on the other end of the line. "General?"

"I can't trust you, Porter."

"Why not?"

"Because you can't protect me! Like I said, you have no idea what's involved here. I want guarantees of protection—and immunity."

"I don't have the power to grant you immunity, General. That would be up to the judge advocate general or the attorney general. But I can protect you."

Porter heard the derisive snort. "The way you protected Garrett and Ostroff? Don't think I didn't know that you had them under surveillance."

"Tell me what you want, General," Porter said quietly.

"If I come to you, I want the FBI there. I want Special Agent Mack." That caught Porter off guard, and Murchison picked up on it. "You're not the only one who can punch a computer keyboard, Porter. Mack's been on your team for a while now."

"He'll be there, General."

"Damn right he'll be there, because I'll be watching. I want him and Ryder, nobody else."

"I'll come—"

"No, you won't. Only Mack and Ryder. If I see anyone else, that guarantees a no-show."

Porter understood that he had no choice. "All right. Where and when, General?"

Murchison's instructions were brief. When the line

went dead, Porter allowed himself a minute, then called in Sloane Ryder.

"Where's Mack?"

"At Bureau headquarters. Why?"

"That was Murchison—"

"*What?*"

"He's back in D.C. I don't know where. He wants a meeting." Porter glanced at his watch. "In exactly seventy-five minutes. Listen to this." He played the tape for her. "What do you think?"

"I think he sounds scared. And what on earth is he doing here?"

"He wouldn't have left the operations theater without a valid reason. Either the President got him back here for a secret briefing, or he manufactured a damn good excuse." Porter paused. "He said only you and Mack. I can't go along with that. Not with what's already happened."

"If Peter brings along support agents, Murchison won't show. He's serious about that."

"And I'm serious about not letting you go there, just the two of you. I don't think Alley would stand for it either."

"What if he came along? With Paco Santana. They're both ex-military. They'd know how to blend."

Porter considered this. The temptation of getting hold of Murchison, who could break the puzzle wide open, clashed with the need to protect Sloane, who was already too close to the two victims—and therefore to their killer. He made his decision.

"Get hold of Alley and Santana and get them in

here. I'll call Mack. Everyone in the conference room, twenty minutes."

Opened in 1982 and located between Henry Bacon Drive and Constitution Avenue, the Vietnam Veterans Memorial, or the Wall, is one of the most stirring monuments in a city filled with landmarks. The names of more than fifty-eight thousand Americans who perished in that war are etched into black granite slabs embedded in the earth. The Wall never closes to those who come to pay tribute. At night, its walk-ways are chastely lit and the light reflects off the cold slabs and the tears of those who stand in front of them.

To Murchison, the Wall was an obvious choice, one that worked in his favor. He often went there, to be among men he'd led and lost. His bodyguards did not think anything odd about such visits, especially the one tonight: The general was there to share his victory with the fallen.

The hum of evening traffic greeted Murchison as he stepped out of his car, parked on Henry Bacon Drive. Together he and his handlers skirted the bottom of the Lincoln Memorial and the giant flag to the left of the Reflecting Pool. As usual, the body-guards fell behind as the Wall came into view. Flowers, keepsakes, and small flags lined the base of the Wall where remembrances had been paid on Veterans Day. But the crowds were gone now, and the bodyguards were relaxed. At the height of the tourist season, there was the occasional mugging at the Lincoln Memorial, but never at the Wall. This was hallowed ground and even thieves were superstitious. Murchison raised the collar of his coat against the night wind and walked on.

At the opposite end of the Wall, the part that runs parallel to Constitution Avenue, Whip Alley sat in the driver's seat of the Suburban, speaking into a headset.

"Paco, can you hear me?"

Dressed in a combat camouflage jacket, Santana was at the eastern edge of the Wall, walking sixty feet behind Sloane Ryder and Peter Mack.

"I see them," he growled into his wrist mike. "It's freezing out here. There's no one around."

"Stay sharp."

Alley did not like this operation. It had been thrown together hastily, with barely enough time to outfit Sloane and Mack. The darkness and terrain also worried him. Lighting around the Wall was poor and there were few places to take cover if something went wrong. Alley had urged delaying the meeting until he could check out the site, but Sloane had vetoed that. Murchison would be there, she argued, and there was no other way to contact him. If they didn't seize this chance to connect, they might not get another one.

Walking side by side, Sloane and Mack were about a third of the way down the Wall, approaching the point where it angles toward the Lincoln Memorial. They heard the exchange between Alley and Santana on tiny receivers tucked inside their ears. Here was Santana again.

"We've got company, approaching along the southeast path. Wait . . . Okay, I see him now. Dressed in spec four fatigues. He's in a motorized wheelchair. Something in his lap, could be flowers ... Yeah, flowers. He's stopping, trying to put the flowers on the ground ..."

Mack watched Sloane's expression relax as Santana dismissed the disabled mourner as harmless.

"Are you okay?" Mack asked.

"Fine."

They had gone over exactly how they would handle Murchison. Sloane was to get what she could out of him as fast as possible. Mack would watch the perimeter. He'd get them walking to the Suburban while Murchison talked. He didn't want Murchison left in the open for any longer than absolutely necessary.

"Up ahead, that's him," Sloane said.

Mack had already spotted the figure in the overcoat. He lowered the zipper on his bomber-style jacket, felt his weapon against the left side of his chest.

Murchison had stopped at exactly the point where the two sides of the Wall intersect. He had his hands in his pockets, watching the pair approach.

"Miss Ryder?"

"That's me, General. This is Special Agent Mack, FBI."

"I want to see some identification."

Mack flipped open his ID, watched as Murchison glanced at it.

"General, it's too cold to stand here," Sloane said. "We have a car to get you to a secure facility—"

"There's no such thing as a secure facility!" Murchison said harshly. "You people have no idea what or whom you're dealing with."

"Then tell us," Sloane said.

Murchison licked his lips. "It's been going on for years, beginning when Kissinger went to China back in '72. Ever since then we've known that China would eclipse Russia as the dominant power, that we'd have to make accommodations for that."

"What kind of accommodations?" Sloane demanded.

"Territorial. What do you think the return of Hong Kong was all about? You think the Brits really wanted to give it up? Not a chance. But they ponied up, to get a place at China's table. We agreed to do the same. Except not everyone sees it quite like that. They want to ignore the secret protocols—"

"What protocols, General?" Mack cut in.

"The ones that guarantee the return of Taiwan to the mainland by the end of this year."

"What are you talking about? The President won't let that happen," Sloane said.

"The President doesn't have any say in what happens! Don't you see it yet? All the information you got from Garrett and Ostroff—don't you see where it's pointing?"

Sloane glanced sharply at Mack. *How does Murchison know what and how much we got from them?* Before she could speak, Mack interrupted again.

"Garrett and Ostroff were feeding you high-grade intelligence that you used to fashion military policy on China. Isn't that right?"

"Yes."

"And that policy was designed not to contain China but to give it what it wanted."

"What was necessary for China to have!"

"But you didn't do this by yourself, did you?" Mack pressed. "You don't have the necessary Chinese contacts. You couldn't afford to be seen at embassy functions where information could be passed along. And the Chinese army brass doesn't come visit you the way the Russians do."

Sloane tried to get in between Mack and the general, but Mack pushed her away.

"*Who did you pass the intelligence to!*" he roared. "What's going to happen on Thanksgiving? Why was that date so important to MacGregor and Yang?" He had Murchison by the lapels of his coat and was shoving him toward the Wall. Sloane heard Murchison gasp.

"MacGregor," Murchison cried. "He was the first one—"

Suddenly he jerked his head. Now Sloane and Mack heard it, too, a steady, high-pitched whine, like a winch, only keener. A figure in a wheelchair was gliding along the path toward them.

"*He was the first . . .*" Sloane desperately needed Murchison to give up the rest.

The man in the wheelchair passed from a pool of light into the shadows. The whine ceased.

"What the hell—" Mack started to say.

Sloane heard a faint popping sound, cried out as Mack fell heavily against her. She grabbed him and tried to hold him up, then saw the hole in his neck, and the blood gushing from his torn throat.

She was turning toward the wheelchair-bound man when something terribly hard and hot slammed into her chest. Her legs flew out from under her and she felt herself falling into blackness, voices chasing her.

Murchison staggered away from the bodies, away from the blood pooling on the frozen earth in front of the granite face. He heard the brief whine of the electric motor. The killer sat very still, looking at him.

"They're dead," Murchison said under his breath. "It's done. Let's get out of here."

"Not quite done," the Handyman said, and squeezed the trigger.

As the life pumped out of him, the last thing Murchison heard was the soft whine of the electric wheelchair as it rolled down the path.

Alley had been listening intently to the exchange between Sloane, Mack, and Murchison. Then came the popping sounds and two soft cries.

"Sloane? *Mack?*" There was nothing but a faint gurgle on the other end. "Paco!"

Alley's voice roared in Santana's earpiece, but he was beyond caring. He lay in a bed of wet leaves next to a tree, the back of his head blown away by the Handyman's first bullet.

Alley threw the Suburban into gear and crashed over the edge of the sidewalk, careening into the park, the fat tires spewing dirt.

The Handyman rolled along, approaching Murchison's bodyguards, who huddled, one looking at his watch. Their charge had been gone a while and they were starting to worry. Looking down at the figure in the wheelchair was the last act of their lives.

The Handyman slipped out of the chair and went through their coat pockets. He found the keys to the car, then returned to the chair and drove himself to the sidewalk that bordered Henry Bacon Drive. He checked to make sure no one was watching, slipped out of the chair, and opened the trunk of Murchison's car.

The motorized wheelchair was heavy, but the Handyman managed to get it into the sedan's deep trunk. A minute later, he was driving toward the Washington marina, closed and deserted at this time of year. The sedan would go into the Potomac. The current and silt would wash away any fiber evidence that he might have left behind.

Sloane took her first breath and felt as though her lungs were on fire. She expelled a weak gasp, then took another breath, a little deeper. Each time she drew in a little more air, she felt her head clear. She tore open her jacket and ripped back the Velcro straps of the Kevlar second-chance vest bound to her chest.

She heard a rasping sound a few feet away and crawled toward it. When she raised her hands, her fingers were slick with blood.

"Peter . . ."

Mack lay on his back, one arm thrown away from his body, the other across his chest. As Sloane pulled herself closer to him, she saw Murchison's body.

"Trap . . . The bastard laid a trap."

"Don't talk, Peter. Whip's coming. We'll get you to a hospital."

She was next to him, felt his short, rapid breath on her cheek.

"Betrayed me," Mack whispered.

Sloane put her arms around him. "Who, Peter?"

A soft sigh escaped his lips. " . . . went to see French."

"What?"

Mack's eyes were wide open, staring up into the night. Beneath his coat she felt the stiff vest that had failed him.

"Had to know if you were right. Told him everything . . . everything about Murchison. Thought that if he was in on it, he'd warn Murchison. Didn't want to believe that. Couldn't."

Mack coughed, blood shooting out in a rooster's plume. His hand tightened around Sloane's. "He betrayed me!"

A final spasm gripped Peter Mack, shook him, then stopped just as suddenly. He lay still, his eyes open, his head cradled in Sloane's lap.

That was how Whip Alley came upon them in the blaze of headlights as he crashed out of the woods, rocking to a stop in front of the Wall.

27

DALE GREER, sheriff of Corona, was coming off the graveyard shift, gliding down the town's wide streets, silent and empty at five-thirty in the morning except for the newspaper boy on his delivery route.

Greer saw the door to the Sik house open. Kyung Sik came out and fired up the minivan he used to haul flats of flowers. Next, his relatives appeared, the sick little boy huddled in a blue snowsuit. The woman—something Cho, Greer recalled—spotted the patrol car and called to Sik.

Greer lowered the passenger-side window. "Howya doin', Kyung? Big day tomorrow."

"Yes, yes. Big day. Drive family to airport."

Behind the smile, Greer thought Sik was nervous. He shifted to catch a glimpse of the woman bundling the child into the van.

"Little fella's going to meet the President. He must be really excited."

"Yes, very excited." Sik glanced over his shoulder. The doors to the van closed. The engine was running. "Must go now, Sheriff. You come by shop after holiday, have beautiful Christmas tree this year."

"I'll be sure and do that."

Greer didn't raise the window, nor did he stop looking at the van. He remembered his years with the state troopers, pulling over vehicles like this one in the dead of night, getting out of his cruiser, the hair on his neck bristling. Greer shivered as that old sensation crawled over him. His cop's instincts screamed at him to investigate.

"Aw, shit!" he muttered.

"Something wrong, Sheriff?" Sik asked.

Too fuckin' tired is what's wrong. This was morning in the town where he lived, not some godforsaken stretch of highway. This was a neighbor from whom his wife bought spring bulbs and potted plants, not some shark-eyed creep behind the wheel, his hands out of sight.

"Nothing's wrong, Kyung. Tell your relatives I said good luck. And make sure they get plenty of pictures of the President. Folks around here will want to see them."

"Yes, Sheriff. Thank you."

There *would* be plenty of pictures, Sik thought. Just not the kind people could stand to look at.

Two months before, Kyung Sik had chartered a small Gulfstream II jet. Because it was able to take off and land on short runways, the plane could use the small regional airport twenty miles west of Corona, avoiding the crush of Thanksgiving weekend traffic at La Guardia, Newark, or JFK.

Sik had the entry permit ready for the guard at the airport perimeter gate and the van was waved through to the private-craft section of the field. The pilot and copilot were waiting by the jet. Sik signed off on the paperwork and listened carefully as the pilot outlined their route from Long Island to Providence, Rhode Island. They would have smooth weather all the way. Getting to D.C. might be a little bumpy if an expected front moved in.

The woman did not relax until the jet was wheels up. She made sure 1818 was comfortable and waited for the sedative that she'd mixed into his hot milk to take effect. When the child closed his eyes, so did she.

Seventy-five minutes later, the jet was on the ground in Providence. Kyung Sik brought the rented van around and drove the Cho family to a wealthy residential area where sprawling, turn-of-the-century houses with widows' walks fronted the sea. He pulled into the garage of one of these and closed the automatic door.

The home, with its fine oriental rugs and period furniture, had been leased a year before by an Asian financier. He had told the real estate agent that he was considering opening a small electronics plant in the city. The financier had paid the full amount of the lease up front, in cash, and was never heard from again. The only people who lived in the house were an Asian caretaker couple. They had left the country yesterday.

The woman held 1818's hand as they walked down the wide hall to the rear of the house. There, in a room that had once been a conservatory, three men waited, surrounded by medical equipment that had been bought at various outlets throughout the year, some of it coming from hospital-supply warehouses as far away as New York and Boston. The surgical table, stainless-steel sinks, stand-up trays, monitors, respirator, and anesthesia gear were the same as those used in the best hospitals. And by tonight, it would all disappear, no hint of it left.

The woman scanned the faces of the three men. They were in their late fifties or early sixties, with broad, Slavic faces. She did not know their names, only that they had once worked for the former Soviet Union's security apparatus, the KGB. In the new Russia, there was little call for their specialized skills, so they farmed themselves out to those still in need of their particular talents. Their cover for being in the United States was watertight: Each man had been invited to attend a medical seminar in Boston. Their visas and credentials were in order. Like most such conferences, this one allowed a good deal of free time between lectures and discussion groups. Most participants indulged in shopping or sightseeing; these three had taken a four-hour ride down the turnpike to Providence.

"Get the others out. You stay," said Vladimir Kirov, the head surgeon. Like the two others of his team, he had already scrubbed and was gowned in surgical greens.

The woman gestured for Sik and her "husband" to leave.

"Take the boy in there and undress him," Kirov said to the anesthesiologist, pointing at a mobile partition screen. "Make sure he is stable."

Kirov went over to the woman, his eyes as bright and hard as polished river rock. "Have you done this before?"

"No."

"But you are familiar with the material."

"I am an expert with the material."

Kirov grunted. "Look at this."

He led her to a stand next to the surgical table and, with his latex-gloved hand, opened a chart showing a large drawing of a child. There were black marks along both buttocks, underneath the arms, and along the calves.

"The incisions will be exactly six centimeters in the buttocks, two point three under the arms, and three point one in the calves," Kirov said. "You will fashion the material to fit these specifications."

"Thickness?"

"Half a centimeter."

"The detonators?"

Kirov removed the tissue paper covering the surgical tray. Next to an array of gleaming instruments lay a small plastic box containing six half-inch-long pieces of wire that looked very much like pieces of a paper clip.

The woman drew in a sharp breath. This was the key. Everything she'd done to bring 1818 to America would have been for naught had the Russians been unable to deliver the detonators. Certainly she could not have brought them in herself, much less procured them in the United States. Doctors, on the other hand, traveled with strange and exotic instruments. Even if U.S. Customs had opened that box, the shiny steel-like pieces, nestled in protective sponge padding, would have been taken for fine surgical drill bits.

The woman knew that the wires were not made of steel but of a very hard plastic treated to resemble that metal. The interior of each one was hollow, creating two minuscule chambers separated by a heat-sensitive alloy that housed a subminiature radio-frequency receiver. One chamber contained a tenth of an eyedrop's worth of fuel accelerant, the other, a similar amount of explosive charge. When the radio signal hit the alloy, it would dissolve, allowing the two components to mix. The result would be a miniature explosion, no bigger than a speck of sulfur ignited on a matchhead. But it would be more than enough.

The anesthesiologist reappeared from behind the screen. "The boy is stable. His vital signs are normal. He is still drowsy from the sedative, but that will make him easier to work with."

"Do you have a gown for me?" the woman asked Kirov.

"You won't need one. I and my team will be the only ones to actually touch the boy." He smiled thinly. "And we are not concerned with postoperative infection in this case, are we?"

"No."

"Then we begin. Bring him to the table. Once he is completely unconscious, you can prepare this." Kirov nodded at a brick of dull-gray substance the size of a quarter pound stick of butter.

The woman went behind the partition where 1818 lay on his side, naked beneath a thin blanket. He was shivering from the cool air in the room and clung to her as she carried him to the surgical table. She had to pry his fingers off her neck to get him to lie down on the table. The anesthesiologist administered a shot and 1818 went limp. His body was arranged on the table, hooked up to the monitors, and the anesthetic began to flow through the mask covering his nose and mouth. When the instrument indicated that 1818 was completely under, the surgical team turned him over. Kirov covered all the exposed skin except the buttocks. His eyes darted to his team, then to the woman, as he reached for a scalpel.

The woman was surprised by how little blood appeared beneath the blade. She watched Kirov make the incision and pull back the skin and fatty tissue. Then she busied herself with the gray, puttylike material. It was plastic explosive, manufactured in the Far East, slightly less powerful than the American C-4 but more stable for her purposes. She pinched off a piece of the explosive, rolled it between her palms like dough, then pinched and rolled it again until it was no thicker than the thinnest strand of spaghetti. She cut the plastique to the exact length, then very carefully wrapped it around the detonator.

As soon as she placed the tiny charge on the tray, Kirov reached for it and began squeezing it into the fatty tissue of 1818's left buttock. He worked with the fat and flesh until he had the tube positioned exactly the way he wanted it. He paused, checking his handiwork. In the course of his service in the KGB—and for more recent interested parties—he had performed this procedure over a hundred times. Had it been possible for it to be written up in medical journals, he would undoubtedly have been given credit as its founding father. Instead of posterity, he contented himself with a very substantial bank account.

By the time Kirov had stitched the wound, the woman was ready with the next charge. It went on like that for three and a half hours, until all six charges had been implanted in 1818. At the end of the procedure, Kirov was drenched with sweat. He ripped off his cap, mask, and gloves and threw them into a plastic-lined disposal tub. He lit a cigarette and smiled at the woman's startled expression.

"The oxygen has been turned off, and the smoke certainly won't affect *him*." He nodded toward 1818, still unconscious on the table.

"You did well," the woman told him.

Kirov shrugged. He was looking ahead to a hearty dinner after the drive back to Boston.

"From now on, you must be very careful," he told the woman. "The incisions were small, but there will be some discomfort. The boy will want to scratch the stitches."

"I already clipped his fingernails."

"I noticed. But while he's asleep, keep him in restraints. Later, use a local anesthetic to deaden the patches of skin around the stitches."

The woman caught the question in Kirov's eyes and was surprised. She'd been told that he was the consummate professional in the building of human bombs. Living, breathing, talking bombs. Now he was flirting with the idea of asking where, or for whom, the boy was destined. But his curiosity passed.

Kirov ground out his cigarette under his heel. "What is it the Americans say? 'Guns don't kill people. People kill people.'" He winked at the woman. "But you and I, we know better."

28

SLOANE WAS DREAMING that she was swimming just beneath the surface of the ocean. She turned over on her back and saw the sun, the rays splintering into a large, glowing fan. She was almost out of breath as she kicked for the surface, arms outstretched, ready to break clear of the water. But the top of the ocean was covered with a membrane that she couldn't penetrate. She punched and clawed but it was hopeless. Her lungs began to burn and her muscles screamed. She couldn't hold her breath any longer. Her mouth opened and the water poured in . . .

Sloane's eyes flew open and she bolted upright. It wasn't water that was holding her back but Whip Alley's arms.

"It's okay," she heard him say. "You're okay."

Sloane let her head fall on his shoulder and dug her fingers into his back. She shut her eyes and let him rock her gently until her heart stopped pounding and her breathing slowed.

"Where am I?"

"University Medical Center."

She sat back against the pillows and ran three fingers over her breastbone. Her chest felt like it had been hit with a sledgehammer.

"You're okay," Alley repeated. "The bullet packed a wallop, but the Kevlar stopped it cold."

Mention of the bullet opened the floodgates to the memories of what had happened at the Wall.

"Peter?"

Alley shook his head. "He didn't have a chance. I'm sorry."

"He was alive," Sloane whispered. "He was very strong. He fought to live, to tell me things." She ignored Alley's startled expression. "Did you get Murchison? Is he safe?"

Alley ran a fingertip down her cheek. "They're all dead. Murchison, his bodyguards. Paco."

"No."

She stared into Whip's eyes, shiny with tears. Her arms reached out to hold him, fingers clutching his hair. His breath was heavy on her neck.

"Before he died, Peter told me he'd gone to see Dodge French," Sloane whispered "He'd laid out what we knew about Ostroff and Murchison, the connections we were making. But his telling French was all a ploy. Peter didn't want to believe that French could be the ultimate traitor, but the only way he could be sure was to give French everything and see what he did with it."

"Then French tipped off Murchison."

"He did more. The killer was there. Who else but French could have told him when and where Murchison would meet us?" Sloane paused. "Peter believed in French and French betrayed him."

"Did you get a look at the shooter?" Alley asked.

Sloane shook her head. "He came up behind us. Peter was hit first. I remember turning . . . Then, nothing. Whip, what was going on out there? What happened after you found me?"

Alley described the madness that had followed after he'd reached Sloane, barely conscious and cradling Peter Mack. He'd sounded the loudest alarm of all, 10–13, officer down. Within minutes, paramedics and squad cars were on the scene, followed by a contingent from Homicide. Because the chairman of the Joint Chiefs and his two bodyguards were among the victims, calls went out to the CID at Fort Belvoir. The shooting of Peter Mack brought in the FBI. Within the hour, the crime scene had become a jurisdictional nightmare.

"Everybody's chasing their tails," Alley concluded. "I didn't mention what we have on the shooter."

"What's the spin for the media?"

"You're going to love this. Some CID guy was thinking aloud and everyone picked up on it: Murchison was the target of an Iraqi hit squad."

"You're kidding!"

"I'm not. And you know, given what's happened over there, it'll play. The Iraqis will fall over themselves denying any involvement, but who'll believe them?"

Sloane thought it was exactly the kind of story that people *would* believe. And be outraged by. A story that would demand swift, unequivocal retribution.

"Where are my clothes?"

Alley pointed at the closet. "The docs want to keep you—"

"I'll be okay. I just can't breathe too well. Whip, listen to me. I need to speak to Porter. Murchison said things before . . . before the shooting."

"It was a trap, Sloane. He would have said anything to keep you in place until the triggerman arrived."

"Sure he would have. And since he knew Peter and I were going to die, what better way to keep us hanging than by doling out the truth? Bullshit might not work, it might make us suspicious. But if what he was telling us jibed with what we already knew, then sure, we'd stick around to hear more."

"You really believe Murchison gave you something genuine?"

"You and Porter can decide that."

Alley slid off the bed. "Porter's right outside. He's been waiting ever since I brought you in."

Lee Porter had arrived at the Wall within twelve minutes of receiving Alley's call. After making sure that Sloane would be all right, he had called the White House. After that, he trailed the ambulance carrying her to the medical center.

"Sloane. You're okay." Porter was surprised to see her dressed. He reached down and hugged her.

"Easy," she cautioned. "I feel like Humpty Dumpty all patched up."

Sloane gave him the short version of what had happened at the Wall. "Now, here's the rest."

At twenty past ten, three and a half hours since the carnage at the memorial, Porter entered the White House. A Secret Service agent escorted him through the chaos that had erupted there as soon as word of General Murchison's shooting had hit. When the door to the Oval Office swung open, Porter saw that Claudia Ballantine was still fighting shock.

"Hello, Lee," Claudia Ballantine said. "Quite a mess we have out there. Word that Murchison is dead has been flashed around the world. I've put Jack Carter in charge over in the Gulf. He assured me that he's ready in case the Iraqis try to take advantage of the situation."

"There's been talk of how Murchison died," Porter said.

Claudia Ballantine nodded. "Everyone's heard *that* rumor. The Iraqis have been screaming at their new best friends, the French and the Russians, that they didn't have anything to do with the shootings. They're petrified that our Tridents have made Baghdad their target packages."

The President fixed her gaze on him. "Problem is, no one's sure of anything: why Murchison was killed, who did it, under whose command? Or maybe I'm wrong."

"Madam President, this will take a while—and none of it will be pleasant."

Claudia Ballantine grimaced. "I already suspected that much."

He sketched out how Sloane Ryder and her team had focused in on Murchison, how Peter Mack had gone rogue, running his own test of allegiance on French, and the bloody results that had followed. He watched Claudia Ballantine pale as he spoke.

When he finished, the President turned and looked out to the gardens, bathed in soft light. She felt like the biggest fool in the world, betrayed by those she trusted absolutely, furious because she had allowed herself to be victimized.

"If Mack was French's creature," she said, "why did French have him killed?"

"Either he suspected Mack was laying a trap, or he was certain that Mack and the others would eventually get to Murchison and he would crack. They both had to die."

"And the others—the bodyguards, the detective?"

"Collateral damage. The killer wasn't leaving witnesses behind."

Porter saw how hard the President was fighting this. Dodge French was a long-standing friend, vested with her complete trust.

"What you're saying makes sense," Claudia Ballantine said slowly. "But it's all circumstantial, Lee. You've got no real evidence against French."

"I have a tape of a phone conversation between him and Murchison."

Her eyes widened.

"I tapped Murchison's phone. He made only one call from his house, to French in Kalorama. Problem is, it was digitally scrambled. NSA's pulling out all the stops, but the decoding will still take time."

The President withdrew something from her drawer, rose, and slowly walked around her desk. "Go on."

"Murchison told Ryder that this—whatever 'this' is—started as far back as 1972, with Kissinger's secret trip to China. Territorial accommodations, secret protocols with Beijing—"

"Lee, I never heard of *anything* like that!"

"Protocols that guarantee the return of Taiwan to China by year's end," Porter continued.

"That's insane!" she whispered.

"It sounds like it, Madam President. But I have no way of confirming that. Such agreements would have been concluded at the highest levels. The security surrounding them would be commensurate."

"We'll damn well find out if they exist!"

"Madam President. According to what Murchison told Sloane Ryder, you will not be able to stop the Chinese advance."

Her eyes blazed. "Why not?" she demanded.

"Consider the situation. For years Dodge French has been the acknowledged China expert—"

"But not with any real power, Lee."

"Maybe he didn't hold power directly, but he had his creatures—Garrett, Ostroff, Murchison. He had the best intelligence available—not only on our side, but also from the Chinese. Garrett, Ostroff, Murchison—maybe others—were the *instruments* of our policy toward China. But they weren't working in the country's best interests; their loyalty was to French. And his goal wasn't to contain China but to accede to its territorial demands."

Claudia Ballantine clenched her fists so hard that what she was holding cut into her flesh.

"So whenever I or my predecessors brought Dodge in to give advice, he steered us to what the Chinese wanted," she murmured. "God, what have we allowed to happen?"

Porter wished he didn't have to say another word, but the President had to hear it all.

"There's also the issue of MacGregor," he said. "According to Ryder, Murchison said he was the *first* one."

"The first what?"

"Maybe MacGregor's death wasn't really a suicide. Maybe he was induced to put himself away."

"The devil's choice: Take your own life, or live in terror of the bullet that'll surely find you, somewhere, sometime," the President said grimly. She kneaded the object in her hand.

"A question, Madam President: Is it your intention to stay with the Iraqi cover story?"

Claudia Ballantine's eyes narrowed. "Speak your mind, Lee."

"In my opinion, going public with *any* of the details we've discussed would be disastrous. Stay with the cover. It gives the press something to feed on and it keeps the pressure on Iraq, maybe enough to forestall any counterstrike that might be on their agenda. It also allows us time to formulate a plan to get to French. I think we have to determine the full extent of his . . . his actions."

"His treachery, you mean."

"If French even suspects that we're on to him, he might manage to spin details about Murchison and the others in a way that suits him. Your presidency would be crippled—at a time when we are preparing for war."

Claudia Ballantine went over to Porter and opened her hand. He was shocked by what lay in her palm. It was the Medal of Freedom, the highest civilian award a president could bestow upon a citizen.

"I was going to present this to Dodge the day after tomorrow, Thanksgiving, after the Hands of Hope ceremony. He was a friend, Lee, to both Robert and me. We always considered him someone we could trust. He gave so much to this country . . . and at the same time he was working to betray it."

"Those who give the most are the hardest men to identify, much less catch," Porter said softly. "Because they have a history of service, their loyalty becomes unquestioned. We never suspect that behind public actions lie private dreams, secret agendas."

"Damn him to hell!" the President said softly.

"Yes, but to put him in hell, we have to be very careful."

Claudia Ballantine listened in silence as Porter explained his plan, interrupting only to pose a question or ask him to clarify a point. When Porter was through, she gave him the go-ahead.

"There's one thing you left out," she told him. "The assassin. I want him found and taken. Preferably alive, but if not . . ."

"I don't have the resources to undertake a hunt like that, ma'am."

"You will. I'm giving you Holland Tylo from executive protection." The smile did not reach her eyes. "She knows who we need, and where to find her."

Dodge French had had his housekeeper prepare him a light dinner of cold ham and German potato salad, accompanied by a half bottle of California Merlot. He had his meal on a tray in the study while watching CNN. At 7:02 P.M., regular programming was interrupted by a news flash. There was the Wall, its marble face streaked with camera and police-car lights. Uniforms everywhere, interspersed with men in plainclothes, gesturing and calling out to one another. There was pandemonium as reporters and camera crews tried to get in close, rebuffed none too gently by grim-faced uniformed police.

Then came the first report. A bizarre shooting at the Wall. Five dead; one critically injured, not expected to live. Among the victims: General Samuel Murchison and his two bodyguards; Detective Paco Santana, D.C. Homicide; and FBI Special Agent Peter Mack. The victim who'd survived was identified only as a woman in her late twenties. Speculation was that she was a tourist who had been caught in the crossfire.

Chewing slowly, French nodded in silent approval. Mai Ling's man had been very thorough. He hoped that the wounded victim was Sloane Ryder who would have accompanied Peter Mack; that would be the best of all.

But what was this? Using the remote, French turned up the volume. The reporter was babbling on about Murchison, the general having secretly come to Washington to brief the President on the situation in the Middle East. An Iraqi hit squad waiting in the wings. The general making a pilgrimage to the Wall, a time-honored habit that was part of his legend. A habit the Iraqis would have known about and capitalized on.

French could hardly believe what he was hearing. There was absolutely no basis for such an account. Even though the reporter had prefaced his account with a disclaimer, the buzz words "informed sources" and "police spokesmen" sprinkled his narrative. Bullshit reporting passing for journalism.

But good bullshit, French thought. Perfect for the occasion. Americans loved nothing more than a clear-cut bad guy. Now they had one: Saddam Hussein. The howl to let slip the dogs of war would be heard across the country. And whatever hard information Sloane Ryder thought she had would be ignored, scattered on the winds of frenzied speculation.

In the eye of the storm, Dodge French was safe. All he needed was another day. Then, on Thanksgiving—

The trill of the phone intruded.

"Mr. French?"

"Speaking."

"This is Joyce McMartin. Please hold for the President."

Well, well.

"Dodge?"

"Yes, Madam President."

"You've been watching the news." It was not a question.

"I have."

"You've no idea what a screwed-up situation this is."

French thought Claudia Ballantine sounded exhausted, edgy. Good. The more off balance she was, the better.

"If there's anything I can—"

"I'm calling together an ad hoc committee to try to get a perspective on what's happened. Tomorrow evening, seven o'clock. I'd like you here."

"And so I shall be, Madam President."

"Thank you, Dodge. I knew I could count on you."

Dodge French stared at the receiver in his hand, listened to the faint buzz of the tone dial.

Of course you can, Claudia. Always.

It was almost midnight when Alley took Sloane back to Brook Hill and the big bed in the master suite. It took all the energy she had to scrub off the hospital smell. The last thing she remembered was donning one of Whip's T-shirts and crawling between the sheets.

Alley turned out the lights and made a phone call. Within twenty minutes, three off-duty detectives had arrived to stand guard. Alley told them he'd be gone only a few hours; they replied that he should take as much time as he needed. With Paco Santana's death seared in their minds, the entire D.C. metropolitan police department was ready to take care of business.

An hour later, Alley was in the coroner's office, going over the preliminary autopsy reports. He was surprised that Santana's was the only body there.

"The army transferred Murchison and his bodyguards to Fort Belvoir," the coroner told him. "The Bureau picked up its own."

"Where's Paco's family?"

The coroner nodded toward the viewing room, venetian blinds closed over the small window.

"You don't have to do an official ID, Whip," the coroner said.

"That's not why I'm here."

He opened the door to a small lounge and embraced Santana's parents and sister. Then he went into the viewing room, raised the blinds, and drew back the sheet. Leaning forward, he made the sign of the cross and bowed his head.

Alley returned home and slept for three hours. He got up at seven and gently roused Sloane from her restless sleep. "Porter's called a meeting for eight," he said, tracing his hands across her face, kissing her lightly on the lips.

After leaving the morgue, he had gone to see Porter, who was still at the MJ-11 offices. Porter had told him about his meeting with the President. Other things too. It was going to be a long, hard day and Alley knew he had to keep his eye on the prize: Dodge French in cuffs, stripped of the power, prestige, and privilege that protected him.

Porter was waiting for them in the GAO garage when Alley drove in. Sloane noticed the razor nick on Porter's chin where he'd cut himself shaving.

"Baltimore-Washington Airport," Porter said to Alley. "We've got a pickup. We can talk on the way."

As Alley steered the Suburban onto the turnpike, he gave Porter and Sloane the breakdown.

"Surveillance on French went into effect at four this morning." He pointed to the police radio in the center console. "The minute French moves, we'll know about it."

"When do we pick him up?" Sloane asked.

Porter explained the way he and the President had set it up. The plan was bold, and it sounded good to Sloane. She wondered about the strength that Claudia Ballantine must have called up to help her set snares for her lifelong friend.

"The problem is, we have nothing concrete on him," Alley said. "He's covered his tracks with dead bodies. We'll be able to hold him for a while on grounds of national security, but the key is to break him, fast."

"What about the assassin?" Sloane asked.

"The President wants to stay with the Iraqi story," Porter answered. "Of course, this means that the FBI and the army CID are looking in the wrong places for the wrong person, but maybe that'll work in our favor. You know that French and his gunman are watching the news. As long as they think everyone's off chasing in the wrong direction, they'll feel safe. I'm not counting on them doing anything stupid, but at least they might not see us coming."

"But when we tag French, the assassin could bolt," Sloane said.

"That's a chance we have to take," Porter replied. "French is the only player left on the board who knows all the details. I want the shooter as badly as you do, but bagging him may not give us what we need."

"Maybe we'll get lucky," Alley said. "Maybe French will give him up to save a piece of his own hide."

Sloane didn't think so. When he was taken, French would keep his mouth shut and play for time.

The lack of a smoking gun linked to French infuriated Sloane. The more she thought about it, the more she believed they were all missing something. It was like looking at a picture hung slightly off center, one she couldn't quite reach to adjust.

Glancing out the window, Sloane saw that they had reached the BWI airport. Alley took the road to the cargo section and had his pass ready for the guard.

"What are we doing here?" she asked.

Alley pointed to an aircraft taxiing into its designated space. But no trucks or forklifts were standing by to tend to it. In fact, the surrounding traffic was giving the jet a wide berth. Sloane craned her neck to read the green and blue logo stenciled on the fuselage and tail. It belonged to an air-freight company she'd never heard of.

A government-issue sedan with Holland Tylo behind the wheel drew up beside the Suburban. She lowered her window and called to Alley, "Follow me."

As the vehicles approached the aircraft, Sloane saw the fuselage door pop open in front of a mobile staircase. The woman who appeared at the top of the steps was about thirty, wearing khaki pants and a fleece-lined bomber jacket. Her hair was the color of a dying winter sun, her skin lightly tanned, as though she'd recently been in the tropics. In one hand she held a rectangular hard-shell box that resembled a musician's carrying case.

"Good to see you again," Tylo said as Sloane went up to her. Then she added, "Although I think we'd both feel better if it were under different circumstances."

"Amen to that," Sloane said, looking up at the woman. "Who is she?"

"Hollis Fremont. She works for a government department—Omega—that operates only outside the United States. Its mandate is to stop assassins with an American target on their agenda."

Sloane stared at Tylo. "What's she doing here?"

"What she does best—on personal orders from the President."

A tall man in his mid-forties joined the woman at the top of the ramp. He looked briefly at the people below, then gently held the woman and kissed her, the way only someone who is leaving a lover would.

Fremont watched him disappear back into the aircraft, then walked down the steps. When she saw Tylo, she set down her case and the two women hugged each other.

"Hollis Fremont," Tylo said, "meet Sloane Ryder."

Fremont's grip was firm. Sloane felt calluses on the woman's fingertips and along the ridge of her hand.

"Tylo has told me about you," Fremont said warmly. "Word is you're a top-notch investigator."

"That's overstating the case."

"You've seen the Handyman's work up close and personal. He took a shot at you, but you're still alive. I know only one other person who's been that lucky: me." Fremont looked at the plane one last time, then asked, "Is there a place where we can talk?"

The vehicles pulled into an empty service hangar Tylo had arranged to use.

"I'm here for several reasons," Fremont said. "First, the man you're hunting is called the Handyman. How he got that moniker is unknown—as are his exact age and nationality. What we *do* know is that he's between forty-five and sixty, in peak physical condition, a superb marksman, and an inventive, lethal, close-in operator. We think he's originally an American who's lived abroad for most his life. And we know that up until four years ago, he never worked in this country.

"Getting close to him—and surviving—is next to impossible. I did it once, in the Statue of Liberty when the President's husband, Robert Ballantine, was murdered." Fremont nodded at Tylo. "That's why, even though he's changed his appearance, I recognized him from those blowups taken off the video footage shot in the park. I'm here because if we get close enough, I just might spot the Handyman before he sees me or any of you."

Alley touched her case with the tip of his boot. "And you'll be the last person on earth that he sees."

"Don't you think the Handyman is finished here?" Porter asked.

Fremont shook her head. "Because of the body count? No. The Handyman was protecting Dodge French by making sure that all those connected to him died before they could implicate or discredit him. Now there's only French left. But is French, at his age, capable of being a physical threat to anyone? I doubt it. He's the kind who issues marching orders. Something big is coming down tomorrow. You can count on the Handyman living up to his moniker."

"Given this guy's specialty, what kind of target are we looking at?" asked Alley.

"So far, he's moved all the way up to the chairman of the Joint Chiefs. Who do *you* think is left?"

Hard glances were exchanged in the cold silence. Finally Holland Tylo voiced their common thought.

"The President? Something related to her husband at the Statue of Liberty?"

"It's never personal with the Handyman," Fremont cautioned. "There may be a connection, but I doubt it. This is a new contract."

The idea that Dodge French could be setting up his old friend the President for the kill shocked everyone in the group.

"The President isn't scheduled to leave the White House for the next three days," Tylo said. "Especially not with Murchison dead and the situation in Iraq still fluid. If she's the intended target, how can the Handyman get to her? The White House is a god-damn fortress now."

"All I'm saying is that the Handyman plays for the highest stakes," Fremont said. "All he's been doing so far is cleaning up and warming up for the finale. My advice? Take French and do whatever it takes to make him talk. He's the only link we have."

FROM THE SUBURBAN, Alley checked in with his surveillance teams. Dodge French had not stirred. Alley told his men to stay sharp. According to Porter, who had this from the President, French would go out at least once before his evening appointment at the White House.

As Alley followed Holland Tylo's sedan back to Washington, he outlined for Sloane and Porter how French would be taken. His plan was as precise as a military operation. French would use his money, means, and influence to elude them. All the hunters had was the element of surprise. They had to make that count.

"If we become separated, whoever has French goes to this place," Alley said, never taking his eyes off the road. It took him a few minutes to explain the details.

"That's good," Porter said.

Sloane agreed. But while she listened to Alley, another part of her concentrated on her little inner voice.

"Lee," she said suddenly, "can you get us into Peter's office at the Bureau?"

Porter looked at her curiously. "It might take some

doing, but we'd get in there." He paused. "Why do we want to?"

"Peter was a note taker. He documented every meeting, made comments in the margins of every memo and report. Maybe he wrote about French."

"The Bureau's internal security team would have taken his office apart by now," Alley said.

"Right. But they'd be looking for anything having to do with Iraq, not French."

Porter shrugged. "We have a few hours until our meeting with Tylo and Fremont—or at least until French moves."

"Then let's play Sloane's hunch," Alley said, spinning the wheel and veering across three lanes of traffic, toward the exit.

On the way to the Hoover building, Porter spoke with the Bureau's chief of internal security, who was waiting for them when they arrived.

"The understanding is that nothing leaves this room without our okay," he said, escorting the trio.

"Fine," Porter replied.

One glance at Peter's office, with its half-open drawers, strewn files, and carelessly piled floppy disks was all Sloane needed to realize that internal security had already been here.

Porter closed the door and asked, "Where do you want to start?"

Sloane looked around. They had very little time and she had to make every minute count.

"Whip, why don't you handle the floppies. Lee, you and I'll get the paperwork. I'll handle these at the same time." She pointed to a stack of cassettes.

In the back of a drawer, Sloane found a Walkman and pulled on the headset. She pushed a chair over to the desk, grabbed a pile of files, switched on the player, and began to listen and read.

Two hours flew by. No one spoke. As Alley went through the stack of floppies, multicolored files littered the floor around the chairs Sloane and Porter sat on.

Four hours later, they had nothing to show for their efforts.

"We've got that briefing with Tylo and Fremont in thirty minutes," Porter reminded them

Sloane had only two more cassettes to check. She slipped off the headphones, placed them and the Walkman in her sling bag, and calmly palmed the cassettes.

When she saw Alley's raised eyebrows, she said, "I'll listen to them in the truck. If I don't find anything, the Bureau's welcome to them."

In the Suburban, she reloaded the Walkman and adjusted the volume on the headphones.

"Take your time getting there," she told Alley, and sat back to listen.

Their destination was the Secret Service headquarters at 1800 G Street NW. Alley dawdled in the mid-afternoon traffic, using the time to check in with his surveillance teams. French still hadn't moved. Alley hoped the President's information was correct. But maybe this year French would break with tradition, which meant they'd have to take him as he left for the White House.

He was about to switch off the speakerphone remote when Sloane ripped a cassette out of the Walkman and jammed it into the dash-mounted player.

"Listen!"

The clipped, patrician speech patterns belonged unmistakably to Dodge French.

"Your job will be to go through everything that Porter's people have accumulated on Martin Garrett. They dropped the ball and let him get killed. Now you're coming in to find out who killed him and whether or not Susan Ostroff is a potential second target. She's your key. Lock in on her. Any suspicious movements, anything out of the ordinary, I want to know about it."

"Son of a bitch!" Alley exploded. "*We* dropped the ball? French had already given Garrett up. Garrett was as good as dead when French was—"

"Whip, listen!"

Sloane rewound the cassette and they listened to French's words again.

Porter shook his head. "All I hear is French screwing over the man who trusted him. Mack took French everything the bastard needed to know about how dangerous Garrett and Ostroff—and eventually Murchison—had become."

"Listen to what French is saying about Ostroff," Sloane said. "Think back to when this tape was made. *How, at that exact moment, could French have known that Ostroff was connected to Garrett? It was too soon!* Ostroff's name had never come up in the meeting with the President, right?"

Porter nodded. "*No* one could have known that she was involved—"

"Except French, her ultimate handler," Sloane finished.

"The smoking gun," Alley said softly.

"Right," Sloane said. "*Now* we have some leverage. Now French will break."

"Do you think Mack was covering himself by making that tape?" Porter asked. "Could he have been suspicious of him that far back?"

"Not a chance," Sloane said softly. "Taping this must have been an accident." She paused. "Peter had the answer all along. He just never knew it. He never saw what was coming at him—and neither will French."

Dodge French had spent the day closeted in the library of his Kalorama house, watching the media chase the story about the slaughter at the Wall. The networks indulged in an orgy of speculation about an Iraqi hit squad until fully 80 percent of Americans believed that Iraq was responsible for the butchery. An equal number were ready to back any retaliatory strike—preferably a massive one—that the President might contemplate.

Meanwhile, the bravado of the Iraqi spokesmen could not disguise their country's fear. French and Russian satellites monitoring revealed intense U.S. military activities at bases in Saudi Arabia and on the island of Diego Garcia. The Americans were making no secret that a strike was imminent. Diplomatic consultations were continuing around the clock, but it was clear that Washington was just waiting for some scrap of evidence that would link Iraq to the massacre. As soon as it had that, the bombers would be slipped off their leashes.

Meanwhile, not a word about China. French thought it a sad commentary on his country's military posture that it abandoned one position when another was being threatened. Murchison's movement of the two carrier groups from the Taiwan Strait to the Persian Gulf had left a soft, exposed underbelly. Lin, the charismatic Chinese nationalist on Taiwan, was organizing a huge rally for tomorrow. Hundreds of thousands would take to the streets. Most public services would cease to function. The police and security forces, although well trained and heavily armed, would be overwhelmed. There would also be some surprises as Lin's agents wreaked havoc in the authorities' lines of communications.

Which brought French to the Chinese. He had made only one call all day, on his secure line, to an upscale greengrocer. The person who'd answered was Mai Ling. In rapid-fire Mandarin, she had described the Chinese military's readiness.

The troop ships were loaded and ready to weigh anchor. The escort warships were firing up their boilers for the short dash across the strait. On the tarmac of military airfields, cargo planes were taking on paratroopers and matériel to be used to take control of the island's airports and defensive positions. Chinese battle planners calculated that a swift strike would meet with hard but brief opposition. All the elements in the equation would create chaos, and chaos always worked in favor of the aggressor.

The joker in the pack rested in Dodge French's

hand. Throughout the day, he reviewed each of his cards very carefully:

—The President continued to juggle the ongoing investigations into the slaughter at the Wall and the potentially explosive situation in Iraq. She had tunnel vision where everything else was concerned. Good.

—The military was still trying to cope with Murchison's death. Murchison's replacement was Admiral Carter, probably the weakest—in terms of character—of all the Joint Chiefs. He governed by consensus and would bend with the wind. Right now that wind was blowing across the Arabian peninsula. Carter would not order the carrier task forces back to the Taiwan Strait. Even if he were inclined to do so, and acted immediately, the fleet would never arrive in time. Good.

—Through discreet inquiries, French had learned that the lone survivor of the massacre was indeed Sloane Ryder. He would have much preferred her out of the way entirely, but with Murchison and the others dead, Ryder had nothing with which to threaten him.

—Anthony Foster, the vice president. He was almost as involved with the current crises as Claudia Ballantine was. He kept busy doing what everyone expected of him, keeping his distance from French as they had agreed. But not so busy as not to wonder exactly what would happen tomorrow. French had no doubt that initially Foster would be shocked and sickened by events. The few minutes of the power vacuum, between Ballantine's death and Foster's being sworn in as the new president, would be critical.

French thought Foster might need some propping up to see him through.

—And 1818, the child who would wreak havoc in the heart of the nation. French had heard nothing about him, but knew that the boy would be ready.

Reviewing his cards, French decided that he held an unbeatable hand.

At four o'clock, French wrapped himself in his favorite old Burberry coat and walked into the garage. There, beneath fluorescent lights, next to his everyday Rolls-Royce, was his toy, a wasp-yellow Porsche he drove himself, strictly for the exhilaration.

French's touch on the wheel was deft and the car responded to it. On I-95, he opened up the Porsche and let it run, the engine screaming on the straightaways. It never occurred to French that the family-size Buick in his rearview mirror or the Suburban with the smoked-out windows might belong to anyone of significance.

The Buick had tailed French, sure he'd come out of the Kalorama house.

"You believe our luck?" the driver had radioed Alley. "We couldn't lose that puppy if we tried."

"Stay close," Alley replied. He glanced at Sloane, in the passenger seat, then changed channels and updated Lee Porter, who was monitoring from the Secret Service communications center.

"Nice and easy," Porter came back. "We don't want to make him suspicious."

Alley, who joined the surveillance once it became clear that French was headed for I-95, kept the channel on the encrypted radios open, talking to his men in clipped, spare sentences. In a car like that, French could unexpectedly dive onto an exit and lose his pursuers.

But he could never outrun the helicopter that fluttered a thousand feet above the stream of traffic headed for Quantico and points south. The Jet Ranger was part of the Secret Service fleet and this afternoon it carried Holland Tylo and Hollis Fremont. The pilot, along with his passengers, was dialed in to the pursuit frequency. Even if he hadn't been receiving continuous updates from the ground, the pilot would have had no problem eyeballing the yellow sports car.

Unknown to any of the pursuit parties, there was already another set of eyes following Dodge French on the ground, but farther ahead. These watched as French came off exit 160, reducing speed when he reached the limits of a village called Occoquan.

In the early eighteenth century, Occoquan had been a milling center and tobacco-trading town. By the mid-1990s, its historic architecture housed over a hundred boutiques, ranging from art galleries to gourmet shops. Thanks to Mai Ling, the Handyman knew exactly which shop French would head for. He had also observed the surveillance on French's home and had reported the same to the old woman. To the Handyman, the surveillance was sophomoric.

The Handyman watched as French climbed out of the Porsche, set the alarm, and strode across the street. The former adviser to presidents did not disappoint; he was going exactly where Mai Ling had said he would.

The Handyman glanced up the main thoroughfare,

crowded with last-minute Thanksgiving shoppers and those already with an eye out for Christmas gifts, and walked swiftly up to where the Buick and the Suburban had parked. Passing the Buick, he palmed a thin, dark strip of adhesive tape to the right-rear tire. It was virtually invisible against the black rubber. He did the same to the Suburban.

The Handyman drifted under the awning of a candy parlor and bought a caramel apple. From this vantage point, he observed the surveillance team. He took note of, then ignored, the pair from the Buick. It was Sloane Ryder and her detective friend, walking on the other side of the street, who interested him.

The Handyman saw the setup. While French approached the front of a shop, Maggie's Puritan Fowl, Ryder and the detective slipped in behind him. The pair from the Buick set themselves up across the street so that they had a diagonal line of sight on the store.

Caramel apple in hand, the Handyman walked up the street and down the ramp of the parking garage where he'd left his vehicle. The garage was deserted and no one saw him change into an outfit that made him all but invisible: white work pants and jacket, and a long apron, each piece suitably bloodstained. The finishing touch was the health-code-prescribed cap over his hair. The pants and apron had baggy pockets that accommodated the ordnance the Handyman had selected for the occasion.

As he went back up the ramp, the Handyman saw the way it was all going to happen, now that the players were almost in position. Except that he had miscounted. In his overconfidence, he had failed to catch the shadow that was creeping up fast behind him.

The Secret Service helicopter landed in a field about three hundred yards from the heart of the town. Hollis Fremont had hopped out, leaving the Super Magnum sniper rifle she favored stowed beneath the seats.

The strategy that she, Tylo, Ryder, Alley, and Porter had formulated was simple. Ryder and Alley would be the close-in couple. This left Fremont the long perimeter, the area *behind* the Handyman, if he was still shadowing French. Her job was to make sure that the detectives' backs were covered.

Fremont tightened the perimeter a little, moving to within sixty feet of the butcher shop. Her eyes scanned in quadrants, taking in everything and everyone. There was a family with a ponytailed dad pushing a stroller; two lovers, the girl's hand slipped into the butt pocket of her boyfriend's jeans; Alley's watchers; the back of a tall man in stained butcher's wear, tossing a snack into a trash bin, hurrying into an alley that ran behind the shops.

Everything was ordinary, just as she'd expected. If the predator was among them, the herd members hadn't sensed him yet. The thought made Fremont sharpen her watch. She had no faith in the instinct of the herd.

Maggie's Puritan Fowl was located in a former ice house, with flagstone floors and walls and a giant walk-in refrigerator that had once been used to store two-hundred-pound blocks of ice. A long, glass-enclosed counter ran the length of one wall, its gleaming trays filled with turkeys, ducks, geese, game hens, and chickens. The shop was crowded, and harried butchers pulled out preordered, prepackaged turkeys as fast as customers clamored for them. At one end of the counter was a high stool where Maggie, perched like a Vegas pit boss, harangued her customers and collected their money.

"Hello, Maggie. Here to pick up my bird."

"Turkey for French! French pickup!" she bellowed.

As French moved down the counter, he never noticed Sloane Ryder and Whip Alley enter the shop in the slipstream of customers.

But the Handyman did.

He stood next to the walk-in refrigerator, half hidden by countermen swiftly moving in and out. In his work clothes, none of the employees gave him a second look, assuming he was a meatpacker's delivery man.

There was Sloane Ryder and her detective, both a little more tense than they'd been when the Handyman had watched them in the street. Looking at her now, he recalled the most intimate details of the night at the Wall, the way her hair had shone in the light, her gestures as she'd tried to persuade Murchison to leave with her, her eyes filled with pinpricks from the reflection of the granite slab.

I should have shot her in the throat, like the other one.

He had never suspected that she would come to the rendezvous wearing armor. The FBI agent, yes. Hence the throat shot. But a civilian? Now here she was pretending to examine the gourmet sauces and condiments on display. Mai Ling had assured him that Ryder was still bedridden, in the hospital.

No matter. The issue would be handled here. Correctly.

The Handyman checked French's position, then that of the trackers. French was about ten feet away, at the end of the meat counter, diagonally facing the door to the walk-in refrigerator, waiting for someone to bring out his bird. Ryder and Alley had edged over to the floor-to-ceiling shelves that held a variety of canned goods. Then the detective split off and began moving toward French in the classic flanking position.

The Handyman glanced past the milling shoppers, out the windows where the backups had taken up position on either side of the front door.

Here was the counterman carrying out a package with French's name written on the white butcher's paper.

That's when they'll take him, as soon as he's holding the bird. He might as well be wearing handcuffs.

From his pants pocket the Handyman withdrew a modified .22 pistol with a custom-made suppressor no longer than his thumb. The gun was hidden under his butcher's smock. He turned his body rather than just his arm to get into firing position.

The counterman stepped in front of him, proceeded over to French, and, holding up the fowl, asked French if he needed help carrying it to his car. French shaking his head, Sloane Ryder stepping forward, the counterman wishing French a happy Thanksgiving before turning to another customer.

Now.

Dodge French thought that the sound he heard was a child's cough. Something rock-hard punched into him, the impact making him stagger and slip. As he fell, French managed to raise his eyes, saw the dirty butcher's smock, then the two small black holes in it. He saw the face, the cold, pitiless eyes fixed on him, then his head struck the edge of the counter, met the floor, and a cold, black wave carried him off to oblivion.

30

THE IMAGES slammed into Sloane: French taking two jerky steps backward, the expression of terror and disbelief frozen on his face, the wrapped bird falling, French's arm swinging out, scattering the glass jars on the countertop. The blood . . . pouring from French's head wound.

He's dead. God help me, he's dead.

As she snapped out of her paralysis and started toward French, Sloane saw Whip Alley straight-arm a customer and draw his weapon. The 9-millimeter Walther was almost clear of his jacket when he was spun around. The gun sailed high in the air as Alley clutched his shoulder and staggered against the counter.

Customers were stampeding out of the shop in a tangle of arms and legs, filling the air with screams. Jars and bottles shattered and curses went up as people were trampled underfoot.

Sloane shoved through the crowd to get to Alley, leaning heavily against the counter, blood seeping from his arm.

"Only a flesh wound." His gaze was still riveted on the walk-in refrigerator.

"Where's the Handyman?" Sloane cried.

"Forget him. Get French out!"

"Whip—"

"Stick to the plan!"

French was on the floor, his skin ashen. Sloane crouched beside him, seized his blood-drenched hands and pried them away from his body. Ripping open his coat, she ran her fingers over his jacket, then reached underneath and touched his shirt. Both pieces of clothing were dry.

"Get up!" she yelled, but he stared at her vacantly. "Get up, goddamn you!"

Gripping him under the shoulders, she heaved him to his feet and pushed him, stumbling across the broken glass, toward the door. The two detectives who'd been standing guard outside had finally made their way through the escaping crush and were inside, weapons drawn. One of them started toward Sloane.

"Help Whip!" she shouted. "I'll handle this one."

With one hand on French's collar, Sloane steered him toward the door. There she looked back, but Whip Alley had already disappeared.

When Hollis Fremont witnessed the uproar in the shop, she knew exactly what was happening. Training made her ignore her first instinct, which was to rush in to help, because that would only trap her in the melee. Certain that the Handyman wouldn't come out the front way, she made sure she could cover and control the alley that ran along the side of the shop from the street to the back entrance.

Weaving through the mob scattering out of the store and into the street, she ran into the alley, her gun

in her hand, pressed against her thigh. When she
turned the corner, Fremont saw that the rear door to
the shop was still closed. She tested the handle. It
didn't budge. The Handyman was still inside.

Taking two steps back, Fremont shot away the lock
and kicked open the door.

The old icehouse's refrigerator had three long runners
set into the ceiling to accommodate the sliding meat
hooks. In one corner was a saw assembly, bolted to the
floor, a large butcher-block table, and a rack of knives.
There were stacks of pans and trays and large plastic
tubs for the scraps and bones. And a series of U-
shaped iron rungs, bolted to the wall, that created a
makeshift ladder to the trapdoor cut into the roof.

Since the Handyman had known exactly where
Dodge French was headed, he'd arrived two hours earlier. This had given him enough time to scout the layout of Maggie's Puritan Fowl, slip into the alley, and
climb up to the fire escape to the roof of the adjoining
building, then leap onto the roof of the poultry shop.
The Handyman couldn't have reconnoitered Maggie's
refrigerator from inside the shop, but he had sprung
the lock on the trapdoor in the shop roof. Satisfied
that he had found his escape route, he left the trapdoor unlocked before taking up his vigil for French.

Now this preparation would save his life.

In the split second it took him to pump the two
rounds at Dodge French, the Handyman had realized
that his mission would fail. At that instant, French, for
some inexplicable reason, had hefted the package he'd
taken from the counterman. The weight of the bird

should have made French's hands lower, exposing exactly that area of his chest the bullets were intended for. But instead of finding human flesh, the .22s, designed to penetrate soft targets before carving up their interior, had buried themselves in the turkey carcass.

By now, the Handyman had seen Whip Alley draw his weapon. The third shot, which would have brought French down, had to be spent on the detective.

The Handyman had no chance for a fourth. Chaos erupted in the shop and he used it as cover to retreat into the refrigerator. The countermen inside had heard the commotion and were pressing past him for a look. The Handyman went the other way, found the makeshift ladder and began climbing the rungs.

Seconds later, he had pushed open the trapdoor and swung onto the roof. He crouched and ran to the edge, then leaped over the low parapet of the adjoining building. From there, it was a short sprint to the fire escape.

Before descending, the Handyman removed the butcher's garb and rolled the apron around the .22, dropping everything down a ventilation shaft. Swiftly and silently he made his way down the fire escape, dropping the last few feet to the ground.

"Hey, Officer!"

The Handyman whirled. Facing him was a boy no more than ten years old, his eyes as wide as saucers as he looked up and down at this Virginia state police trooper who'd materialized from out of nowhere.

"What is it, son?"

The boy gulped. "You better come quick. Somebody's been hurt in that store."

The Handyman approached the boy. "Maggie's?"

The boy bobbed his head furiously.

"Are your folks around here?"

"Across the street. My mom's—"

The Handyman dropped one hand on the boy's shoulder, the other on the butt of the .44 Magnum in his holster.

"Go tell her that I'll need to talk to you when I'm done with the bad guys. Now scoot!"

The boy took off like a jackrabbit. He made it across the street, all the way to the store, before curiosity got the better of him. When he looked back, the trooper was nowhere to be seen.

"What the hell do you mean he's not here? Where could he have gone?"

Clutching his bleeding shoulder, Whip Alley stared wildly around him. The huge refrigerator seemed to mock him.

"There," Hollis Fremont replied. "It's the only way out." She pointed to the U-shaped iron rungs.

"Son of a bitch!"

As Fremont hoisted herself up to the ladder, Alley radioed his two men, alerting them that the Handyman was likely on the roof of a nearby building. Gritting his teeth, he climbed the ladder and emerged through the roof. He found Fremont atop the next building, holding up a butcher's apron, her eyes bright with anger.

"We missed him," she called out.

"He couldn't have gotten far—"

"Far enough. I'm heading for the chopper. Tell Ryder to contact me."

Before Alley could reply, Fremont dropped out of sight. Slowly, he sat down on the parapet and slumped forward. Shock was setting in. He fumbled with the radio and brought his lips close to the microphone.

"Sloane? Are you there?"

Sloane drove along I-95 toward Washington, the big tires humming along the blacktop, eating up the miles to her destination. She'd made it from Occoquan to the interstate in twenty minutes flat, using the Suburban to bully other cars out of her way. All the while she kept thinking about Whip, wondering how badly he was wounded. She was relieved when his voice crackled over the radio speaker.

"Are you there?"

Sloane jabbed the transmit button, opening up the channel.

"I'm here. Are you all right?"

"I'm okay. Do you have French?"

Sloane glanced at the figure slumped against the door. "Yes. He's pretty shook up, but he'll make it."

"Where are you now?"

"On I-95, about twenty miles north of the 123 intersection. Whip, the Handyman—"

"We missed him. Listen, Sloane. Fremont and Tylo are in the chopper. They'll find you in ten, fifteen minutes. Stay on this frequency. Once they have you, you'll be covered all the way to the city. Tylo's scrambling a Secret Service detail as additional escort. You got that?"

"Got it."

"I'm hitting the road right now. I'll be on this same channel. With a little luck, I'll catch up with you before you reach the city." A burst of static cut him off, but Sloane caught the words she needed to hear: "—love you."

The radio fell silent and Sloane heard a dry, raspy chuckle.

"A friend?"

Sloane took her eyes off the eighteen-wheeler she was following. French had propped himself up in the passenger seat and was staring at the dark stains covering his coat.

"Ruined," he muttered. "Do you know how many years I've had this coat? Now I suppose I'll have to buy a new one."

His banter cut Sloane. "Your man has killed seven people so far. You would have been number eight—set up by whoever knew you'd be coming here today."

"It may appear that way to you."

"It *was* that way!"

"You're Sloane Ryder, aren't you?"

"Yes."

"You've been very clever, Miss Ryder. Pity your efforts are all for naught." French paused. "May I ask where we're going?"

"The White House. The President wants to talk to you."

"Yes, I expect she does."

Radio chatter flooded the air as Holland Tylo checked in from the chopper.

"We're about three minutes behind you, Sloane. Everything okay?"

"So far."

"How's your passenger?"

"Okay, so far. Where's Whip?"

"Moving fast to you. Sloane, you did good back there. Now we'll cover you all the way home."

Sloane signed off and concentrated on the road. The semi she was tailing signaled that it was pulling off. She slowed, watched it drift to the right, then pulled up behind a minivan.

"You seem to have everything under control," French remarked.

"Tell me why you did it," she said suddenly.

French regarded her as he might a mildly interesting archeological specimen. He glanced at the dashboard, then poked his finger into the cassette player.

"Looking for something?" she asked.

"Merely taking precautions. I wouldn't want to think you had a tape in there intruding on our privacy. You see, I know that you're not wearing a wire. Given the nature of your little operation back in Occoquan, you wouldn't have needed to. So, we can talk freely."

"Why?" Sloane repeated.

"Don't be pushy," French admonished her. "Otherwise you'll learn nothing. And don't think you'll hear very much when we reach the White House." He paused. "Tell me, what finally prompted you to take me? I *know* that I gave you nothing concrete to work with."

"Peter Mack did."

French's surprise was genuine. "What?"

"A tape. One of the times he was with you, he had a microcassette recorder in his pocket, one of those voice-activated units. He probably didn't even realize he had it on him."

"Serendipity," French murmured. "And what was on that tape—exactly?"

"You arranged for Peter to work with MJ-11. You had him come out to your home right after the White House meeting the President asked you to attend. By then Garrett was already dead. You had no idea how much MJ-11 knew, and you were going to use Peter to find out. You gave him Susan Ostroff's name because he had to know what to pick up on. You wanted him to alert you the minute she came on our radar."

Sloane paused. "The problem was that *no one* had ever mentioned Ostroff, much less connected her to Garrett. You were telling Peter something only you could have known."

French lightly tapped a front tooth with his fingernail. "How fortuitous for you that Peter made the tape—and that you managed to find it. But then again, you used to be his lover. You knew his habits, his little idiosyncrasies."

Sloane ignored French's taunt. "What Peter left behind will be enough to hang you. My turn. Why?"

"You've deduced a great deal. You're so close. Surely you can take that last step. So tell me, Miss Ryder, what was the nature of my work?"

"Treason. You set up your own spy network within the government: Garrett to Ostroff to Murchison to you. You had minimal direct contact with the first two. Garrett fed Ostroff; Ostroff fed Murchison."

"And my objective?"

"To sell our policy secrets to the Chinese."

"*'Sell?'* For money? I didn't need that."

"Ideology, then. You were—are—the ranking expert

on China. Maybe you love China more than you do your own country."

"Love, Miss Ryder, does not enter into this equation. We are talking about affairs of state, not of the heart."

"Your actions still make you a traitor."

"Do they? I've found the distinction between treason and patriotism to be quite thin. I have not been undermining my country's policies in regard to China, merely *guiding* them. There are those in the White House who believe that China is an entity we must be wary of, the second evil empire, if you will."

"James Trimble."

French nodded. "And the President."

"Which is why she has to be eliminated."

It was as though French never heard her. "All China wants is for us to live up to already agreed upon protocols."

"What protocols?"

"Those secretly signed by the heads of some of our biggest corporations, agreements which, over their lifetime, would be worth tens if not hundreds of billions of dollars. The late H. Paul MacGregor was the point man in those negotiations. Of course, you never knew that, but still, it was unfortunate that some correspondence between MacGregor and Mi Yang came to your attention."

"MacGregor?" Sloane shook her head. "But I didn't *know* anything. I saw one cover letter. It was meaningless."

"On the contrary, Miss Ryder. It mentioned a specific date, one which I believe you asked General Murchison about."

"Thanksgiving. Tomorrow . . ."

"Exactly."

"Is that why you had MacGregor murdered and you destroyed my career—because you were afraid that the Thanksgiving reference might mean something to me?"

"There were other considerations where MacGregor was concerned. But you—you had to be humbled." French barked out a laugh. "Ironic, isn't it? I ruined you only to drive you into the arms of Lee Porter and his bloodhounds."

Sloane's mind was spinning as she tried desperately to retain every detail French was imparting.

"The protocols," she said. "What do they involve? If they were already in place, that means the deal had been cut. Payment—whatever that was—would have already been made."

"You assume that. Perhaps you might consider the possibility that payment had *yet* to be made."

A sick realization crept over Sloane. "You're guiding our Chinese policy—that's part of the payment, isn't it? Nothing sudden or dramatic. Just a word here, a nudge there. Even though technically you were no longer in government service, you still had your people. Garrett in national security, Ostroff at State, Murchison to cover the military. You knew what our policies would be, you passed that information to the Chinese, who then altered *their* position in order to dispel our concerns."

"Bravo, Miss Ryder. You *are* a quick study."

"But there's one more step, isn't there? You corrupted and used Garrett not only for the information he could provide, but because that information could later be used to discredit Trimble. And you killed Murchison. . . . You used him to get our naval forces out of the Taiwan Strait and into the Gulf."

For French, the realization on her face was like the dawning of the sun over the ocean. "Go on. Finish it."

"Which is where the Chinese wanted the fleet to go because it meant Taiwan would be defenseless."

"Exactly."

"And you managed all this while pretending to stand in the service of the President, a woman who calls you her friend."

Sloane shuddered, as though throwing off the cobwebs of a nightmare.

"You're an exceptional woman, Miss Ryder."

"But leaving Taiwan exposed to satisfy the protocols is not the last play." Sloane noted how French's eyes narrowed. "The President might still find a way to stop you. So she has to go. Tomorrow."

French's expression held no pity, no remorse, nothing at all.

"Which means that you're expendable," Sloane continued. "You've already played your part in what's to come. Otherwise the Handyman wouldn't waste his time. The Chinese don't need you anymore. You've become as much a threat to them as Murchison and the others were to you."

The lights from other cars washed the cabin of the Suburban, alternately illuminating French's face and casting shadows over it. He sat very still, his features as stark and lifeless as those of a graveyard alabaster angel.

"You had everything," Sloane said. "Pedigree, wealth,

recognition. Everything except a sense of shame. But you still have a chance to stop this thing. Show me that you're better than I think you are."

"You're wrong," French replied, his voice grating on each word. "Tomorrow the world will be a new place, entering a new age, and I will see my life's work reach fruition." The stillness in the vehicle seemed endless, then he said it all: "Are you familiar with the writer Lawrence Durrell? Probably not. You might do well to peruse *Justine*, where, among other things, it is written, 'We are the children of our landscape; it dictates behavior and even thought in the measure to which we are responsive to it.'"

The quotation meant nothing to Sloane. She was about to press French to explain when she noticed something in the side mirror: a car moving up fast, on her left. She was reaching for the radio transmit button, then drew back. It was all right. The car had roof-rack lights and, looking down, she could see the decal on the door: VIRGINIA STATE POLICE.

The car the Handyman had parked in the Occoquan garage was a White Crown Victoria, a model preferred by law enforcement. From the driver's door, he'd peeled off a nearly invisible piece of white plastic to reveal the shield of the Virginia State Police. He repeated the process with the passenger door. From the trunk he removed a rack of bubblegum lights and affixed it to the roof, running the wires through a crack in the driver's window and into the electrical panel underneath the steering column.

After starting the engine, he activated the Global

Positioning System and was rewarded with two blips
on the screen. One was turning off on I-95; that had
to be the Suburban. The second was stationary in
Occoquan—the backup car, the Buick, which the
detective would eventually use.

The Handyman had pulled out of the garage and
taken the back way out of town to Route 123. By the
time he'd reached the interstate, night had fallen and
he was able to increase his speed without worrying
about a legitimate state trooper passing him in the
opposite direction and wondering what all the hurry
was about.

As he wove his way through the thickening traffic,
the Handyman replayed the debacle at the shop. Bad
enough that he had failed in his attempt on French;
worse was the fact that during his escape across the
rooftops, he had glimpsed a ghost: Hollis Fremont.

Several years before, she had been the innocent who
had unwittingly brought the Handyman out of Paris
and into New York. Once she'd done her job, she was
to have been killed, at Kennedy airport, but there had
been complications. With the help of Omega's top
assassin hunter, she had managed not only to escape,
but later to surface and wreck the Handyman's assignment. That day at the Statue of Liberty, it should have
been Claudia Ballantine, not her husband, who died.

Now Fremont, the one person who might be able to
see past his disguises, was again part of the equation.
The Handyman felt her tendrils probing for him
somewhere out in the darkness and the sensation
made his skin prickle. That Fremont was here, in
America, meant that the rules had changed. Omega's

activities were limited to areas outside the United States. Presidential dispensation must have been granted to bring Fremont in and her pursuit would be relentless. He had to deal with French immediately.

The Handyman glanced at the GPS display and increased his speed. The Suburban was about a hundred yards ahead. He reached into the canvas bag on the passenger seat and began taking out the things he would need.

"Sloane, how are you doing down there?"

The sound of Holland Tylo's voice over the speaker snapped Sloane out of her reverie. The enormity and the implications of what French had told her had left her stunned. She forced herself to respond.

"Traffic's getting heavier, but we're still moving."

"I can see that from up here. We're a little behind you over on the left. You're looking good."

"Where's Whip?"

"About ten miles back. Traffic's staring to pile up around him, but you'll see him in a few minutes. We're going to do a flyby and see what the flow's like up ahead. How's your passenger?"

Sloane glanced at French. "Sitting tight."

Seconds later, she heard a roar overhead and through the windshield saw the chopper dart over the highway.

Her eyes strayed to the side mirror. The state police car was still there, on her left bumper. Then it accelerated and Sloane heard a muffled sound, like someone trying to talk underwater. She lowered the bullet-resistant window an inch and heard the metallic echo of the trooper's voice coming through the bullhorn bolted to the fender.

"Move past the minivan into the center lane. I'll go around you and clear the way."

There was no light inside the trooper's car. All Sloane could make out were vague features behind the wheel. But she recognized the unmistakable silhouette of a Smokey hat.

As she reached for the turn-signal lever, she never thought to ask herself why Holland Tylo hadn't mentioned the trooper.

The Handyman watched the Suburban ease into the center lane, moving past the minivan, giving him just enough room to slip into the right-hand lane.

The Handyman had to act quickly. Ryder would be watching for the police cruiser to come up on her left, pass her, and settle in front to act as escort. When that didn't happen, she would wonder why, and reach for the radio.

The Handyman tapped the accelerator and came abreast of the Suburban. Looking up at the dark, armored glass, he saw the outline of Dodge French's profile. He lowered his window and with his right hand reached across for the explosives.

When the Handyman had tagged the Suburban with the specially treated tape, he had discovered exactly the kind of vehicle he might have to deal with. The oversize tires, the reinforced rear axle, and the customized body panels indicated armored modifications.

The Handyman chose his weapon accordingly: three thin, I-shaped sheets of explosives resembling a honeycomb. The top sheet was impregnated with a separate timing device designed to ignite a microsecond before the bottom two. The effect would be to drive the blast down. The explosion would ignite the fuel line, causing it and the gas tank to blow. If the first explosion and resulting loss of control didn't kill Ryder and French, the incendiary fuel and subsequent fireball would.

The Handyman took his right hand off the steering wheel for the three seconds it took to peel the plastic backing off the sheets of explosives and expose the adhesive. With those in his left hand, he edged closer to the Suburban, until the two vehicles were only a foot apart. Stretching out his arm, he pasted the sheets of explosives just above the wheel well, on the fender.

Fifteen seconds had elapsed since he'd peeled off the plastic backing, automatically setting the timer. The Handyman pulled away from the Suburban, counting under his breath, *1016, 1017, 1018.*

Whip Alley was in the passenger seat of the Buick. Beside him, the driver cursed the growing traffic and the sloppy way the big car handled. The detective in the back was checking the load in the Heckler and Koch MP-5 machine gun he'd retrieved from the trunk.

Alley had a pressure bandage on his shoulder and had swiped a small bottle of painkillers when the paramedic wasn't looking. The throb of the wound balanced out the narcotic effect of the painkillers. He was alert and knew that he could stay that way until Sloane had reached safety.

"That's gotta be them up ahead," growled the detective behind the wheel.

Alley scanned the road and saw the top half of the Suburban floating above the traffic. As much as he'd hated to, he'd stayed off the air, knowing that it was more important for the helicopter, with its overview, to stay in touch with Sloane. Now he dialed himself in.

"Sloane, do you read me?"

"Whip!"

"I'm six car lengths behind you, in the fast lane. I'll be alongside in a minute."

"What happened to the state trooper?"

Alley went numb. "What trooper?"

"He came up beside me a minute ago and told me to follow him. Now he's disappeared. Wait." Her voice broke up into static and Alley thought he'd go mad. "Speed it up!" he snapped at the driver. "Sloane, talk to me!"

"I see him now. He must have been on my right. He's out in front, but I don't see his lights. He's supposed to escort me—"

Alley cursed. "Sloane, listen to me. Get off the road. Right now. Get on the shoulder—"

"But the trooper—"

"The trooper's a fake. He's the Handyman. For God's sake, Sloane, get off the road and out of the car!"

1026, 1027, 1028 . . .

"Sloane, do you understand? Get out of the car!"

Sloane looked at French, who was smiling slightly. "He's coming to get you, Sloane," he whispered.

He's crazy, Sloane thought. *Certifiable.* "No. He's coming for *you.* I'm just in the way."

Sloane heard honking behind her, checked the side mirror and saw the big Buick moving up fast. It would have made better progress had it not been an undercover vehicle, no lights except for a small bubble on the dashboard. Sloane spotted an opening and cut into the right lane. A quarter turn of the wheel and the right-side tires began throwing up pebbles and grit from the shoulder. She hit the power locks.

"Get ready to jump," she shouted at French, slowing her speed, getting ready to ease the truck off the pavement.

. . . 1029, 1030.

The force of the blast made the truck heave. In that split second before she saw the hot-white flames, Sloane thought that she'd somehow run over a giant log. The Suburban's front end lifted, allowing the secondary charges to plow into its guts. The right half of the engine compartment crumpled, the steering and speed controls ripping away as the explosives tore through the armor, demolishing the engine mounts and shredding the front tires. The passenger-side floor was carved open, the scimitarlike steel petals cutting and chopping into French's legs. Blood flew from Sloane's nose, her sinuses ruptured, and her eardrums popped. She was spared the sound of French's terrible screams.

The carcass of the Suburban was thrown into the center lane, where it ground up a small Toyota Camry.

There were multiple squeals and crashes behind the car but Sloane heard none of them. Both the steering-wheel air bag and her seat belt had kept her alive. Then she felt the impact of a rear-end collision as something plowed into the Suburban, then a second and a third hit. Metal screeched against blacktop as the truck, its entire front end gone, was pushed across the road. One last shove and it rolled, rocked back and forth, and settled on its roof.

The Secret Service helicopter had reached the end of its perimeter run and was swinging back in Sloane's direction when the pilot's shout came over the headsets.

"Over there! Jesus Christ, what's going on?"

Tylo and Fremont stared at the fireball ballooning in the middle of the interstate. Tylo reacted instantly, trying to raise Sloane on the radio, getting nothing but static.

"He's down there," Fremont shouted into the mike. "We've got to find him."

"We're going back for *her!*" Tylo replied fiercely. She didn't need to tell the pilot to hustle.

Tylo changed frequencies. "Whip, are you down there? Can you hear me?"

". . . hear you fine. It was a car bomb. I'm on it. Sloane reported a state trooper car pulling up beside her. It had to be the Handyman. He can't have gotten far in this mess. Go get him!"

The pilot looked over his shoulder. Tylo glanced at Fremont and made the call.

"Wheel around!"

* * *

Rivulets of flame inched their way under and around the wreck. Sidestepping them, Alley raced for the Suburban, which lay on its roof. The smell of oil and gasoline was so strong it almost made him gag.

"It's gonna blow, Whip!" one of the detectives shouted.

Alley ignored him. He got a handhold on the truck's underbelly and hoisted himself up, then maneuvered his way to the passenger compartment. The glass on the driver's door had splintered but not shattered. Inside, Alley saw Sloane hanging upside down, like an astronaut at rest. He roared out her name, thought he saw her stir.

"Get me the tire iron!" he screamed at his men.

Alley would never remember how the iron came to be in his hands. He was never conscious of the searing pain in his shoulder as he lifted the tire iron, drew back, and smashed its squat butt through the window. Then he attacked the layers of glass with his bare hands, peeling them back like an orange's rind. Struggling to reach her, he smelled the fire retardant his men were spraying on the wreck, buying him precious seconds. Finally he got a grip on Sloane's jacket and pulled. Her torso was hanging out the window, the rest of her caught in the seat belt.

"Knife!" Alley called out to his men.

Alley reached inside and sliced through the restraint. With a final, jarring pull, he dragged her out of the wreck.

One of the detectives lifted her over his shoulder in a fireman's carry.

The other grabbed Alley and said, "Come *on!* We gotta get out of here!"

Then Alley heard it, the whimpers through the crackle of the flames. He shook off the detective and staggered to the other side of the truck.

"Talk to me, Harry," Tylo shouted at the pilot.

"A minute . . . Gimme a minute."

"Don't have a minute. He's down there somewhere. Find him!"

Hollis Fremont had broken out her sniper's rifle and jacked in a ten-round box magazine. She pulled open the door, the wind tearing at her face and hair, and scanned the traffic below. The telescopic sight, with its beta light reticle illumination, turned the night into a pale-green sea. The car headlights were emerald pinpricks. Six hundred feet below, a father driving his family to his parents' for Thanksgiving never noticed the red dot wavering on his forehead.

"You find him, I'll take him," she said to Tylo.

"Okay. Okay, I got him!" The pilot made a stabbing motion with his hand. "On I-395, just passing the Fashion Center at Pentagon City."

Tylo snatched up the night-vision binoculars and trained them on the highway.

"My ten o'clock!" the pilot shouted.

There was the patrol car, the only one on the road, moving at a steady forty-five miles an hour.

"You want me to light him up?" the pilot asked, his thumb over the button that would illuminate the fifty-thousand-candlepower belly lamp.

Tylo glanced at Fremont, who shook her head.

"If he sees us, he'll bolt. Given his present direction, where's he heading?"

"Into the city. The only exits left would take him to the Pentagon. There's nothing for him there."

"Getting into the city means crossing a bridge."

"The George Mason. He'll come out by the Jefferson Memorial."

"It's the bridge," Fremont said softly. "Your people block off the D.C. end. We'll come behind him."

Tylo was reaching for the radio when she felt a hand on her shoulder.

"You'll want a river patrol too," Fremont said. "I lost him once in water."

The Washington-bound half of I-95 was now a grave-yard of twisted, broken metal. Seconds after Whip Alley had dragged Sloane and Dodge French from the Suburban, the gas tank had blown, destroying not only the SUV but four cars that had piled into it. Miraculously, those drivers and passengers had had the time and presence of mind to abandon their vehicles. All were badly frightened, none was seriously hurt.

Because police, fire, and rescue vehicles were still fighting their way to the scene, Alley's two detectives became the law and order. They set up a perimeter around the Buick and one by the burning wrecks. Drivers who'd gotten caught in the snarl were ordered to return to their vehicles. The injured from cars in the pileup behind the Suburban were taken to a large motor home that had quickly been commandeered as an emergency shelter.

Alley sat in the driver's seat of the Buick, the door

open. He'd just gotten off the air with the police helicopter that was en route, carrying a team of firefighters and investigators. A medevac was also on the way. Landing wouldn't be a problem since traffic couldn't get around the accident sites. I-395 eastbound was unnaturally still and silent.

"How is he?" Sloane asked.

Alley looked at Sloane stretched out on the rear bench seat, propped against the door. He reached over and took her hand. Her skin was cold, her pulse still racing. She had survived the wreckage with only a few cuts and some nasty bruises. Dodge French hadn't been so lucky.

"Not good," Alley replied.

French's legs had been severed in the explosion. What was left of him now lay on the lower half of a bunk bed in the motor home. Working frantically, Alley had fashioned tourniquets to stem what he could of the blood flow. There was nothing he could do to still the screams.

"Will he make it?" Sloane asked.

Alley checked the sky. He thought he heard the flutter of rotors in the distance

"If the medevac gets here soon, maybe."

"We need to keep him alive, Whip. The things he knows . . . things the President needs to know."

He rubbed the back of her hand with his thumb. "You said he talked to you. You'll be on the first helo out of here."

"He told me so little," Sloane whispered.

"Maybe he told you enough." Alley paused. "It's a wonder that he said anything at all."

"It was his ego talking. French is a megalomaniac. The idea that he might be killed never crossed his mind. He still believes he will live to see the final piece of his grand design."

"God might have other plans."

They both heard the flutter. Sloane winced as she sat up.

"French told me what he did because he believes he *is* God," she said. "The Handyman came for him and missed—proof that French's time wasn't up. But riding beside me, he really believed that mine was."

Using the resources of the D.C. police, the Secret Service cut off traffic at the junction where I-395 empties onto U.S. 1. Then they forced all the motorists between U.S. 1 and the George Mason Bridge to turn around. At the foot of the bridge, within sight of the Jefferson Memorial, the road was blocked by six Secret Service vehicles, including several armored utility vehicles. A picket fence of agents was strung across the road while snipers slipped into position on both sides of the bridge.

A police vessel out of Buzzard Point took care of the Potomac watch.

A mile behind the Handyman, Virginia state troopers were preventing motorists from going around them. The procedure served to clear the highway ahead, allowing undercover police sedans to move up to the remaining traffic and cull the motorists one by one. The idea was to have as few cars around the Handyman as possible. No one wanted a high-speed pursuit or a hostage situation.

"We have ten cars, a semi, and two small trucks around him," Tylo said, holding the binoculars to her eyes. "If we take any more, he'll get suspicious."

"Thank God it's night," Fremont replied. "Otherwise he'd have already noticed that there's less traffic behind him."

Neither woman mentioned her worst fear: that the Handyman *had* already noted the diminishing number of headlights behind him.

"How's the flow ahead of him?" Fremont asked.

"Steady at forty, forty-five miles an hour. The troopers have staged a small accident at the exit to Memorial Parkway to siphon off the cars."

"That means traffic will be slowing down. Look. It's already happening. Even if he sees the flares and the accident, he won't buy the coincidence. He doesn't believe in them."

"The bridge is blocked off on the other side," Tylo said tightly. "He tries to cross it, he gets nowhere. Same thing for the parkway exit. And we're sitting on his ass. Where else can he go? What else can he do?"

Fremont didn't know, and that was the worst of it. The Handyman always planned for contingencies. At the Statue of Liberty, it had seemed that he was trapped. But the Handyman had come prepared, had created spectacular diversions, had used the subsequent confusion to make his getaway. Fremont glanced down at the inky Potomac, at the reflection of the city's lights shimmering on the waves, and cursed the slow progress of the police boat.

"Traffic's down to thirty-five miles an hour," Tylo said. "If he's going to bolt, this is when he'll do it."

"Tell the pilot to bring us down a little closer, two hundred feet."

Tylo's stomach tightened as the helicopter lost altitude. Now she didn't need the night-vision glasses; the overhead lamps along the highway were enough.

What little traffic remained had come almost to a stop. Tylo saw the highway flares, the flashing bubblegum lights on the police cruisers, the state troopers waving cars toward the exit.

And there was the Handyman's car, distinctive because of the roof-rack lights.

Tylo turned to Fremont. "Something's wrong. Look!"

The Handyman's car crept past the flares, toward the troopers directing the traffic. Past them, now, only two car lengths from the exit.

"Call it," Tylo said urgently. "He can't jackrabbit across the bridge now and I can't get my people to the bottom of the exit in time. Either the troopers take him—"

"Let them," Fremont replied.

Tylo's first call was to the Secret Service contingent. Even before she finished speaking, the first cars had streaked across the George Mason Bridge. Next, Fremont saw the state trooper cruisers moving up the exit.

"Let that last car ahead of him go by, then drop everything you've got on him," Tylo said into the mike. She switched frequencies and spoke to the pilot.

"Get us in closer, Harry. And lower. Closer . . . Okay, light him up!"

The beam of the fifty-million-candlepower belly

lamp shot through the night, painting the Handyman's car a dazzling white. Fremont listened to the shouts of troopers coming over her headphones, braced herself by the open door as the pilot brought the chopper in like an angry dragonfly. Very carefully she brought the rubber rim of the telescopic sight against her right eye.

"We got him! Got 'im! He's down. Covered."

The state police cruiser's door opened. A man, his hands held high, was getting out. On his knees now, leaning forward, lying facedown. One hand came behind his neck, then the other. Four troopers ringed him, the barrels of their weapons no more than three feet from his body. One of the troopers stepped forward, cuffed the man, then pulled him to his feet.

"Got 'im!" Tylo said triumphantly, punching the air with her fist.

The helicopter settled and she was about to jump out when she noticed Fremont's slack expression.

Fremont tapped the sight on her rifle. "I saw his face. It's not him. That's not the Handyman."

31

"I'M TELLING YOU, that's the way it happened!"

"Tell us again."

Tylo stared at the suspect sitting on the hard wooden chair in the interrogation room at the Virginia state trooper barracks on Old Jefferson Davis Highway.

His name was Billy Waterstone. He was black, thirty-four years old, with coffee-colored eyes and a face pocked by childhood acne. His hands were rough, with dirt under the fingernails, and he wore a thick red-and-black-check jacket over two sweaters. Billy Waterstone was a bricklayer; a union card and a recent pay stub had been found next to the Maryland driver's license in his wallet.

Tylo glanced at Fremont and the state trooper commander, then said, "Give it to us one more time, Mr. Waterstone."

On the table bolted to the floor was a tape recorder, its spools turning slowly.

Waterstone shifted in the chair. "Okay. I'm driving alone, minding my own business—"

"Driving your pickup."

"Right. With a Brahma cab. Anyway, I'm driving along and I see this Smokey come up behind me, lights flashing. I know I'm not speeding and last time I checked, my taillights were working just fine. But I pull over."

Tylo noted the resignation in his voice. To Billy Waterstone, a black man being pulled over for no apparent reason was just the way things were in America at the beginning of the new millennium.

"The trooper pulls up behind me, comes over, and all very polite says *he* has a problem. He needs my help." Waterstone shook his head. "Now, *that's* a switch."

"Did he show you any identification?" Tylo asked.

"He was *wearing* it. The uniform, the badge, the gun. His car. I mean, what *wasn't* I supposed to believe?"

"Then he said . . ."

"He said that he was on an emergency run and his engine was acting up. He needed my truck. Said I could take his cruiser, drive it as far as it'd go. If I made it all the way to the city, I was to pull in at the fifth-precinct station and wait for him there."

"None of this sounded strange to you?" the commander broke in.

"You gotta understand, it was all happening so fast. I get pulled over, here's this guy telling me he has an emergency. Okay, he wants to take my truck, but he's leaving me *his* wheels. It's not like I'm being car jacked."

"It didn't occur to you to ask if he'd radioed for help?" Tylo asked.

"Like I said, things were happening too fast. He opened my door, I got out . . ." Waterstone shook his head.

"What is it?"

"If he was someone else, maybe I would have asked questions. But not this dude. He was real polite, but cold. His eyes—they were dead. Listen, I did my stint in Desert Storm. I met guys who worked behind the Iraqi lines. Never said what they did there, didn't have to. They had eyes like that."

"Then he took your car," Tylo prompted.

"Took my *truck* and barreled down the highway. I go to the cruiser. The keys are in the ignition, just like he said. I get in, sit for a minute—I never been in the *front* seat of a cop car. I'm looking for the radio and the fancy computer they have on the dash, but there's nothing. Not even a shotgun rack. I'm thinking maybe this is a different kind of trooper's car. Anyway, I fire it up. The engine sounds just fine and I'm rolling."

Waterstone smiled faintly. "I tell you, it was a rush driving that thing, catching the looks people gave me when I passed them, looking twice because I'm not wearing the uniform, because I'm black."

"And you headed for the city," Tylo said.

"That's it. The car's purrin' along. Whatever problems he had, they're gone. Now all I'm thinking is I hope he don't wreck my truck in some chase."

"You followed the trooper's instructions to go to the fifth-precinct station."

"Sure did. I get close to the bridge and traffic's all backed up. I see the flares, what looks like a bump-and-scrape, cops waving people off." Waterstone looked up at the commander, his voice becoming hard, stopping just short of accusatory. "Then it's my turn. I'm pulling off nice and easy and suddenly the hammer drops. Cops fall out of the sky, I'm down on the ground, and all I'm thinking is, 'They think I stole this damn car.'"

The commander's neck was turning red. "That's not what my men assumed."

Tylo saw trouble in the making and got between them.

"Mr. Waterstone, the trooper was an impostor. He's really a wanted felon."

"Yeah," Waterstone replied. "I kinda figured that out for myself."

"I'm sorry that you became involved in this matter."

"I'm a little more than involved, ma'am. This guy has my truck."

But maybe not for long, Tylo thought. An APB for the truck had been flashed across six states right after Waterstone had told his story the first time. The alert was flagged with caution: If spotted, the vehicle and its driver should *not* be approached. The officers involved were immediately to contact the Secret Service, maintain surveillance, and request backup. Seventy-five minutes had elapsed since the flash but Tylo remained hopeful.

"We'll get your truck back to you," she said. "The commander will have you driven to wherever you need to go."

Waterstone looked suspiciously at the faces around him. "You mean I'm out of here?"

"With our apologies."

Waterstone rose. "You mind my askin' or you gonna make me wait to hear it on the news: Who is this guy? What did he do? Kill a cop or something?"

"Or something like that." Tylo opened the door for him. "You're a very lucky man, Mr. Waterstone."

The crush of media vans around the White House kept the uniformed Secret Service agents busy. Reporters lined up in front of the black wrought-iron fence to do their stand up. Across the darkened lawn, lights blazed in the Oval Office. The Iraqi cauldron was threatening to boil over; it was reassuring that the President was on the job this night before Thanksgiving.

What the media couldn't possibly know was that the activities in the White House and the arrivals of grim-faced military and civilian advisers were not in any way related to the situation in the Middle East. As camouflage, the Iraqi question was perfect.

"A saving grace," Claudia Ballantine said, staring out the window, knowing that just beyond the lights, reporters were keeping vigil.

She turned to Sloane Ryder, sitting near the crackling fire, one of the only two other people in the room.

"You look dead on your feet. Are you sure you're up to this?"

Sloane looked down at the cable-knit sweater she wore. She and the President were about the same size and Claudia Ballantine had sent her up to the family quarters to change into something that didn't have blood on it.

"I'll be fine, Madam President," Sloane replied. "How is . . . Mr. French?"

"Officially he's still very much alive," James Trimble cut in. The national security adviser shook his head. "The doctors at Johns Hopkins can't believe he's still hanging on, but they're not guaranteeing he'll last through the night." He paused. "Madam President, I'm sorry to have to press you, but it's almost noon tomorrow in Taiwan."

"I know."

Claudia Ballantine gazed at Sloane. For the past two hours, this young woman had told her the most incredible story, one so obscene and treasonous that the President could scarcely believe it. But the truth of Sloane's words was etched on every cut and bruise on her face, and in the words themselves.

When Sloane was escorted from the family quarters, she had found the Oval Office filled with people. Key members of the President's cabinet were present, along with high-ranking military officials. Some had regarded her with suspicion, others with incredulity, but that had changed when the President prompted her to repeat her story. After that, the air was filled with muttered curses; the whispered exchanges were punctuated by swift, fearful glances.

As the debate about what to do had heated up, Sloane had withdrawn to a chair by the fireplace. She'd stared at the flames and time had dissolved. The next time she'd heard her name spoken, the room was empty except for the President and James Trimble.

"Tell them we're on our way," the President said.

Trimble spoke briefly into the phone, then followed the President and Sloane into the hall. Because of the very real possibility that the Handyman had targeted the President, the Secret Service had doubled its White House detail. The small elevator between the Oval Office and the Cabinet Room was crowded with big men whose jackets were open to allow for easy access to their weapons.

As the car descended the three hundred feet to the subbasement, Sloane tried to prepare herself for what lay ahead. But as she had already learned, nothing could ready one to deal with the world she'd suddenly been plunged into.

The elevator glided to a smooth stop and the agents escorted their charge to the nuclear-blast door, open to reveal the presidential nuclear command center.

The purpose of the room, as much as the atmosphere in it, chilled Sloane. It was the size of a small auditorium, with three tiers. On the lowest were three monitors, each the size of a multiplex theater screen. One displayed a Mercator projection of the globe; the second, a satellite shot of the South China coast and Taiwan; the third, an even tighter shot defining various Chinese ports and airfields.

The second tier was filled with computer stations manned by thirty-odd military officers outfitted with headsets; on the third and highest tier were comfortable leather chairs set in front of a long console. In the center was the President's chair, facing a bank of telephones.

An air force general escorted the President to her seat and whispered something to her. Claudia Ballantine shook her head and mouthed no. Sloane wondered if the military was still trying to change her mind.

Back in the Oval Office, there had been a heated debate over whether or not to remove the President immediately, by helicopter, to Mount Weather in the

Virginia Blue Mountains. It was a self-contained shelter from which she and her senior advisers could direct a nuclear confrontation and, if it came to that, use Mount Weather's television studios to reach out to survivors. Or, Sloane thought, the issue could be the visitor.

A moment later, Claudia Ballantine waved away the general and said to Trimble, "Bring him in."

The man was dwarfed both by the two marine escorts and by the enormous vault door. As soon as he was inside the command post, the door began to close. A slow shudder rolled through the room as the door locked and the foot-thick reinforcing rods slid into place.

Li Peng, the ambassador from the People's Republic of China, stared around as though he'd been transported to another world. He was tall for a Chinese man, with handsome features and pitch-black hair. His postgraduate degrees from two American universities and his pleasant manner had earned him a network of high-ranking friends in both government and business. Because he was familiar with things American, and a devoutly loyal Party member, Li Peng had been tapped for the post of ambassador. But nothing in his experience had prepared him for this. The urgent call from the White House and the quick drive over had unsettled him. Looking around, he realized that he was well out of his depth.

"Mr. Ambassador," the President said, rising as Trimble guided the diplomat to her chair.

"Madam President," Peng said softly.

He couldn't take his eyes off the giant screens and the calm young personnel arranged below him.

The President indicated the chair beside hers.

Sitting down, Peng now had the same view of the world that the President had. He felt that in some inexplicable way she was making an accomplice of him.

"Do you know why I asked you to join me here, Mr. Ambassador?"

"No, Madam President. I was told only that the matter was of the utmost urgency."

"It is." Claudia Ballantine fixed her eyes on him. "Fifty-eight years ago, December 7, 1941, to be exact, two diplomats representing Japan met with our secretary of war. They, too, professed not to know why they had been summoned, although they carried with them a formal declaration of war. A little too late, as it turned out. The bombs had already fallen on Pearl Harbor."

"Madam President—"

"Please look at the monitor on the left."

Peng gasped. There was Dodge French, lying in a hospital bed, surrounded by life-support systems. A young male nurse stepped into the frame and placed a small mirror to French's lips. The camera zoomed in to catch his breath fogging the mirror.

"You might not believe the machines," the President said. "But the mirror does not lie. Dodge French is alive and we will keep him that way."

She did not add how long that might be or enlighten Peng to the fact that the lumps under the covers where French's legs should have been were actually rolled-up blankets.

"He's already given us many details," she continued.

"We expect more. But for our purposes, we have enough. Would you care to hear some of them?"

Peng licked his lips. "Madam President, I'm at a loss as to what to say. Really, I think I should contact my government for instructions—"

"Later. Now is a good time to listen. Sloane?"

Sloane collected her thoughts and repeated for Peng what Dodge French had told her during their escape from Occoquan.

"Madam President, I find all this quite incredible!" Peng said vehemently. "These charges are preposterous! My country has no knowledge—"

"It does now," the President said, silencing him. "It's known for a long time exactly what we'll do now. And this is what will happen."

She leaned forward and said into the microphone, "Captain."

Somewhere below, an officer punched in an entry code. The image of French in the hospital bed disappeared, replaced by the Mercator projection. Small red dots pulsated in an area bounded roughly by the Philippines, Okinawa, and Thailand.

"Most of my military advisers were dead set against my showing you this," the President said. "They didn't even want you in this room. I, on the other hand, want you to see *everything*, so that your report to Beijing will be complete and accurate.

"Those red dots, Mr. Ambassador, represent our current forces in the Far East. As you can see, they are slowly converging on Taiwan. The Taiwan Strait is, at the moment, defenseless, but we all know the reason for that. It may appear that our resources are quite far away. However, you and your principals should understand the following: Our bomber armadas, including the B-2 Stealth, are currently being refueled in midair."

The President checked the digital clock suspended from the ceiling. "In fifteen minutes, Chinese mainland ports and airfields will be within range of our cruise missiles. At the same time, the captains of our nuclear submarines, which also have cruise-missile capability, will break out their attack orders and retarget their packages to include any Chinese warship or troop transport that enters the Taiwan Strait."

"Madam President, that is provocation of the basest kind!"

The President leaned closer to Peng.

"No, sir! This is a *measured response* to a potential attack on a sovereign state. Your intelligence people know that our forces never carry only conventional weapons. In this case, the first strike would be conventional, targeted only against your military headed for Taiwan. But it doesn't even have to go that far.

"Tell Beijing to pull back, Mr. Ambassador. We know that the attack is slated for Thanksgiving Day. But we're not sure whether it's *our* time or yours. If yours, then the attack will begin very shortly and you must act quickly. If tomorrow, then we will have even more deterrence in the area."

The President drew back. "China doesn't have to do this. China doesn't need to do it. You waited decades for Hong Kong to revert. Soon, the old men of Taiwan and the old China hands here will disappear. Then maybe the Chinese of Taiwan and those of the mainland will want to be one again. Let *them* decide, not some industrialists and money changers who seek only profit. Such people never had, nor will they ever have, the authority to create such protocols."

The President rose and swept her hand to embrace the room. "You know what we know. You've seen what we see. You understand what will happen if Beijing stays its course. Talk to your leaders, Mr. Ambassador. Make them understand that this nation will not tolerate the kind of treachery that Pearl Harbor symbolizes. Not on my watch. Not ever again!"

On Thanksgiving eve, Chinatown was deserted except for the elderly, who'd never embraced the American holiday, and the most recent immigrants.

Mai Ling sat in the kitchen of the butcher shop, watching the cooks gamble quietly in the corner. The owner of the shop and his wife sat next to the cold ranges, tallying up the day's receipts. No one looked up when the back door opened and a tall white man entered. He simply did not exist.

"Good evening, Mother," the Handyman said.

Mai Ling took her time screwing a cigarette into her holder, fitting it between her teeth. Then, lightning quick, she slapped the Handyman across the face.

The Handyman felt the sting of her palm linger on his cheek and knew it was because he had allowed French to live.

"He will not live long, Mother," he said quietly. "Certainly not long enough to say anything. Maybe he's dead by now."

Mai Ling snorted. "You are mistaken. He lived long enough to say a great deal."

She launched into the account Li Peng had provided her with upon his return to the embassy. Li Peng, with his braying voice, wringing his hands.

"You say that Li Peng saw French on a monitor, lying in a hospital bed," he said. "He didn't see him in person."

"And he was breathing," Mai Ling added.

"The mirror, yes. Interesting that the President would go out of her way to demonstrate that. Isn't it possible that Li Peng was the victim of a hoax? I know disguises and special effects. The mirror could have been sleight of hand."

"Peng believes the Americans would not have brought him into their innermost chamber just to perpetrate a hoax."

"What better way to do it? You wrap the small lie in a very large truth."

"Maybe what you do not wish to believe is that you failed with French."

The Handyman shook his head. "Yes, the Americans have learned about your intentions for Taiwan. But as Peng reported, they remain uncertain as to the time. They reacted as they did because they think that the operation might be under way right now, running on Taiwan time, instead of tomorrow."

"And . . . ?"

"And what is to occur tomorrow shall still come to pass. Whatever French may have told the Americans, he didn't give them the Chos, did he?"

Mai Ling shook her head. She had contacted the

Chos less than an hour before. They and 1818 were safely ensconced in a nearby Embassy Suites hotel, having flown in from Providence.

The Handyman rose and buttoned his coat. There would be no further face-to-face contact between him and Mai Ling. There didn't have to be. The Handyman knew exactly what was left to him to do.

"May fortune favor you tomorrow," Mai Ling said, then added. "I should have let you deal with that Ryder woman!"

The Handyman glanced over his shoulder. "Yes. But now is not too late."

WHILE SLOANE RYDER tossed in a restless sleep in the White House guest quarters, the digitally encrypted satellite link between Taipei and Washington hummed.

Even before Claudia Ballantine and the Taiwanese prime minister finished speaking, units of the Taiwanese navy steamed out of their berths to take up positions just inside their territorial waters.

Under the guise of "joint military exercises," they were joined by the Taiwanese air force. F-16s and F-18s, fully armed, left their reinforced bunkers to patrol the skies. They were refueled by aerial tankers and touched down only for pilot rotation.

At the same time, the U.S.S. *Virginia,* carrying, among other things, an array of cruise missiles, broke the surface just long enough to allow Chinese satellites to get a peek at her. It was a none too subtle signal to Beijing that the Americans hadn't been bluffing about their presence in the strait.

Meanwhile, U.S. satellites and SR-71 spy planes crisscrossed the Chinese coast, searching for military movement.

In Washington, preparations of a different sort were under way, aided by the cover of darkness.

Holland Tylo and Hollis Fremont returned from the state trooper barracks and reported that neither the Handyman nor Waterstone's truck had been spotted. The President decided to increase the pressure.

Since state troopers already had the Handyman's description out on the wire, she called the head of the FBI and the chief of the D.C. police. It was possible, she told them, that the attempt on Dodge French's life was linked to the death of General Sam Murchison and, by implication, that this was the work of the same assassin or assassins who might be bankrolled by Saddam Hussein. Since there was no way to avoid a leak with so many people in on the hunt, the media would at least tie the news about French into an existing story. The President figured that if the Iraqis denounced the news reports, who'd believe them?

While Fremont waited for word of a Handyman sighting, Tylo worked at intensifying the security arrangements around the President. All the sensors—audio, eye, electronic, pressure, and infrared—that surround the White House grounds were double-checked. Secret Service SWAT teams armed with machine guns were positioned on the roof. Three agents monitored the digital locator box that tracked the President's movements both inside the White House and out. Claudia Ballantine's entire Thanksgiving Day schedule was reviewed. A hundred and thirty children would arrive later today, along with their parents. Tylo ordered that the profiles of all the accompanying kin be run through the computer again. Even remotely unusual details were to be brought to her attention immediately.

At 3:00 A.M., the President finally went upstairs to sleep. A half hour later, Tylo, who'd been reviewing the profiles of the parents as they were forwarded to her, did the same.

The hunt was up. All around him, the Handyman saw an increased police presence. The news carried stories about a possible connection between Dodge French's accident and the murder of the chairman of the Joint Chiefs of Staff. That meant the FBI and other federal authorities were out in force. Even in the hotel, security had been stepped up, with desk clerks and plainclothes guards paying greater attention to the faces in the lobby and other public rooms.

The Handyman had slept in the living room of the Chos' two-room Embassy Suites accommodations. Now, looking through the window, across to the park, and farther, to Rock Creek Parkway, he saw a perfect Indian-summer day.

He entered the bathroom that separated the two rooms and critically examined the man he saw in the mirror. The paunch, a special-effects device used to make actresses appear pregnant, created the illusion that he was shorter and out of shape. The baggy pants and the tweed jacket with shiny leather elbow patches fit right in with the gray beard, trimmed mustache, mock tortoiseshell glasses, and pipe. The sum of the parts produced the desired effect of a dusty scholar.

Returning to the living room, he thumbed through a well-worn wallet that included a California driver's license, a UCLA faculty ID, the return portion of an

American Airlines ticket to Los Angeles, a Social Security card, and credit cards all bearing the name of Joseph Pularski. If he were stopped, Joseph Pularski would pass more than a cursory examination.

"You are ready?"

The Handyman turned to the North Korean woman. "Yes."

"You are better than the chameleon."

He smiled. "The boy?"

"As well as can be expected. The sedative I gave him last night is wearing off." She checked her watch. "Two hours to the ceremonies. If he's still drowsy, I'll give him five milligrams of Dexedrine to make him act like the other children."

She reached into her purse and handed him a Motorola cell phone.

The Handyman hefted it in his palm. "Heavier than the real one."

"Marginally so. The transmitter adds to the weight. To use it, pull the antenna, press the power button, then the pound sign, then the send button."

The Handyman stared at the tiny phone whose guts had been replaced with a transmitter powerful enough to reach its target despite the enormous amount of interference the signal would encounter.

"Range?"

"Two hundred yards. It is only ninety-five yards to the Zero Milestone, across the South Lawn, to the doors of the Diplomatic Reception Room." She glanced outside. "In this weather, they will set the party on the lawn, according to the newspaper. Easier for you."

The Handyman pocketed the cell phone and picked

up a well-thumbed copy of *Moby-Dick* from the coffee table.

"Safe flight home," he told the woman and started to leave.

"*Will* it be safe?"

The Handyman had his hand on the doorknob. "You think I will kill you because you have seen my face?"

She nodded.

"You will be on your way to the airport by the time I'm done, too late to interfere or stop me. Yes, you are safe."

The woman was an expert at detecting lies and could not sniff one out in his words. But neither did she know how perfectly sincere the Handyman's promise had sounded to the colonel who'd run the camp where 1818 had been found.

As the Handyman left the Embassy Suites, final preparations for the party were under way.

Over breakfast in the informal dining room, Holland Tylo had argued that the entire affair should be held indoors, in the secure confines of the Diplomatic Reception Room. The President would not be swayed. She had planned to have the children eat and play outside; now that the weather was cooperating, she would not change her mind. Besides, that room had been reserved for the parents to mingle, chat, and sample the buffet.

By noon, the White House staff had set up the tables, chairs, portable heat lamps, and serving carts on the South Lawn, between the two exterior stone staircases that curved down to the double doors of the Diplomatic Reception Room. From there, parents could look out and watch their children play.

In the kitchens, White House chefs were in the last stages of preparing lunch. Due consideration had been given to the dietary requirements of both the children and the parents. Fortunately, turkey and the traditional trimmings were accepted fare in the majority of cases. In some instances, fish or lamb was substituted; a rabbi had overseen the preparation of a kosher meal for the Israeli family.

At half past twelve, Tylo made her final perimeter check. Bomb-sniffing dogs and their handlers were stationed at every vehicle checkpoint. Agents in camouflage silently patrolled the wooded areas behind the ten-foot-high fence that separates the grounds from the public sidewalks. The concrete barriers along Pennsylvania Avenue had been checked at dawn to make sure no explosives had been secreted. Glaziers used by the Secret Service had gone over the panes in the doors and windows of the Diplomatic Reception Room to ensure that there were no seams or hairline fractures. Two helicopters carrying Service sharpshooters patrolled the restricted airspace around the White House. The radar used by the Service to follow aircraft coming into and out of national airport was tested.

"How's it looking?" Fremont asked Tylo when she finished her walk around at the Fifteenth Street guard post.

"We're as ready as we'll ever be. The Handyman?"

Fremont shook her head. "He's out there, waiting. Watching, maybe."

Tylo glanced up Fifteenth Street. A tour bus had pulled up at the corner of Pennsylvania and a group of adults and children filed out.

"We're on," she said.

"So's the Handyman," Fremont replied.

They walked down to where Executive Drive curves in front of the South Lawn. Behind the wrought-iron fence, the fountain was shooting spray high into the air.

"Your idea?" Fremont asked.

Tylo nodded. The greater the water pressure, the higher the spray, helping to spoil a possible shot.

Even on Thanksgiving, clusters of tourists posed by the fence, using what could be seen of the White House as a backdrop for pictures. Close to the fence were two chase cars, a Bronco and a sedan. The windows of the Bronco were down so that the agents with field glasses could pan the tourists.

"He can't do it," Tylo said quietly. "No damn way he could line up a shot from here. And that's the only shot he has."

Fremont said nothing. As a former Secret Service agent who had been betrayed and in the process had lost an individual on her watch, she understood how Tylo felt. It was true: Checks had been run and rerun on every person associated with this event, all the way down to the pot scrubbers in the kitchens. No flags had gone up; no alarms had sounded. Maybe because of that, the silence seemed unnatural, the wait for this ceremony to begin—and end—unbearable.

"What's your post?" asked Fremont.

"I'm a floater. The President never gets more than

four feet from me. What about you? Any special position you want inside?"

"I'll stay out here a while. I missed him going in at Occoquan. He's not going to be that lucky twice."

The Chos and 1818 boarded the bus under the portico of the Embassy Suites driveway. They were the last pickup and moved all the way to the back. Both North Koreans smiled and nodded at the people they passed. The woman was glad that the parents appeared nervous. Nervous people never remembered anything.

The drive to Fifteenth Street took less than ten minutes along the traffic-free streets. The Chos and 1818 were the last to disembark. They stood at the end of a line that numbered sixty-odd people. When another bus pulled up and more people got out, the Chos became indistinguishable from the rest of the crowd.

As they approached the guard station, the woman forced herself not to stare at the uniformed Secret Service agent inside, or the cameras mounted on guard. She told herself that she was just another mother, nervous, excited, starry-eyed by everything around her. She tugged her "husband's" sleeve and began to chatter, pointing at the Treasury building. The man responded to her ploy. They chatted like that as the line moved slowly toward the guard station, all for the benefit of eyes and ears they could not see but knew were there.

"Your invitation and identification, please?"

The guard's tone was polite, but his gaze was coolly professional, sweeping over the Chos without a hint of apology.

The man handed over the letter and the passports. The guard matched the passport photos with the three faces in front of him, passed the Hands of Hope invitation under a scanner that revealed watermarks and a likeness of George Washington that were invisible to the naked eye. These were genuine and in the right places. The guard then made his final check, bringing up the Chos' passport numbers and photos on his computer.

"Thank you, folks. You can go in. Have a great time."

The woman's smile masked her sigh of relief. She glanced down at 1818, who was looking around, fascinated by the squirrels that raced along the branches of the trees.

"We have tons of them—squirrels, I mean." A young woman came forward. "Hi, I'm Jenny, one of your guides."

She tousled 1818's hair. "Aren't you just the cutest little guy. Ma'am, sir, if you'd like to follow me, I'll show you the way to the reception room. Isn't it just a *fantastic* day?"

The North Korean woman ached to tell her just how fantastic a day it would really be.

Lee Porter found Sloane in the library in the family quarters, seated at a desk with a notebook computer, a notepad, and an open book in front of her. His features tightened when he saw the swelling on her face, the way she winced when she raised her hand to greet him.

"How are you?" he asked.

"I'll be a whole lot better when this day is over, or when they catch him." She cast him a hopeful look.

Porter shook his head. "He's vanished. I'd like to think he saw the security and called it off."

"He didn't. He wouldn't." Sloane paused. "What about the Chinese?"

"Not a murmur. All flyovers indicate they're sitting tight. Not even a protest over the Taiwan exercises.

"They're waiting." He nodded at the desk. "What do you have there?"

Sloane tapped the bright-blue screen with a fingernail.

"Zero, so far. I've been going over the analysts' reports. All we have are assumptions based on interpretations of what French said to me. We know there's a killer out there. We know that the President is his target. Everything is being done to protect her . . ."

"But not enough."

Sloane shook her head. "We're missing something. It's there. We just don't see it."

"What's the book?"

Sloane showed him the copy of Lawrence Durrell's *Justine*. "There wasn't a copy in the White House library. I got it from Olsson's in Georgetown."

Porter read the underlined sentences aloud. "We are the children of our landscape; it dictates behavior and even thought in the measure to which we are responsive to it."

"Out of everything French said, this, I think, was the most meaningful. He was throwing out a clue to the way his mind works. I just can't figure out what to do with it, what it means, or how it relates."

"He could have been messing with your mind," Porter said quietly. "French loves his games."

"Yes, he does. But I don't think he was playing then." She glanced past Porter to the window. "What's going on out there?"

"Come see for yourself."

The Hands of Hope party was in full swing. Some children between the ages of seven and twelve were racing around the South Lawn, shrieking, while the Secret Service agents who had formed a cordon around the festivities looked on. Other kids were lined up by the food carts, holding up plates for turkey and trimmings. One by one the chairs at the tables filled up and the conversations tapered off as people started to eat.

"The President?" Sloane asked.

"Inside with the parents." Porter checked his watch. "She'll give the kids forty-five minutes, then come out and give her speech before the pumpkin pie and ice cream."

Sloane had to smile. The only alternative would have been tears. Children already condemned, playing under God's sky like they had all the time in the world ahead of them and not a care in the world. Her eyes swept over the lot, then focused on the stragglers who were being guided into the food line by parents. There was a little Indian girl with the distinctive caste dot on her forehead; an Asian boy in a sailor's outfit, being coddled by his mother. The child seemed angry or upset, his face streaked with tears. The woman leaned close, and, without warning, the child struck at her with his small fists, catching her in the eye, making her head snap back.

Sloane caught her breath. The woman's arm was snaking out at the child, poised to either strike or grab him. But at the last minute, like a shoplifter who senses a floorwalker nearby, she caught herself, kneeled, and reached out slowly. The child shook his head, then began to scratch at his buttocks. The woman caught his arms and held them tightly. She hugged the child, and he threw his arms around her neck. Then, in a motion that puzzled Sloane, that made her feel queasy, the woman slipped her hand into the boy's pants and moved it around his buttocks, the way one might check a baby's diaper.

Is he incontinent? . . . More likely, it's a reaction to his medication.

Sloane watched the woman calm the child, then slowly walk him to the food line.

"What's so interesting down there?"

Sloane hadn't realized that Porter had moved from the window.

"Nothing . . ."

Once in line, the woman did not leave the child. She helped him hold up his plate and, when it was full, steered him to a table where there were plenty of empty seats.

"Sloane?"

"We are the children of our landscape . . ."

Sloane stared down at the carnival scene. It was unthinkable. Not even remotely possible. *Or was it?*

Still, she pulled out her cell phone, finger jabbing the key pads. Tylo answered on the half ring.

"It's Sloane."

"What do you have?"

Sloane hesitated, knowing that the words sounded outrageous as they raced through her mind. Then: "You checked everybody going in, right? *Everybody?*"

"Everyone had to have the watermarked invitation. And passports that we scanned against the master list."

"Children—most of them—don't have passports. Their names are on the ones issued to the parents."

After a beat: "Sloane, where are you going with this?"

"You checked all the *adults*. What about the children?"

"Everyone had to go through a metal detector—"

"French said, 'We are the children of our landscape.' I found the reference in *Justine*. Durrell was talking about the adult characters in his novel. But what if French wasn't? What if he was referring to children literally?" Sloane heard Tylo's rapid breathing on the other end. "Holland, what's the President doing—working the crowd?"

"Yes."

"Okay. You know what to look for in that situation. But what happens when she goes outside and stops beside a child, picks him up, holds him?"

"But the kids went through the detector too!"

"Look, I don't know how or even if any of this is real. You made sure you checked the parents. But are all the children who're here *supposed* to be here?"

"Hold on, Sloane. I'm going on another line."

In the Diplomatic Reception Room, Tylo edged away from the President and signaled for another agent to take her position. Then she spoke into her wrist mike.

"Ladybug base. Raise to level two. Repeat, level two."

The message flashed across to every agent on duty. Hands dropped into jackets and flipped open the latches of briefcases designed to hold automatic weapons. Level two meant there was potential danger within the security zone.

Tylo watched the President handshake her way through the crowd. Claudia Ballantine must have sensed that the agents were crowding her; she shot Tylo a curious look.

"Tell Ladybug we're still okay—for now," she said into the mike, and watched an agent lean close to the President and relay the message.

Tylo hit the speed dial. "Hollis?"

The crowds in front of the South Lawn had grown, people taking advantage of the weather and lack of traffic to enjoy a leisurely stroll.

"Right where you left me," Fremont replied. "On Executive Drive."

Tylo didn't waste a word describing what Sloane had just told her. "What do you think? Did we miss something with the kids? Is it even *possible* that one of them could have been used to smuggle in a weapon?"

Fremont's mind raced. In her work for Omega, she had access to the latest intelligence, collated from sources around the world. Children . . . Something to do with children. There'd been a reference and now she dug furiously to retrieve it.

Children carrying weapons . . . No, that's not it. Come on. Come on. Children, children, children . . .

As weapons.

Fremont failed to stifle her gasp. Two years before, a report from Israel's Mossad had crossed her desk. A new radical terrorist organization had been spawned. Their twist: to send human beings with dynamite strapped to their bellies into a busy Tel Aviv shopping area. Explosions, bodies dismembered, arms and legs flying. Shrapnel cutting down victims as far away as two hundred feet.

Addendum to the report: Mossad confirms that children, some as young as seven, are present in the training camps. Being taught how to carry bombs. *Become* bombs.

Wrong! If a child was fitted with explosives, the detectors and dogs would have picked it up. Think!

The training camps . . . Who else did the report mention? Advisers: Vietnamese, old KGB Russians, North Koreans—

"Holland, is there a family from North Korea?"

"Negative. Only South Korea. The Chos. Why?"

"Hold on."

North Koreans. KGB advisers. *Medical* advisers. *Implants.*

"Where's the President?" Fremont asked.

"In the reception room. She's ready to go outside."

"*Don't let her.* Have her shake a few more hands. Make it seem natural. Do it now."

Tylo raised her wrist to her mouth. "Alert three. Tell Ladybug to make one more pass around the room. Do *not* let her go outside."

The agent closest to the President stepped up to her and smiled as he spoke. *Good move,* Tylo thought.

Then the President smiled and nodded and began chatting with another couple.

"Okay, she's staying put," Tylo said.

"Listen to me. It's possible that one of the children has been implanted with explosives. These would not have shown up on the scanners. The dogs wouldn't have picked them up either."

Tylo's voice was cool and controlled. "All the children are outside. A few of the parents too."

"The parents—if that's what they are—would stay close to the child. The implant procedure is very painful. The child is most likely drugged in some way, either to keep him calm or to make him seem lively, up, to look and act as normal as possible. But if the drug is wearing off or the wrong dose was given, he'd exhibit unusual behavior."

"You say 'he.' It could be a girl."

"Could be."

"I'm going outside to look around. Sloane's in the library. She has the bird's-eye view. See if she's spotted anything unusual."

Sloane saw Tylo step outside just as her phone rang.

"It's Hollis. Are you still at the windows?" Fremont asked.

"Yes."

"Describe what you see."

"All the kids are eating. There are the cooks and the waiters. Two clowns, the guy in the dinosaur suit moving from table to table—"

"Parents?"

"A few. A couple at one table with a little girl. Two mothers at another. Wait. A man just walked out, he's going over to a boy. One table with only a few people . . . A boy sitting with his mother, at the far end."

Fremont caught the change in Sloane's tone. "What about them?"

Sloane hesitated. "I can't say for sure. All the other kids seem . . . normal, I guess. They're laughing and playing, having a great time. But this one's funny, like he's having a reaction to medication, something like that."

"What race is he?"

"Asian."

"The mother too?"

"Yes."

"Sloane, can you tell if they're Japanese, Chinese—"

"Definitely neither of those. Thai, Korean?"

Fremont felt cold fingers curl around her heart. "Sloane, keep this line open, and keep your eye on them. Tell me if they move."

"Why? What's—"

"Sloane, wait one second. I need to talk to Holland."

Fremont switched channels. "There's an Asian boy and his mother, possibly Koreans, on the lawn," she told Tylo, then quickly filled in the details Sloane had passed along. "They could be the ones."

"Let me check."

Moving as quickly and unobtrusively as she could, Tylo made her way to the Map Room. A temporary workstation had been set up there and she began scanning the computerized guest list. South Korea. The Cho family. Clearances issued as far back as June. Background checks all positive.

Tylo hesitated. She could not keep the President in the reception room indefinitely. She could not approach the Cho boy or his mother until she was certain that they were the ones. *If* they were the ones. If the boy was implanted and moved toward the President, Tylo would throw herself on him. But how much explosive was he carrying? How far away would Claudia Ballantine have to be to escape the blast?

Is he the one?

Tylo knew she had time for only one shot. She took it. Within seconds she was connected to a Korean-speaking agent. She rattled off the number on the screen and told him to call it.

Seconds dragged and the minutes flew. When the agent came back on the line, he said, "I spoke to the grandmother. She says her daughter, husband, and grandson are in Washington to meet the President."

That's it. They're clean.

The agent was still talking. "But she's been trying to get hold of them over here and no one's been answering the phone at their hotel room. She's worried that something's happened."

"Something has," Tylo said tightly. "Call the grandmother back. Get as many details about the family as you can."

Tylo channeled back to Fremont. "The implants. What would they be? How could they be detonated?"

"The boy got past the dogs and scanners, so I'm thinking plastique. For the same reason, it's certain he's not wearing the trigger. That means remote control, an electronic signal."

"What kind?"

"You name it: radio, phone, pulse."

"How can we kill it if it's sent?"

"Jesus. We don't even know the transmitter's range. You'd have to kill every electronic transmission in the area to be sure to stop it."

"If that's what it takes." Tylo paused. "If the boy isn't wearing the transmitter, neither is the father or the mother. That leaves—"

"The Handyman. I know. He's out here. It's two hundred feet from the street to where the kids are. His signal has to be strong enough to cover that plus more. But he won't be too far. He'll want to see as much of the explosion as possible."

"Voyeur?"

"No. He'll just want to be sure. I'm going to keep working the crowds out here. Maybe I'll get lucky."

"Be careful—and keep this channel open."

Tylo punched in the number for the Ready Room at Andrews Air Force Base. A crisp voice answered immediately.

"Lieutenant Matthews."

"This is Agent Tylo, Secret Service. Stand by to verify ID."

"Standing by."

"Delta, kilo, niner, niner, three, seven, eight, alpha."

Tylo heard Matthews's breath on the line, heard the clicks of his keyboard.

"ID verified. How can I help you?"

"I have a level-three situation at the Nest. I need an immediate Starburst."

"Roger that. Starburst."

"Time to impact?"

"Scrambling now. I estimate impact in four minutes, maybe less."

"Less would be better."

"Is . . . is the President—?"

"She's alive and going to stay that way."

"I'll keep you posted, ma'am." After a pause, "God bless."

Forty-five seconds after Starburst had gone red, a pair of F-16 interceptors screamed down runway L-29, went into a steep climb, and leveled off at ten thousand feet. Ahead of them, all air traffic out of Dulles International and Ronald Reagan National Airports had been contained. Takeoffs were delayed, incoming flights were put into a holding pattern or, if fuel was a problem, rerouted to alternate airports.

One minute behind the F-16s was an AWACS aircraft. Distinctive because of its roof-mounted revolving radar dish, the AWACS is designed as an electronic clearinghouse in the sky, directing fighters and bombers to their targets, monitoring incoming enemy forces, watching troop movements on the battlefield. It also has one other distinctive ability.

Two minutes and twelve seconds after takeoff, the AWACS was approaching its escorts. Using Lieutenant Matthews in the Ready Room as a conduit, the pilot was able to talk directly to Tylo.

"This is eyeball flight to ground leader. You read me, Agent Tylo?"

"Five by five."

"We're approximately ninety seconds to target. Starburst systems are armed. We'll be good to go on your command."

"Eyeball flight, confirm good to go. I'll be looking for you."

Tylo sensed the pilot hesitate before he spoke his next words.

"Uh, Agent Tylo? Are you familiar with the mechanics of Starburst?"

"Your aircraft is equipped with a high-energy radio-frequency device that shoots out a radio signal to disable electronic targets."

"Right. We're carrying the HERF gun. That means we can coat a much smaller area than, say, an entire city. But the effects won't cover just the White House. Only military and other hardened units will be unaffected."

"Do it." Tylo changed radio frequencies, "Take him down."

Almost before the words were out of her mouth, two agents who'd been acting as stewards moved toward the Korean man. That the Korean was holding a plate would help. As Tylo approached, she saw the Korean smile at one of the stewards, gesture at his plate as if he wanted a refill on the broiled shrimp. He never saw the second agent come up on his left, felt only the iron grip as both men grabbed him, pinning his arms behind his back.

Tylo was close enough to catch the plate as it fell from the Korean's hand, close enough to feel the heat of his rage before he was twisted around and duck-walked out of the room. She looked around quickly, relieved that none of the other guests had noticed the takedown.

Tylo went out the doors that opened up on the

South Lawn. She hadn't heard anything from Sloane and realized why: The Korean woman was still at the table with her son. But she appeared nervous, her expression tense and suspicious.

She's wondering what's holding up the President.

Tylo stopped at the first table and said, "Folks, I just want to let you know that the President will be out here shortly. She'll be speaking over there," she pointed to a small podium with a lectern. "We're arranging the chairs so that you all have a better view. If you'd like to take your seats . . ."

As the parents started to move, Tylo went to the second table, repeated her little act, then on to the third. Now she stood at the woman's table, talking to the families, encouraging them to move along. She made sure her voice was loud enough so that the Korean woman heard every word.

When the woman and the boy were the only ones left sitting, Tylo turned and raised her wrist mike.

"Alert three, alert four. The Korean woman with the boy. Drop her."

With a disarming smile, she walked up to the woman.

"Hi there. Everything okay? Having a good time?"

The woman bobbed her head. "Yes, good time."

Tylo slipped behind the woman. With her left hand, she pointed in the direction of the podium and the woman's eyes naturally followed. Which was exactly what Tylo wanted. Her right hand snaked into her jacket, reappeared with her Sig Sauer, the barrel jammed against the base of the woman's neck.

"Don't you even *think* of moving," she said in a low

voice. "Now, slowly, bring both hands around the back of the chair."

The woman obeyed. One of the two agents who had appeared beside Tylo quickly cuffed the woman's wrists.

"Get her out of here," Tylo said, holstering her gun.

The boy was staring at her, holding a spoon of dripping ice cream. She never took her eyes off him as she radioed, "Get Ladybug out. Now! Then get everyone off the lawn."

As the agents hustled the woman away, Tylo slowly backed away from the boy. Looking around, she saw that everyone was in the reception room. Then her heart caught in her throat. A lone figure approached the boy, holding out her hand to him. Sloane Ryder.

33

THE HANDYMAN stood in the sunshine near the Zero Milestone, on Executive Avenue. He had already spotted Hollis Fremont and, using a small group of French tourists as cover, tracked her movements.

The Handyman wanted very badly to dispose of this meddlesome woman once and for all, but there was far more security than usual along Executive Drive. He could get close to Fremont, but he could not take her down without being seen.

But Fremont could prove useful. The Handyman had seen her on the cell phone and on the radio link. After each conversation, she moved in a different direction. By watching her, the Handyman thought he might get an indication of where the watchers were focusing their attention.

He saw Fremont coming his way, around the curve of Executive Drive that runs into Seventeenth Street. Drifting away from the French tourists, he found a black family taking pictures. He cheerfully obliged them by snapping a photo of the whole group standing in front of the White House fence.

Handing back the camera, the Handyman glanced at his watch. The President should be making her way outside to the podium right now. The boy, 1818, would be seated in the front row, no more than ten feet away.

The Handyman fell in behind Fremont as she walked around the curve, staying twenty feet behind her. He saw a stretch van pull up on the corner of Seventeenth Street and disgorge a party of chattering tourists. The Handyman fell in with the group as they strung themselves along the gate to look across the expanse of lawn.

It was perfect. From this particular angle, the Handyman could follow the slope of the lawn all the way to the White House. He saw red, white, and blue balloons—they must have been tied to chairs—bobbing in the wind. But there were no people, no children, none of the noise that several hundred bodies and voices should generate.

The Handyman's eyes flitted to Fremont, who was still circulating among the tourists. He decided he had to take the risk. From his jacket pocket he removed a pair of opera-style binoculars and trained them on the White House. No one would have noticed anything had the sun been positioned at a slightly different angle.

Bobby Ryan was one of four men stationed in the Bronco parked on Executive Drive. He, too, had binoculars, and was scanning the crowds along the drive all the way to the Ellipse. So far, the only person who had caught his attention was a dumpy professor type. Ryan wondered why the professor mirrored Fremont's every move, but stayed in her blind spot. He decided to take the initiative.

"Alert twelve to alert one. Copy?"

"Copy, twelve."

Tylo was the only person left in the Diplomatic Reception Room. The President had been taken to the Situation Room, the children and their parents spirited away to the East Room, on the other side of the White House.

"Your floater, Fremont—is she supposed to have cover?"

"Negative, twelve. No cover. What do you see?"

Ryan trained his binoculars on the Handyman. "The subject is male, appears to be in his late fifties, Pillsbury Doughboy body type, smoking a pipe, carrying a book. He has a set of small field glasses and is looking across the lawn in her direction. He's been moving whenever Fremont moves, always staying behind her."

Tylo closed her eyes lightly. "Alert, twelve, do not—repeat *not*—attempt to make any contact with this individual. Do not let him feel that he's under surveillance. I'll get back to you stat."

Tylo immediately contacted Fremont and passed along Ryan's report. "Do you see him?" she finished.

"Yeah. Fifty feet away, by the fence. There are a lot of people around him. I don't have a clear shot."

"Hollis, don't let him see you! If he does, he might send the signal right away." She looked up at the sky. "Wait one second."

Tylo patched through to the AWACS jet. "This is alert one. What's your status?"

"Ten seconds to target," the pilot replied.

"Do it now."

"If I do, there's no guarantee that the designated area will be covered."

"Screw the guarantee. Do it now!"

"Okay. Make sure your people are dialed in, because nobody else will know what hit them."

The pilot pushed the throttles of the big jet to the limit. Out the window, he could see the Washington Monument coming up. *Still too damn far!* But he was already relaying commands to the crew of ten in the main compartment of the plane.

"On my mark, gentlemen. Three, two, one . . ."

The Handyman heard the roar of the approaching craft even before he saw it. Looking up, he noticed the distinctive revolving radar dome and immediately reached for his cell phone. It took a split second to pull up the antenna, then his fingers danced across the pads.

Power. Pound sign. Send.

"Hi. Are you okay?" Sloane saw the ice cream dripping from the spoon, running onto the boy's sailor suit. "Here, let me help you with that."

Slowly, she pulled out a chair, picked up a napkin, and drew the boy to her.

"Want to give me your spoon first? Great . . ."

She placed the spoon on the table, wrapped the napkin around her finger, and gently wiped away the ice cream on his sleeve. When she touched the boy's thigh, he winced and drew back.

"Sorry, honey, sorry. I didn't mean to hurt you."

Sloane noticed a dark stain—not from the ice cream—on the seat of the boy's pants. Then he began scratching his buttocks feverishly.

"Baby, don't do that," she whispered.

The boy stopped. His eyes glistened with tears and his gaze, filled with pain and pleading, tore at Sloane's heart.

She cupped his face. "Let me look at it, okay? Then I'll get you to a doctor."

She knew the boy didn't understand her, but he seemed to respond to her soft tone.

Carefully, Sloane reached out and undid the button at the waistband of his pants. Then, suddenly, the boy pulled them down himself, exposing two ghastly incisions whose sutures had ruptured.

"Oh my God!"

The boy's buttocks were soaked in blood that had mixed with a clear, viscous liquid, like egg white. Two fat tears slid down his cheeks.

"Baby, what have they done to you?"

Sloane was on her knees. The boy gasped, then flung himself at her, his arms tight around her neck as she rocked him.

Overhead, Sloane heard the rumble of an approaching jet, then Tylo's voice over her shoulder.

"Sloane, don't turn around. Don't look at me. Just listen. The boy is implanted with explosives. There's a bomb disposal unit coming—"

Suddenly, it seemed as though the entire city went still. Traffic noise diminished, then ceased. No horns, sirens, or alarms were heard. The only sounds were those of nature—the wind snapping the flags, leaves rustling, the birds . . .

Tylo raised her wrist mike. "Hollis, are you there?"

"Still here. Something's wrong. He's holding a cell

phone, acting like there's something wrong with it."

"That's a transmitter. The HERF gun worked."

"He's moving away from the crowds."

"Drop him, Hollis."

"What's going on?" Sloane called, still clutching the boy.

"We're safe. Sloane, you have to move away from the boy. Now."

"He doesn't need a bomb truck. Get a doctor and an ambulance!"

"Sloane, he might still be a danger—"

"Dammit, I'll drive the ambulance myself. Just get it!" The boy started to cry and she gently shushed him. "Holland, please!"

The Handyman didn't waste time reentering the sequence on the cell phone. Detonation should have occurred the instant he'd pressed the send button. It hadn't. Which meant that the AWACS plane, with its laser-guided pulse, had been close enough to blanket this area of the city. Nothing electrical was working now—car engine turbines, lights, computers, telephones. *His phone.* The shock waves from the invisible blast had knocked out communications and transportation. Except for one alternative.

The Handyman did not have to turn; he sensed Hollis Fremont coming up behind him. Others too. He dipped into his pocket for the tobacco pouch and flipped it open. Holding the pouch in one hand, a lighter in the other, he spun around.

Fremont was no more than ten feet away, gun drawn, charging him. The Handyman shook his head and smiled as he dropped the lighter into the pouch and tossed it at her feet.

Only the fact that she saw the objects in his hand saved her life. Redirecting her momentum, she leaped left. The flame burned through the tobacco and ignited the small concussion bomb nestled at the bottom of the pouch. Fremont was already down, her body tightly curled, when the bomb exploded.

The shock waves kicked the air out of her lungs. Through the ringing in her ears, Fremont heard the screams of the tourists who'd been hurled to the ground or against the wrought-iron fence.

Gasping and coughing, she staggered to her knees. Hands grabbed her by the shoulders and pulled her up.

"Are you all right?" Bobby Ryan demanded, his voice hoarse from the smoke.

"Yeah." Fremont steadied herself. "The Handyman?"

"Who?"

"The guy you pinpointed!"

Bobby Ryan shook his head. "Gone."

Only specially-hardened government communications devices and relays escaped the effects of the HERF gun pulse. All other electronics—from radios to car ignitions and entire grids—went black. In a matter of seconds, the core of the nation's capital plunged into chaos.

It took the Handyman only a few minutes to reach the Farragut West subway station on the corner of I Street and Seventeenth. All around him were stalled cars and trucks, with plenty of accidents clogging the streets as drivers, caught off guard when their engines died, slammed into other vehicles. The victims—those who could still move—leaned against their cars or wandered aimlessly, in shock. They were joined by hundreds of people spilling out of office and apartment buildings.

The Handyman knew that Fremont had not been killed by his blast. She'd been very quick. Nonetheless, the aftermath would slow her down—and the Secret Service cavalry charging to her side.

The Handyman made his way through the traffic snarls, careful to appear as bewildered as everyone around him. There were a lot of police around and he did not want to draw attention to himself.

Finding a subway station, he headed down the steps. By now, Fremont would have put out his description along the dedicated government lines and to all parts of the city unaffected by the pulse. That meant the first order of business was to lose the professorial disguise. Then, escape, by riding the Orange Line as far as Metro Center, and there, switching to the Red Line.

Reaching the first escalator, the Handyman discovered that the steps were frozen. Something was wrong, and suddenly he knew what it was. There were no rumblings coming from the tunnels below. No draft. No sounds associated with moving subway cars.

Then he saw why. Pounding up the motionless escalators were panicky crowds, herded along by uniformed patrol officers. The subway had been shut down.

* * *

The instant Holland Tylo had heard the blast on Executive Drive, she wanted to rush to the site. But she could not—would not—leave Sloane alone with the boy.

"What was that?" Sloane shouted, huddling the child.

"An electromagnetic blast," Tylo called back. "Everything in a twenty-block radius is down—cars, trucks, phones, the works. Except for our communications. Sloane, there's an army medical team on the way to take care of the boy."

Before Sloane could reply, she heard boots pounding toward her. She placed her hand over the boy's face so that he wouldn't see the soldiers, bulked out in hard-shell armor, trotting toward them.

Stopping fifty feet away, they quickly broke out a large, half-sphere tent of bright orange fabric, the kind used in arctic training. Equipment and a cot were set up inside under the watchful eye of an officer whose insignia identified him as a battlefield surgeon.

Looking at Sloane, he called out, "My name is Colonel Powell, from the 2833 MASH unit. Are you all right, Ms. Ryder?"

Sloane nodded. "Thank God you're here. Has anyone told you what was done to the boy?"

"Yes—though I can't believe it. Listen, I have to give him a sedative before we move him inside."

"What do you want me to do?" Sloane asked.

"Just hold him. Believe me, he won't feel a thing."

Powell brought out a pneumatic inoculator, loaded and ready. Moving slowly, he approached the boy, who was clinging to Sloane's waist. He would have preferred to shoot the sedative into the boy's arm, but he wasn't about to risk a struggle. The exposed thigh would do.

Crouching, Powell pressed the inoculator against the boy's thigh and squeezed the trigger. Sloane heard the boy's sharp cry, felt him stiffen, then go limp.

Quickly, Powell scooped him up in his arms. His face paled when he saw the incisions.

"Who did this?" he whispered.

"Maybe you'll get a chance to meet him," Sloane replied.

She watched Powell carry the child into the tent, then ran to Tylo and Fremont.

"Where did he go?" Sloane asked as the Secret Service sedan, siren and lights on, swerved around the stalled vehicles that littered Pennsylvania Avenue.

"We know where he *didn't* go," Fremont said, turning around in the front seat. She was still shaken from the blast, but recouping fast. "National airport is closed and Dulles is too far away. He'd never make it out of the city."

"The subway," Sloane said. "He may be headed for the outskirts—Bethesda or Falls Church."

Tylo, behind the wheel, shook her head. "The minute Starburst was put in play, the entire subway system was shut down."

She pointed out the window at the military convoy rolling down the avenue. "Marines from Quantico. They'll take up positions around all federal buildings and help the cops handle traffic."

Tylo pointed through the window. "See that Humvee? Looks like a command car to me. Pull him over."

She turned back to Sloane. "He's got to be holed up in this six-to-ten-block area. The military can throw up a cordon, then help us go in and find the son of a bitch."

The Handyman turned around the instant he saw the police. But he didn't walk back up the steps until the crowd was almost upon him. He emerged from the subway station surrounded by anxious voices and jostling bodies, just as a convoy of army trucks roared down Eighteenth Street.

Seeing army vehicles, the crowd slowed, milling about the entrance to the subway station. The Handyman shouldered his way through and followed the trucks as far as H Street and Pennsylvania, where they stopped. As soon as the soldiers began jumping out, he knew that a cordon was going up.

The Handyman drifted over to an accident site where a man was slumped by the open door of his wrecked car, pressing a handkerchief to his bleeding forehead. He stared at him for several seconds, his thoughts racing. The squeal of tires broke his concentration.

A government sedan pulled up next to a Humvee. An officer in battle dress jumped out, joined by a woman from the sedan. Holland Tylo, Secret Service. Then Hollis Fremont, Omega. And finally Sloane Ryder.

The Handyman slipped closer to the wrecked car and its dazed victim. Kneeling, he asked the man if he was all right, but he never lost his line of sight across the hood of the car. Tylo was talking to the officer, gesturing at the street corners. Fremont and Ryder were scanning the area, their eyes searching faces in the crowd, pausing, moving on, relentless.

The Handyman was unarmed. But he realized that even if he had a weapon, he would get only one of the women before the military returned fire. He forced himself to concentrate on the soldiers.

The officer was speaking into a radio. Two trucks roared up Eighteenth Street to I Street and blocked off the intersection. A third proceeded down Pennsylvania. Watching the cordon go up, the Handyman saw an opening.

"I can seal off this entire area in twenty minutes," the colonel told Tylo.

His name was Redwing and his Apache ancestry was etched into the creases of his dark skin. He hadn't appreciated this civilian interference in his duty, even though it had come from the Secret Service. But his attitude changed after Tylo had handed him the phone and Redwing found himself listening to his commander in chief.

He had a map spread out on the hood of the Humvee. "No one, nothing, gets in or out," he continued, tracing a finger around the perimeter. "Plus, we get a chopper for rooftop surveillance."

Getting on the radio, Redwing ordered the chopper up, then checked on the deployment of his troops. He turned to Tylo. "I'll need a description of your man."

Fremont gave it to him, along with a warning. "This guy is a master of disguise. That potbelly and hair are gone by now. He'll be thirty pounds lighter and not look like an academic at all. The eyes will give him away. He won't appear lost or afraid—just looking for a way out."

"What did he do, exactly?" Redwing asked.

"Tried to assassinate the President."

Redwing's eyes narrowed. "Am I authorized to use deadly force?"

"Drop him any way you can," Tylo replied.

The Handyman walked west along H Street, moving around the cars and trucks that had mounted the sidewalks and crashed into fences or ended up in the courtyards of government high-rises. Ignoring the moans of the injured and the cries of the Samaritans trying to help them, he zigzagged his way to the George Washington University Medical Center on Nineteenth Street.

The Handyman drifted into the hospital like the Grim Reaper. The chaos there soothed him; the shouts of nurses and doctors over the groans of the injured were his balm. He already knew where to find the orderlies' locker room. Inside, he removed his wig and the prosthetic padding around his waist, then scrubbed off the makeup. In the linen closet, he found a crisp uniform that fit. Dressed in whites, he stepped into the melee, invisible.

The emergency-entrance driveway was clogged with ambulances, civilian and military. Ignoring the soldiers, the Handyman concentrated on finding the things he needed. The first was a paramedic's navy-blue jacket, which he plucked off a chair in the emergency room. The second took a few minutes longer.

The Handyman scanned the incoming ambulances, waited until he spotted one that was being parked by the emergency doors. Two paramedics flung open the back doors, pulled out a gurney with a pregnant woman strapped to it, and rolled her into the emergency room. The Handyman thought this was as good a bet as any—and he was right. In his haste, one of the paramedics had left the keys in the ignition.

Slipping behind the wheel, he drove carefully into the streets of the paralyzed section of the city.

"We've moved down one block from the north, south, east, and west," Redwing told Tylo. "No sign of him."

Tylo was staring at the helicopter drifting just above the tallest buildings. In the Huey were two spotters and a pair of marksmen. One of them was Hollis Fremont.

The city blocks that had already been checked were a disaster zone. Soldiers had gone into each of the buildings and, starting with the roof, worked their way down floor by floor. Whether office workers or apartment dwellers, the occupants had been herded into the halls, their IDs checked, then they had been escorted into the streets. Now they stood huddled in small knots, their coats wrapped tightly around them, staring in mute incomprehension at the relentless military machine that had invaded their privacy, watching as neighbors and coworkers stumbled out, equally dazed.

Redwing followed Tylo's gaze as it swept the street.

"He's not going to make it out of here," he said, as if intuiting her unspoken fears. "Nothing except military and emergency vehicles is moving. We have the sewers covered. Anyone who even remotely resembles him is being stopped. We're tightening the noose."

Tylo wished she were as confident. She looked around, then asked Redwing, "Have you seen Ryder?"

"Thought she was heading over there." He pointed to the intersection of H Street and Pennsylvania.

A message crackled over the radio. The search parties were prepared to move into another block.

"Tell them to stay sharp," Tylo said.

The Handyman returned to the accident site where he'd watched the three women huddle with the army officer. As he'd hoped, the wrecked car and its lone, injured occupant were still on the corner of H Street and Pennsylvania. The driver had crawled back behind the wheel, his head slumped against the padded rest, the bloody handkerchief covering his forehead.

The Handyman broke out a gurney and wheeled it up. "Take it easy, buddy. You're going to be just fine. Can you stand up for me?"

The man pulled away the handkerchief and blinked, beholding the Handyman as he might a divine apparition.

"Thank you," he whispered. "My head . . ."

"I know. Here, let me help you."

The Handyman lowered the man onto the gurney, affixed a neck brace, and fastened the straps. Using the sodden handkerchief, he bloodied the gurney sheets for effect, then rolled the gurney into the ambulance. Before getting behind the wheel, he checked the ambulance's call number, stenciled on the door. He reached for the radio mike and raised the dispatcher at the George Washington University Medical Center.

"Medic 1072 to center."

"Center receiving. Go ahead."

"Male Caucasian, early forties, blunt-head-wound trauma. Severe bleeding. I'm solo and need to run him in fast."

"Copy, medic 1072. Be advised we are unable to accept your patient—"

The Handyman had been counting on the fact that the hospital was overwhelmed and was rerouting patients.

"Then give me an alternate or this guy won't make it!"

The Handyman had put steel into his voice, not to prod the dispatcher, but because he knew that the army was monitoring all transmissions.

"Medic 1072, be advised that your alternate is Georgetown University Hospital on Reservoir—"

"I know where it is!" the Handyman snapped. "But I'm in the quarantine zone."

The dispatcher was becoming harried. The Handyman imagined how the calls were backing up on the switchboard.

"Medic 1072, I'm clearing you at the checkpoint on H and Twentieth. Good luck."

"Thanks. Medic 1072 out."

The Handyman was replacing the mike in its clip when he heard a voice behind him.

Hollis Fremont had been whisked away in the army helicopter; Tylo was busy with Colonel Redwing.

Armed with only a radio, Sloane found herself walking along Eighteenth Street, searching the faces in the crowds. When she reached Pennsylvania Avenue, she saw the ambulance, and the paramedic wheeling an injured man and thought she could help.

Sloane quickened her stride. Because of the din around her, she did not think of calling out to the paramedic. She was only ten feet away, watching him as he spoke on the radio. Then he made a half turn and she saw him in profile. The composites created from the video shot on the day of Martin Garrett's death exploded in her memory. In spite of herself, she spoke.

"I know you."

The Handyman whirled around. Sloane saw him drop the mike and his hand dip into the open medical chest. The next instant, he spun on the ball of one foot and thrust his arm at her. A glinting steel scalpel slashed the air. Sloane felt a searing pain as the blade slid across her collarbone.

Her knees buckled from the shock and she fell, hitting her shoulder on the street, rolling over on her back. When she looked up, the Handyman was looming over her, the scalpel held high.

He's going to cut my throat.

The Handyman needed only a few seconds to rip the blade through Sloane's flesh, but the roar of a diesel motor startled him.

Swerving around the corner was an army Humvee, the machine gunner riding in the "high chair" behind the driver. The gunner's vantage point gave him a clear view of the Handyman—and the Humvee was coming in his direction.

The Handyman hesitated, then dropped the scalpel. He looked deeply into Sloane's terror-stricken eyes.

"You owe me a life!" he whispered, then brought the edge of his right hand down hard behind her ear.

Racing to the ambulance, he jumped behind the wheel. Within seconds, the siren and lights were on. The Handyman grabbed the radio mike.

"This is medic 1072 to the army vehicle behind me. Do you copy?"

"Copy, medic 1072. What's the problem?"

"I have a critical head wound on board. The medical center has cleared me for Georgetown University Hospital, but I'd sure appreciate an escort. My guy's in a bad way."

"Medic 1072, wait one."

The Handyman had expected the Humvee to contact the checkpoint.

"Medic 1072, we confirm medical center's alert. But you're gonna have to pull over."

The Handyman pretended to protest. "But—"

"We gotta check your load, mister. *Then* we'll ride shotgun."

Of course they had to check.

Two armed soldiers jumped out of the Humvee. The Handyman came around the ambulance and pulled open the doors. He was pleased that not only had the injured driver lost consciousness, but that the wound to his forehead had reopened and seeped blood. The soldiers looked closely, but were careful not to touch the victim.

"He have any ID?" one of them asked.

The Handyman produced the wallet he'd lifted from

the injured man. The soldiers glanced at the Maryland driver's license.

"Okay. Button it up and follow us," one of them said.

The Handyman threw them a two-finger salute and hopped back into the cab of the ambulance.

Sloane fought against the blackness threatening to engulf her. She was aware of the street grit against her scalp and the pounding at her temples.

She moved her fingers, then her hand, reaching into her pocket for the radio. Her finger trembled over the transmit button, then found it.

"Hollis. Hollis, can you hear me?"

The Huey was a quarter of a mile away, holding at seven hundred feet. Hollis Fremont flinched as she heard Sloane's feeble voice over the headset. She didn't waste a word.

"Give me your location, Sloane. Now!"

Fremont pressed the headset to her ear to better hear the reply.

"I'm coming for you, Sloane."

She spoke briefly to the pilot and her fellow sniper. "He's down at H and Pennsylvania."

The Handyman watched the Humvee approach the checkpoint and veer right. But the two military vehicles blocking off the street did not move apart. The Handyman slowed; then, on instinct, he hit the siren.

The drivers of the double deuces fired up their diesels and created an opening. The Handyman touched the brim of his cap in a farewell gesture as he swept through.

* * *

Straining against her harness, Fremont leaned out of the helicopter. Through the sniperscope she saw Sloane, lying in the street like a broken doll. Fremont was about to radio Tylo when Sloane's broken voice filtered through the headphones.

"1072 . . ."

"Sloane, don't talk. I'm right above you!"

"1072. Ambulance number. He's in an ambulance . . ."

"Hang on, Sloane. I'm going to call that in. I'll get back to you pronto."

Fremont switched frequencies and told Tylo what had happened.

"I'll send out an alert to the military to stop all medical transports," Tylo replied. "I'll get a unit over to Sloane—"

Fremont heard Redwing's voice on another channel.

"The checkpoint at H and Twentieth reports an ambulance passing through sixty seconds ago," he said urgently. "It was cleared by the medical center for Georgetown University Hospital. A patrol stopped it inside the quarantine zone and checked the patient. He wasn't our man." He paused. "But they didn't check the driver."

"Get someone over to Sloane," Fremont told him. "I'll head for Georgetown and call you from there."

She tapped the pilot on his shoulder and the helicopter wheeled to the west.

On the ground, Holland Tylo was already behind the wheel of her sedan. Soldiers and civilians scattered as she tore down Eighteenth Street.

In less than a minute, the helicopter was over the bridge that traverses Rock Creek, connecting George-town to the rest of the city. Fremont spotted the ambulance immediately, caught in the snarl of traffic on the bridge, its flashers spinning. On the roof, in bold, luminous paint, was the ID number 1072.

"Go low so I can get a better look," Fremont ordered the pilot.

The chopper made a stomach-churning turn, then dove at the ambulance. Fremont set her sights on the cab. She swore when she saw that it was empty.

"Hover and get ready to lower me," she said, then turned to the sniper. "Cover me."

The pilot held his machine steady at a hundred feet above the ambulance. Fremont slipped into a harness that was attached to a winch. With her rifle pointed at the ambulance, she gave a thumbs-up and the winch motor began to hum. A moment later, her feet hit the roof of the ambulance. She touched the quick release on the harness and, crouching, jumped onto the hood, swinging the barrel of her rifle across the windshield. The cab was empty.

By this time, the second sniper was on the ground. Fremont motioned him to follow her around to the back of the ambulance. She pointed at the wide double doors, received a nod of acknowledgment, then gripped the handles and pulled.

Fremont had two pounds of pressure on a four-pound trigger when she heard the groan. She saw a raised arm, then the bloody face of someone strapped to a gurney.

* * *

The Handyman was less than two blocks away, at the back entrance of the Georgetown Four Seasons. He'd stopped the ambulance and darted away only seconds before hearing the helicopter rotors, leaving behind confused and angry motorists.

The Handyman stepped into the hotel. He realized that he was conspicuous in his paramedic's jacket, but it also lent him authority. Better to keep it.

He strode purposefully past the news kiosk, registration desk, and concierge station, mixing among well-heeled guests talking in a half dozen languages. The topic, however, was the same: What had overtaken the city? Rumors ranged from a massive electrical failure to a terrorist attack.

As the Handyman passed a television that had been set up in the small lobby, he heard a news anchor announce that the President would be addressing the nation in a few minutes. This was his first confirmation that Claudia Ballantine was alive, that he had failed.

The Handyman shook off the news. His only objective was to get out of the city. A busy hotel provided certain opportunities. There was the physical plant, with its heating, air-conditioning, and plumbing network, pipes that connected to city sewers that led to a vast honeycomb of tunnels under the city. The Handyman had spent hours at the Smithsonian studying this underground maze that could take him far underneath the Potomac and into Virginia where he had numerous opportunities to escape the country.

The Handyman heard the faint wail of police and emergency vehicle sirens. The helicopter's reinforcements were on the way. Soon, even the congested traffic and narrow streets of Georgetown would not stop his pursuers. He needed to get into the city's ancient catacombs.

He was marking the positions of the hotel's security guards, working out a way to slip past them, when he saw an alternative: Near the front doors sat an elderly gentleman in a wheelchair. The bellhop had loaded several large suitcases onto a cart and was wheeling them to a limousine parked under the portico. A coiffed, well-preserved woman in her early fifties supervised the loading. *The wife.*

The Handyman straightened his paramedic's jacket and approached the disabled man. The British Airways baggage tag on a handsome alligator-skin briefcase read J.E.M. Sykes.

"Mr. Sykes?"

The man's face was like old crepe, the skin sallow, ravaged by disease. His eyes appeared dulled by medication.

"And who might you be, sir?" Sykes whispered hoarsely.

"Charlie Landon, sir. I'm a registered nurse. The hotel manager has arranged for me to accompany you to the airport."

The Handyman's tone was suitably deferential. He wanted Sykes to see him as nothing more than a servant.

"Jeremy, who's this?"

Swathed in sable, silk, and gold, the leggy Mrs. Sykes appraised the Handyman as she might a mildly interesting eighteenth-century chamber pot being offered at auction.

"Belongs to the hotel," Sykes rasped. "Says he's supposed to come out with us and help tuck me into the plane."

Mrs. Sykes pounced on the offer. "How very thoughtful. Your name is . . . ?"

"Charlie, ma'am."

"The car's waiting, Charlie." She gestured in the direction of the black limousine. "Now if I can just get that porter to take the rest of these bags . . ."

The Handyman gripped the handles of the wheelchair and walked smoothly to the doors. He heard Mrs. Sykes's rapid-fire instructions to the bellhop about how to handle the Louis Vuitton carry-on; he smiled at the two doormen, one of whom hurried to assist the Handyman as he lifted Sykes out of the chair and into the car. The doorman was surprised by the paramedic's strength; he lifted the old man as easily as if he were a child.

The Handyman was breaking down the wheelchair and storing it in the trunk when he heard the wail of sirens again, much closer now. A few seconds later, he caught a glimpse of police car-rack lights, then two cruisers and an unmarked car pulling up the feeder road that connected the hotel property to Rock Creek Parkway.

The Handyman's pulse raced when he saw Sloane Ryder's detective, Whip Alley, step out of the plain-Jane sedan. His thick sweater had been cut away at one shoulder to accommodate a thick bandage.

A moment later, another car pulled up and Holland Tylo stepped out.

Holding his breath, the Handyman drifted behind a pillar. Alley had seen him up close and Tylo would have his description. If either looked his way, they couldn't help but recognize him.

Out of the corner of his eye the Handyman saw Mrs. Sykes, striding imperiously ahead of a bellhop. The Handyman slipped in front of her just as the detective glanced in their direction. Instead of a shout of alarm, the Handyman heard Alley snapping orders at the uniformed officers.

Give me just another minute . . .

Mrs. Sykes went to the trunk of the car to supervise the loading of the last pieces of luggage. The Handyman saw Alley's reflection in the tinted window as he opened the rear door of the limousine and, smiling at Sykes, adjusted a blanket over the elderly man's knees.

"We'll be out of here in a moment," he said reassuringly.

The limo driver stepped past the Handyman to close the trunk, then opened the door for Mrs. Sykes. Four police officers were talking to the doormen and bellhops, checking the guests milling under the portico and behind the front doors. The Handyman slipped past the driver, almost stepped on Mrs. Sykes's ankle, and settled himself in the seat that faced the rear of the limousine. Through the smoked-out window he saw a shadow, heard the tap on the window.

"All this fuss," Mrs. Sykes muttered. She lowered the window several inches and spoke to a policeman the Handyman couldn't see. "Yes, what is it?"

"You heading out to the airport, ma'am?"

"We certainly are, Officer. I assume that in spite of this commotion, it's still open."

"Dulles is open. Excuse me, ma'am, is that your husband?"

The Handyman saw Sykes's rheumy eyes dart from his wife to the officer to the Handyman.

Don't look at me. I'm not here.

"Of course, he's my husband," she snapped. "Officer, really. I don't know what's going on, but we're going to be late."

The Handyman watched the officer's shadow retreat, then heard: "You have a safe flight, ma'am."

"Yes, yes, thank you." She pressed the intercom button. "Driver, why are we still waiting?"

The Handyman didn't move until the limousine turned onto Rock Creek Parkway. He was so still that he didn't realize that the old man was addressing him.

"I said, how will you get back from the airport?" Sykes brayed.

"Not to worry," the Handyman replied politely. "The hotel provides cab fare."

"Decent of them, don't you think, dear?"

Engrossed in the latest issue of *Vogue*, his wife didn't pay any attention to him.

For the first time in hours the Handyman allowed himself to relax. Dulles International Airport would be his avenue out of the country too.

Upon arriving in Washington, he had taken a number of precautions. These included money and completely documented identities tucked away in lockers at Ronald Reagan National Airport, Baltimore-Washington International, and Union Station. A fourth, in a locker at Dulles International, held the papers to his French-Canadian identity, a change of clothes, money, a ticket to Montreal, and a small makeup kit whose contents would subtly alter his image to fit the passport photo.

The Handyman had no doubt that the Chos had been taken. But even if the Americans used chemicals, it would still take time to make the Chos talk. The description they'd give up would in no way match his new appearance. Naturally, security at Dulles would be on heightened alert, but the agents would be searching for a man who'd already ceased to exist.

Listening to the hum of the tires, the Handyman thought back to everything that had happened. A small frown furrowed his brow. Mai Ling had paid him for results that had not been delivered. That meant returning the front money he'd received. For a time, the Chinese would be too busy trying to find a way to silence or disavow the Chos to worry about him. But they would get around to him eventually. Questions would be raised, answers expected.

The Handyman thought that the Chinese couldn't hold very much against him. They, not he, had been in complete control of the operation; his primary function had been to protect Dodge French until his usefulness had run out. He had done exactly that.

Detonating the bomb was something he'd agreed to later. That it hadn't gone off as planned, well, that was the Chos' fault for allowing themselves to be exposed.

The Handyman concluded that the threat was not the Chinese, but the women. First, there had been only Hollis Fremont of Omega, a constant threat.

Now, because he'd made an attempt on the life of the President, Holland Tylo might join Fremont's hunt. And he shouldn't overlook the gosling of the three, Sloane Ryder, who'd been savaged too much to ever forget him.

The Handyman thought it was prudent to get as much information on the three of them as possible, then pass it to the astrologer Fat Lee. He smiled faintly. The portents, he imagined, would not be entirely favorable.

The Handyman felt something nudge his foot—old Sykes's cane.

"Something strike you as funny, young man?" Sykes demanded.

"Just thinking about my girls," the Handyman said, and looked into the smoked-out window, as opaque as his heart.

Mrs. Sykes stirred. Something about this nurse, his rough edges and the musk of danger, appealed. He wore no wedding band, and he didn't look like a father. She wondered briefly if he'd ever had it on Pratesi sheets between sips of champagne. Her musing was fleeting and she returned to her magazine. He was, after all, only a flunky.

EPILOGUE

THE ARMY MEDIC who ministered to Sloane wanted to send her directly to the nearest hospital. Sloane told him to bandage the wound and give her painkillers for her pounding headache.

The unit's radio operator patched her through to Holland Tylo, who ordered the officer in charge to drive Sloane to the White House.

As soon as she walked through the doors of the West Wing, Whip Alley rushed to her side. His eyes widened when he saw the field dressing between her neck and shoulder.

"Sloane . . ."

"I'm okay," she said, kissing him lightly.

"Thank God you're alive," he whispered. "I thought—"

She pressed a finger against his lips. "Any sign of the Handyman?"

Alley shook his head. "Vanished."

Sloane couldn't believe it. "With all this security?"

Alley took her elbow. "Come on."

Fremont, Tylo, and Lee Porter were waiting in an office a few doors down from the Oval Office. Clearly relieved, the two women fussed over Sloane; Porter hugged her gently.

"Whip told me that we don't have a line on the Handyman," Sloane said.

"It's true," Tylo replied. "His description is out to everybody—local, state, federal authorities, the army. So far, no sightings."

"He's on the run," Sloane said. "Are the airports closed?"

"Only Ronald Reagan National," Porter told her. "Because it was briefly affected by the HERF blast."

Sloane shook her head. "I don't understand. Why not the others too?"

"Besides those of us in this room, and the army surgeon who looked after the Korean boy, no one else knows what really happened today," Porter explained. He paused. "And that's the way it stays."

"The boy," Sloane said. "How is he?"

"The surgeon managed to remove the implanted explosives," Fremont replied. "But stage-three infection had already set in. Given how sick he is, it's unlikely he'll make it through the night."

"What about the woman who was with him?"

"A North Korean agent—like her phony husband. She gave us nothing, but he cracked."

Sloane's eyes blazed. "Those two are just the tip of the iceberg. There must be something we can do to punish the people behind them."

"There is," Porter said. "But first, this thing has to blow over. We can never allow any country to learn how close the North Koreans and the Chinese came to killing the President. After that, we start working on a little payback for what they tried to do."

He pointed to the television and turned up the volume. "Listen to what the President has to say. Later, we'll take a little ride."

In spite of the chaos inflicted upon the central core of Washington, D.C., the government continued to function.

From the Oval Office, the President broadcast a statement to the nation. The incident in the capital had been the result of a military training exercise gone awry. The details, cloaked in the aegis of national security, were vague.

However, the President emphasized that no nation should believe that America was in any way weakened or crippled, and she warned against anyone taking advantage of the situation. Satellite feeds and reconnaissance overflights reports indicated that the world was heeding her words: No vessels left the Chinese coast, no aircraft departed the airfields. The silence from Beijing was deafening.

After the broadcast, the President boarded the helicopter designated *Marine Two* for the short flight to another hospital, Johns Hopkins in Baltimore. There, in a room that was equipped with the latest medical technology, she came face-to-face with her nemesis.

Dodge French lay in bed, wasted, his breathing coming in short, frail gasps. Claudia Ballantine realized that it wasn't the machines that were keeping him alive; it was his formidable will. But the instant he saw the woman who had called him a friend, it was as though his soul began to shrivel and decay.

"Yes, Dodge, I'm alive," the President said. "I wanted you to see for yourself."

French managed a smile. "You're a survivor, Claudia. Always were."

"You didn't set this up by yourself, Dodge," she said. "I want the names of the men in Beijing you were working with."

The enigmatic smile didn't change.

"We have the man and the woman. And the boy." The President shook her head. "I can't believe the cruelty you allowed to be inflicted on that child. Was that piece of rock called Taiwan so important to you?"

"You never appreciated the big picture," French managed weakly.

"Yes, I did. The big picture was our friendship, built on a trust going back thirty years. That's over. Give me what I need to know, Dodge."

French's smile twisted into a rictus. He opened his mouth, but only a dry rattle emerged from his throat. His head rolled across the pillow, and his eyelids fell across the mirrors of his treason.

Claudia Ballantine took a moment to compose herself, then left the room and went into the lounge where Ryder, Fremont, and Tylo waited.

"He's gone," she said.

"Did he—" Tylo started.

Claudia Ballantine shook her head. "He gave up nothing. Uncovering hard evidence of Chinese involvement—and using it—will take time. But there is something we can do right now."

She looked in turn at Ryder, Fremont, and Tylo.

"The Handyman is still out there. He knows everything French did—maybe even more."

She glanced from Ryder to Tylo to Fremont. All three women nodded, as though knowing exactly what the President would say.

"Find him," Claudia Ballantine said. "Whatever it takes, so that he can never hurt us again."

ABOUT THE AUTHOR

PHILIP SHELBY studied international affairs and strategic studies at McGill University. After graduate work at the Sorbonne and the University of London, he returned to the United States, where he worked as an analyst for various government and private groups. He is the author of *Days of Drums, Last Rights, Gatekeeper,* and *The Cassandra Compact* (with Robert Ludlum).